For Anne,
who always wanted to read this book,
but unfortunately never got the chance.

"People are trapped in history, and history is trapped in them"

James Baldwin

The Matheson and Grant Families 1924–1944

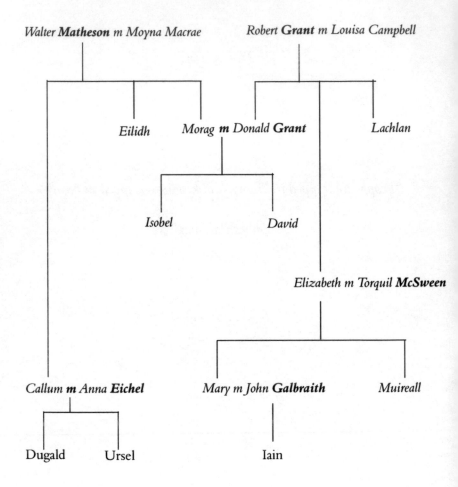

Prologue

Glendaig, Scottish Highlands.
July 1930

Dugald Matheson perched awkwardly upon the substantial granite boulder he'd proclaimed to be his own *special place*. That had been eight years before. No one else in the family had been permitted to sit there since, not even his younger sister Ursel. The family had named this hulking relic of the glacial age, "Dugald's Rock" and it was here that the quiet fifteen-year-old boy could often be found, his head buried in a book, or on occasions scanning the shimmering surface of Loch Coinneach for the tell-tale wake of an otter.

Today was no different; Dugald had clambered up to his special place with a well-thumbed copy of the Hardy Boys mystery, *The House on the Cliff*. He'd reclined against the trunk of an old rowan tree and had settled down for a good read. The late afternoon sun felt warm upon his face and everything would have been perfect, had it not been for the squealing and laughter emanating from the distant figures further along the beach.

Dugald repositioned his long legs and shot a disapproving glance in the direction of his distracters. Irritated by the din, he ran a freckled hand through his mop of red hair, as if to rid himself of an imaginary insect. The truth of the matter was that he was a vain individual, and the realisation that his normally slicked locks had taken on a life of their own concerned him deeply. Realising there was nothing he could do to improve his appearance, his attention returned to the group running about on the beach.

Why couldn't he be alone… with just the sound of the gulls for company? He shook his head a couple of times and turned the page of his book.

For the rest of the family, it had been the perfect day. They'd all been together for the first time since 1928. The younger generation were playing cricket on the sand, whilst two women watched from the shade of nearby trees.

Anna, Dugald's mother, beamed as she and her older sister Katharina relaxed upon a colourful tartan rug. The remnants of a picnic lay spread out about them, and as they laughed and chatted they looked up periodically to watch the entertainment. There could be no mistaking the two women as siblings, both were tall and slim and both shared their mother's dark piercing eyes. Katharina especially looked forward to these holidays in the Highlands. She was at her happiest when she was walking in the mountains, laughing with her sister and reminiscing about their happy childhood back in Zürich before the Great War.

Anna, too, looked forward to these times. There was always an atmosphere of euphoric excitement present in the house when Katharina and her sons were soon to arrive. Visits home to her native Switzerland had become an increasingly rare occurrence, so the times she spent with her sister were always precious, helping to dull the frequent pangs of homesickness she still experienced when receiving letters with news from home.

There was no sadness present in the hearts of either woman today, no worries about the future. They were just happy and contented watching their offspring running around the sandy beach, enjoying themselves in the late July sunshine. Anna, her face and dark bobbed hair shaded from the sun by a wide-brimmed linen hat, handed an empty glass to Katharina.

'So when is Otto going off to Mürwik?' she asked as she removed her hat and reclined onto the rug.

Katharina closed the lid on the picnic basket. 'Oh, sometime in

October, after his eighteenth birthday has passed.'

'He must be looking forward to it?'

'*Ja*, immensely, his grandfather has prepared him well with stories of his time at the *Marineschule*. I think he'll adapt well to life in the navy.'

'That's good... and Max, what plans does he have for the future?'

Katharina raised a hand to shield her eyes from the sun. 'He seems happy enough in his current employment, but I don't believe he has found his calling working for Meier and Stahl.'

Anna looked puzzled. 'Meier and Stahl?'

'They're a shipping company in Kiel. Bruno got him a temporary job there when he completed his studies at the Christian Albert Gymnasium. He tells me he'll be joining the navy as soon as he can, so I don't believe it will be long before he joins his brother at Mürwik too.'

'He's never wavered from his dream to become a submariner then?'

'Not at all, we must thank Bruno and his grandfather for that!'

Max came trotting back to the two women. 'Is there any lemonade left Aunt Anna?'

'Yes dear, help yourself. The bottle's in the basket.'

Max dropped to his knees and poured himself a generous glassful. He had turned sixteen, and had grown considerably since his last visit, now topping six feet. He'd become a handsome youth, having inherited his father's prominent angular jaw and athletic physique. But for all his masculine features, there was a softness to his young face and a hint of a smile every time he spoke. He was always well groomed, and even now, after the physical exertion of a game of cricket, not a dark hair was out of place. Similarly, his white shirt and cotton shorts maintained the appearance of having just been laundered and pressed with military precision.

'Have you managed to master the game of cricket yet?' his aunt enquired of him.

'Not really Aunt Anna, the bat they use seems far too narrow to me.' Draining his glass, he padded off across the sand towards his fellow cricketers.

'Don't you worry about them both joining the navy Katharina?' Anna asked.

'No, not really, not when the world is at peace with itself I suppose, but who knows what the future holds?' She picked up that day's edition of the *Scotsman*. 'There's little in here to worry us, thank God. It seems the British Navy have been sent to Egypt to help quell some rioting...' She turned the page '... and here's a piece about this new airship, the *R101*. Apparently, it's commenced its maiden flight across the Atlantic.'

Anna eased herself up from the rug and began clearing the leftover food from the picnic. 'What do you know of this man Adolf Hitler? He seems to be gaining popularity in Germany.'

'Yes, I do believe he is,' Katharina agreed. 'The economy's been in such a mess lately, so the voters are looking for an alternative. There will be an election in September and the word is he will do very well.'

'Is there a chance his party will win?'

'I don't know. They say that if he were to become Chancellor, it would be a disaster and he wouldn't last long. Personally, I believe he could be good for Germany. If things remain as they are now, we could be heading for a very bleak future.'

The sun had begun dipping in the west, pausing momentarily behind a ragged streak of purple cloud. Anna beckoned to the cricketers to join her. 'The best of the day's gone I'm afraid. Perhaps we should think about heading for home?'

Katharina shook the sand from their blanket and folded it into squares. 'You are right dear, in fact I do believe there's a hint of a chill in the air now.'

The youngsters plodded towards them, kicking sand at each other amid shrieks of laughter.

'Where's your brother?' Anna asked, whilst Ursel searched the basket for the bottle of lemonade.

'Oh, he's still over there Mother, sitting on his rock, reading.'

'Can you please go and get him, we're going up to the Manse now.'

'Aye, I will, but you know he won't listen to me. Perhaps *you* should go and get him?'

'Just tell him I want him to come home right now Ursel.'

Katharina smiled, amused at the ease with which Anna switched from speaking their native German to perfect English, but with just a hint of an accent. Whether it was German or Scottish, she couldn't quite be sure.

Ursel started off across the beach. 'Are you coming with me Isobel?' she called out. Isobel Grant stood up, having adjusted the buckles on her shoes. 'Aye, I'm coming,' she replied and ran to catch up.

Ursel and Isobel were cousins, but also best friends. Ursel was a little taller than Isobel. Her long auburn hair shone as it tumbled about her shoulders, framing her pale elfin features and vivid green eyes.

She struggled to sweep her hair away from her face as she walked purposefully across the sand towards "Dugald's Rock". 'He won't come with us you know, he's beastly. I can't believe he's my brother.'

Isobel suppressed a grin. She too had long flowing hair that hung like a cloak about her narrow shoulders. 'We'll just have to pull him off his silly rock then, won't we?' she giggled.

Ursel stopped abruptly. 'Are you mad Isobel? He'll probably punch you.'

Isobel shook her head and took Ursel by the arm. 'Come on, I'm not frightened of him… even if you are.'

As they approached the rock, Dugald looked up from his book. 'What do you two want?' he scowled.

'Mother wants you to come home with us Dugald… *now.*'

'Tell her I'll be up later.'

'Come on, she'll only get angry with you again.'

'Fine by me.'

'Och, let's just leave him here,' said Isobel. 'We've done what your mother has asked.' She stood glaring at Dugald as her dark hair thrashed about in the strengthening breeze. He ignored her and continued to read, so Isobel turned and walked away.

Dugald shot her a sly glance from behind his book and called out to her. 'If you ask me nicely, Isobel, then I'll consider coming with you.'

Isobel stopped and looked back. 'I don't care whether you come or not Dugald,' she said and walked briskly on. Ursel followed close behind.

Dugald waited for a few seconds, then snapped his book shut and slid down the face of the rock. On reaching the sand, he jogged after the two girls. 'What's wrong with you Isobel, don't you like me?' He put his arm around her shoulders, but she twisted away, intending to keep her distance from him.

'Get off me Dugald, you can be so annoying at times.'

He laughed. 'Oh, and little girls can be so tiresome.'

As they approached the rest of the group, Anna beckoned to them to hurry up. 'Murchadh wants to take a photograph of us all before we go,' she announced.

Dugald raised his eyes skyward, an undisguised gesture of his displeasure at the prospect. But not wishing to push his luck, he nevertheless did as he was told.

'Let's all look as though we know each other,' said Katharina, as she shepherded the little group into position.

Eight-year-old Murchadh attended the village school with Isobel and Ursel. He was a pleasant boy, always grateful for any attention and had become a favourite of Anna's. His parents were poor crofters with a large family, so she'd taken him under her wing, ever conscious of his frugal existence.

For a few seconds, he fumbled with the catch on his camera case. Then, easing his small Box Brownie camera from its canvas receptacle, he cradled it against his stomach, checking the image in the viewfinder. The little group was now in position. Katharina stood with her two sons, their arms draped casually around her shoulders. Anna stood to her right, her arm through Dugald's, although he looked particularly uncomfortable in such a pose. Kneeling in front of Anna were the girls, Ursel and Isobel with two of Isobel's cousins, Muireall and Mary. The group held themselves stock still waiting for the camera shutter to click.

Isobel protested. 'How long are you going to be Murchadh? We can't keep smiling forever.' At that moment the camera's shutter let forth a distinctive hollow clunk.

'You were talking when I took that!' Murchadh complained.

'Sorry,' said Isobel.

He settled the camera against his body for a second time and checked his composition. 'Smile everyone!' he called out. 'Even you, Dugald!'

Dugald reluctantly expanded his mouth to form a smirk and the shutter clunked again. The grainy monochrome product of Murchadh's little black camera would, unbeknown to those present, be a final poignant record of those happy family reunions.

Anna and Katharina would never have believed on this of all days, that their chosen paths to a life of happiness and fulfilment would eventually trigger such a tragic series of events. In a few short years, their lives and those of their families would change forever. They would face the ultimate test of a family's loyalty and entrust the population of the small highland community of Glendaig with a secret that many would take to their graves.

2 0 0 9

Chapter One

Sunday 24ᵗʰ May
Stac Coinneach Dubh

The plaintive mewing of a solitary buzzard stopped Tamsin Kirkwood in her steps. She craned her neck, hoping to spot the graceful creature, but always mindful of the danger that the steep scree slope presented. High above, silhouetted against a slate grey sky, the giant raptor wheeled and soared, as if maintaining a holding pattern above the heads of the two hill walkers.

Tamsin lifted her binoculars to view the display. She called out to her husband, Mike, who'd progressed further down the rocky slope. He paused, thankful of the opportunity to rest his aching feet and glanced back. Realising that his wife was some way behind, he shielded his mouth with his hands and called out. 'Time for a break don't you think?'

He swung his rucksack away from his shoulders and placed it by his feet. His back felt cold as the wind-chill cooled the sweat that had soaked through his shirt. By the time Tamsin had caught up with him, Mike had already taken his first bite from a substantial baguette. The feast had been supplied by Fiona, the vivacious landlady at the Invertulloch Inn. It was a welcome service she offered her guests, many of whom were climbers or hill walkers.

'These are bloody marvellous!' Mike announced, struggling to form his words as he swallowed the last of his mouthful. He reached into the open sack and pulled out another monster, still wrapped in foil. 'Don't eat it all at once,' he joked, as he tossed the package to his young wife.

The couple huddled together in the lee of a large boulder as they ate their lunch. They would have been easily visible from the road below, dressed in their matching fleeces, two red dots against a backdrop of sombre granite. Mike wiped the crumbs away from his goatee beard. He settled his sunglasses atop his head, and absorbed the view through his binoculars. 'This is the life,' he declared with a wide grin.

They'd driven up from Lincolnshire two days earlier. Mike, a computer programmer, had been looking forward to this break. Life had been pretty hectic at work since the spring, and he'd needed to get away. He was an avid Munro bagger, and had already climbed eighty of the highest Scottish peaks listed by the Victorian baronet of the same name. It had always been his dream to conquer all 283 of them, and he was well on course to succeed. This holiday would help him add to his tally, and by the end of the week, he would, weather permitting, have another four under his belt.

Tamsin had been introduced to the hobby following their marriage three years earlier. She'd often remind her friends at dinner parties how she'd spent a good deal of her honeymoon, picking her way gingerly up the near vertical sides of mountains with unpronounceable names like Liathach or Braeriach.

A petite brunette, Tamsin had been slow to appreciate her husband's love of the mountains, but she'd discovered that walking in wild places was a welcome distraction from her job as PA to the director of a pharmaceutical company in Lincoln. For Mike, it was a match made in heaven!

On this trip, they'd planned to conquer the two Munros along the northern rim of Loch Coinneach, Ben Caisteal and Stac Coinneach Dubh. They'd climbed the former the day before, and were now half way down the latter, having reached the summit two hours before. Tomorrow they would move on to Glen Torridon, where two more monsters beckoned.

Tamsin was experiencing that buzz she always felt when she'd conquered another peak, and was now on her way to a hot bath and a bottle of wine. She called it her "post-summit experience", but Mike preferred to call it motivational melt down. Whatever the case, the worst was over!

Tamsin lay back against the warm rough surface of the granite and closed her eyes. The sun had broken through temporarily, and was rapidly heating the rock behind her head. For a second, she considered removing her fleece, but the keen breeze blowing onto the hill prompted her to refrain from doing so. She was half way up a Scottish mountain, after all.

Mike could be heard ferreting around in his rucksack, then she heard the sound of pages turning, and knew he'd found his favourite guidebook. She counted quietly to herself, and then right on cue, out it came.

'That little place down there on the side of the loch is called Glendaig. It says here there's a castle on the edge of the village, hidden in the trees down by the water.'

'Really?' Tamsin replied, her eyelids clamped shut, but still trying to sound interested.

'There's an entry here about Glendaig, listen to this.'

'Go on then…' As if she had a choice!

He read to her.

'"…Picturesque fishing village, situated on the northeast shore of the prominent sea loch, Loch Coinneach, north of Knoydart peninsula. Glendaig is a small linear settlement, built on lands once held by Tormod Macleod, son of Leod, Chief of the Macleods of Harris. A renowned soldier, who was present at Bannockburn, he built a castle at Glendaig in 1315. The stronghold, now in ruins was besieged in 1489 by Kenneth Macdonald, Earl of Knoydart, who took it as his seat. Kenneth, known as 'Black Kenneth', due to his harsh treatment of those who opposed him, gave his name to the loch and castle (Coinneach)…"'

Unperturbed, he rambled on about the Jacobites and the affinities of the local village folk during the 1745 rebellion. Then came the story of the clearances, and finally a summary of the local economy in modern times.

Tamsin had had enough. She raised herself up from the boulder, and interrupted him.

'Let's get going eh?'

'Okay,' Mike agreed. 'Shouldn't take us long to get down to the road now.'

The pair packed up their things and continued the trek down the mountainside, eventually coming across a stalker's track that twisted and turned as it descended steeply between the plethora of glacial debris.

It took them twenty minutes to reach the road and its comforting smooth surface. Visible relief washed across Tamsin's face, relief that her feet were now back on that hard, smooth and horizontal surface. Then she remembered where the car was. They'd parked it in a lay-by just outside of the village and had commenced their climb from there. *Shit!* she thought as she took a swig from her water bottle.

Mike had walked across the road, and looked down towards the loch. 'According to the guidebook, that little island down there is where Black Kenneth is buried. Apparently, there's a cairn at the eastern end to mark the spot.'

Tamsin joined him. 'It's certainly a beautiful place to be laid to rest. No doubt you'll be wanting to go down onto the beach and see if you can find this bloody cairn?'

She was right. 'But of course!' said Mike with a mischievous smile. 'Come on Tams, it won't take long. Or you could wait here?'

'No, no, I'll come with you,' Tamsin sighed.

They scrambled down the steep slope from the road, negotiating clumps of broom and eventually stumbling onto the shingle beyond. Tamsin clattered across the loose pebbles and stood at the water's edge, permitting the briny contents of Loch Coinneach to lap at the soles of her dusty walking boots.

The topography along the northern rim of the loch was gentler than that further inland. Here, its dark waters gently scoured the steep rocky banks of a string of small islands. Each island had a Gaelic name, as unpronounceable as the mountains that towered above them, and each was crowned by a sparse copse of windblown Caledonian pines. These islands protected the beaches of numerous small coves, similar to the one they were standing on. Some had sandy beaches, backed by high rocky cliffs, where only the odd clump of broom or heather struggled to maintain a precarious footing. Others were carpeted in loose rock, the debris from centuries of land based erosion.

Tamsin scanned the jagged profile of the island they'd seen from the road. It was a lonely, sinister place, with sheer glistening cliffs of granite that were liberally draped in kelp and seabird droppings. 'I can't see anything, only a few trees,' she called out.

Mike had walked further along the beach so he could observe the eastern end of the island more clearly. He too, could only see the small copse of wind sculpted pines clinging to the grassy summit. 'I can't see anything either,' he called back.

Then, as his view widened to take in the rocky beach on the south side of the island, he saw the neatly stacked cone of stones. Protected by a muddy bank where the soil and peat had been eroded away, the cairn had been hidden from view, except from the very end of the island.

'Found it!' Mike called out, with a sense of pride somewhat disproportionate to the level of his achievement. Tamsin caught up with him and they both stood in silence, absorbing the Arthurian atmosphere that hung about the place.

'You can easily imagine the scene centuries back, when the low wooden boat carrying the body of Earl Kenneth was rowed slowly across to his final resting place.' Mike closed his eyes, savouring the atmosphere.

Tamsin shook her head. 'You really are an incurable romantic aren't you?'

'You know, I do believe I can hear the pipes,' said Mike, shielding his ear with the palm of his hand.

'Oh, I suppose that'll be Black Kenneth's personal piper playing his sad lament from the prow of the boat. What about the rhythmic swishing of the oars, can you hear them too?'

'Yes, I do believe I can.' He yelped as Tamsin landed a playful punch on his arm.

'They call this lump of rock Eilean Ceann-Cinnidh, "Island of the Clan Chief". You know, I think I'd like my ashes sprinkled here,' said Mike thoughtfully.

'I'll bear that in mind,' Tamsin replied. 'Now, can we go back to the car?'

They strolled back across the shingle towards the path that led up to the road. Mike hesitated before commencing the final climb. 'You go on ahead Tams, I need a pee.'

He hurried off towards the tangled mass of broom that lined the edge of the beach. Once he'd reached the safety of the shrubbery, thereby providing himself a degree of privacy, he felt for the zip on his trousers. He heard his wife call out, 'I don't know why you're hiding in there, unless you're worried about a seagull watching you… and *I've* seen it all before.'

Mike glanced back at her and grinned. She did have a point he supposed, as he returned to the task in hand. Seeking a suitable spot to aim his flow, he casually scanned the pebbles lying about him.

Then something caught his eye, just a momentary flash, as if the sun was reflecting on something shiny. When his eyes focussed on the spot, he realised the source of this momentary distraction was the clouded glass face of an old wrist watch. For a second, it crossed his mind that another unfortunate rambler must have passed this way, and had somehow mislaid their old timepiece. He bent down to retrieve it, then recoiled abruptly, standing bolt upright, staring down at the spot wide eyed, disbelievingly. A shiver ran through his very soul, prompting the hairs on his neck to stand on end; the watch, complete with decaying leather strap, was seemingly secured to the wrist of a skeletal hand.

He blinked and squatted again to take a closer look, almost fearful that the yellowing bones may come to life and reach up to him. There was no mistaking it, this *was* a human hand. All the bones were intact, the phalanges forming the fingers, and the metacarpals of the palm. It projected up through the sand, claw like, clutching at the pebbles as if it were frenziedly attempting to free itself from a dark abyss beneath. The urge to urinate had now deserted him. He looked up to where he expected Tamsin to be. She was standing up on the road studying her map. Mike called out and waved furiously.

Eventually hearing his call, she spun around to see him beckoning to her to join him on the beach. 'Oh no, what has he seen now,' she murmured. She raised her arms, priest-like with palms raised, indicating that she was having difficulty with his bizarre method of communication. But there was no cessation in his frantic waving, and she soon realised that whatever it was he'd seen, it was most definitely important.

Begrudgingly, she started off down the slope, her eyes fixed on her husband who was squatting again, one hand to his mouth as if deep in thought.

Tamsin appeared next to him, annoyance etched upon her face. 'What on earth have you got me…?'

'Shut up will you, and look at this.'

He was in no mood for one of her lectures. Her protestation firmly checked, she stooped over his shoulder. 'Oh my God, is that a hand?'

'It most certainly is, complete with wristwatch.'

They both fell silent, desperately trying to make sense of the discovery. Tamsin was first to speak. 'Do you think there are any other bones under those stones?'

'I don't know whether I should look any further, what do you reckon?'

'Just carefully remove a couple of those pebbles. Let's see if there are any arm bones beyond the hand,' Tamsin suggested.

'Okay, but just a couple.'

Mike gingerly reached out and lifted first one, then two stones from around the hand. It soon became apparent that there were indeed other bones present, a radius and ulna from the forearm extending downward through the shingle and into the ground.

'That's it, no more. Let's go and call the police.' Mike replaced the stone he had in his hand and stood up.

Tamsin pulled out her mobile phone and checked the screen. 'No signal here, surprise surprise.'

'We'll have to walk back to Glendaig and call from there.'

Still reeling from the shock, they climbed back up to the road. Mike stopped and glanced back, as if to remind himself of the location of the bones, and then they started walking eastward.

Having marched along in silence for ten minutes, the monotonous rhythm of their footfall was interrupted by the sound of a car approaching from behind them. A small red van came into view some way off. It was then lost from sight for a while before reappearing onto the straight stretch of road they were walking along. As the vehicle came closer, Tamsin thought she recognised it as a Royal Mail van. She was soon proved to be correct when the van slowed to pass them. Mike stepped out and waved, prompting the single occupant to pull up next to them.

The driver's window was already wound down and peering through at them was the cheerful face of a young woman in her mid-thirties. 'Hello there, can I help you two?' She spoke confidently with a soft highland accent.

'I hope so,' said Mike, noticing the Royal Mail logo on her tee-shirt. 'We've been out hill walking this morning and ended up on one of the beaches back there. The one with the island just offshore. It has a cairn at one end.'

'Och Aye, that'll be Eilean Ceann-Cinnidh.'

'Yes, that's the one.' He took a deep breath. 'Whilst we were down on the beach, we came across what we think is a body… well a skeleton actually, partly buried under the shingle.'

The woman's eyes narrowed in disbelief. 'Are you sure?' she enquired.

'We're sure alright,' Tamsin protested, still visibly shocked, and a little irritated that their account had been questioned. 'He, or she, was still wearing a bloody wristwatch. Look, we need to call the police, but we can't get a signal on our mobile, can you help?'

'Aye, of course,' said the woman, her smile now gone. 'I'm on my way home to Glendaig. You can come with me and call from my house. It's only five minutes away.' So they set off for Glendaig, Mike crouching in the back of the van with the rucksacks and Tamsin sitting next to the post woman.

'My name's Siobhan Stuart,' their chauffeur divulged, interrupting an uneasy period of silence. 'I'm the postie at Glendaig... if you hadn't already guessed. Pleased to meet you, but perhaps not in these circumstances.' She smiled again, reassuringly this time. Tamsin now began to relax a little, disarmed by the post woman's congeniality.

Siobhan was a strikingly attractive woman. Curly dark hair cascaded around her porcelain smooth features, pierced only by her vivid green eyes. Tamsin glanced across at her, wondering whether the catwalk may have been a far more lucrative choice of workplace for her than a Highland mail van!

Siobhan turned to her passenger, mindful of her continued silence. 'Where are you two from then?'

'Oh sorry, I'm Tamsin Kirkwood, and my husband's Mike. We're up here on holiday from Lincolnshire.'

'Some holiday you're having! I just can't believe you've found a... a skeleton. This sort of thing just doesn't happen around here.'

As she stopped speaking, they passed an ageing white sign, informing travellers that they were entering Glendaig. A short distance further on and they came across Tamsin and Mike's silver Volkswagen Golf, still parked in the lay-by where they'd left it earlier that morning.

'That's our car, parked there,' Tamsin said, pointing.

11

'Okay, well I live just along from here. It'll only take you a minute or so to walk back.'

The van sped into the village, past the old stone Manse and small parish church. Then, as they began to lose speed, Siobhan announced, 'Here we are at last.'

They pulled up on a gravel hard standing, outside a slender looking single storey cottage. It's dark granite walls sheltered beneath an equally dark slate roof, upon which stood three small chimneys. The flaking white paintwork on the sash windows provided Tamsin with a foretaste of what she might expect inside, and she wasn't to be disappointed. Having released Mike from the rear of the van, Siobhan led the couple through the crumbling wooden gate. An elderly cabin cruiser stood before them, propped up precariously on stacks of sleepers. *The Pride of Knoydart,* according to the name just discernible upon the stern, had definitely seen better days. Peeling paint revealed the grey of partially decayed wood, whilst the cabin windows had become obscured by grime and the webs of countless spiders. Tamsin glanced up at the vessel and came to the same conclusion that previous visitors had no doubt reached – that the rotting hulk was far from being a source of *pride*! Yet she could imagine the vessel in its heyday, slowly plodding across the loch, its white paint sparkling in the spring sunshine and its progress closely monitored by scores of hungry seagulls.

Next to the lobster pots guarding the front door was a tangle of green fishing net, surmounted by several plastic marker buoys. The small orange spheres lay draped in strands of dried seaweed, relics from their last immersion in the cold waters of the Sound of Sleat.

'Come on in,' said Siobhan, kicking a couple of lobster pots to one side as she inserted the key in the lock. 'The phone's on the table over there.' Mike didn't delay, and picked up the grubby plastic handset to dial 999. After a short wait, he said 'Police please.'

Tamsin followed Siobhan into a kitchen teeming with everyday clutter.

'Cup of tea, Tamsin?' Siobhan asked, as she filled the kettle.

'Thank you, if it's not too much trouble.'

'Never too much trouble to make a brew!'

Tamsin sat down at the kitchen table, having first removed a ginger tomcat that had been sleeping on the chair she'd selected.

'It'll take the police ages to get here. You've got plenty of time,' Siobhan advised.

'Tell me,' asked Tamsin, 'have you ever heard of anyone going missing around here, perhaps a long while ago? Those bones seemed quite old to me.'

Siobhan pursed her lips. 'No, not that I can recall. Gordon, that's my husband, and I have been here for the last four years. I certainly don't recall anyone going missing during that time.'

'Well I suppose the police will eventually get to the bottom of it.'

'I hope so, it's not something they get much practice at out here,' said Siobhan. She sighed as she poured the tea. 'Everyone in the village will be really shocked when they hear about this.'

Mike eventually entered the room. 'The police are on their way, but they've got to come from the Skye Bridge, so they'll be about forty-five minutes. We've been asked to go back to the place where we found the remains and wait by the road for them.'

'Well, drink this before you go,' demanded Siobhan, as she handed him a steaming mug.

'I wonder what on earth could have happened to that poor devil on the beach,' said Mike.

'Who knows,' Siobhan replied as she stirred her tea. 'One thing's for sure, now you've found him, or *her*, our usual humdrum existence is set to change… at least temporarily!'

The Kirkwoods drained their mugs, grateful for the refreshment. 'Well you never know, they may well be old bones and perhaps the story behind them isn't quite as dramatic as we assume it to be,' suggested Mike. 'Thanks for the tea Siobhan, we'd better get off I suppose, and wait for the police.'

Outside, the breeze had strengthened significantly. Leaves that still lay in abundance around the sleepers supporting the cabin cruiser swirled about their feet as they walked to the gate. Mike and Tamsin exchanged glances. 'The day hasn't quite panned out as I'd quite envisaged,' Tamsin sighed, as she grasped Mike's hand. They turned right and walked down the deserted road towards their car. He smiled back at her, squeezing her hand. 'That's probably what the owner of the wristwatch would be saying, if he could speak,' he retorted.

Chapter Two

It had seemed an age since Mike Kirkwood first called the police. According to his watch, it was now nearly one thirty, and not one solitary vehicle had passed by. They'd been waiting for nearly an hour.

Mike opened the car door and eased himself out. The muscles in his calves had begun to tighten, and he felt the need to stretch his legs. As he leant against the door post and exercised the offending muscles, he noticed movement in the distance. A car was approaching from the west, sunlight glinting on its bodywork. It was travelling at speed and, like the mail van, was passing in and out of view as it negotiated the numerous bends and blind summits that littered this lonely stretch of road. It was unmistakably a police car, trimmed garishly in blue and yellow, the now familiar Battenberg livery that adorned police vehicles up and down the country.

By the time he'd slipped back into the driver's seat and given Tamsin the good news, a Volvo patrol car had pulled up on the layby in front of them. The two front doors slowly opened as if harmonised, revealing Celtic crests and an equally inspiring Gaelic motto.

In contrast, Mike and Tamsin leapt out of their car with a good deal more urgency, a sense of anxious excitement rising within them. Two uniformed policemen climbed out of the police car, their demeanour almost leisurely, each pulling on a flat cap.

'Don't hurry yourselves,' Tamsin growled under her breath.

Mike glared at her. 'Shhh, for God's sake.'

'Mr and Mrs Kirkwood?' Sergeant Duncan Strang approached the young couple and shook hands.

'I'm sorry about the wait folks; we were a wee bit busy with an incident up on the Skye Bridge. Couldn't get away as quickly as we'd hoped.'

He was joined by another officer, a constable who was a little older and larger than himself. The sergeant continued his introduction.

'I'm Sergeant Duncan Strang, this here is Constable Alisdair Drummond. Now, I understand you've found some human remains?' He looked firstly at Mike, and then Tamsin enquiringly.

Mike's mouth was dry, whether it was nerves or excitement, he couldn't tell. Whatever the case, it took him a second or two to find his voice. He swallowed hard several times, before nervously explaining how he'd come across the skeletal hand. Then, at the officers' request, he led them across the road and down the rocky path to the beach. They trudged across the pebbles towards the point where he'd made the grisly discovery. His heart was pounding, his mind racing... *oh God, what if I've dreamt it... what if the hand is no longer there?*

There it was though, still reaching up through the sand, an almost sinister stillness about it. Mike sighed, experiencing a strangely perverse sense of relief. It was just as before, the grubby face of the wristwatch still glinting in the sunlight.

'Well, well,' said Strang, 'what do we have here?'

He pushed his crumpled cap to the back of his head and squatted down to examine the bones. For several seconds, the forty-five-year-old Glaswegian pondered over the scene before him, his twenty years of policing experience immediately being brought to bear. However, his eventual assessment was the only one possible and could just as easily have been made by a rookie! He rubbed his chin before sharing his conclusions.

'My initial thoughts are that these bones are quite old. Having said that, the watch clearly indicates they're not ancient. I think we can safely say, he, or *she* I suppose, wasn't a Viking!' He stooped lower to get a better view of the timepiece. 'This'll no doubt help us date the remains relatively accurately.'

Drummond then joined him on the shingle, also dropping to his knees and joining his supervisor to examine this most important clue.

'*Hanhart, seventeen Steine* is inscribed on the face. Then there's the word *tachymeter* in red on the inner dial. I'm surprised it's still here; the strap is almost completely gone. Looks like it was brown leather in an earlier life.'

The sergeant heaved his large frame back up to a standing position. He dusted the sand from his knees. 'We'll call this in, and start the ball rolling. I'm not going to disturb the scene any more… we'll leave our Scene Investigators to do that.'

He glanced back towards the sparkling water of Loch Coinneach. 'At least we're well above the high tide mark. Otherwise we'd have to recover the bones on the hurry-up. Doesn't look like they were washed up though, being this far up the beach.'

Drummond was instructed to return to the police car and call in the details of the find to the Force Control Room. As the constable retreated across the beach, Strang stood with the Kirkwoods. 'I wonder how he ended up here… I think we can assume it's a *him* for the time being, from the style of watch. The bones seem quite bulky too.' He turned back to the couple. 'We'll obviously be treating this as a suspicious death enquiry for now, so we'll need witness statements from you both.'

'That's fine,' said Mike. 'Do you want us to wait here?'

'Where are you staying?' the sergeant enquired.

'The Invertulloch Inn,' said Tamsin, arms folded against the freshening breeze.

'Och aye, I know it. That's Fiona Garvie's place. She's a larger than life character is she not?'

He produced a muted chuckle, no doubt recalling some previous experience with their convivial landlady. 'Well we can send someone up to see you there or you can wait here with us and I'll get them taken as soon as the reinforcements arrive.'

'We'll stay here if you don't mind. We can sit in the car out of the way,' suggested Mike.

'That's fine, let's go back up to the road now and leave this beach to the experts. We don't want to disturb the scene here anymore than necessary.'

When they returned to the cars, PC Drummond joined them. 'All sorted Sarge; they're sending a DC out from Fort William, and informing the duty SIO at Inverness. I got the impression they were thinking we'd found some ancient Pictish warrior, but they changed their minds fairly rapidly when I told them about the wristwatch!'

'I bet they did,' said Strang, dismissing the jape. 'What about uniform support?'

'A couple of units en route, one from Broadford and another from Fort Augustus, they'll be some time though.'

'Well luckily we're not inundated with onlookers or the media just yet,' said Strang. 'Start a scene log Alisdair, and we'll tape off the approach to the remains whilst we are waiting.'

Drummond returned to the police car and began ferreting around in the boot. 'What's an *SIO*?' Tamsin asked. Strang, impressed by her interest, was happy to explain.

'Oh, it's a term we use for a senior detective, someone trained to manage major crime investigations, like murders. It's police jargon for "Senior Investigating Officer". We have a pool of them, so one's always on call. They're based at our headquarters over in Inverness.'

The Kirkwoods, reflecting on Strang's words, particularly that of *murder*, returned to their car, still numb from the day's unexpected turn of events. They sat in silence as the policemen went about their business. Drummond had now retrieved a large roll of blue and white plastic tape and was carefully unravelling it as he made his way down the slope to the beach. Strang followed on behind, twisting the tape around sticks and branches that he'd pushed into the soft ground beside the path. Soon a corridor of blue and white was snaking its way down to the point where the remains had been found. Flapping wildly in the breeze, this macabre pathway now seemed to dominate the scene, as if an affront to the stunning beauty of its surroundings.

A couple of cars had passed since the arrival of the police. The inquisitive occupants had craned their necks to see what was going on, but hadn't had the courage to stop and ask. As he sat huddled behind the steering wheel of his own car, Mike doubted whether the peace they were currently experiencing would last for long.

Another patrol car eventually pulled into the narrow lay-by and parked up behind the first. Sergeant Strang clearly knew the occupants well and briefed them through the driver's window. Shortly afterwards the Kirkwoods were invited to join the new arrivals so that their witness statements could be obtained. Strang then busied himself making notes in his own car, leaving Drummond to do the manual work. The constable, happy to remain industrious, marched off up the road with *Police Slow* signs under each arm.

Time passed quickly whilst Mike and Tamsin recounted their experience to the two young constables. In fact, another thirty minutes had passed by when a third patrol car arrived, occupied by a lone female officer. She was closely followed into the parking area by a small dark blue hatchback, driven by another young woman. The second driver was smartly dressed in beige slacks and a matching waistcoat. Her immediate priority was the removal and protection of her shiny brown court shoes, as she hopped around on one leg at the rear of her car. The shoes were duly replaced by a pair of green wellington boots, trendily trimmed with tweed around the rims. Aged about twenty-five, if that, she was greeted by Sergeant Strang who then beckoned to the other woman who'd just arrived. He then repeated his briefing speech, before accompanying the trendily dressed woman in the wellington boots down to the beach. They passed between the fluttering blue tapes, deep in conversation, and then stopped close to the site where the remains had been found.

'What d'you reckon then, Pepper?' Strang asked.

'I think you're right Sarge, these bones do look quite old.' DC Holly Anderson had been dubbed "Pepper" by her older male colleagues when she initially joined the CID. Apparently, her surname was identical to that of a female TV cop of the seventies – long before her time, of course! Initially the name had niggled her, but then she'd figured that to be given a nickname meant that she'd been accepted in the office, especially as all the male DCs had also been given one!

This was her first day flying solo as duty DC, and she was acutely aware of the responsibility that had been bestowed upon her. Draping herself over the long spidery fingers, she endeavoured to examine the watch as closely as she could without disturbing the remains. She swept away strands of barley-coloured hair from her face with a latex-gloved hand and looked up.

'Have you heard the name *Hanhart* before?' she asked.

'Not that I can think of,' the sergeant replied, shaking his head.

Anderson jumped up with an energy that Strang considered had long since abandoned him. She wiped the sand from her gloves and peeled them off to reveal tiny childlike hands. 'It looks sort of old, but not that old… if you know what I mean? It may well be Swiss. We'll just have to do some digging.'

She looked about her, taking in the surroundings. 'Umm, good place to bury a body I suppose. I don't expect anyone comes down here much.' She glanced across at Strang, who was unwrapping a boiled sweet. 'Thanks for offering, Sarge.' She held out an expectant hand. 'Is this exactly how the Kirkwoods found it?'

Strang handed her one of his foil-wrapped humbugs. 'They removed a few stones to see if there were any other bones attached, which as you can see there were, then replaced them.'

'What about the rest of the beach, have you had a look around yet?'

'Not really, only a cursory check.'

'Okay, that's fine; we'll have it searched properly at some stage. I've spoken to DCI Brodie over at Inverness. Think I must have caught him at the nineteenth hole!' She stuffed the sweet wrapping in her pocket. 'The Major Enquiry Team seem to be interested in this. He's the duty SIO, says he'll get here as soon as he can.'

Strang sucked hard on his humbug. 'There's not much more we can do I suppose, not until the Scene Investigators arrive.'

'You've done well Sarge, securing the scene,' said Anderson, scribbling into her pocket book. Strang shot her a disbelieving glance.

'It's very good of you to say so Pepper; it's only taken me all of twenty years to reach this level of competence. In fact I do believe I was probably attending scenes like this when you were in nappies.'

She laughed. 'Och, don't be so sensitive Sergeant Strang, you know I'd be no good with duty rosters or staff appraisals! Horses for courses eh?' Strang produced a low chuckle and made a playful gesture of smacking the back of her head. The spirited young DC reminded him of his own daughter, who'd just gone away to university. Anderson ducked, instinctively avoiding his hand, and trotted away ahead of him, intending to stay out of range.

Back at Strang's patrol car, the veteran sergeant and rookie detective sat together theorising as to the origins of the remains and how the investigation should progress. She drank periodically from a bottle of mineral water, willing her colleagues from the Scientific Support Unit to arrive and commence their examination of the beach. In the meantime, the statements from the Kirkwoods had been completed and Strang passed the time reading them, emitting the odd expletive when he came across a spelling mistake.

Anderson grinned. 'Did you not know Sarge, they don't teach them spelling in schools now.'

'They probably didn't even when you were at school, which probably wasn't that long ago.'

'They did *so*, and I consider that to be an ageist remark Sergeant, shame on you.'

'Sue me then.' They both laughed, and the conversation switched to in-force gossip.

It was well after three when a pair of white vans appeared in the distance. When they finally pulled up in the lay-by, Senior Scene Investigator Fraser Gunn emerged from the leading vehicle.

'Afternoon Pepper, sorry about the delay, it's these bloody Sunday staffing cuts. I've been chasing my tail all over the place today.'

Gunn was an experienced Scenes of Crime Officer with a reputation for his attention to detail. He was also well known for his complaining nature and his failure to suffer fools gladly, particularly those in senior management positions. Now aged forty-four, his wispy auburn hair was receding rapidly to reveal more and more of the heavily freckled scalp beneath. He was a tall, lean man with prominently high cheekbones and sunken eyes. These gaunt features combined to present a somewhat cadaverous appearance, considered by many to be well suited to his line of work. Anderson could well understand why some of the younger lads on the Force had dubbed him "The Skull".

'What have we got then?' he enquired as he opened the rear doors of his van and began the vaguely amusing ritual of climbing into a white all-in-one suit. Anderson talked him through the circumstances, assisted by the odd interjection from Sergeant Strang who was, by now, well-rehearsed on the subject. Gunn nodded in silent acknowledgement before releasing the rims of his purple latex gloves with a loud *thwack*. 'Right,' he said grinning, 'let us go to work.'

Laden with a number of steel cases, tripods and various other items of equipment, he led his small team across the road. They paused by the dutiful PC Drummond, who was eager to interrupt the boredom of the previous hour or so by making a further detailed entry in his scene log.

Once on the beach they trooped along the marked pathway towards their target. To the casual passer-by it would've been a strange, if not surreal, sight. Four white-clad figures, attired like aliens, marching steadily across the beach one after the other.

Having arrived at the location of the find they immediately went to work. Anderson looked on from the road, content that the scene was now in good hands. She turned and made her way back to the Kirkwoods' car.

'The statements are fine,' she told them. 'We've got all your details if we need to speak to you again, so you're free to go if you wish.'

Mike and Tamsin agreed that it had been a long day and the prospect of a long hot soak in their bath at the Inn was becoming more and more attractive. 'Okay, we'll get going,' said Mike. 'Thank you for your help.'

Anderson smiled. 'No problem at all, thank you for yours! We'll certainly let you know how things progress.'

As the Kirkwoods drove slowly away towards Glendaig she returned to her viewpoint by the side of the road. Two of the white-clad figures were painstakingly removing stones from the burial site, overseen by another who was videoing the proceedings. Fraser Gunn was setting up some camera equipment on a tripod whilst his colleague, trainee Scene Investigator Lynn Cowan, scribbled furiously on a clipboard.

Anderson took another slug from her bottle of water, and ambled over to Drummond who was still diligently standing guard at the top of the path. News that the sometimes prickly DCI Brodie was en route had significantly heightened his attention to duty.

'I wonder why that hand became exposed, Alisdair.'

'Perhaps it was animals,' said the constable, grateful that his humble opinion had been sought.

'Well it wasn't the tide, that's for sure. Perhaps it's been exposed for years, who knows? I suppose it's just a stroke of luck that anyone found it at all.'

Gunn could now be seen making his way back between the tapes. He zigzagged his way up the steep slope clutching a number of evidence bags in his right hand. When he reached the road, he paused to get his breath back.

'Well, all I can say is…' he panted, 'this is not your average crime scene. We've partially uncovered what appears to be a complete skeleton, probably male due to the size of the bones.' He took another lungful of air, and was looking even more deathly than usual. 'The remains are old, but not ancient, taking into account the watch and some other stuff we've found. I'd say we're looking at half a century, perhaps a little older. The pathologist will be better placed to give you an age.'

'So what have you got there?' Anderson asked, gesturing towards the polythene bags.

'We've recovered a number of items of interest located amongst the remains. You've already seen the watch I gather? Well, we've bagged it up now, so you can see both sides of the casing.'

He handed her the evidence bag, inside of which the watch lay forlornly amongst the crumbling remains of its leather strap. She lifted the bag to face level and studied the contents for several seconds, her eyes darting from side to side, seeking any potential clue from this vital exhibit. She flipped the bag around to reveal the back plate of the watch. Inscribed in the centre of the plate was the name *Hanhart*, beneath which was a serial number. Around the edge was the faint inscription – *Hergestellt in Deutschland, 100m wasserdicht, stossfest, Edelstahl-Gehäuse,* and *Saphirglas.*

'*Deutschland.* So it was made in Germany then?'

'Looks like it,' Gunn concurred. 'Now look at this.' He handed her another bag. In it was a small four-pointed metal cross, dull black and trimmed in faded silver. The arms of the cross widened towards the ends in the cross pattée style. In the centre was the unmistakeable shape of the swastika, and the date 1939 was inscribed at the base of one arm.

'There was another cross lying next to this one, slightly different, and with some sort of leaf arrangement in the form of a clasp mounted above one of the arms. We found them next to the right thigh bone.'

A third bag was produced. Sure enough, inside there was another cross, on the face of it identical to the first, but with a small burnished clasp, clearly shaped in the form of oak leaves attached to the uppermost arm. On the rear of the cross was the date 1813 and there were several small hallmark-like stamps on the rim, the figure *800* on one side of the clasp ring and *20* on the other.

'They look to me like Iron Crosses,' suggested PC Drummond, peering over Gunn's shoulder.

'Iron Crosses?' The young detective looked round at him, surprised by his contribution.

'Yes, German medals from World War Two. They used to wear them around the neck sometimes, or on their uniform tunics. You must have seen them in films on the TV?'

'I prefer the soaps myself,' said Anderson, acknowledging her lack of knowledge of all things military.

Gunn nodded. 'Yes, Alisdair's stolen my thunder, but I'm sure he's right; that's certainly what they appear to be. I've often seen them being worn in wartime photos. I've just never handled one.'

'Well it all makes sense, taking into account the German watch,' Anderson concluded. 'What else have you got there?'

Gunn produced a fourth bag. It contained a tattered remnant of dark material, decorated with what appeared to once have been three faded strips of gold lace, surmounted by a small star. 'We've found a few fragments of this type of cloth around the remains, together with some thicker blue-grey woollen material. Obviously clothing at one time… and we also found this.' He handed her another smaller bag, containing a single button.

She examined the corroded object through the clear plastic. Green with oxidisation, the button bore the image of an anchor laid upon a wavy length of rope, the edge worn away but still retaining some of its original patterning. 'Looks like we possibly have ourselves a German sailor from World War Two then.'

Anderson sensed that her newly acquired detective skills were not being tested quite to the extent that she'd hoped. 'Anything else of interest?'

'I'd guess he was a naval officer of some seniority.' Gunn pointed towards the bag containing the gold lace. 'But to answer your question, not really. Just some fragments of what was possibly a leather wallet, nothing with it of course.'

'Seems to me this is more a case for the historians than us,' said Drummond, still hovering in the background.

'It's beginning to look like it,' Anderson agreed. 'But it's a little strange that he ended up here. Is it at all possible he *was* washed up, Fraser?'

'Not a chance,' Gunn replied, his eyes twinkling as if he were about to deliver a bombshell. 'The circumstances here really don't support that theory.'

'Go on then, don't keep me in suspense Fraser... what circumstances?'

'Well, firstly he was buried in a shallow grave...'

'Fair comment, but he still could have been washed up initially.' She pursed her lips, seeking at least some support for her theory.

'You haven't asked me for a cause of death yet,' he declared with a degree of haughtiness. Anderson coloured slightly, her discomfort evident.

'I would've got round to that Fraser. I didn't think you'd have a clue that's all... so enlighten me then.'

'I believe he was executed. Single shot, very close range to the front of the head, just above the eyes. My guess is that a small calibre weapon was used, probably a handgun. I don't know about you, but I can't see there being too many instances of combat related injuries bearing that hallmark!'

Chapter Three

Neil Strachan's brow crinkled into a lingering scowl. He attempted to shift his reclining form to a more comfortable position, but it was never going to happen. Sharing a two-seater sofa with a sleeping dog *and* a broadsheet newspaper was always going to be awkward. He raised the sports supplement just enough to reveal a long furry snout and two intensely focussed brown eyes. The three-year-old chocolate spaniel lay stretched out between his legs, his silky head resting nonchalantly on his master's lap.

'For Christ's sake Tam, do you have to lie between my legs like that?' The newspaper dropped back onto his chest, and he returned to the article on Europe's top ten golf courses.

This was Neil's first Sunday off for three weeks. He'd been the Duty Detective Inspector the weekend before and had been called out the Sunday before that to a missing child from the beach at Dornoch. So today he was going to chill out. That meant walking the dog, watching some of the Monaco Grand Prix and reading the Sunday paper. He'd overindulged when they'd eaten at lunchtime and sleep was very much on the agenda. Utopia! So far all was going to plan, the eyelids were becoming heavier and the paper was slowly beginning to concertina onto his chest.

'Look at the pair of you; you're like a couple of old lovers.'

One eye half opened from beneath the dog's distinctive sun bleached fringe and the tail wagged a couple of times. Neil's long-time girlfriend Catriona Duncan strolled into the room wiping her hands on a towel.

'Well, are you going to lie there all day, or shall we take Tam out and walk off lunch?'

'Aye, I suppose so.' Neil heaved himself upright and carefully lifted his leg over the dog's inert body. The tail wagged again, this time furiously against the leather seat cushion. Catriona looked on in amusement as the dog stretched and slid off the sofa like a snake. Her partner, now vertical and yawning protractedly, had stretched his arms above his head, accentuating his full height of five feet ten. Neil had just turned thirty, however, he could be mistaken as being several years younger. His mop of chestnut brown hair, loosely parted in the centre, and expensive rimless spectacles gave him something of a scholarly appearance. It was an image that wasn't entirely undeserved. He did, after all, have a BA in modern history and politics.

Cat, as Neil preferred to call her, had tried to persuade him to lose the glasses and use contact lenses, but he'd protested that without them he looked far too young. She knew that this was rubbish. He secretly preferred to wear glasses because the thought of inserting contacts repulsed him. Glasses or not, he was a handsome young man with an athletic build. Watching him tuck his shirt back into his jeans had reminded Cat that he'd been quite a catch all those months before.

The couple had met at school in Fortrose. They'd both been brought up on the Black Isle, not an island, but a low narrow peninsula lying between the Moray and Cromarty Firths. Cat had lived all her young life in a small hamlet near Fortrose itself. She'd moved on to college in Inverness before landing herself a job in the local procurator fiscal's office. Now aged twenty-eight, she rented a small flat in the city centre. However, most of her friends knew the best place to find her, and it wasn't at the flat off the Old Edinburgh Road.

Neil was born and raised in nearby Cromarty, an ancient sea port at the tip of the Black Isle peninsula. He'd moved south to Stirling after school, and had studied at the university there before joining the police service in 2002. He'd always wanted to be a police officer, inspired by the stories of his Great Uncle Euan, who'd retired from the force a year before he was born.

Neil had always been attracted to Cat, but had been too shy to take things further. She'd always turned heads, with her piercing blue eyes inconspicuously framed by long blonde hair that fountained about her shoulders, and an intensely convivial nature that had always placed her top of the popularity league as a teenager. He'd convinced himself he was never going to be in the running as far as she was concerned, but then they'd been reacquainted at a party two years earlier. He'd rightly detected the subtle signs of attraction flowing from Cat that evening. Buoyed up by her flirtatious remarks and a generous intake of alcohol, he'd asked her out on a date. The rest was history.

He knew she wanted more from the relationship and she kept reminding him that time was marching on! He knew she was right, but somehow felt he couldn't commit for the time being, perhaps wary of the disaster that befell his own parents' relationship, but more so due to the long hours he'd committed to in his newly acquired rank. Nevertheless, their bond was strong and thriving, and Cat was known for her patience!

Neil shuffled out into the hallway followed by his trusty hound, tail still wagging rapidly in expectation. He opened the cloakroom cupboard, scratching his scalp through still compacted hair. The tail of his shirt still hung crumpled over the back of his jeans. Cat shook her head in disbelief. Having leant into the dark void for an inordinate period of time, he re-emerged with Tam's lead in his hand. 'Let's go then, son,' he called out to the dog.

The view from Neil's unimposing new build, high above the Moray Firth at Culloden, was far-reaching. Beyond the Firth lay the Black Isle, and his childhood home. Beyond that were the mountains of Sutherland, dark purple against a backdrop of towering white cloud. In the foreground sprawled the Royal Burgh of Inverness, its ancient heart now swamped by modern housing schemes, a sure sign of the emerging popularity of the Highland capital. Red anti-collision lights capping the towers on the Kessock Bridge glinted in the distance, beneath which a relentless flow of ant-like traffic sped in both directions over the narrow channel that separated Inverness from the Black Isle.

The couple strolled out from the driveway arm in arm, Neil struggling to control the excited spaniel. They'd just turned left onto Culloden Road when the rhythmic beat from Neil's mobile phone interrupted the couple's conversation.

'Hello, Neil Strachan.'

His boss's voice boomed from the earpiece. 'Neil, it's Alex Brodie, can you talk?'

Neil closed his eyes in disbelief. 'Aye sir, I'm all ears.'

'Neil, some human remains have been found on a beach over on the west coast. I'll be taking the SIO role, but I thought you might like to come with me to visit the scene, you being the new boy on the team, eh?'

There was a pause, whilst Neil digested the proposal; a pause that he knew could not linger for too long if he were to remain in favour with the head of the Major Enquiry Unit. Detective Chief Inspector Brodie didn't do rejection.

'Aye Sir, I'm up for it. I'm out with the dog at the moment though.'

'No bother Neil, just get yourself over to my place soon as. I'll brief you on the way. Oh, and do you mind driving? Only the wife needs the car this evening. Thought it might be a nice afternoon for a run in that wee MG of yours.'

'No problem sir, see you shortly.'

Neil returned the phone to his pocket. 'I'm sorry Cat, that was the DCI. Seems they've found a body on a beach over in the west. He wants me to go over there with him.'

'Sounds interesting,' replied Cat, trying hard to mask her disappointment. 'This could be your first murder case in the new job, eh?'

'I don't know about that, probably a Russian fisherman fallen overboard from a trawler or suchlike. One thing's for sure though, If I want to go anywhere in the new job, I can't piss the boss off.'

'Don't worry, I understand. You get off and I'll see you later. Come on Tam, you'll have to make do with me as your walking companion I'm afraid.'

Neil planted a kiss on Cat's cheek. 'I'm really sorry; I'll try not to be late.' He dropped down, and having satisfied Tam with a disproportionate level of affection to that just afforded to his partner, he strode off purposefully towards home. 'I'll ring you later on,' he called after her as she headed off in the opposite direction.

'So what's your gut reaction Neil? Was our mystery man the victim of a mutiny, or perhaps a spy, landed by submarine to keep an eye on what the military were doing up here in the Highlands? Hardly likely I suppose, spies don't often wear medals.'

Alex Brodie chuckled to himself as he studied the Ordnance Survey map depicting the area around Glendaig. He adjusted his large frame so that he could open the map fully. Neil shot him a concerned glance, mindful of the strain that the big man from Stornaway was inflicting on the ageing seat springs.

Neil had travelled to Leeds to buy the mark one MG Midget just after he'd joined the police. It had first come off the assembly line in 1964, one of the last of its type, and had been left in a sorry state within an equally sorry looking garage for nearly ten years. The restoration process had become an obsession, but now the little sports car hummed like a bird, resplendent in its original British Racing Green livery and gleaming chrome trim.

Neil tapped impatiently on the steering wheel, stuck behind a slow moving truck. 'It all seems a bit strange to me. The obvious theory would be that he was washed up, but clearly that's not the case in these circumstances. Your agent theory would be second on my list, but as you say, agents don't normally wear medals. Perhaps he's not who he appears to be at all and we're barking up the wrong tree completely.'

Neil was trying hard to project a level of enthusiasm above that which he was truly experiencing. The facts suggested that any enquiry into the origins of these bones would end up in the hands of a team of military historians, rather than hard-pressed police officers. Nevertheless, there was a small part of him that relished the challenge of discovering whose bones these were and why they were buried on a Ross-shire beach. No doubt, he reasoned, it was because of his deep routed and on-going fascination with the past. As much as he loved his work as a policeman, the historian still languished within him from his university days! They were happy days, and the lure of academia often still seduced him.

'Aye, you may be right,' Brodie replied. 'Still, I suppose it's a wee bit of a departure from the usual domestics or fight-related deaths.'

'What's the fiscal going to make of it do you think?'

'We'll find out when we get to the scene, I've asked Jack Tait, the on-call man from Fort William, to meet us there. My guess is that he'll have no option initially, but to treat this as a suspicious death and for us to investigate it as such.'

They swung right at Invermoriston and began heading west. His boss had fallen silent and Neil glanced across at him in a bid to discover why. Brodie was gazing out of the window, deep in thought. His military-style cropped red hair glowed in the late afternoon sunlight. He looked older than his forty-six years, probably because he was carrying too much weight. Then again, it could have been his lengthy military service with the Queen's Own Highlanders in Northern Ireland and Kuwait that had left its mark. One thing was for sure, his personality definitely matched his physical appearance.

'Who's out at the scene?' Neil asked.

'Some of the local uniform boys and a DC from Fort William, Holly Anderson. Do you know her?'

'Aye, I've heard of her, bit of a looker I'm told, and keen as mustard. The boys call her "Pepper", from that American cop show *Police Woman*.'

'Umm, I recall that series, what was her name… Angie Dickinson? The actress who played the character Pepper Anderson?'

Neil grinned. 'Bit of a fan were you sir?'

'Christ no, I'm not a fan of American cop shows.' His jowls reddened as he urgently dismissed the suggestion.

The sun had dipped behind the dark jagged tops of the Five Sisters by the time the two detectives turned onto the steep narrow road that twisted and turned its way across to Camuscraig. It was nearly five o'clock, but the air was still warm and Brodie had no concerns about fading light. The MG laboured as it tackled the steep gradient, new mountain vistas opening up with each hairpin bend. As they reached the top of the climb the road fell away before them, threading its way down between green pastures towards the sea and the distant village of Camuscraig. Beyond, the Cuillin mountains of Skye stood pencil sharp like fangs against a backdrop of azure blue.

Camuscraig had grown little over the years, with only the odd new-build property springing up on the edge of the village. The centre, however, retained its old-world charm, dominated by the neatly maintained fishermen's cottages that lined the narrow street. The throb of the MG's engine echoed off of the little stone dwellings as the shiny green sports car headed ever closer to the shoreline. As they emerged from a series of bends, bordered by a mass of tangled rhododendron bushes, the war memorial came into view, standing tall against the backdrop of the Sound of Sleat. Next to the memorial was the old concrete slipway, surrounded by the beached hulks of the local fishing fleet. Beyond, a row of seventies' bungalows lined the potholed road. Then they were out of the village and speeding along the single-track route that hugged the north shore of Loch Coinneach. There was no mistaking their final location, as the bright yellow and blue markings of the three marked police cars came into view a mile further on.

'I think I'll stick with the Volvo,' said Brodie as he negotiated his bulk out of the little sports car, smoothing his crumpled suit jacket as he did so. Neil certainly wasn't going to disagree. It was exactly the response he'd been hoping for! Thankfully, the novelty of travelling in a sports car was to be short-lived. Brodie, for all his excess weight, was always immaculately turned out and any disruption to his crisp appearance would never be tolerated.

Holly Anderson appeared from nowhere, clutching the plastic evidence bags. She was accompanied by a smartly but casually dressed man around forty, with ash grey hair and a friendly smile.

'Hello sirs, DC Anderson from Fort William, and this is Mr Tait, the duty fiscal.'

Introductions over, the two men from Inverness were briefed and shown the contents of the evidence bags. Neil studied the old watch, running his thumb across the face through the plastic. He could feel a heightened sense of excitement rising within him. *Who on earth owned this watch and why did he end up here? What was his story?*

There was a curious angle to this case, an additional element that was missing from the others he'd worked on. History had left its mark on this beach and he again felt the sense of wonderment that had once motivated him to study the subject at Stirling.

'Well let's have a look at the grave site shall we Holly?' said Brodie; there was no way he was going to use silly nicknames!

'Yes sir, come this way.'

The foursome halted to provide the now erect and annoyingly overly attentive PC Drummond with their names for his log before descending onto the beach. Stumbling over the loose shingle, they headed for the white-suited figures still beavering away at the end of the tape-lined pathway. Fraser Gunn had been tipped off that the group were approaching and rose stiffly to his feet before strolling out to greet them.

'Afternoon Mr Brodie, Neil. Do come and meet my mysterious friend!'

'Hello Fraser, Holly's brought us up to speed, let's have a wee look then.'

'We've fully excavated the grave site now. I believe we have a youngish male, large build as you can see, over six feet tall. We've managed to recover some more fragments of clothing, but the significant finds are in the bags you've no doubt been shown.'

'Aye, we've just been having a look at them.'

Brodie stood, head cocked to one side as he took in the scene in front of him. The shingle had been carefully removed to reveal a shallow grave in the underlying sand. It measured approximately two feet deep, and about the same in width. The skeleton lay fully intact on its back and as Gunn had already pointed out, the individual it once supported had certainly been well built. The skull's lower jaw had dropped open revealing lines of surprisingly white teeth. Neil felt a momentary shiver pass through him as he surveyed the scene. The yellowing skull grinned back at him, reminiscent of a prop from a ghost train ride; its empty eye sockets gazing skyward, revealing the void behind them where sand deposits had built up over time.

Neil squatted to examine the skull more closely. Just above and between the eye sockets was a small round hole. The bone around its rim had been forced inwards, indicating an entrance wound. Directly in line with the nasal cavity he could just make out the corresponding exit hole at the rear.

'Any thoughts on the weapon used, Fraser?'

'I was saying to Holly earlier, small calibre handgun, probably nine millimetre, and at close range.'

Neil clambered to his feet. 'Why is the left arm at that angle?' he asked. 'Was it found in that position?'

'Yes, as you can see the right arm was laid in the grave, positioned at the side of the corpse. The left arm which was poking out through the stones was positioned at a wider angle, actually extending outside of the grave, hence the find by the witness who saw the watch face reflecting the sunlight.'

'So what does that tell us?' Brodie mused. 'A particularly hasty burial?'

'Very possibly,' Gunn agreed.

'Well, we'll leave you to it and discuss a plan of action. Seen enough Jack?'

'Yes, I'm more than happy,' Jack Tait replied.

The little group retraced their steps back to the road where Drummond was waiting. Brodie thanked him for his efforts and promised a relief at the earliest opportunity. Then he invited Tait and Anderson to join Neil and him in Anderson's CID car.

'So how do you want to take this forward?' Brodie asked Tait.

'It's a difficult call, Alex. They're clearly old bones, possibly dating back to the last war. If we'd found them in France, say, or elsewhere in Europe, I think we would be justified in relating them directly to the conflict. In those circumstances, we could let the historians or the war graves people deal... but *here*, well that's different. There was no such military action in this part of the world that could account for this death, so therefore we have no option but to treat it as suspicious, certainly for now.' He smiled almost apologetically. 'Taking account of the evidence uncovered so far, I feel we have no option but to leave this with your team and to investigate this matter as thoroughly as we can. I appreciate the chances of a successful conclusion are remote. However, we owe it to the victim of this apparent shooting to at least try to identify him, if nothing else. You never know, we may even be able to return his remains to his family.'

He waited for a response, but there was none initially, so he continued. 'Another issue to consider here is the media. I can see them becoming very interested in this case. You know how they love a mystery, especially one such as this.'

Now Brodie did have something to say. 'I had a feeling you were going to go down that route,' he said, his deep voice tinged with disappointment. 'I would have thought we'd got enough on our desks presently without taking on some excursion into the world of *Time Team*.'

'Yes, I know Alex, but I do believe our hands are tied here. I'll speak to Hugh Jardine at the Inverness Office but I think he'll agree with me on this.'

Brodie knew the area procurator fiscal at Inverness well. The smooth-talking Highlander was usually supportive of the police, but never a man to cut corners. 'Aye, I'm sure Hugh *will* agree with you,' said Brodie, his mouth crumpled at the corners.

Tait, somewhat relieved that Brodie had accepted his decision with a modicum of good grace, pressed home his advantage. 'We'll have the remains removed to the mortuary and I'll arrange for them to be examined as soon as possible. Then we can move on from there.'

Neil left Brodie and Tait to discuss the ongoing management of the scene with Holly Anderson, and returned to speak to Gunn. He stood in silence, gazing down at the forlorn remains before him as the shutter on Fraser Gunn's camera clicked away incessantly.

'I'll find out who you are, and that's a promise,' he mouthed under his breath.

'What was that, Neil?' Gunn momentarily shifted his eye from the camera's viewfinder.

'Nothing at all Fraser,' Neil replied. 'I was just thinking out loud, that's all.'

Chapter Four

Monday 25th May

After a disappointing start, Monday had slowly evolved into a pleasant but windy late spring day. Overhead, a few frayed wisps of high-altitude cloud graced an otherwise clear blue sky above the Highland capital.

Neil was once again acting as driver as he and Alex Brodie left the modern landscaped environs of their Force Headquarters in the Old Perth Road. They were heading for the mortuary at the nearby Raigmore Hospital, and a meeting with local pathologist Dr Adam Carnie.

The location of the mortuary was no mystery to the two detectives and, having parked close by, they navigated their way through a network of pipe-lined basement corridors towards the main examination suite.

Having emerged through the swing doors and into the bright, artificially lit environment beyond they quickly located the larger than life pathologist. He was sporting one of his garish bow ties and clad in a green plastic apron whilst hunched low over one of the examination tables. With him was another man of a similar age, also clad in greens. He was an austere looking figure, peering over metal rimmed spectacles at the display of bones on the table.

'Ah, Chief Inspector Brodie and Inspector Strachan. Long time no see.' He flicked off his surgical gloves and shook hands with the two men. It was a ritual that had to be endured every time they met, one that irritated Brodie, and he showed it, much to Neil's embarrassment.

'This is all rather exciting isn't it?' declared Carnie, gesturing towards the table.

'Well I'd rather be dealing with a crime in this century than the last,' was Brodie's dour reply.

'Yes, yes, I'm sure you would Alex, but a small deviation from the tedium of normality is never a bad thing. Keeps us all on our toes, don't you think?'

'You're absolutely right Adam,' Neil agreed. Brodie immediately shot him a disapproving glance, as if accusing his DI of disloyalty.

'So, what can you tell us? asked Neil.

'Firstly, let me introduce you to my colleague Dr John Patterson. He knows a lot about bones. Most eminent in his field.'

'Nothing like a good introduction. Good to meet you,' Patterson interjected, his frosty façade melting just a little. 'My *field* as Adam describes it, is forensic anthropology. He's invited me along for a second opinion.'

Introductions finally complete, the four men positioned themselves around the table upon which the "Glendaig skeleton" had been laid out, each weathered bone precisely in its rightful place.

Patterson leant forward, scooped up the skull with a large hand, and sat it on his gloved palm.

'Male,' he declared assertively. 'Definitely male, with a skull this size. Female skulls are generally far more delicate. The frontal bones of the female forehead are more rounded than this. See how it slants away on our friend here.' He ran his finger across the surface of the skull, as if to make his point. 'Then there's the pelvis. The size of this one is clearly indicative of a male and the sub pubic angle just here confirms this.' He leant across the table and pointed to the base of the pelvic bone, all the while keeping one eye on his tiny audience as if to check that they were paying attention. 'V-shaped you see, whereas in the female it's broader and more rounded.'

'Okay, we assumed that to be the case,' Brodie interrupted,

recalling Fraser Gunn's comments. 'What else have you gleaned that might help us?'

Patterson's brief excursion into the world of congeniality faded away. He glared across at Brodie, injured by his curt dismissal. It was highly unlikely these two would ever be going out for a curry together, Neil mused.

Patterson resumed his appraisal in a more matter of fact style. 'Well for what it's worth we believe he was a white male, again evident from the features of the skull. He was also quite a big fellow, at least six feet tall, possibly a little over, six feet two say. The length of the femur here and some clever arithmetic has given us his height. Having all the long bones has helped, and so we can deduce this with some accuracy.'

'How about age – of the bones generally I mean and of the victim at time of death?' Neil spoke softly, not wishing to rile the good doctor any further.

'We were just coming on to that,' Carnie interjected, clearly not wishing to be side-lined by his colleague. He turned his attention back to the skeleton. 'We can give you an estimate of his age at time of death and the *overall* age of the remains, based on experience, but we'll need to send bone samples off for tests to be more accurate. We'll do fluorescence and nitrogen tests for starters, then possibly check for blood pigment and amino acids.'

'What about carbon dating?'

'Perhaps,' said Carnie, nodding, 'but I have a feeling it may not be so helpful in this case. If the skeleton was centuries old, then maybe.'

'Okay, so what's your gut instinct?' Neil was impatient, dismissive of all the scientific jargon.

Patterson spoke again. 'Well the evidence of deterioration within the bone material is minimal here. There's evidence that the epiphysis on the sternal end of the clavicle has fused.' He pointed to the end of the collarbone. 'This usually happens around the age of thirty. The degree of pitting on the fourth rib, and the condition of the teeth, would lead me to suggest the age at time of death to certainly be around that mark, perhaps a little older, perhaps slightly younger. As for the overall age of the skeleton, well, from its general condition I would say fifty plus years. Acid erosion from the sand is minimal here, so he's no cave man! Of course cavemen didn't have dental fillings or wear watches.' He interrupted his assessment to allow himself a brief chortle, before resuming a more professional persona. 'It's difficult to be more specific at this stage, but I'm confident he wasn't born a Victorian! Definitely younger than that.'

'That's very helpful, thanks,' said Neil.

'Anything else of interest. What about the hole in his head?' Brodie was the enquirer this time.

'Ah yes, the bullet wound. Well, it wouldn't take much of an expert to have a guess at cause of death,' suggested Carnie, the corners of his mouth curling to form a wry smile.

'So is there anything interesting you can tell us about the wound?'

'There are certain facts we can deduce from the entrance and exit sites. Clearly he was shot from the front. This is a typical entrance site with a sharp-edged punched-out hole in the outer table. The skull has two layers you see, we call them tables. There's a larger, corresponding bevelled-out hole on the inner table. It's a perforating wound with a corresponding exit site to the rear. We can tell it's the exit as the cranial damage shows bevelling on the outer table.'

'I think I'm still with you,' Brodie chipped in with a pronounced sigh.

'Good. The fact that the bullet has exited leads me to believe that it was a full metal jacketed type, probably nine millimetre from the measurements we have taken. Interestingly, the track of the projectile seems to have been on a slightly downward angle.'

Carnie lifted the skull and ran a long metal rod through the entrance site and out of the exit site at the rear. He lifted the skull to eye level, and peered at it.

'Our friend here appears to have been kneeling, or similar, when his killer approached and shot him clean between the eyes… this is not a combat wound, gentlemen. This appears to be cold-blooded murder.'

Patterson removed his gloves and walked across to the sink. 'There's nothing else of specific interest. It seems he was relatively young and physically fit, not too dissimilar to you, DI Strachan.' He turned on the tap. 'We've taken samples of bone and tooth enamel for isotopic analysis; should tell us something about where he came from. It's not an exact science though. Anyway, we'll keep you posted with the results of all the tests just as soon as they come in. Until then, I think we've provided you with all the information we can… for now.'

'I believe the personal effects found at the scene are your biggest clues,' said Carnie, arms folded. 'The evidence seems to suggest that he was a wartime German sailor, does it not?'

'So it would seem, yes,' Neil replied. 'But we'll keep an open mind for now.'

Patterson glanced back as he washed his hands. 'Well, I wish you the best of luck gentlemen. Not every day you get a murder enquiry quite this old to get your teeth into. Like I said, we'll keep you posted with the test results.'

The hand-shaking ritual was repeated, much to Neil's amusement, and armed with a copy of the pathologist's preliminary report the two detectives took their leave. They strolled back to the car park in silence, and once out in the warm sunshine, Brodie erupted.

'This is going to be a bloody nightmare,' he carped, having undoubtedly been festering since they left the mortuary, 'There's no way I'm committing any serious resources to this. We're never going to get a bloody result in a month of Sundays.' Before Neil could mouth a reply, he exploded again. 'And you know what, that wee devil Jardine will expect us to pull out all the bloody stops as usual, I know he will. He's about as flexible as my bloody golf clubs.'

'Well don't you think that poor devil lying on that table deserves some effort from us sir? He does, after all, appear to have been executed. Surely, even if we can identify him, that will be a result?'

Brodie pulled up and frowned. 'Aye, I suppose so, but those buggers in the Crown Office have no concept of police workloads. I'll be making that clear to them.'

Neil smiled as he slid into the driver's seat. He looked forward to the forthcoming spat with the straight-talking Procurator Fiscal. 'I've no doubt you'll be doing that in a way that only you can sir.'

'Bloody right.' Brodie stared out across the car park before turning to Neil. 'What have you got on just now, work-wise?'

'Just the usual mountain of paperwork, why?'

'I mean *now*, this morning.'

'Nothing that can't wait I suppose.'

'Do you fancy a coffee out at Fort George?'

'Aye, no problem, you're the boss. Why Fort George?'

'I want to visit an old army buddy of mine from Stornaway, Jim Morrison. We served together in the QOH, Queen's Own Highlanders to you, during Operation Granby.'

'Operation Granby?'

'The liberation of Kuwait. Jim was a warrant officer at the time. I was a lieutenant. He helps run the regimental museum out there now.'

'So is this connected to the Glendaig job, or do you just want a cup of coffee and a *war story* session?'

'This is strictly business you cheeky wee sod. You do want to find out who our skeleton was don't you?'

The traffic along the A96 was heavy as usual. Neil tapped impatiently on the steering wheel as he crawled along behind an Aberdeen bound HGV. 'Thank God, at last!' he uttered with relief as he turned off the main road, signposted *Ardesier* and *Inverness Airport*. There was no response from his passenger. Brodie was chewing his lower lip as he struggled to compose a text to his wife. Neil gazed out into the distance, wondering what Brodie's army friend could possibly tell them about their skeleton.

Once past the imposing seventeenth-century tower of Castle Stuart, the road turned east along the Moray Firth. Fifteen minutes later they were pulling up in the car park at Fort George, remote and windswept at the end of a curving promontory extending out into the Firth. Today there was little in the way of a breeze. The choppy waters that flowed around the fort, home to a colony of bottle-nosed dolphins, were unusually placid. During winter it would have been different, with only the grassy ramparts and massive granite walls to protect the visitor from the relentless easterly gales. The detectives marched purposefully through the defensive ravelin and past the old guardhouse. Ahead of them, across a white-fenced drawbridge, was the ornately decorated main gate, emblazoned with the royal coat of arms of the Hanoverian King George the Second.

Inside the fort, built in the wake of the Jacobite rebellion of 1745, one could fully appreciate the boast that this was once one of the mightiest fortifications in Europe. Neatly arranged within its walls, standing sombre and grey, stood a gloomy complex of barrack blocks, approached along a wide driveway bordered by extensive lawns.

Neil soon found himself outside the Highlanders Museum, housed in the former home of the Lieutenant Governor. Once through the half-glazed doors, Brodie asked one of the staff as to the whereabouts of Jim Morrison. His enquiry was immediately answered from the top of a nearby staircase. 'Well, if it's not my old mucker Alex Brodie, how the devil are you pal?'

Jim Morrison trotted down the stairs and shook hands with his old colleague. 'What brings you to this neck of the woods Alex? Having a few pangs of nostalgia?' Morrison grinned widely, revealing a gleaming row of uneven white teeth. He was a large man, upright and ex-military in every sense. There was a hint of silver flecked through his close-cropped hair, but other than that, little to indicate the onset of middle age.

'I thought we'd drop by for a brew and pick your brain,' said Brodie. 'This is my colleague, DI Neil Strachan.'

'Good to meet you Neil, so is this official police business then?'

'You could say that, Jim. Lead us to the kettle and I'll explain all.' Brodie gestured towards a door marked *Private*.

'Och, no, you deserve better than that. We'll go up to the café and have a chat there. Follow me lads.'

Morrison led the way back out into the sunshine. There followed, a short walk around the corner and along a narrow avenue shaded by the lofty barrack house walls. Morrison ducked through a doorway in one of the imposing granite structures. 'Here we are, what can I get you?' They were now standing in a large canteen area. Uniformed soldiers sat at some of the tables, mingling with groups of tourists also taking refreshments. Having made their selection at the counter, they headed for a table close to the window. Morrison joined them soon after with three steaming mugs and sat down next to Brodie. 'Fire away,' he said as he poured a heap of sugar into his coffee.

Brodie explained the circumstances of the discovery at Glendaig in some detail, his eyes remaining fixed on Morrison as he stirred his coffee to the point of excess. When Brodie fell silent, Neil asked, 'I know it's a long shot, but are you aware of any events up here in the Highlands during the war which may have involved the landing of German military personnel for whatever reason?'

'None that I know of,' came the immediate reply. 'I've no doubt the Germans would have been very interested in the comings and goings from places such as the naval bases at Scapa Flow and Loch Ewe, or perhaps the naval air station at Invergordon. We know they landed a number of agents in the UK, but the vast majority, to put it bluntly, weren't very good. As I understand it, they were all captured very quickly. I suppose it's not inconceivable that the odd one remained undetected, but *your* man appears to have been wearing a uniform complete with medals. He doesn't exactly come across as a spy, does he?'

'Okay,' said Brodie. 'What about escaped prisoners of war. Is it possible one of them remained unaccounted for?'

'There were a considerable number of POW camps scattered around Scotland, and I've read about various escape attempts, but I'm not aware of any being successful. Those prisoners who actually broke out of camps found themselves in pretty inhospitable terrain, and were all recaptured, I believe…'

'Well, this line of enquiry isn't proving too fruitful, is it?' Brodie muttered under his breath as he drained his coffee mug and returned it to the tray.

'I'm sorry I'm not being much help, Alex,' said Morrison apologetically. 'I'll certainly go back to the museum and speak with my colleagues. We can also have a look at our archive material. Don't forget, I'm only speaking from personal knowledge here. There may be something of interest amongst the mountain of documentary records we keep in the museum.'

'Och it's no big deal, it was just a thought.' Brodie got up and patted him on the shoulder.

Neil handed Morrison one of his business cards. 'Thanks for your time Jim, perhaps you can you give me a call if you find anything?'

'Of course, Neil. One other thing I can suggest is to speak with the curatorial staff down at the Imperial War Museum in London. If there *was* anything at all going on up here during the war, they're bound to know about it.'

'Good idea, thanks for that, I'll certainly give them a call,' said Neil. The three men parted company at the main gate, then Brodie and Neil hurried away over the wooden bridge and back towards the car park.

'You know what, Neil,' Brodie announced suddenly. 'I reckon there was a mutiny on one of those German submarines, U-boats they called them didn't they? Must've all been nutters sailing around encased in one of those bloody things… Anyway, I reckon they shot the captain and put his body overboard. Then the body washed up on our bloody beach. I'm not so sure anything happened on British soil at all.'

'I doubt that sir, he was buried in a grave above the high-water mark, wasn't he?'

'I know, but someone could've buried him later on, couldn't they? You know, as an act of decency perhaps.'

'I'll certainly look into that possibility when I go down to London.'

'Aye, well I was only thinking out loud… what do you mean, *go to London?*'

'Well I think I should go down to the museum and show them the artefacts. They may be able to help, or at least have some documentary stuff that I can go through.' Neil studied his boss, as if seeking his approval, before continuing to make his case. 'I don't know. It's always better to do these things face to face; that's what you keep telling me.'

Brodie looked at him disbelievingly. 'You just want to look around that bloody museum… and in my bloody time… don't you? I bet you ex-history students get off on anything that's in a glass case, eh? Well if you *do* go, you'd better be back the same day. I won't be authorising any overnight *jolly*.'

The Chief Inspector's spiky red hair slipped below the roof of the car, leaving Neil gazing out across the car park, an incredulous expression etched upon his face. 'Aye sir, I'll certainly do my best.'

Chapter Five

'That's it… *iwm.org.uk*.'

Neil sat hunched over his desk, scanning the pages of the Imperial War Museum website on his PC. Having navigated around the site for several minutes he eventually figured that *Collections and Research* should be his first port of call. He dialled the contact telephone number and waited. A pleasant young woman answered and connected him to his chosen department. Next came a male voice confirming that he had the right extension. 'How can I help?' asked the educated voice.

Neil recounted the details of the find and enquired whether someone at the museum would be good enough to inspect the objects found at the grave site. The voice at the other end of the phone certainly seemed excited at the prospect.

'Yes, of course we can. The person you need to speak to is Dr Paul Miller. He's our resident expert on the *Kriegsmarine*…' He quickly provided a translation for Neil's benefit. '…the wartime German Navy… he has a particular interest in the U-boat arm.'

'I see,' Neil replied. 'I can only *assume* our man had naval connections. We're really only surmising at present.' There was a short pause at the other end. Then came the condescending response.

'Well I think there's a strong possibility, don't you? Your skeleton appears to have been wearing a watch that was worn by U-boat officers. You also seem to have collected some standard issue *Kriegsmarine* buttons and you say the piece of material you have found was sporting three bands of gold lace. Are the bands all the same thickness?'

Neil frantically sorted through the plastic bags on his desk until he found the one containing the lace fragments. 'Yes, looks like it, and there's a small star stitched into the material above them.'

'Well there you have it then. What you appear to have there are the sleeve rings of an officer with the rank of *korvettenkapitän*, or commander in English. A little unusual if he was serving on a U-boat, but Paul will explain more.'

'Right, thanks very much. When would it be convenient to come down and see Dr Miller?'

'Well, he's away at the moment advising some TV producers about a new documentary. He'll be back on Friday. I'll ring him and let him know you're coming, if Friday's okay? He'll be most interested in your find.'

'Friday it is then. I'll let you know what time I'll be arriving.'

'Marvellous, look forward to it... bye.'

The line went dead. Neil reflected on the information he'd been given. His concentration was interrupted by a presence behind him, and the placing of a hand firmly on his shoulder. 'Come on laddie,' boomed Brodie, his furrowed features appearing in Neil's peripheral vision. The distinct aroma of digested coffee hung in the air as the DCI spoke. 'We've got an appointment with that bugger Jardine at eleven o'clock. Grab us some car keys will you.'

Neil rose from his desk and donned his jacket. 'I've got some here sir. Ready when you are.'

Brodie was striding back from his office. 'Let's be on our way then,' he said as he breezed past, struggling to fit his large frame into his own suit jacket.

Twenty minutes later they were sitting in the functional, air conditioned office of the area procurator fiscal. Two chairs had been pulled up to the large uncluttered desk that dominated the centre of the room. Neil and his boss now occupied them, perched uncomfortably like a couple of wayward schoolboys called in to the headmaster's office.

Hugh Jardine stood by a low cedar wood unit on the other side of the room. He poured himself a cup of coffee from the glass jug that had been simmering on the hotplate of his new coffee maker. Jardine was a tall man, and looked particularly fit for his fifty-five years. His hairline was rapidly receding and what hair he had left amounted to little more than grey stubble. Beneath the stubble, his unusually tanned face was not typical of a resident of such a northern latitude. It was more likely to have been windburn, built up from years of jogging along the beach near his home in Nairn. Like Brodie he was immaculately turned out in a crisp blue suit with perfectly complimenting shirt and tie.

'Jack Tait has brought me up to speed with the events on Sunday. It's a difficult one to call in terms of where we go from here. How are things progressing, Alex?'

Brodie was about to reply, but then held back. 'Neil will explain, Hugh; he's heading up this enquiry.' He gestured to Neil, who looked back in bewilderment, before commencing his extemporaneous briefing.

'And the cause of death?' asked Jardine. 'I assume it was the gunshot wound to the front of the head?'

'That would appear to be the case,' Neil confirmed. 'The items we have found at the scene tend to suggest the remains are those of a German naval officer, possibly of some seniority.'

'Umm, well that may help us to identify him at least. How have you come to that conclusion?' Jardine studied Neil over the gold rims of his half-moon spectacles. His narrow lips pursed to form a probing smile that left Neil with the impression he was attending a job interview.

'Well firstly, we've recovered two wartime German medals believed to be Iron Crosses,' Neil explained, placing the exhibit bags on Jardine's desk so that he could examine the items personally. He then recounted in detail the conversation he'd had with the man at the Imperial War Museum.

'I see,' said the fiscal, examining the bags from various angles. 'So no doubt you'll be referring these finds to the appropriate authorities, with a view to coming up with a name then?' The smile was there again, Neil could almost feel the irritation seeping out across his face.

'I'm going down to London to see a Dr Paul Miller on Friday,' he responded, with a degree of curtness. 'We'll have to see where that takes us.'

'It seems to me this is fast becoming a case of historical research, rather than a murder enquiry in the normal sense,' Brodie interjected.

'Quite so,' Jardine replied, stirring his coffee. 'And I expect you'll be suggesting to me that we don't go committing too many of your valuable staff resources to this enquiry, Alex.'

'Well, that is a very real consideration for me, bearing in mind current workloads.'

Jardine cleared his throat. 'I'm not here to dictate to you how you manage workloads, Alex. That would certainly be remiss of me. But let me clarify the situation as I see it. I have a duty as Procurator Fiscal to investigate suspicious deaths. This is without doubt a violent and suspicious death, to all intents and purposes, perpetrated within my geographical area of responsibility. We cannot confirm in these circumstances that the death was combat related, certainly not at this stage in the enquiry. Equally the time element here, although a matter for consideration, is immaterial from my perspective. I still have a duty to investigate this matter, whether it be five years or indeed fifty since the poor fellow's demise. I'm sure you will understand that.'

'Of course,' Brodie replied. 'But surely you can't expect me to pull out all the stops on this one Hugh, not with such a slim chance of success.' Brodie could not disguise the frustration in his voice.

'All I can say, Alex, is that I will be requiring the *stops*, as you call them, to be pulled out sufficiently to ensure a satisfactory outcome to this investigation. What is satisfactory for my purposes will depend upon the result of your enquiries. I agree this case is different, but I do need to satisfy myself that this death, like any other, has been enquired into fully. If there's a possibility that justice can be delivered for this apparent victim of crime then all efforts, however challenging, must be made to achieve this.' His smile faded. 'It would be conjecture at this stage, would it not, to suggest that delivery of justice in this case amounts to an impossible task?'

Neil glanced anxiously at his boss. Surely this would be a good time to dispense with any debate on the issue.

'Fair enough,' Brodie conceded. Neil sighed almost audibly with relief.

'Excellent,' said Jardine, his smile reconstituted.

'We should also take account of the media interest in this matter. I've had several of the national dailies on the phone since yesterday. Naturally, I've referred them to your press officer.' He picked up a scrap of paper that had been lying on his desk and scanned the note that was written on it. 'I'm told there are television crews at the scene as we speak. There's nothing like a historical murder mystery to whet their appetite.'

Brodie passed a sheet of A4 across the table to Jardine. 'This is the holding release we've issued for the moment. I've arranged a meeting with the media tomorrow. Would you like to be there?'

'Och no,' said Jardine. 'I think I can leave that side of things to you for now.' He read the press release he'd been given.

"About midday on Sunday 24th May 2009, Police attended an incident by Loch Coinneach, close to the village of Glendaig.

Skeletal remains had been discovered on a beach adjacent to the road by tourists walking in the locality.

The remains have now been removed for detailed examination by a pathologist. Initial investigation has revealed that they may have been in situ for a number of years, and are believed to be those of an adult male. A full investigation into the incident is now underway,

and police are currently treating the death as suspicious. Anyone with
any information is asked to contact their local police.
Ends"

'That's fine for the time being,' said Jardine with a nod. 'I assume you'll be more forthcoming regarding cause of death when you meet with our friends from the press tomorrow?'

'Yes, we will,' Brodie confirmed with a wry smile. 'We'll also repeat our appeal for information, if indeed there's anyone alive who can give any.'

'Well you never know, Alex,' said Jardine, wanting the last word. 'So what's the plan from here on in?'

Neil fidgeted on his chair, prompting Jardine to look across at him. 'The search of the scene is on-going as we speak,' Neil explained. 'There's a search team out there now, and we've arranged for a forensic archaeologist to assist the SOCOs, chap by the name of Dr Ben Moss. We'll be getting out to Glendaig tomorrow to make some local enquiries, and of course I'll be going down to London on Friday to do some historical research.'

'And exactly what level of staffing do you consider appropriate to this enquiry, Alex?'

'For the time being I'll be asking Neil to act as SIO. He can oversee things from here, no need to base himself out on the west coast. He can get some assistance from our office in Fort William if need be.'

Neil could hardly believe his good fortune. He was sure Brodie would be breathing down his neck, him being the new boy, but Jardine had obviously put him on the spot and it looked like he was going to get a free rein.

'Well, I look forward to hearing how things progress, Neil.' Jardine appeared happy with the arrangement… for now.

Neil smiled back. 'I'll certainly keep you in the loop Hugh. I'll relish the challenge!' The two detectives rose from their seats and bade farewell to Jardine before making their way back downstairs to reception. As they emerged into the semi-darkness of Baron Taylor's Street, Neil enquired; 'So am I to assume that I'll be running this enquiry from today. You're going to take a back seat?'

'That's about the sum of it,' Brodie replied as he checked his phone for messages. 'See how you go. I'll arrange for some assistance if need be.'

Neil didn't reply. They turned right and made their way towards Academy Street, passing between the numerous rubbish-filled skips that littered what was little more than an alleyway. This wasn't the Inverness that the tourists normally see, Neil mused as he sidestepped a vagrant squatting in a doorway and supping from a can of Tennents lager…

'I assume you *are* happy to run with this enquiry, Neil?' Brodie asked as he returned his phone to his pocket.

'Aye, of course I am sir; we've got to give it a go, whatever the outcome.'

'That's the spirit, give it your best shot, but don't waste your time chasing shadows mind, is that understood?'

'Of course, sir.' Neil tried to suppress his sense of excitement. He was more than happy with Brodie's apparent confidence in him, and had no intention of jeopardising his new SIO role, even though he would probably be leading a team of one!

His boss patted him on the arm. 'I'll speak to the DI at Fort William and ask him to release DC Anderson to assist you if required. You know I can't give you anyone from our office, what with leave, sickness and suchlike.' He scowled as he edged his way between two wheelie bins. 'Managing people is a bloody nightmare, and the higher your rank the worse it gets, mark my words.'

Neil didn't consider that a reply was warranted and opted just to smile instead. They'd now reached Academy Street and were making for the multi-storey car park at the Eastgate Centre. 'You're on coffee duty when we get back to the office, Neil.'

'I might even grab a couple of cheese scones from the canteen?' Neil suggested.

Brodie paused. 'Are you buying?'

'Aye of course.'

'There must be a catch, you must want something... or perhaps you're just rewarding me for letting you run with this job.'

'No,' said Neil, 'but I wouldn't mind a lift to the airport on Friday!'

'Oh, I think my busy schedule will extend to that,' Brodie replied as they disappeared into the car park's stairwell.

It was nearly six o'clock when Neil pulled up on the driveway of the neat but unpretentious semi on the edge of Culloden Forest. He turned off the ignition, and the throaty drone of the MG's engine died away. Only the evening birdsong and the distant sound of rush-hour traffic on the Culloden Road disturbed the relative peace of the little cul-de-sac. He removed his glasses and massaged the bridge of his nose. Looking up, he followed the track of a small ragged cloud as it cast a lingering shadow across the quiet street. It had been a long day, and tomorrow would probably be longer, yet there was a sense of expectation building within him. He would at last be able to get to grips with the investigation at Glendaig and possibly put a name to the face of the mysterious German. In fact he felt like a pig in shit, to use one of Brodie's preferred expressions. Historical research and police work combined. It couldn't get better than that.

Cat was sitting on the sofa working on her laptop when Neil breezed in and dropped his jacket on the top of the armchair. Tam had been lying next to her, but leapt off the two-seater to greet his master, a well chewed bone extending equidistantly from his soft mouth. As Neil knelt down to engage in a play fight with the excited dog, Cat looked up from her laptop. 'I hear you were at the office this morning talking to Hugh Jardine.'

'Aye, that's right,' he replied. 'News travels fast!'

'Nothing much gets past me, even on a day off. So come on, spill the beans then.'

'Oh, Alex Brodie and I went in to discuss this case over at Glendaig. Alex was beating his gums about resources, and all the usual excuses he comes up with when he's under pressure covering workloads. Jardine was having none of it. He wants a comprehensive enquiry into the find.'

'So is that good or what?'

'It is for me. Much to my surprise, Brodie's appointed me as investigating officer, the only one I hasten to add, so he's sticking to his guns on the resources front. Still, he's right I suppose; we may never get to the bottom of this case.'

'Well, it'll be up to you to prove them wrong then. Surely this sort of thing is right up your street?'

'Aye, of course, but the odds are definitely stacked against me. Not least that Alex Brodie will be on my back, reminding me that the clock is ticking and that the funds for this enquiry will be coming straight out of his own personal current account.'

Cat sat forward and placed a supportive hand on her partner's knee. 'I have every confidence in you, Neil. Even *I'm* intrigued as to how this case will develop. So where are you going from here?'

'Well, I'm driving over to Glendaig tomorrow. I want to see how the Scene Investigators are doing at the scene and then I'm going to start talking to the locals. That'll certainly be interesting.'

Chapter Six

It had been the early start he'd reluctantly committed himself to, but now Neil regretted climbing out of his warm bed and hurrying out of the house in the half-light before even the dawn chorus had fully commenced. He'd missed breakfast, and now the tell-tale sounds of hunger were becoming ever more vocal. The unrelenting growls that were rising from his empty stomach had prompted him to stop at the village store in Invermoriston for coffee and a sandwich.

Rain had been falling steadily for an hour and the temperature had dropped away noticeably, so he was content being back in the MG, sipping the takeaway coffee through a slot in the plastic cover. Frustrated by the lack of fluid reaching his lips he finally dispensed with the offending lid and took a long slug from the steaming cup. Then he sat quietly, contemplating the reception he'd receive from the residents of Glendaig.

Ahead, through the rain-spattered windscreen, the clouds seemed darker than ever. A leaden sky hung as backdrop to the lush green tops of the roadside forestry. It was not a day to be working outside and Neil wondered whether the search team at Glendaig were making any headway at all.

Sandwich and coffee consumed, he resumed his journey westward. As he progressed, he became heartened by the streaks of lighter grey appearing in the western sky. However, in Glen Shiel the rain continued unabated, falling in sheets through the misty cloud that hugged the mountain tops. The glistening, wet granite closed in around him as he drove deeper into the Glen, prompting him to turn up the heat to de-mist the car's windows. The month of May was certainly not ending as it had started in the Highlands.

At the top of the ascent from the road to the Kyle, the silvery waters of the Sound of Sleat once again came into view, defining the mist shrouded coastline of Skye. Neil stopped the car in a passing place and reclined in his seat, relieved that he'd broken the back of the journey. As he sat taking in the scenery the windscreen began to blur as his warm breath collided with the cold glass. He reluctantly used his sleeve to restore its clarity and drove on towards the brighter skies that were spreading east from beyond the Cuillin Mountains.

Twenty minutes later, and he was pulling up in the same lay-by that he'd parked in three days before. He'd been lucky to find a space on the cluttered strip of compacted scree, and had just managed to manoeuvre the little sports car onto the end of the stationary convoy behind a mud-spattered Subaru. Two white vans stood unattended beyond the Subaru, and in front of them, a marked police Land Rover.

Rain was still falling steadily, but there was now clear evidence of a forthcoming improvement in the weather. A few small patches of blue were beginning appear between the billowing columns of *cumulonimbus*. Clad in a battered waxed jacket, he made his way across the road to where a young policewoman was standing, her chin buried deep into the collar of the fleece liner of her reflective jacket. She greeted him rather more cheerfully than he would have expected and, once his details were entered in the scene log, he took the short walk down between the blue and white tapes towards the small cluster of figures on the beach.

He was greeted by a hunched Fraser Gunn, cocooned in his own wet weather gear. 'Morning Neil, hope the summer's going to be better than this.'

'Aye, so do I. How's it going then?' Neil pulled up the collar of his jacket and thrust his hands into his pockets.

'Not so bad. I think we're almost finished here, and I've got some interesting news, hot off the press this morning. Come and have a look.'

He led Neil over to the edge of the beach where the skeleton had originally been found. Completely obscuring his view of the grave site was the rain-soaked back of a tall, heavily-built man. Tight curly hair, liberally streaked with grey cascaded over the raised collar of his equally battered jacket. Hearing the approaching footfall on the shingle, the man turned about to reveal a weathered face obscured by a full beard. Standing next to him was Gunn's colleague Lynn Cowan.

'DI Strachan, this is Dr Ben Moss, forensic archaeologist and anthropologist.' Gunn's introduction was delivered with an uncharacteristic degree of formality.

Dr Moss held out his hand. 'Fraser asked me to come up and have a look at the site. I think he was a tad worried that we'd find buried Germans all over the beach!'

'Stranger things have happened, no doubt!' said Neil grasping his hand. 'So where are you based Dr Moss, that's not a local accent?'

'Oh I'm a Sassenach Inspector, up from Cranfield University in Bedfordshire. I lecture down there...' But Neil was only half listening. His attention had switched to the area of shingle visible beyond the spot where Cowan and Moss were standing.

'Oh right,' he replied almost half-heartedly, then turned to Gunn. 'Is that what I think it is?' He manoeuvred himself around the little group to get a better view.

'I'm afraid so Inspector,' said Moss. 'You appear to have a *second* grave site. The good news is, this one's empty.'

Neil squatted to examine the shallow pit in the sand. Standing up again, he gazed at the two graves side by side. The new discovery appeared slightly smaller than the first. They were separated by a distance of about four feet, and dug at a ninety degree angle to the shoreline.

'Are you sure about this, Fraser?' Neil was still taking it all in.

'No doubt about it,' the Scene Investigator replied. 'I asked Ben and his team to do a geophysical survey of the entire beach site with their ground penetrating radar. We weren't really expecting anything. I just wanted to be certain that there hadn't been multiple burials, or anything else lurking under the surface here. In fact, we thought we'd found nothing, but this anomaly appeared on the survey map.' He handed the glossy document to Neil who stared at it fixedly.

Moss looked over his shoulder. 'The features of both graves appear identical in terms of general depth and dimensions, although this new site had been filled in with shingle.

'And there's no evidence of any other grave sites on or around the beach?' Neil wanted confirmation.

'Absolutely none,' Gunn replied.

'So what are the possibilities here, I wonder?'

'Well, the grave may have been dug but not used for some reason. It's unlikely our skeleton was moved from one to the other, bearing in mind the measurements. Besides, it wouldn't make sense. The other more sinister possibility is that whoever once occupied this grave has been moved to another location, who knows where.'

'Christ, Brodie's going to love this!' Neil murmured, almost to himself. He turned to look out across towards the eastern side of the beach. A group of black-clad search officers were crawling, side by side, towards the rocky cliff at the far end of the bay. A sergeant walked slowly behind them carrying a clipboard.

'They're nearly done,' said Gunn.

'Have they found anything of interest?'

'Only this.' Gunn motioned to Cowan, who produced a small evidence bag and handed it to Neil. Inside was a small black cartridge case, corroded in places, but still clearly identifiable.

'Do you think this is connected to our remains?'

'Well it looks old, and I would say it's nine mill. Not the sort of ammunition used by the local stalkers. We'll send it off to the ballistics boys. They may be able to tell us more.'

'Where was it found?' Neil held the bag up to the light and shook it gently.

'About ten feet due east of the grave site, just above the high water mark,' said Moss. 'We got an indication with the metal detector and the search team dug it out of the sand, a few inches down.'

Neil handed the bag back to Cowan. 'I'm on my way across to Glendaig. How long will you be here Fraser?'

'Another hour at the most, then we'll close the scene down.'

'Okay, I'll ring Brodie from the TK at Glendaig and give him the good news. See you back at the office.' He probed around in his pocket for his car keys. 'Good to meet you, Dr Moss. Thanks for your help.'

'A pleasure, any time Inspector,' came the amiable response.

Neil retraced his steps up to the road, shared a joke with the young log keeper, and hurried back to his car. He sat for a while reflecting on the latest developments and Brodie's potential reaction to them.

Out on Loch Coinneach, a small fishing boat was battling through the westerly stampede of foaming white caps. It was, Neil surmised, heading for the tiny pier at Invertulloch several miles to the south-east. The distinctive red and white vessel rose and fell as it struggled against the tide, trailing a long fan-shaped wake from its stern. A flock of excited seagulls trailed the little boat in the vain hope of a snack being provided by the fishermen.

Neil wondered whether the fishermen's expedition had been a fruitful one. It would have been in times gone by, for this area had been one of the major herring fisheries in Scotland. Evidence of the industry still survived in these parts. Abandoned, dilapidated herring sheds, built in the dry stone style still lined the shore in several local villages. Their rusting iron roofs and crumbling walls now contained nothing more than rubbish or the odd bale of animal feed.

Changes in fishing methods and regulations had eventually put an end to the herring trade. Now long line fishing for eel, skate, mackerel and cod provided a few men with a livelihood, but the glory days were long gone. The old fishermen could now be found seated outside their stone cottages, sucking on their pipes and reminiscing about times past. According to them, it was once possible to walk around the many small bays, stepping from boat to boat without placing a foot on the ground.

Neil turned the ignition key and secured his seatbelt. He manoeuvred the MG back onto the road and headed east towards Glendaig. The dark mountains of Knoydart lay ahead of him, guarding the southern shore of the loch and providing an impressive panorama as the road dipped towards the village. The battered sign bearing the name *Glendaig* soon came into view on the left and then the Manse, grey and uninviting, standing within a treeless compound and enclosed by a dry stone wall. A footpath ran along its western boundary from the road. On the roadside verge, leaning precariously, stood a wooden fingerpost pointing across the field towards the distant mountainside. Neil just caught the words *Stac Coinneach Dubh, 2 miles* inscribed on the weather-bleached finger together with the image of a walker carrying a stick, thereby indicating a hikers' trail.

Fifty yards further on from the Manse was the church, clearly built at the same time as the minister's residence and also enclosed within a similar boundary wall. A number of ageing trees stood within the enclosure, their gnarled, lichen-encrusted branches reaching out like witches' fingers from the prevailing wind. Gravestones, leaning at similar angles to that of the finger post, dotted the environs of the church, mostly of granite but with the odd polished stone memorial indicating a more recent interment. On the eastern side of the building was a gravel car park surrounded by a stock fence.

Neil turned left into the car park and pulled up next to a newly painted red gate. From here, a gravel path extended into the graveyard carrying churchgoers to the imposing arched wooden door of the building, also painted red.

He leant forward to see the wording on the sign displayed next to the gate. Under the colourful burning bush emblem of the Church Of Scotland, he read the words:

Presbytery Of Lochcarron and Skye
Parish Church of St Columba, Glendaig
Minister – Revd Duncan Mackay BA

Beneath this bold introduction to visitors were details of the times of Sunday services and the contact address of the minister. A laminated, computer-generated notice hung from the wooden frame. The size of the text posed too much of a challenge for Neil's eyesight, even with glasses, so he left the warmth of the car and walked over to read it. If he was expecting something exciting, he was to be disappointed. The grubby yellowing document merely provided details of a craft sale at the local community hall, held two weeks previously. As he scanned the impressive list of stalls included at the foot of the notice, he became aware of footsteps disturbing the gravel behind him.

'I'm afraid you're too late for the sale.'

The voice was that of a male with a soft highland accent. Neil spun around to encounter a beaming smile spread across a youthful face, short and blunt, resembling that of a cat. Beneath it was a dog collar, partially obscured by a green Arran jumper.

'Duncan Mackay, I'm the local minister.' He extended his hand. Neil grabbed it and shook it firmly.

'Detective Inspector Neil Strachan, over from Inverness. Pleased to meet you.'

'Unusual choice of police car. More suited to tourism I would've thought. But I suppose it would be naive of me to think you were just passing by, Inspector.' Mackay strolled around the MG, hands clasped firmly behind his back, then stooped to peer through the open driver's-side window.

Neil shrugged. 'Well actually I *was* as it happens, and I suddenly felt inclined to have a look at the church.'

'Ah, the power of the Lord, no doubt.' The minister glanced heavenward, arms outstretched, as if acknowledging a miracle. 'It's a shame he hasn't been so successful enticing other passers-by!'

Neil responded to the minister's quip with a brief grin. 'As far as being in Glendaig is concerned, I'm afraid it's business. I'm investigating the discovery of some human remains down on one of the coves by the side of the loch.'

'Aye, I first saw it on the news, terrible business that. I can't believe the pour soul was lying there all that time. Everyone's talking about it round abouts. Have you any idea who he was?'

'Not as yet. We have a few lines of enquiry to follow up, but I expect you've also heard that the remains are a number of years old?'

'Aye, I did hear that.'

'So what are the views of the locals? Do they have any theories as to who he was?'

Mackay scratched his scalp through a thick mop of jet black hair. 'Not anything that I'd consider credible.'

'Well, anything's worth considering at this stage,' Neil suggested.

There was a pause, then another smile spread across MacKay's face. 'How does Glaswegian gangster from the sixties grab you? Or then there's the Jacobite soldier hunted down by *Butcher* Cumberland's murdering government redcoats.'

'Perhaps that's a wee bit too far back,' Neil replied, struggling to remain straight faced.

'The imagination runs wild around here, Inspector. Och, we've even got a monster in the loch, according some of our older residents.'

'Haven't all lochs these days?'

'Aye, that's true! But on a serious note, the locals do seem flabbergasted by the news. The word is that it was murder, is that right?'

'We're certainly treating the circumstances as suspicious, yes.'

'No one can actually believe such a thing like this could have happened around these parts. The belief is that there hasn't been any violence in Glendaig since the *45*.'

'Tell me Reverend, who would I talk to locally to get the lowdown on who's who around here? Perhaps *you* can help?'

'I could, but probably the best person to speak to is Siobhan Stuart, the local postie. I never fail to be amazed by her knowledge of the comings and goings around this village; best have a word with her. If I can help at all though, with anything, please let me know.' He pointed back to the road. 'You'll find Siobhan along the way at Seal Cottage. If her van's outside she'll be at home.' Then he looked at his watch. 'She should be there about now if you want to speak to her.'

Neil thanked the minister and headed back to the MG. He wanted to look around the church and graveyard but, more importantly, didn't want to miss the opportunity to speak to Siobhan Stuart. Clearly his departure had not caused offence and following a wave of the hand, the Reverend Mackay breezed through the red gate and marched away purposefully towards the church door.

Seal Cottage was less than a minute's drive from the church. Neil cursed himself for not having left the car in the car park and walked the short distance. Sure enough, just as Mackay had predicted, the red Royal Mail van was parked on the stony hard standing outside the property. He pulled up behind it and reached for his mobile phone. As expected, no signal, not even one bar. Brodie would have to wait.

He opened the gate, inducing a high pitched squeal from the rusty hinges. A dog barked nearby, but no animal appeared. Reassured that he was not about to be savaged, he edged cautiously past the *Pride of Knoydart* and knocked several times on the front door. The door was opened almost immediately by Siobhan, who was drying her hair with a large white towel. Dark twisted strands of it still hung wet about her face.

Neil introduced himself. 'Perhaps this isn't a good time,' he suggested. 'I could always come back a little later.'

'Nonsense,' came the reply. 'Come on in Inspector, I'll put the kettle on.'

Chapter Seven

Siobhan ushered Neil into her chaotic world. He followed her into the kitchen, where she hastily removed the ginger tomcat from the same chair Tamsin Kirkwood had used four days earlier. She indicated to him to sit down, then deposited her towel on the worktop and went across to the sink to fill the kettle. 'Tea or coffee, Inspector?'

'Sorry? Oh, coffee please, two sugars.' Neil had been distracted by the scale of clutter in the room. His attention now switched back to his host as she placed the kettle on the range.

'So how can I help you?' Siobhan turned to face him, her arms loosely folded in a leisurely fashion.

'I'm told you are the person to talk to about the locals,' he replied, hoping not to offend her.

'Well I deliver their mail, if that's what you mean. And I suppose I do stop for a chat with people when I see them. In fact, I'm awash with tea by the time I get home most days!'

'Can you tell me a wee bit about the current residents living in the village? I'm particularly interested in those who may have been living here during the war.'

'That's easy enough, but why during the war?' Siobhan deposited a mug of coffee on the table in front of Neil.

'We think the remains found along the road date to around that period.'

'Oh, I see.' She took a sip of coffee whilst she considered the question. 'The two people who immediately come to mind wouldn't have killed anyone, I can assure you of that.' Siobhan was now busy, vigorously brushing her wet hair as if it were the mane of a horse.

'No, I'm not digging for suspects, but they might be able to help me get a feel for what was going on here at that time.'

'Okay,' Siobhan sighed, happy with the reassurance. 'Well, firstly there's my father-in-law, Murdo Stuart. He's eighty-eight now. He's lived here all his life, well here or roundabouts. He was born on a croft along the road towards Invertulloch. I believe he started working as a ghillie on the Glendaig Estate in the thirties, and worked his way up to Head Stalker. He retired in the mid-eighties after fifty years loyal service to the estate... so he likes to remind us.'

'So did he not get called up during the war?'

Siobhan laughed. 'No, his boss put in a good word for him, made the case that he was engaged in important work on the land and so his job fell within the remit of a reserved occupation. Then there was his asthma, I assume that strengthened his case.'

'Who was his boss at the time?' Neil sipped his coffee thoughtfully.

'Sir Brodric Macleod, the local Laird. He was a retired diplomat and one time lawyer. Had a lot of friends in high places, both in Edinburgh and down in London apparently.'

'So your father-in-law must have been well respected on the estate.'

'Aye he was, very well respected.'

'Do you know where was he living during the war?'

'Still with his parents at their croft. He married his wife Ursula just after the war and they moved into a ghillie's cottage on the estate. They eventually moved to Caisteal Cottage, here in the village, back in the seventies. They changed the name to Lochview, Ursula's decision, and have remained there ever since.'

'And where's Lochview?' Neil asked.

'Just follow the road through the village towards Invertulloch. You cross an old stone bridge over the burn and Lochview's the second on the left. You can't miss it, they've painted it pink.'

'Does Murdo have any brothers and sisters?'

'He had three, two sisters and a brother. Two of them are dead. His younger sister Moira lives in London. I think they only speak periodically.'

'That's great, do you think he'll mind if I pay him a visit?'

'Och no, I shouldn't think so. They're around most of the time.'

'Is there anyone else that I should know about who might be able to help me, Siobhan?'

'Well, there's Mary Galbraith. She lives with her son Iain along at Rowan Cottage. Just before the bridge over the burn there's a track on the left that leads up to Glendaig Mains, Tom Buchanan's farm. Mary's place is just up there on the right-hand side.'

'Okay.' Neil toyed with his mug as he shifted his position on the wooden chair. 'Tell me about Mary.'

'What can I tell you about old Mary? She's about the same age as my father-in-law I would say. Her father, Torquil McSween, ran the farm for years and she's lived there all her life. Torquil was a puritanical figure so I'm told, an avid churchgoer. They say everything stopped up at the farm on the Sabbath. Apparently he used to read from the Gaelic bible most of the day and only stopped to attend church.'

'And does Mary have any siblings?' Neil wanted to steer the conversation back from its digressive path.

'She had a sister, Muireall. I believe they were very close. Muireall died about six years ago. I think she lived in Aberdeen.'

'What about Iain's father?'

'Mary doesn't speak about him much. I do know he was killed during the war, not long after Iain was born. They were childhood sweethearts, so I'm led to believe. Met when he was a labourer on the farm.'

'So has Iain never married then?'

'No, his fish farm is his life. He's a dour wee man. If you ask me, I don't think anyone would have him. Mary fusses over him like a wee child... More coffee Inspector?'

'No, thanks,' Neil replied, reinforcing his response with a raised hand. 'I won't keep you, but just quickly, can you give me a brief rundown on the other residents currently living in the village?'

'Well that shouldn't take long. There aren't many left these days,' she chuckled. 'Let me see now.' She raised a finger to pursed lips and peered out of the window in contemplation. In a second her attention had returned to Neil. 'You've seen the Manse, no doubt?'

'Aye, and I saw the minister up at the church just now. Duncan Mackay.'

'That's right. He lives there with his wife Fiona and two kids. I bet it was Duncan who sent you down to me.'

'I'd hate to tell tales.'

'Och, it's not you who's the wee clipe, it's him. He always does it. I reckon he thinks I'm the village gossip.'

'I'm sure he doesn't,' Neil said, a little embarrassed. 'I suppose it's a logical deduction that the postie knows everyone.'

'That's very diplomatic Inspector, but we'll just have to agree to differ.' Siobhan's green eyes were now fixed on her guest, her lips spread to form a disbelieving smile. 'Then there's Gordon and me. We don't have any children.'

'And Gordon is Murdo's son?'

'Aye, he works along at the fish farm at Invertulloch. Iain Galbraith is his boss. Then, along from us there's Tam and Margaret McDonald. They live at Ardmhor. He was the local postman here from 1968 until around 2000. They're a lovely old couple, keep themselves to themselves.'

She paused as if consulting a mental map of the village.

'Across from the McDonalds, at Burnside, are Mary Forbes and her son Cameron. She's in her mid-forties, works at the Invertulloch Inn; cleaning, waitressing, you name it. Cameron's in his twenties, works for Iain Galbraith too. Then up at the farm are Tom Buchanan and Theresa, and their three kids. They've been up there since the mid-eighties.'

'Do they have any connection with the McSweens, who had the farm previously?'

'No, none at all, Torquil and Elizabeth were long gone before Tom came along. He's from Perthshire, so not local to here.'

'Okay, and there's Mary and Iain Galbraith at *Rowan Cottage*, just down from the farm.'

'Aye, that's right. Then, as you follow the road to Invertulloch, you cross the burn and there's the Old School House on the right. An Englishman from London has it now as a holiday home. His name's Giles Fordyce. He gets up quite regularly, as do his family, nice people.'

'Okay, and beyond them…'

'Murdo and Ursula at Lochview, and next to them at Ben Caisteall is Patricia Simms, a university lecturer from Newcastle. She's another holiday home owner, but going on the amount of time she spends here I think the house must just be an investment!'

'So not a regular visitor?' Neil deduced.

'Once or twice a year at the most. The place must be awfully damp inside being left like it is, such a shame. The last house on the right, Skye View Cottage, is Godfrey and Denise Roland's. He's a nice chap, a retired artist. They moved here in 1990.' She took a deep breath. 'So that's about it, Inspector.'

'Thanks Siobhan. You're right, the only people living here now who could possibly help me are Mary Galbraith and your father-in-law. The rest seem to be relative newcomers.'

'That's right. I could tell you about some of the other folk living round about, but I can't think of anyone who may be sufficiently elderly, *and* have lived here long enough to be of assistance to you. I'm afraid many of the properties are now holiday homes, or owned by people moving up here to escape the rat race down south.'

'No, that won't be necessary for now, thanks. It's really *this* village I'm interested in.'

'So do you think someone who was living here back then killed the man you found on the beach?' Siobhan was eager to pick up on any morsel of information that she could distribute on her next morning's round.

'We must keep an open mind, but you and I both know that in those days people wouldn't have travelled the distances they do today. I might be way off the mark though, so don't quote me on that one.' Neil got up from the table and placed his empty mug on the drainer. 'Thanks for the coffee, and the information. I'll try not to disturb you again.'

'Any time,' Siobhan replied, beaming seductively. 'You know where to find me.'

Neil sensed that Siobhan was flirting with him and felt himself blush as he made haste towards the front door. The truth was he had nothing to fear from the vivacious postwoman, everyone knew that she was completely besotted with her Gordon!

With a brief wave of the hand, Siobhan had disappeared into the darkness that engulfed the hallway and the door closed behind him with a dull thud. He stood still for a minute, a little relieved, listening to the birdsong flowing from the trees behind the house. The sun had burnt through the canopy of cloud now and large swathes of blue had appeared in the western sky, indicating a return to fair conditions.

Neil skirted round the *Pride of Knoydart* and opened the gate. He glanced left and right. Nothing, not a human or a vehicle in sight, only the MG, and Siobhan's Royal Mail van parked outside the cottage.

Across the road stood a telephone kiosk, one of the old red ones, paint peeling from the roof and a variety of flora invading the interior through the glassless window panels. Fixed to a telegraph pole nearby was a small letter box. The royal cypher of George the Fifth remained visible through the copious coats of red paint that been applied over the years. Nearby, the grey walls of Burnside sheltered under a roof of dark slate. In the garden, a line of washing tossed and turned in the breeze, no doubt soaked by the recent rain. Neil turned left and walked along the edge of the road, past the neat flower beds and newly cut lawn at Ardmhor. Ahead was the old stone bridge Siobhan had spoken of. He could hear the icy mountain water rushing beneath the ancient structure, a comforting relentless tone that increased in volume as he approached. He peered over the parapet into the gurgling water as it tumbled and frothed its way downstream from the upper slopes of Beinn Caisteal. The 3,000 foot peak towered over the village together with its near neighbour Stac Coinneach Dubh. Both were magnets for climbers like the Kirkwoods. Today, their summits were lost in a swirling fog of wispy grey cloud that clung to the glistening rock like fairground candy floss.

Neil had noticed the track to Glendaig Mains as he approached the bridge. A painted metal name sign in the shape of a cow confirmed Siobhan's directions. A wooden fingerpost stood behind the glossy black beast, indicating the route to a series of ancient brochs, mysterious dry stone structures dating back to the Iron Age.

Beyond the bridge stood the Old School House, a typically grim example of a Victorian temple of learning. Only its brightly painted front door, floral curtains and satellite dish suggested a change of use to that of a dwelling.

Further along the single track road the pink walls of Lochview came into view through a screen of yellow broom. Gardens that could only be the work of a perfectionist surrounded the neat little cottage. Neil glanced to his right, where far reaching views across Loch Coinneach opened up between the Old School House and the harled white walls of Skye View Cottage.

Beyond the Stuarts' property and the dour-looking exterior of the Roland's home opposite, he found himself at the eastern limits of the village. A *Thank you for driving carefully* sign graced the verge outside the low gate to Beinn Caisteall, another harled, white-walled property with dormer windows. The house looked sad, every inch the little-used holiday home. The gardens sorely needed attention and a wheelie bin, its lid plastered with bird droppings, sat outside the gate, grass climbing around its small plastic wheels.

The road onward to Invertulloch stretched away to the east. Bordered by dry stone walls, this lonely route passed between fields on the seaward side, and pine forest on the other.

Whilst Neil stood taking in the view he became aware of the sound of a vehicle approaching from behind him. He turned in time to see a green Land Rover rush past and disappear into the distance trailing a cloud of dust. Other than the Reverend MacKay and Siobhan Stuart, it was the first sign of life he'd seen in over three hours.

Retracing his route, he was able to take in a different perspective on the village. For the first time he became aware of the imposing castellated tower of Castle Coinneach peeping out from above the trees on the south side of the road. He assumed the castle must be accessible from somewhere near the church and made a mental note to take a walk out to the ruins at some stage.

On reaching Lochview again he stopped, checking for any sign of life at the property. The only clue was the presence of a silver Ford Escort standing on the paved driveway to the prefabricated garage. It was a model that dated back to the nineties, but its overall condition befitted that of a new purchase.

Neil opened the iron gate and approached the front door. He pressed firmly on the doorbell button and heard a distant chiming tone somewhere deep within the cottage. Then there was silence. He waited for a few seconds, listening, but there was no sound. He turned to leave, convinced that the property was unoccupied but then, as he stepped away into the sunlight, he heard footsteps marching along the hallway.

Chapter Eight

'Can I help you young man?'

A woman, probably in her early eighties and unusually voguish in appearance for her age, peered out from a gap between the door and frame. Neil caught his reflection in the conspicuously large lenses of her bifocals, lenses so large in fact that the greater part of her heavily made-up cheeks could be seen in magnified detail.

'My name's Detective Inspector Neil Strachan, I'm with the Northern Police Major Enquiry Team.' He presented his warrant card through the gap in the doorway. 'Would you be Mrs Ursula Stuart?' The door then opened wide to reveal a short woman, dressed trendily in corduroy trousers and cotton tee-shirt. Her curly grey hair rested upon her shoulders, accentuating her youthfulness.

'Aye that's me. Do come in Detective Inspector, please.'

She led him down the hallway to a neat but cluttered sitting room. The walls were adorned with numerous framed photographs depicting the work of the stalker. It soon transpired that the common theme in all these images was the subject; a fit looking man, smartly dressed in tweeds and matching deerstalker hat. He carried a rifle slung over his shoulder and appeared in different locations, and obviously at different times of his life. As Neil studied the display it became obvious to him that the man in the photographs was becoming older, facially, but certainly not in stature. His hair had gradually turned to white, but he remained powerfully built and it was clearly the same man.

'Sit down please,' said Ursula, busily clearing away some

knitting from the sofa. 'We don't often see the police out here, I have to say.'

Neil sat as requested, sinking into the sumptuous sofa. 'I'm making enquiries about the human remains that were found near here a few days ago,' Neil explained.

'I see, Detective Inspector. I wish we could help, but I'm afraid I can't see how.'

'Well, you never know. I'm really interested in speaking to any of the local residents who lived here during the war. I believe your husband, Murdo, might be one such resident. Is that correct?'

'Aye, you're right there, he did live locally throughout the war years; on his parents' croft just outside the village. I'm afraid he's away out with our son at the moment, he has a hospital appointment in Fort William.'

'That's a shame, I hope everything's alright.'

'Oh aye, he has angina, something he's lived with for years. It's only a routine appointment with the specialist.'

'I don't suppose *you* can help me then? Were you living in Glendaig during the war?'

'Me? No, I'm afraid not. I was living with my parents in Camuscraig during the war. Murdo and I weren't married until 1948. I only came to live here then.'

'Did you ever come here at all during the war?'

'Aye, a few times I suppose. I first met Murdo at a dance in Camuscraig in 1943. We saw each other for a while, and then I started seeing another chap, a local boy from my village. I didn't see Murdo again until 1947, about a year before we were married.'

'I see. Do you recall any unusual events occurring in this area, Camuscraig included, around that time... people going missing perhaps, or talk of German agents landing, anything like that? I know it all seems a bit dramatic, but I can assure you the question is relevant to my enquiry.'

'No, nothing so exciting I'm sorry to say.' The old lady laughed. 'The strangest thing I recall from back then was the minister's wife at Camuscraig running off with her brother-in-law after a ceildh in the village hall. Autumn of 1944 that was. He was a soldier, due to be shipped out to the continent, but he deserted and they ran off up to Ullapool. Everyone from the Kyle to Invertulloch was talking about it.' She interrupted her story for a moment, as if searching her memory. Then she was off again… 'Young Jackie MacIver, that was him. He got caught of course, and ended up in a military prison, silly wee bugger.'

Neil was amused by Ursula's gamy use of language. 'So what happened to the minister's wife, then?'

'Och, she went back to her man, as expected. Her mother told her to.' The conversation hung silently in the air for a second. Then she shook her head. 'No, nothing more interesting than that, Detective Inspector. Sorry to disappoint you.'

Neil glanced at the photographs hanging around the room. 'I take it the photos are of Murdo?' he asked, gesturing towards them with a nod of the head.

'Aye, that's my Murdo. He ended up as head stalker on the Glendaig Estate. Started out as a wee ghillie at fifteen years old, then worked his way up.'

'And did he live on the croft with his parents up until you were married?'

'Aye, we moved into the ghillie's cottage on the estate in 1948, when we married, and then in 1957 we got the stalker's cottage when Donald Grant, the previous incumbent, retired.'

'How long have you lived here at Lochview?'

'Oh, since 1974. We wanted something for our retirement, something we owned outright. This place was up for sale so we grabbed it!'

Neil patted his thighs, signalling the end of his questions. 'Thank you for your time Mrs Stuart. Can you tell your husband that I called, and I'll come back to speak with him as soon as I can?'

'Well we're here most of the time, don't venture far these days.' She tilted her head slightly. 'So where are you off to now?'

76

'I thought I'd drop in on Mary Galbraith. Your daughter-in-law tells me she's lived here for a long time.'

'That's certainly true,' said Ursula. 'Well I hope she can help you more than I have. You may find her a little deaf though.'

Neil thanked her for the advice and made his way down the path and through the gate. On reaching the road he glanced back at the little pink house. The window to the left of the front door stood partially open. Within the darkened room, the curtains swayed gently in the breeze. Behind them, Ursula stood in silence, supervising his departure. On seeing him focus his attention on the open window she withdrew immediately, as if she'd been caught in the act.

Neil wondered whether her furtiveness warranted the pangs of suspicion that began to surge through him. It was an intuitive response that he felt content to dismiss... for now at least.

The track up to the farm, Glendaig Mains, was pitted with pot holes, most of them filled with muddy water. Neil picked his way gingerly between the craters, trying to protect his shiny new brogues. The gradient became more acute as he neared the grubby, low-set stone property that he assumed was Rowan Cottage.

A thin column of blue grey smoke arced away from one of the two chimneys, eventually being dispersed by the prevailing wind. Reassured by this tell-tale sign of occupancy, Neil let himself through the gate and headed for the front door. The cobweb-encrusted light in the porch remained on, even though it was nearly midday. Neil knocked several times on the door. Turning away to survey the garden, he listened intently for any audible clue that someone may be in residence. A large rowan tree provided a canopy over much of the front garden, such that it was. Patchy grass bordered by a few wilting shrubs were all that remained of a once well-tended curtilage.

A dog barked from behind the house, followed soon after by the thunder of paws on mud. A black and white collie hurtled around the corner of the property, barking frantically. The dog skidded to a halt in front of Neil; its head dropped onto its front paws and its rear end swung from side to side as the black tail wagged furiously. Neil squatted to stroke the dog, hoping to God he wouldn't lose his hand. As he did so, he sensed someone tugging at the front door from within. The wood appeared to be swollen, and whoever it was seemed to be experiencing some difficulty. Then suddenly the door released itself and swung open. A tiny woman with a distinct stoop stood in the doorway. Neil estimated her age to be somewhat greater than that of Ursula Stuart, but she still had a certain presence about her and he was certain that her physical frailty belied a far more powerful spirit.

She stood, supporting herself on a hand-carved walking stick, looking down upon Neil with narrow, suspicious eyes.

'Come away Cadha,' she called, clearly irritated by the dog's behaviour. The collie shot into the cottage, its rear end narrowly missing a misaimed sweep of the stick.

Neil stood up and introduced himself to the stern-faced old lady. 'Would you be Mary Galbraith?'

She scowled. 'Aye, I'm Mary Galbraith. I'd heard you fellows were swarming all over the place.' She studied him with dewy blue eyes, awaiting a response from her visitor.

'I expect you've heard that some human remains have been found near here. We think they date back to the war. I gather you lived here at that time, and thought you might be able to help me with my enquiries?'

She glared at him from beneath a shock of white hair pulled up into a bun. 'Perhaps,' she said dismissively. 'Do you want to come in?' Neil thanked her, but not before she'd turned stiffly and shuffled away indoors, correctly anticipating his answer.

'Excuse the mess,' she murmured, softening her tone as she approached a wing-backed chair near the fireplace. She eased herself down into it and gestured to Neil through the peaty haze that hung heavily within the gloom-filled room. 'Sit down, laddie.' It was more of a command than an invitation, reinforced by the raising of her trusty stick that directed him to an old leather two-seater. Once he was seated it was *she* who fired off the first question.

'So do you think you'll discover who those bones belong to?'

'I hope so, Mrs Galbraith.' He spoke in a raised tone, mindful of Ursula Stuart's advice regarding the old lady's deafness.

'You don't have to call me *Mrs* Galbraith, laddie. I haven't been a *Mrs* since 11th September 1944. You may as well call me Mary. That's my name after all.'

'I'm sorry Mary. I take it your husband was killed during the war?'

'Aye, that he was.'

'May I ask what happened to him?'

'You can, but it probably wouldn't mean anything to you, you're too young.'

'Actually, I'm very interested in history, Mary. I might surprise you… and I'd really like to hear about him.'

Mary's features softened again, as she gazed dreamily into the fireplace. 'It'll never be just history for me laddie, it's *my* present. It always will be.'

Neil cursed himself for being so insensitive. 'I'm sorry Mary. I hope I haven't upset you.'

She looked up, her eyes displaying sadness rather than anger. 'No, no, it's just me, take no notice. Sixty-four years of being alone, bringing up a child single-handed, it leaves its mark.' She clasped her hands together and rested them on her lap. Neil noticed the presence of a slight tremor as she did so and wondered whether she was suffering from Parkinson's disease.

'I met John, that's my husband, when he first worked on the farm up here. We were in our late teens then, not a care in the world. He joined the army in '39 and went with the Gordon Highlanders to France.' A weak smile crossed her lips. 'He was one of the few lucky men in the 51st Highland Division to escape back to Britain. Then he went to Africa after that and was wounded. No sooner had he recovered, when they sent him back to France again in 1944. He was sent to help relieve Le Havre in the September, Operation

Astonia they called it. The letter from his commanding officer said he'd been shot by a German sniper as they entered the town on 11th September. Good soldier, well-liked by all. Very matter of fact. So there you have it.'

Cadha trotted back into the room and sat by Neil's leg. He stroked the dog's silky head with his left hand. 'Did you live in Glendaig throughout the war, Mary?'

'Aye, I did that.' She produced another smile, stronger this time. 'I think I only left once, to help my father take some sheep to the market in Fort William.' She seemed manifestly proud of her achievement. Neil, on the other hand, couldn't imagine being confined to this remote corner of the Highlands for years on end.

'Do you remember anything significant happening here during the war?' he asked. 'Something that may give us a clue as to the identity of the remains we found on the beach?'

'Not much has ever happened around these parts; certainly nothing that I would say was *significant*. As for the war, you wouldn't have known that there was one if you lived here. Yes, there was rationing and such like, but life went on as normal. It was only when the telegrams arrived telling us that our men were dead... that's when we knew there was a war on.'

'Did many men from Glendaig lose their lives then?'

Mary was slow to respond. 'Well there was my John of course, and James Grant. He was in the navy. His ship was torpedoed during the D-Day landings. James lived down at Caisteall Cottage, it's called Lochview now.'

'Where Murdo and Ursula Stuart live?' Neil interrupted.

'Aye, that's right. He was a lovely laddie, James. So was his wife Eleanor, and their two wee ones. Then there was Ruaidhri Macrae, the doctor's son. He was torpedoed in 1940, spent the rest of the war in a prisoner of war camp and died of some illness just before he was liberated. He was only twenty-four. There were others, you know, from other villages along the coast. You've only got to look at the names on the memorial at Camuscraig.'

'Where did the doctor live?'

'Beinn Caisteall, the last house in the village, next to the Stuarts. Alpin Macrae was his name. It was weeks before they got word about Ruaidhri being taken prisoner. Alpin and Meg had given up hope. Then they had good news, that he was alive, only to have their hearts broken a second time a while later.'

Neil heaved himself out of the sagging sofa, and brushed the dog hairs from his trousers. 'If you think of anything that may be of interest to me Mary, however irrelevant it may seem, please give me a call.'

He placed one of his business cards on the arm of Mary's chair. She attempted to get up to see him out, but he gestured to her to stay where she was. 'Don't get up, I'll see myself out,' he said as he turned towards the door.

The cottage was filled with dark and oppressive furniture, no doubt handed down through generations of the McSweens. One such example standing to the left of the doorway was an ancient dresser, its dusty shelves filled with blue and white china. Dinner plates leant precariously on their rims so as to fully display their intricate designs.

'That was my grandmother's,' Mary called after him when he paused to examine the piece, running his hand over the age battered wood.

'It's a fine piece of furniture, Mary,' said Neil as he examined a group of black and white photographs displayed on the lower shelf. He pointed to one of them and moved closer for a better look. 'Is this John?' he asked. The posed portrait was that of a young soldier wearing a dice-patterned Glengarry bonnet bearing the stag's head insignia of the Gordon Highlanders. The handsome young man with his cheeky grin and shiny, bead-like eyes clearly had no inkling of the horrors that were soon to befall him.

'Aye, that's my John, just after he'd completed his basic training. I was so proud of him.'

Neil nodded politely, but wasn't really listening. He'd moved on to the next photograph, another old black and white print of a family group. The little cluster of individuals was standing in front of a wooden door. Two middle-aged couples and two young women in their twenties. They were clad in heavy coats and snow lay around about their feet. A middle-aged man smoking a pipe was embracing one of the younger women. Neil immediately sensed that both bore a remarkable resemblance to his host.

'Who's the man with the pipe?' he asked.

'That's my father, Torquil McSween. He farmed up at the Mains.'

'And who are the other people in this photo?'

'My older sister Muireall, and mother Elizabeth. The other couple are my uncle and aunt, Donald and Morag Grant.'

'And who's the attractive young lady with the shoulder-length hair?'

'Isobel Grant, my cousin on my mother's side.'

'She seems to be looking at someone, away to her left.'

'I don't know, perhaps. Does it matter?' Mary seemed irritated by Neil's comment, a degree of curtness returning to her voice.

'No, not at all. It just seemed a strange pose for a photograph, that's all'.

'It was a long time ago Inspector, Christmas 1943 as I recall. I wasn't there when it was taken. I believe Isobel's brother David took it.'

Neil remained intrigued by the photograph, but he couldn't quite think why. 'How are all these people related, Mary?'

'Donald and my mother were brother and sister.'

'I see, Donald being the estate stalker before Murdo Stuart?'

'Aye, that's right. You've been doing your homework Mr Strachan. So why all these questions about an old photograph?'

'No reason. I'm just interested. Tell me; are any of these people alive today?'

'Well, the older ones are long gone. Muireall died in 2003 and Isobel may be dead too, I don't know.'

Have you never kept in touch with Isobel?'

'Not for years, no.'

'Do you know where she lived?'

'No, I've no idea'.

'What about your cousin David. Tell me about him.'

'There's not much to tell. He grew up in Glendaig. Worked on the estate as a ghillie until he was called up later in the war. He joined the navy and after he was demobbed he lived in Camuscraig and became a fisherman. He was married to a local girl there and died tragically in 2000, in a car accident.' She rose stiffly from her chair. 'Now if you have no further questions, I have to prepare a meal for my son. He'll be in soon.'

'Of course, thank you for your time Mary.'

Neil sensed he'd probed deeply enough on this occasion. He bade the elderly lady farewell and pulled the swollen front door closed behind him. Cadha was nowhere to be seen as he ambled down the track to the road. Only a solitary sheep was aware of his presence, giving him a cursory glance as it continued to feast on the grassy verge.

Once back in the MG, he just managed to execute a one-eighty degree turn from the hard standing outside Seal cottage. Siobhan's van was missing, out on her afternoon collection round he assumed.

As he headed out of the village the church once again came into view, prompting him to pay the old place a further visit. Pulling up outside the gate, he donned his jacket and entered the churchyard. There was still a chill in the air and as he fumbled with the zip, the sound of finches darting about amongst the yellow broom filled his ears. There was an atmosphere of stillness about the place accompanied in equal measure by a sense of desolation. Closing the gate behind him, he made his way along the weed-strewn path towards the building's main door. He glanced about him at the gravestones leaning serenely at differing angles as the earth surrendered reluctantly to their weight. Encrusted in yellow lichen and casting shadows on the coarse, roughly mown grass, they were inscribed with names that you'd expect in this part of the world: *MacDonald, Macrae* and suchlike. Some of the inscriptions had been ravaged by time, some were in Gaelic; a language that he'd never really mastered but had always intended to learn.

Then, as the large arched door came into view, he was drawn towards a large Celtic cross, far more grandiose than the other simple memorials he'd passed and sufficiently impressive to warrant closer inspection. He stood before the cross, hands clasped to his front in respectful contemplation. It was hewn out of rough granite and bore an inscription on the base in black.

In memory of Callum James Matheson
Born 2nd May 1890. Died 15th May 1965.
For 36 yrs, Priest of this Parish.
Also Anna, his wife.
Born 28th July 1890 in Kreuzlingen, Switzerland.
Died 9th January 1979. Together at last.

'*Kreuzlingen.*' The word had a strangely exotic ring to it; so unexpected in such a remote backwater as this. Even reference to a native of Camuscraig would have amounted to the interment of a *foreigner* in these parts.

Neil stared at the inscription, endeavouring to elicit every possible morsel of information from those few words. So here lay the local minister who most probably officiated in this parish throughout the war, together with his Swiss wife, Anna. His concentration was broken by the hollow thud of the church door closing.

'Christ,' he muttered under his breath, struggling to stabilise his heartbeat.

The Reverend Mackay marched along the path towards him. 'Back so soon?' he enquired with a broad grin.

'I was just reading this inscription. One of your predecessors I see.'

'Aye, he was one of the longest-serving ministers in this Parish. His father, Walter, served here before him. He's buried in the plot directly behind this one. Between them they occupied the Manse for over fifty-five years. Some feat, eh?'

'Do you know anything about Callum's wife, Anna?'

'Only what *you* know from reading that inscription. Why do you ask?'

'Oh, it just seems unusual in these parts for someone to have travelled so far to live out here, especially back then... what would it have been... the twenties?'

'I suppose it would have been, yes, if not before.'

Neil skirted around the cross to read the inscription on the memorial directly behind it. The elements had rendered the wording partially illegible, but he could just make out the name *Walter Matheson, died 21st May 1924.* He leant forward, attempting to decipher the extensive epitaph beneath the name. To his disappointment, the erosion of the stone made this impossible. The most that could be gleaned was that the words were inscribed in the Gaelic language.

'Most of the family have been buried here.' The minister joined Neil by the grave. 'His wife Moyna is buried next to him and Callum's son Dugald is buried over there, under that tree.'

Neil looked over his shoulder towards the unpretentious granite headstone that stood in the shade of a nearby birch tree. Its thin leaves whispered softly in the breeze, casting fleeting shadows that danced across the dark stone. Neil walked across to read the words on the memorial. This time they were clear to see.

In loving memory of Dugald Iain Matheson
Born 2nd July 1915. Died 1st January 1942
Lieutenant
6th Morayshire Battalion TA
Seaforth Highlanders.
Tragically taken from us.

'Do you know what happened to him?' Neil asked, reflecting on how peaceful the young soldier's plot seemed. 'Poor devil appears to have been killed early in the war.'

'Och no, he wasn't killed in action. I believe there was some sort of accident here in Glendaig. Mary Galbraith may be able to tell you more about him.'

Mary was already featuring in Neil's thoughts. 'I was only speaking to her just now. I was asking her about the men from Glendaig who'd been lost during the war, and whether anything significant had occurred here during that time. I'm surprised she didn't mention Dugald Matheson.'

'Perhaps she'd forgotten. It was a long time ago after all… and she is getting on a bit.'

'Aye, I'm sure you're right' said Neil, pulling his car keys from his pocket. 'I'd like to have a quick look in the church if I could, and then I must be getting back to Inverness.'

'Be my guest,' said the minister, extending a welcoming arm towards the church door. 'It's always open.'

Chapter Nine

Friday 29th May

The journey south had been surprisingly uneventful. The flight to London Gatwick had departed Inverness on time, and the Gatwick Express had been waiting in the bay platform of the airport's railway station, seemingly just for him. The doors hissed and slid shut as he leapt aboard just after 9.30am.

Fifty minutes had since passed and Neil was now travelling deep under the streets of central London, swaying gently to the motion of the southbound Bakerloo Line train. Supported against the warm bodies of his travelling companions, he kept a firm hold on the shiny handle of the hanging strap above his head. He'd spent the short journey from the Embankment people watching. It was an activity that had clearly preoccupied him for the duration of the journey as, to his surprise, he'd now reached his destination. The train was emerging from the darkness into the brightly-lit environs of Lambeth North Station. The string of silver coaches whined to a halt and, with a gasp of compressed air, the doors eased aside, allowing the mass of compacted bodies to flow out onto the platform and head towards the exits.

A warm draft rushed in from the tunnel as another train clattered along somewhere in the distance. The breeze gently caressed his face and agitated the few discarded items of litter that lay in the void between the rails. Neil unwittingly became drawn into the crowd and followed the surge of chattering tourists up to street level. As he emerged onto the street, he failed to notice a youthful looking busker crouched on the concrete steps.

'Watch where you're goin' mate,' the youth protested, and Neil raised a conciliatory hand, keen to get on his way.

Outside in the glare of the morning sun he walked briskly along Kennington Road. Traffic rushed impatiently along nearby Lambeth Road, an endless flow of whining red buses and impatient black cabs, their drivers taking full advantage of the opportunity to make some progress through the cluttered streets of the capital.

Like a fearful child, Neil jogged across the busy thoroughfare craning his neck back and forth, hoping to remain unscathed amongst the mad frenzy of speeding metal. His mind flashed back to his visit to Glendaig two days previously and he recalled the solitary Land Rover rushing past him. For a second or two he yearned to be back in that place where the only discernible sounds were the trickle of chilled water flowing down from the mountains and the relentless wind in his ears. The dream was shattered as a taxi driver nearby leant on his horn, a pointless rebuke to the motorcycle courier who'd just cut him up. He raised a smile as the leather-clad rider shook a fist in defiance and sped off between two buses.

'No, this isn't for me,' Neil said to himself as he turned his back to the traffic and made his way through some nearby gates. He was now in the relatively peaceful sanctuary of an established park. Rising up behind tall shrubs stood a majestic-looking building with an impressive entrance portico and topped with a copper-clad dome. Outside, the visitor was greeted by two enormous naval guns; impressive relics from a bygone era. He checked his watch, ten minutes early, but at last he'd reached the leafy grounds of the Imperial War Museum.

He sauntered around the huge gun barrels, once the fifteen-inch armament of the old battleships *Ramilles* and *Roberts*. Then, having checked his watch again, he climbed the stone steps to the impressive portico of the museum. Beyond the towering columns were glass doors to the main vestibule. Inside, the drone of distant traffic died away, replaced by the whispered voices and distant echoes that he remembered from childhood visits to the great museums.

He approached a uniformed security officer and presented his warrant card, asking for Dr Paul Miller. Glum-faced, the ageing official shuffled off to find an internal telephone, leaving Neil to absorb the hushed atmosphere of the museum. He could see through to the atrium where large exhibits graced the extensive display space, illuminated by shafts of bright sunlight from high above. Tourists and awestruck children hung over the rails of the balconies studying the silent forms that hung suspended from the roof, ghosts from nearly a century of past conflicts.

Neil felt a hand press heavily on his shoulder. 'Inspector Strachan? Pleased to meet you. I'm Paul Miller.' Neil, taken aback by his host's stealth, turned abruptly. He found himself face to face with a small rotund man, his dark wavy hair, shot through with grey, cascading down over rather prominent ears. He had the features of a predatory bird; hook nosed with large, intense eyes. Neil considered his age to be over fifty, possibly younger, it was hard to tell. Undoubtedly, the ageing process had already got to grips with the good doctor.

'I'm sorry, I was just admiring the exhibits over there. Pleased to meet you, Doctor Miller.'

'Oh, please call me Paul.' He gestured towards the atrium. 'Perhaps you'll have time to have a look around before you head back to the airport.'

'I hope so, my flight's just after seven, so I might just have time for a quick peek.'

'Well you'll just have to come back then. A quick peek will never do! In the meantime, let's get down to business. Follow me.'

Miller led the way through an innocuous looking doorway and up several flights of stairs to the administrative wing of the museum. 'This is all very impressive,' said Neil as they made their way along another long corridor.

'We're in part of the old Bethlem Royal Hospital. The current building has been here since 1815, but the hospital itself dates back to the 1200s. It's renowned as being one of the world's first institutions specialising in mental illness.'

Miller ushered his guest into a small meeting room. A long table encircled by metal-framed chairs took up the greater part of the room. A projector sat at one end of the table, aimed at a large wall-mounted screen. At the other was a tray with two cups and a coffee pot. A collection of old photographs and yellowing folders lay spread across the carpeted floor, some propped up against plastic storage boxes.

'Coffee, Neil?' Miller pulled out a pair of half-moon spectacles and planted them on the end of his beaked nose.

'Thank you. So what exactly is your position here Paul?'

Miller carefully poured coffee into the two cups. 'I work under the Director of Collections in the department of Exhibits and Firearms. Sounds very grand doesn't it? We look after the museum's collection of three-dimensional artefacts: firearms, ordnance, vehicles, medals, you name it. I also have a particular interest in the German Navy during the two World Wars. I'm referred to here as the *resident expert.* That usually means that I've read a few more books on the subject than my colleagues.' He laughed, providing Neil with a glimpse of his yellowing dentures. 'No doubt you're about to put me to the test.'

He sat down with his coffee, having removed his bold checked jacket to reveal a matching waistcoat. Neil surmised that the garish caramel brown combination may well have been fashionable in an earlier decade, and he mused as to what Cat's assessment of this eccentric combination of garments might be. Several non-flattering adjectives immediately sprung to mind as he unzipped his holdall. He scooped out the plastic evidence bags, and placed them on the table. 'You've read the stuff I emailed you about the case?'

Miller crouched forward like an eagle protecting its kill and pushed his glasses back along the ridge of his nose. 'Oh yes, of course,' he replied dismissively. 'It all sounds incredibly exciting. Now let's have a look see.'

He picked up the bag containing the fragment of cloth bearing the gold bands and examined the contents for a few seconds. 'I think I can say with some certainty that these three wide bands of gold lace surmounted by this small gold star are the sleeve insignia of a *korvettenkapitän* in the German Navy. A relatively senior rank to be commanding a U-boat. The British equivalent would be a commander.'

Neil sipped his coffee. 'When I contacted your colleague initially he also intimated that it would be unusual for an officer of this rank to be serving on a submarine... *if* a submarine was involved, of course.'

'Well, yes and no I suppose. So why do you think he arrived in Scotland on a submarine?'

'Just a guess really, I would consider it unlikely he arrived on a surface vessel. In fact, if I'm honest, I'm at a complete loss as to why a German naval officer should be wandering around Scotland in full uniform! What do you think?'

'Well I'm in total agreement; it's all very strange indeed. He wouldn't have been a spy, for obvious reasons. There are only three other possibilities as I see it.'

'Three possibilities! That's a start. Please enlighten me,' said Neil.

'Well, he possibly landed as part of a raiding party, perhaps from a submarine, or he may have been put ashore by his own crew for some reason, a mutiny on board perhaps, I don't know. I've never heard of such an event occurring. Then there's the possibility he was a prisoner of war, an escapee; the one us experts never knew about, because as far as historical record is concerned, no German serviceman ever remained unaccounted for.'

'So going back to your original point, could he have been a submariner, holding such a senior rank?'

Miller let forth a thoughtful sigh. 'I think it's fair to say that the majority of U-boat commanders were either lieutenant commanders – *kapitänleutnants* or in a number of cases they would have been senior lieutenants. Having said this, there *were* some operational U-boat commanders with the rank of *korvettenkapitän*, more often the case a little later in the war. Let's just say it wouldn't have been entirely commonplace.'

He picked up a second bag containing a fragment of blue grey woollen material. 'This is interesting. It's a fragment of standard-issue British battledress... but dyed.' He stooped to open a plastic crate lying beside him and retrieved a swatch of cloth from within. 'Here you are, the very same but in its original khaki form.' He held it up against the exhibit bag, as if comparing the two specimens.

'That's not what I wanted to hear,' said Neil looking bewildered.

'Oh don't worry, I think I can explain this so-called red herring,' said Miller, not wishing to be outwitted. 'It may surprise you, but it was quite common for U-boat officers to wear British battledress. Have a look at this.' He ferreted through his photographs and held one aloft. 'Here's an example. This is *Kapitänleutnant* Fritz-Julius Lemp wearing captured British battledress. Considerable quantities of the stuff were seized at Dunkirk in 1940 and distributed to U-boat crews. They re-dyed much of it before re-issuing it. So I'd say this find fits perfectly with your theory that this chap was a U-boat man.' He raised a constraining finger. 'Having said that, I would expect him to be wearing one or the other, not necessarily tunic *and* battledress together.'

'I see.' Neil studied the old black and white image in which the officer was dressed entirely in the captured British garments. Only his cap appeared to be German issue.

'Now let me see the watch, that's most interesting.' Miller examined the timepiece through the clear plastic, running his finger over the scratched, clouded face.

'I've seen a number of these. *Hanhart* was a leading German watch manufacturer in the run up to World War Two. Their watches were used extensively by *Kriegsmarine* officers and the *Jagdflieger* – that's fighter pilots to you and me – of the *Luftwaffe*. This example of the chronograph was used specifically by U-boat officers. It differed from the *Luftwaffe* version in one particular way; both versions could perform basic navigation and timekeeping calculations, but this one... see here... incorporated scales to reference time against distance. It was this so called *telemeter* that helped them make accurate projections as to the running times of their torpedoes.'

He produced another old photograph. 'Here's a photograph of Reinhard Hardegan, one of the top U-boat aces of the war. See, he's shown here wearing one of these little beauties.' Miller handed Neil the photo, together with a large magnifying glass. 'As you can see, I've come prepared.'

Neil peered at the photograph through the lens. He could just make out the detail on the face of the watch being worn by the bearded naval officer in the image. He checked the watch in the plastic bag. Yes, they were most definitely one and the same.

Miller's attention had switched to the two bags containing the metal crosses. He picked them both up and looked at first one, and then the other. 'This example is an Iron Cross, First Class, shame it's a bit battered. You can see the reverse side is solid silver and so differed from the Second Class version of the award. Incidentally, the holder of this medal would have held the Iron Cross Second Class as well. Don't suppose you found any red, white and black ribbon amongst the remains?'

'No, I'm afraid not,' said Neil.

'Pity, still hardly surprising I suppose, after all this time. Recipients usually wore the ribbon through the second buttonhole of their tunic or service jacket.'

'I'm surprised we've found *any* material, to be honest,' said Neil.

'Quite, quite,' came the reply. 'Anyway, as I was saying. The Iron Cross First Class was awarded regularly to U-boat commanders, mostly for feats of courage beyond those which earned them the Second Class variant. Often it was awarded upon sinking 50,000 tons of shipping, so quite a prestigious piece of metal don't you think?'

Neil took the bag from Miller and examined it again. 'So we're not dealing with just any old German sailor here?'

'Absolutely not, dear boy. Which brings me on to this other cross. The *pièce de résistance*. You see the small clasp at the top here in the shape of oak leaves?'

'Aye, I noticed that when I first saw it.'

'This, my dear fellow, is the *Eichenlaub zum Ritterkreuz des Eisernen Kreuzes*, bit of a mouthful don't you think?' Translated, it means *Knight's Cross with Oak Leaves*. This here is the biggest clue to the identity of your skeleton. It was a hugely prestigious award, only presented 850 or so times. Less than thirty went to the U-boat men. We're talking ace of aces here Neil. Hitler himself liked to award these medals to the lucky recipients.'

Neil could feel his heartbeat quicken. The possibility of identifying the remains had suddenly become a distinct reality.

Miller turned the bag over and pointed to the rear of the oak leaf cluster. 'There is just a trace of the manufacturer's silver grading marks. The suspension loop here allowed the recipient to wear the award around his neck from a red, white and black ribbon, similar to that of the Iron Cross Second Class.'

'Okay,' said Neil thoughtfully. 'Can you give me some indication from this medal, or the list of recipients, who the owner was?'

'I doubt from the condition of the medal we can link it to a named recipient. There were many private copies struck as well. Having said that, I can confirm it is the genuine article, and perhaps I can introduce a name here... but there are some caveats attached.'

He was clearly excited by this particular exhibit, and hastily produced a book from under the table, placing it in front of him. Neil leaned across to view the colourful artwork on the cover. Above the dramatic picture of a submarine crashing through heavy seas, presumably somewhere in the Atlantic, was the imposing title, *Leading the Wolfpacks, by Matthias Fuchs*. Miller thumbed through the pages, stopping about a third of the way through the book. He ran the palm of his hand firmly along the spine, intending that it remained fully open, before sliding it across to Neil.

Neil looked down into the face of a young naval officer. He was posing proudly in what must have been his dress uniform, presumably for an official portrait. He was impeccably smart, and probably in his late twenties or early thirties, it was difficult to be precise. Neil's mind strayed momentarily to the old family photographs his mother had shown him. He remembered the portrait of his great-grandfather, taken during the Great War, and his mother remarking that he was a boy of nineteen at the time. His disbelief had made her laugh.

The young man in the book had short dark hair, incredibly shiny, no doubt heavily slicked with pomade. His skin appeared flawless, possibly due to the slight blurring effect of the old film. However, if there was one distinctive feature it was his nose, unusually long and as straight as a blade.

Neil found himself strangely drawn into the photograph. Had this handsome young man been the victim of a brutal murder on a Scottish beach? Was it possible? He was portrayed in an austere pose, his dark eyes focussed on something, or someone, slightly to his right. It reminded Neil of the publicity photos taken of black and white film stars. He wore a dark jacket and white shirt, but the head and shoulders shot had been taken from too close a range to reveal the full insignia of the uniform. He clearly was wearing one, as around his neck hung the very same Knight's Cross with oak leaf cluster that now lay on the table beside Neil. He could just make out the multi-coloured ribbon from which the award was suspended, neatly tucked away under the collar of his shirt.

Neil formed the impression that the statue-like persona concealed a very different man. Strip away the formality and he suspected this character was possessed of an outgoing and amicable nature. His features revealed a softness that one certainly wouldn't have expected from a man who plied the oceans, coldly sending merchant seamen to their watery graves.

The page was headed *Chapter six*, and under the photograph in bold type was the name *Korvettenkapitän Max Friedmann*. 'You think this is the man whose remains were buried near Glendaig?'

'I can't be sure of course, but he seems to be the only recipient I can think of that might fit the bill,' Miller replied.

'Why him then?'

'Well, it's a matter of elimination really. Of the thirty or so U-boat men who received the Knight's Cross with Oak Leaves, only seven are recorded as having died during the hostilities. Ironically, most of the holders lived on for many years after the war. Of the seven who died, only four held the same rank as your man, *korvettenkapitän*, at the time of their death. One was shot trying to escape from a POW camp in America. Another, Gunther Prien, was lost in the North Atlantic with all of his crew. It is thought his boat was sunk by one of his own circling torpedoes. Then there was Johann Mohr, killed when his boat was sunk with all hands, west of Portugal in 1943... which leaves Max Friedmann.'

'So what happened to him then?'

'To put it simply, he disappeared.'

'*Disappeared*?' Neil's gaze dropped onto the open pages in front of him. 'So how come you include him in the *"dead"* list?'

'Simply because he must be presumed dead after all these years. He's been the subject of much debate by historians. It was thought that he may have even committed suicide.'

'What were the circumstances of his disappearance?'

'Well, during April 1941 he returned to his base in Lorient from one of his most successful patrols. To summarise, he'd snuck into the Irish Sea and caused absolute havoc. I should add that he was already one of Germany's youngest U-boat aces at this stage. Anyway, he succeeded in sinking the British merchant cruiser *HMS Narborough* and three large tankers; about 49,000 tons in all. In fact he was nicknamed "Irish Max" when he returned to Lorient. Unfortunately his boat was later caught on the surface, recharging the batteries of its electric motors, and was attacked by British aircraft. Friedmann was wounded quite badly during the engagement. When he returned to France he spent a considerable period of time in hospital. Soon after, he was promoted to *korvettenkapitän* and awarded the oak leaf clasp to his Knight's Cross. He became a hero of the Reich, and was paraded about as the Führer's favourite propaganda tool. Hitler decreed that he shouldn't return to operational duty, firstly because his brother had already been killed earlier in the war and secondly, more importantly, he was more valuable to the politicians in Berlin as a celebrity. You have to understand that around this time some of the *Kriegsmarine*'s best men had been lost; Prien and Schepke killed and the highest scoring ace of all, Otto Kretschmer, captured.'

'So he became frustrated, being wrapped in cotton wool by his masters, and depressed that he couldn't return to active duty, eventually taking his own life. Is that the theory?' Neil interjected.

'Well, yes, that's the sum of it. He'd been office bound for several months, working on *Vizeadmiral* Dönitz's staff in Lorient. It's recorded that he left there on the 14th of December 1941 and flew to Berlin, reason unknown. He was never heard of again, and no body was ever found.'

'And what are these *caveats* you were talking about?'

Miller shrugged, not wishing to pour cold water on his own theory. 'Firstly, Berlin and Glendaig are some distance from each other. There's no actual supporting evidence, not even these medals, to confirm your remains may be those of Friedmann.' He tapped the table with his finger. 'The recovery of these medals also poses questions. Why on earth would a senior German naval officer be wandering around Scotland dressed in full uniform, medals and all? It just doesn't make sense.'

'What if he'd been taken prisoner… and perhaps escaped?' Neil asked.

Miller smiled. 'Highly unlikely, to be honest. Firstly there's no record of it. We Brits would have been dancing in the streets. Can you imagine it? Germany's golden boy captured! Secondly, there are the medals. If he'd been taken into captivity, he would have been searched and all his property removed, *especially* his medals. In fact many U-Boat commanders didn't wear any of their medals on operations anyway.'

Neil leaned on the edge of the table and massaged his temples. 'Could he have found his way ashore after his submarine had been sunk... is that a possibility?'

'It's conceivable, but there are no records of him sailing with any U-boat on operations after his patrol in the Irish Sea. Then of course there's the question, who shot him in the head?'

'Aye, you're right of course. So where the hell do I go from here then?'

'I'm sorry I can't really be of any greater assistance, but I do know a man who *may* be able to assist you further.'

Neil looked up, appreciative of any suggestions. 'Who would that be?'

'The author of that book in front of you, Matthias Fuchs. He's currently a *kapitänleutnant* in the German Navy. He was a submariner in an earlier life, but now he has a position as naval historian and lecturer in advanced training at the German Naval Academy at Mürwik. He flits between there and the German Naval Office in Rostock.'

'So how do I get in touch with him?'

'No need, dear boy. I'll give him a call for you. I'm sure he'll be very interested in your discovery. I'll get him to call you when you get back to Inverness, how does that sound?'

'Great. Thanks very much.'

'There isn't much Matthias doesn't know about the *Ubootwaffe*, and the men who served in it. In the meantime please take this book with you. It'll give you some background on Friedmann. You can return it when you come back to visit the museum at some stage.'

'Sounds like a deal, thanks.' Neil gestured towards the bags containing the buttons. 'I suppose it goes without saying that they are German naval buttons?'

'Absolutely, standard issue *Kriegsmarine*. There were a few slight variations, but I can show you some identical specimens if you like.' He opened the plastic crate and produced a small clear box containing a brass button resting on cotton wool.

'There you go,' he said, placing the two items next to each other. 'Bingo.' His narrow lips formed a smile. 'Oh, and before you ask, I let a colleague of mine have a look at the photos of the cartridge case your chaps found on the beach. You'll be pleased to hear that it too appears to be of German origin, probably manufactured early in the war.'

'How does he know that?'

'Well, during the early stages of World War Two, Germany developed two new bullets in an attempt to conserve lead. The first of these was designated the *08mE*, iron core encased in lead. The designation *mE* meant *mit Eisenkern,* or with iron core in English. Anyway, this type of cartridge was initially identified by a black jacket, certainly up until 1944. Your casing is an example of this type. The headstamp on the casing bears this out.'

'What calibre are we looking at here?'

'Sorry, I should have explained. It's a nine millimetre parabellum round, used with the Walther PP series, or P38, and of course the Luger. All weapons in use with the *Wehrmacht* during the war.'

'So we're saying, that in all probability, firearms of German origin were discharged on that beach at some stage?'

Miller raised a hand, indicating the need for caution. 'I don't want to confuse you, but this type of bullet could have been used with other handguns, the Browning Hi-Power for example. This was an allied weapon, but the German Army were known to have used it too. Particularly the *Waffen-SS* and *Fallschirmjäger* – parachute troops.'

'Okay, we'll leave it there before I get too confused. So the finding of this cartridge case tends to suggest that one or more firearms of German origin may have been discharged on that beach?'

'Oh yes, without a doubt,' said Miller. 'Now how about some lunch? Then you can have a look around whilst I do copies of some of these documents for you.'

The two men strolled back along the corridor towards the stairs. Their voices faded away as they entered the stairwell, but there was no doubt in the mind of the young woman who followed them that a young man called Max Friedmann was predominantly the topic of their conversation.

1 9 4 1

Chapter Ten

Atlantic Ocean, Northwest of Ireland
Saturday 20th December

Breathing through the mouth had become the accepted norm for the past twelve hours. By doing so, one could just about tolerate the stench that lay putrid and heavy within the confined atmosphere of a submerged U-boat. For Werner Hahn, the thirty-two-year-old commander of U-500, it had quickly become second nature.

At last, the draft of damp salty air drifting through the boat from the open bridge hatch was beginning to take effect. He sniffed cautiously, running his grubby fingers through the tangled beard that now encased his pallid cheeks. There was no doubt about it, the composite aroma of sweat, diesel oil and mould was at last beginning to fade.

Hahn unbuttoned his battledress jacket and threw it over the chair that stood by his desk in the captain's berth. He eased himself down onto his bunk with a contented sigh. The wall clock showed the time to be 1840 hours. That meant twenty minutes' peace and quiet before his officers would be joining him to discuss their next move… if indeed there was one to make! So he closed his eyes, and listened to the rhythmic lapping of water against the submarine's casing. Unfortunately, this sleep-inducing melody meant only one thing; they were dead in the water, a sitting target. His mind strayed from the worries of the present, and he began to reflect on the events that had occurred earlier that day…

It had seemed an age since they'd slipped quietly out of the old Prussian naval base at Kiel. Their routing to the north of Orkney had taken them through frequent snow squalls and heavy seas, but the 740 ton type nine U-boat had cut through the heaving Atlantic breakers with relative ease. The watch crew had huddled behind the ice-encrusted panels of the conning tower, enduring the worst that the Atlantic Ocean could throw at them. Below, there had been some seasickness, primarily amongst the more junior members of the crew, but the journey had otherwise been uneventful.

Kapitänleutnant Hahn's orders had been perfectly clear: '*To avoid enemy shipping unless a significant target had presented itself during passage to his designated area of operations.*' And all had gone according to plan. The vast, empty expanse of ocean rising and falling around the submarine as it forged it's way westward had remained exactly that... *empty*. Then it had all changed, shortly after midday.

The youthful yet punctilious *matrosengefreiter*, Otto Lempke, scanning his designated watch quadrant through powerful Zeiss binoculars, had detected smoke on the horizon. The able seaman had made a good call. The grey smudge to the northwest had slowly evolved into the 11,000 ton British tanker, *Falkland Star*. She was a straggler, trailing a thirty-ship convoy out of Halifax, Nova Scotia. The old vessel was struggling along at around ten knots, making the best speed her ageing boilers could give her. It was 11,000 tons not to be missed; a target that would provide a valuable boost to Hahn's tonnage rating... *and* his eligibility for a Knight's Cross.

According to the crew he'd long had a serious case of *Halsschmerzen*, or "itchy throat", as the U-boat men called it. The condition was common amongst many young U-boat officers, and one that ostensibly could only be relieved by wearing the prestigious decoration around their neck.

There had been no sign of any escorts and Hahn, having weighed up his options, had decided to attack. He'd set a course to intercept the tanker amidships, remaining on the surface and maintaining a maximum speed of eighteen knots. His plan was to engage the target initially with his powerful deck gun, hopefully inflicting sufficient damage to send her to the bottom. Besides, he wanted to preserve his stock of twenty-two torpedoes for the mission ahead. Some good shooting would be required, as he knew this would be a challenging task for the gun crew alone.

Tactical options filled his head as he watched his second watch officer, *Leutnant zur See* Hans Kessel, mustering his five-man gun crew upon the sea washed forward deck. Clad in oilskins, they'd broken open the waterproof ammunition locker, and the first round was being eased into the gun's breech.

Then, as the submarine raced towards its quarry, its diesels churning out full power, a second watchman up on the bridge had cried out from behind raised glasses: 'Alarm! Warships, bearing two four zero, long range, closing fast.' Six other pairs of lenses flashed around to seek confirmation of the approaching threat.

'*Scheisse*, British V and W destroyers.' Bruno Faust, the first watch officer had them clear in his sights. The old relics of the Great War had come from nowhere, dammit! He turned to his Commanding Officer, his tanned face glistening from the salt spray.

'What are your orders *Herr Kaleun*?' He always preferred to use the shortened title for his captain's rank.

Hahn considered his position for a moment, then came his clipped response. 'Secure the deck gun. Watch crew, clear the bridge, prepare to dive.'

He dropped through the conning tower hatch followed by Faust, as the boat was hurriedly prepared for evasive action.

Beneath them, the tension was now tangible. A frenzy of activity filled the cramped vessel as both junior officers and the quartermaster barked out their respective orders. As their raised voices echoed around the dingy control room, the commander, now stationed by the periscope, bellowed out his own directions above the screech of the klaxon. Both inside the boat and up on the deck plates above the clatter of men's feet, moving urgently over metal, added to the pandemonium.

Outside, as hatches were closed and locking wheels spun, the urgent chatter of the anxious men died and finally faded away. Only the sounds of nature, the wind and the sea, now hung in the air. The U-boat's nose tipped gently downward as the Atlantic swell washed across her rusting deck plates swallowing her pencil-like form. Then, last of all, the conning tower disappeared from sight... just as the first four-inch shell from *HMS Wareham* struck the water off her port quarter.

Hahn turned onto his side, his pillow firmly sandwiched between his head and arm. Much had happened since then. First there'd been the *wasserbomben*, "*wabos*" as the U-boat crews preferred to call them. Wave after wave of them, dull grey depth charges sinking silently around the submarine like deadly snowflakes. All the while, U-500 hummed along at no more than three knots. Hahn had ordered that she be secured for *schleichfahrt*, silent running, but the British were undeterred. Time and again the old destroyers' screws thrashed through the churning water directly above them. Their passing was marked several seconds later by the violent shockwaves from the detonations of the *wabos* as they erupted one after the other. The solemn faced U-boat men held on to whatever they could, white knuckled, their reddened eyes raised heavenwards as if expecting the damned things to burst through the casing at any time. The low distant grumble then became progressively louder, akin to an approaching thunderstorm. Next came the series of mind-blurring explosions that shook their very souls. It was then that their lives lay in the balance. The boat bucked and rolled as the shockwaves ripped through the pressure hull. Only the sounds of breaking crockery and men quietly praying interrupted the brief silences between explosions. The torment went on for what seemed like hours, then at last it stopped as quickly as it had begun.

The distant sound of hissing water and the comforting hum of the electric motors re-emerged from the chaos of before. The hydrophone operator's voice broke the silence.

'Screws fading astern of us, sir.' He delivered the news in a whisper, whilst wiping the back of a hand across his sweat-moistened brow. They had mercifully survived for now, thank God, hopefully to fight another day.

But the circling predators one hundred metres above them had no intention of giving up the hunt. The two British destroyers were now homing in for the kill, responding to the faint *ASDIC* contact that their experienced operators had identified as a lone submarine.

'Screws astern, range 600 metres, closing fast.' The *funkmaat* sat hunched over his set, his left headphone pushed clear of his ear so that he could still communicate with the commander.

Hahn riposted without hesitation. 'Maintain this course; give me all she's got. Let's keep the British on a stern chase.'

Faust promptly relayed the command to the *steuermann* at the helm. As the hum of the electric motors became louder, Hahn surveyed the anxious expressions on the faces of his crew. They in turn gazed up at him, silently seeking his reassurance. But it was the unassuming figure steadying himself against the chart table towards whom Werner Hahn was looking for reassurance. It was the look of a man seeking approval from his mentor… and perhaps an acknowledgement that his decision making was sound.

The shadowy figure returned his gaze, a half smile emerging from within the stubble that clung to his cameo-like profile. He stood tall, legs splayed, grasping the edge of the table with one hand. From his appearance and dress, one would perhaps consider him insignificant, a new boy in the *Ubootwaffe*; certainly not an imposing figure. The sloppy grey pullover and baggy dark trousers certainly gave nothing away. Only the black officer's cap, bearing the peak braid of a *korvettenkapitän*, indicated his seniority.

The reassuring grin and kindly eyes of his senior officer was sufficient to put Hahn at ease. There was no indication of fear on this young man's face. He had clearly been here before – many times. Hahn knew he could expect no more, indeed a smile from *Irish Max* was more than enough encouragement. *He* was the commander of the boat, and his crew's fate was down to him. There was no way *Korvettenkapitän* Max Friedmann was going to interfere in the running of his boat.

Hahn called out. 'Range of contact?'

'400 metres,' came the reply.

Hahn chewed on his lower lip, knowing that he must hold his nerve.

'300 metres,' the *funkmaat* called out dutifully.

'Left full rudder,' Hahn snapped, the urgency clear in his voice.

'Thirty degrees of left rudder on sir,' the helmsman confirmed, his voice contrastingly calm and business-like as always.

The boat began to turn, its plates creaking and groaning as it went. They all held their breath.

Above, the second destroyer, *HMS Voracity*, was charging up behind them, its bows scything through the foam-crested breakers at an impressive twenty knots. Closed up at action stations expectant crewmen, clad in duffel coats and steel helmets, braced themselves for the next round of engagement.

As the warship passed rapidly over the submarine's estimated position another wave of depth charges were ejected from their launchers, crashing through her churning wake and sinking slowly towards their prey. Then there was the waiting, as the pattern of charges descended into the darkness.

The anticipated series of *crumps* soon came, followed by plumes of white froth as shockwaves from the explosions pulsed across the ocean's surface. Unknown to those seamen crowded along the destroyer's rails, one had found its mark, detonating close enough to the stern of the turning submarine to seal its fate.

The blast had rocked and bucked the U-boat, tearing off the stern, port-side dive plane and rudder plate. Then came the shockwave buckling the vessel's plates and popping rivets. The faces on the instruments in the control room shattered, showering the crewmen monitoring them with shards of broken glass. Finally, the control room lights were extinguished leaving only the red glow of the emergency bulbs to illuminate the nerve centre of the boat. Hahn rapidly gathered his thoughts. The sound of rushing water filled his ears as the boat slowly settled.

'Depth,' he called.

Faust tapped the depth gauge, now minus glass. 'The gauge is damaged sir, no reading; I'll check the gauge in the torpedo room.'

'Chief, do we still have steering?'

'Yes sir, just about, but it's very sluggish.'

'Good, trim the boat, maintain current course.'

The Engineering Officer, *Oberleutnant* Ernst Rethmeier, appeared through the hatchway from the engine room carrying a flashlight. He waded through the ankle-deep oily water now washing through the control room before recognising his commanding officer in the dim red light.

'How's things aft Ernst?' Hahn asked.

'Not good sir, there's water coming in everywhere, the floor plates have been wrenched loose in the aft torpedo room and there's water in the bilges. The electric motors are still operational... for now, but there's some flooding in the motor compartment. No sign of gas at the moment, but we're going to have to surface.'

'Sorry Ernst, I can't oblige, they'll blow us apart up there. Any other obvious damage?'

'The aft dive planes appear to have been damaged. That's only an initial assessment though. I fear we'll not be able to proceed submerged for much longer.'

'Are the pumps working?'

'Yes, for the time being.'

Faust joined the conversation. 'We've levelled off at one twenty metres sir, still managing four knots.'

'Good, steer one seven zero, we'll maintain a southerly track for the next four hours, it'll be getting dark by then. Maintain this depth and speed for now. Ernst, let me know if things deteriorate aft, or if there's any whiff of *chlorgas*. I'll surface immediately if need be.' Rethmeier nodded and disappeared back through the bulkhead hatch to reassess the damage.

Faust issued the order to change course. 'Helmsman, steer one seven zero.'

Hahn turned his attention to the hydrophone operator. 'Any trace of activity on the surface?'

'No sir, the wheel's sticking though, there could be a problem with the equipment. Perhaps they've finally used up all their *wabos*.'

U–500 limped on whilst her crew occupied themselves with the increasingly hopeless task of keeping her systems operational. Hahn and Faust, torches in hand, pored over the *Kriegsmarine Marinequadratkarte* set out on the table before them. Faust poked the large grid map of the North Atlantic with a pair of dividers. 'We are here, currently still in grid AL27 sir.'

'Miles from anywhere,' Hahn concluded with a shake of the head.

'Yes, *Herr Kaleun*. We need to make a decision soon as to what course of action we take in respect of the operation. Personally, I feel we cannot continue to…'

'Yes, yes, I know what you're saying Faust.' Hahn glared at his First Watch Officer. 'Just remember, I'm the commander of this boat. I make the decisions here. I just have to be sure. When we surface and Rethmeier has had the opportunity to make a full assessment of the damage, then I will make a decision, and only then.'

'As you wish, sir. If you'll excuse me, I'll go and find Ernst. He might need some support back there.'

'Yes, fine, you do that; make sure Kessel joins me in here.'

'Yes, of course sir.'

'And Bruno…'

'Yes sir?'

'Sorry, I snapped at you, I've got a lot on my mind just now.'

Faust acknowledged the apology with a nod then disappeared, leaving Hahn staring down at his chart, leaning heavily on his knuckles and once again biting nervously at his lower lip. His train of thought was broken by a tap on the shoulder, prompting him to spin round. 'What is it?' he snapped. 'Oh it's you, Max.'

The young *korvettenkapitän* was holding two steaming mugs of cocoa in his right hand, his fingers curled awkwardly around the two handles. 'You'd better take this, before I burn my fingers.'

Hahn accepted one of the mugs and placed it on the chart table. He grinned. '*Smutje* always comes up trumps at times like this.' He was referring to his veteran cook, *Matrosengefreiter* Dieter Wimmer, who'd sailed with him on every patrol since he'd taken command of U-500.

'You did well, Werner. Nearly pulled it off too... force the enemy into a stern chase so that their ASDIC's pinging through your wake, then turn radically, just when they're losing contact... classic tactic, you were just unlucky.'

'Would you have done the same, Max?'

'Yes, I believe I would have in that situation.' He sipped from his mug then looked hard at his colleague. 'Faust is right you know. We're going to have to pull out of Operation *Paukenschlag*. We'll never make it across the Atlantic in this state. And yes, I know what you are thinking: here's an opportunity for the *Ubootwaffe* to pass into legend, to be able to say I was part of it, I was one of the *Drumbeaters*. It's true, the Americans are disorganised and have no idea how to effectively protect their merchant shipping. It'll be a turkey shoot for those who follow us Werner... but not for us old friend... not this time.'

Max placed the mug gently on the table and looked about him, lowering his voice to almost a whisper. 'Then there's *Seeadler*, surely it's better to delay the trials than lose the initiative now?'

Hahn took the hint, replying in a hushed tone. 'I know Max, it's just...'

Max interrupted. 'Look, there are other boats going across later.

They can carry out the trial. One thing's for sure, we mustn't allow the *Tommis* to get a sniff of what we're up to with this technology. If all had gone according to plan, you and your crew would be wallowing in glory. I'd wager you'd not only get your Knight's Cross, but the oak leaves, crossed swords *and* diamonds to go with it! It's just that fate has turned against us; nothing more, nothing less. You mustn't blame yourself, Werner.'

'I just hope you don't consider my actions reckless Max… going for that merchantman, I mean.'

Max shook his head. 'Don't be a bloody fool Werner, you're just feeling sorry for yourself.'

'Of course, this is an historic opportunity to strike at the Americans. Particularly when they are still licking their wounds from Pearl Harbor. But I know I must think firstly of my crew, and that includes you Max. If you are lost, heads will roll!'

'Forget me Werner, your priority is to get this boat back to Lorient intact, and with your crew all alive. Like I said, there will be other times when we can deploy *Seeadler*, and with equally devastating results… that's if we can be sure that the project is not compromised. If you can achieve that Werner, then you will have served the Reich well. As Aristotle once said; "where your talents and the needs of the world cross, lies your calling".'

'I just hope I won't be hung out to dry for attempting to sink that damned tanker.' Hahn took a long slug of cocoa.

'It was a reasonable call, Werner. Like I said, I would have done the same. A lone straggler with no escort; you could have sunk it with forty rounds, no more than gunnery practice for Kessel and his boys. How were you to know the *Tommis* were going to come charging over the horizon?'

Hahn smiled in recognition of Max's vote of confidence. He pushed his cap to the back of his head; its white cover, indicating that he was the boat's captain, seemed grubbier than ever now. Having swept the plastered hair away from his brow, he called out. '*Funkmaat* Kasper, come here please.'

The petty officer telegraphist made his way gingerly across to the chart table. 'Yes *Herr Kaleun*.'

'Send this signal to *BdU* immediately.' He waited impatiently until the gangly youth had produced paper and pencil, then continued... '*U-500 engaged by enemy warships. Have sustained serious damage, possibly critical. Will attempt to make for Lorient. Please advise re: availability of friendly units to support within range of grid reference A L 2758. Stop.*'

Kasper swished his way back through the oily water to transmit the message to the headquarters of the *Ubootwaffe* at Kernével on the French coast.

Having made the fateful decision, Hahn left the control room and took himself aft, wishing to inspect the damage and rally his hard-pressed crewmen. He returned ten minutes later, grim faced, and discussed his findings with Max. Kessel then briefed them on their latest position. Hahn looked at his watch. They'd been heading south for three hours, and with no further hydrophone contacts.

'Kessel, bring the boat up to periscope depth.'

The second watch officer complied, issuing a string of orders that were repeated and confirmed by his subordinates. To Hahn's relief the submarine began to rise slowly whilst Faust counted off the depth readings from somewhere aft.

A tense silence followed, then Kessel turned to Hahn. 'Boat trimmed at periscope depth, sir.'

'Good, raise the observation scope.'

The observation periscope began its slow climb to the surface. Hahn straddled the small seat provided for the observer and rested his feet on the pedals. He swung his cap around so that its peak draped down behind him and peered into the rubber-shrouded eyepiece. His tired eyes scanned the horizon. The daylight was fading rapidly in the east and the sea state had reduced to a gentle swell with scattered whitecaps. He struggled to gain a view due to some fogging of the lens, then withdrew, blinking repeatedly. The damned depth charges must have caused a fracture in the airtight casing of the scope. He tried again; nothing, just dark ocean.

'Get *Oberleutnant* Rethmeier up here,' he snapped.

Someone shouted '*LI* to the control room,' using the abbreviated title for the *leitender ingenieur*. Rethmeier soon appeared flashlight in hand, soaking wet, his anxious face crisscrossed by streaks of oil.

'I'm going to surface the boat, Ernst. That should make life a little easier for you, eh?'

'It certainly will, sir. There are big problems with the diesels, oil leaking everywhere, and the fuel feed lines have been damaged. I can't guarantee I can give you any power on the surface.'

'Well let's see what happens, at least we'll be better placed to assess the damage. How's the flooding?'

'We've stopped a fair amount, but not all.'

'Good work Ernst, pass on my thanks to your *Maschinisten*.' He turned to Kessel.

'*Leutnant* Kessel, surface the boat.'

'*Jawohl Herr Kaleun*.'

He turned away. 'Blow tanks five, four three and two...'

The wounded submarine groaned and creaked again as she slowly began to rise to the surface. At last Kessel announced: 'Boat surfaced. Conning tower hatch clear.'

'Opening hatch.'

'Equalise pressure!'

With the hatch open the cold Atlantic wind swept into the submarine. Residual water from the bridge slopped through the opening, soaking the crewman on the ladder and adding to the flood that swilled around the floor.

'*Wachoffizier* and watch crew to the bridge,' Hahn ordered. Kessel was ahead of the game, already donning his leather all-weather *U-Boot Päckchen*, and his *schiffchen* side cap.

Faust had returned to the control room, attracted by the aroma of fresh salty air wafting through the boat. He glanced up through the hatch to the bridge, now filled with the bodies of the watch crew clattering up the metal ladder. 'Looks like we made it,' he grinned.

Hahn was less optimistic. 'We're a long way from having *made it* Bruno.' He handed Faust a copy of a signal from *BdU* that *Funkmaat* Kasper had just passed to him. Faust read the short signal.

From BdU: 16.15hrs 20.12.41 – Maintain current course for Lorient. U-654 at AL34 engaging enemy convoy. Will make towards your position when able. Take all measures necessary to protect Seeadler apparatus. Scuttle if necessary. Good luck. Ends.

'They're effectively telling us we're on our own for the time being. The nearest boat to us could be committed for days.'

Hahn tapped the map. 'Bruno, I would like a meeting of all the officers in my berth at 1900hrs. That'll give the *LI* more time to assess the damage. You have command of the boat. You know where I'll be if you need me.' He turned to Max. 'Are you okay here?'

'Yes, I reckon I'll stay in here and keep an eye on Bruno.'

The 1WO looked across at him with an air of consternation. Max grinned. 'I'm only joking Bruno,' and patted Faust on the back.

Chapter Eleven

Max crouched behind the bridge screen, seeking shelter from the sou'westerly breeze. He stuffed a gloved hand into the pocket of his leather sea coat and pulled out a crumpled pack of Eckstein cigarettes. With some difficulty, he managed to tip out the one remaining cigarette, and eventually lit the thing after several failed attempts. The silver lighter his brother Otto had given him as a birthday present two years earlier had never let him down yet. The ash at the tip of the cigarette glowed red as Max sucked hard to keep it alight. He ran his thumb over the smooth side of the lighter, recalling the day his older brother had passed out from the *Marineschule*. He'd posed proudly in his dress uniform next to their mother on the steps of the academy. Max had recorded the moment for posterity with his bulky *Contax* camera. Otto's beaming smile briefly filled Max's subconscious, but then faded all too quickly. It was a painful reoccurring memory that had haunted him for months. Otto had been killed over a year ago, serving on the cruiser *Blücher* at the Battle of *Drøbak* Sound. His life had been snuffed out when the first shell from a Norwegian shore battery had struck the cruiser amidships creating a devastating inferno.

Max clutched the lighter tightly, his eyes clamped shut as he beat back the tears. He wiped away the moisture from his cheek just as the young watchman standing nearby glanced down and enquired; 'Are you alright sir?'

Max straightened up, wincing momentarily as a dull ache spread through the muscle in his right thigh. 'Of course I am,' he growled. 'Don't watch me boy, just keep your eyes on the horizon'.

'Yes sir, sorry sir.' The young man snapped to attention before thrusting his eyes back into the rubber guards on his binoculars.

Kessel, standing nearby, lowered his own binoculars and snarled, 'For God's sake Kremer.'

This was a clear opportunity to demonstrate to Max that he could effectively maintain discipline, and he wasn't going to miss out on the opportunity.

Max turned and leant on the side of the bridge. He took a long pull on his cigarette and stared out to where the horizon should be. The white tops that scarred the carpet of grey ocean were gradually being swallowed by a developing harr. The wet mist, verging on drizzle, would be a welcome form of cover once the submarine became shrouded in its cold damp grip, but for now it was way off to the west, seamlessly merging with the pale sky.

There is no damned horizon, he thought to himself, *pointless scolding the youth!*

He raised his own binoculars to his eyes and estimated the visual range from U-500's conning tower to be less than ten kilometres. The watchmen would really need to be on their toes.

The hollow thud of boots on metal interrupted the dull symphony of the wind. Hahn's grubby, salt-stained cap appeared in the bridge hatch. He looked up as he emerged into the daylight. 'Everything alright Max?' he enquired as he straightened up and brushed himself down.

'Yes thanks, nothing happening up here Werner. It's good to get some fresh air into the lungs is it not? How's work progressing down below?'

'Difficult to say whether it's progressing at all. Rethmeier is doing what he can with the diesels, but whatever he *is* doing, it's not happening very quickly.' He looked at his watch. 'It's been too long.'

The engineering officer had delivered a particularly dismal

assessment the night before. The damage was worse than first thought. When an attempt was made to start the two nine cylinder M.A.N diesels, the engine room had filled with black smoke, and the starboard engine had failed almost immediately. The port engine was leaking oil at an alarming rate, and it was this that Rethmeier was attending to at present.

As initially thought, the divers had discovered severe damage to the port-side rudder and propeller shaft. The starboard shaft had suffered to a lesser degree. In fact, it had been a miracle that the boat had continued to move through the water. The list had gone on... flooded bilges, jammed hydrophone wheel, electrical failures in a number of areas.

The monotonous sound of banging now rang out from deep within the submarine as efforts were made to do something with the one potentially reparable diesel engine.

'It's going to take several hours,' said Hahn, now scanning the horizon with his own binoculars. 'The electric motors are almost fully depleted and Ernst doesn't want to risk using the starboard prop shaft until he's examined it further. So here we sit, waiting for the *Tommis* to finish us off. At least we made it to the surface!'

Max threw the stub of his cigarette over the side of the tower. 'We'll just have to be patient, nothing else for it. Hopefully Ernst can work his magic sufficiently for us to limp home.'

'You're ever the optimist Max. I only hope you're right.' Hahn was glum faced.

'Let's change the subject for a minute eh?' Max leant over side of the tower's wind deflector and patted the once brightly painted crest adorning the side of the conning tower. 'Tell me about your emblem. I've been meaning to ask you.' He tipped his head to one side to get a better view. 'Winged figure, red castellations, blue sea, what's that all about?'

Hahn knew what Max was up to. It wasn't really working, but he went along with it. 'It's the city crest of Emden, my home town.'

'Ah yes, Emden. I've been there a few times. Some good bars along *Am Delft* as I recall.'

'Yes, there are, my sister's husband has a restaurant along there.'

'Have you lived there all your life?' Max enquired.

'Pretty much, my father was in the navy so we moved around a bit when I was young.'

'Like me then,' said Max, arms extended in celebration of the coincidence. Their conversation was interrupted when the banging down below started again, but still there was no hint of the diesel bursting into life. The two men listened in silence to the muffled hammering, neither being under any illusion as to the hopelessness of their situation.

The gentle rise and fall of the submarine seemed only to add to Hahn's anxiety, rather than provide the soothing, sometimes sleep-inducing effect that it usually did. They were stationary, helpless, and still the sound of that infernal lapping water filled his ears; an ever present reminder of how vulnerable they were.

'It's just turned eleven,' Hahn announced. 'I'll be happier when it gets dark again, or when that *harr* reaches us.'

The lustreless sky had now merged with the sea, accompanied by a noticeable drop in temperature. Hahn blinked away a trace of sleet. 'I'm going down below, better get Kasper to put something in the *KTB*.' Completion of the commander's war diary was often delegated to the radio crew. Crouching over the hatch, he carefully extended his legs into the void, and was about to disappear.

'*Smoke, bearing green 060, long range!*' The watch crews' binoculars swung around as Hahn heaved himself back out of the hatch. The young seaman, earlier scolded for his inattention, was on the ball alright. A feathery wisp of pale grey had emerged from the distant mist.

'What is it?' Hahn demanded, raising his binoculars.

'Looks like a destroyer,' said Max. 'I'd say she's about eight kilometres range and not hanging about'.

'My God, we can't let them get hold of that.' Hahn gestured

towards the complex angled framework of dull steel bolted to the casing behind the conning tower. He yelled at Kessel, his words partially lost in the wind. 'Sound the alarm. Man all the guns Kessel, open fire with the deck gun when you have their range,'

'*Jawohl, Herr Kaleun.*' Kessel thrust his head into the open hatch and screamed 'Alarm! Gun crew, man the deck gun!'

Hahn then called down the voice pipe, 'Action stations! Enemy warship closing fast, *LI* to the bridge.'

'Get the men off and scuttle the boat Werner, that's your only choice. They're either going to capture us or blow us out of the water. There are no other options.' Max now spoke with the authority of his rank.

'I know Max, I know. I just need to buy myself some time. You'd better get down below and collect anything you need to dispose of. I'd guess we have only a few minutes before the shells start flying!'

'Okay Werner, just keep your head down, eh?'

Max moved towards the hatch, but jumped aside as Faust hurriedly emerged with Rethmeier hot on his heels. The din of the klaxon drifted up from below.

'Ernst, can you get us moving?'

'Not a chance sir.'

'Then you know what to do. Set the scuttling charges. Forward torpedo room, control room, and engine room. Give us a fifteen minute delay. When you're ready, we'll open the vents and get the men off. Bruno, ensure that the *funkmaat* signals *BdU* that we are under attack and intend to scuttle the boat. Make sure the cipher machine is destroyed, together with the *kurzesignalheft* and *wetterkurzschlüssel*. The short signal and weather short signal books were the most important code books on the boat. Their capture, and that of the cipher machine, would be unthinkable; an invaluable intelligence resource for the enemy.

Max hung over the bridge rail and indicated to Kessel with a reassuring thumbs up. The young officer waved back, his gun crew waiting nervously. The auto-cannon on the boat's lower *wintergarten*, and the twenty millimetre flak cannon on the upper platform had also been manned and trained on the approaching destroyer.

Faust and Rethmeier returned below, followed by Max, who tapped Hahn reassuringly on the shoulder before clambering down the ladder to the control room. On reaching the foot of the ladder, he pushed his way impatiently past crewmen busy preparing for the impending showdown. Rethmeier crouched near the map table, busy setting the first of three sets of scuttling charges.

As Max passed the radio shack, one of the *funkers* was gently placing a record onto the turntable of the boat's phonograph. The remnants of the enigma cipher machine lay at his feet, the wooden casing smashed and the rotors removed. Onwards past Hahn's quarters, he came to the ward room he'd been sharing with the three other officers. He hurriedly opened the small locker he'd been allocated for his personal belongings and removed his battered leather briefcase. The case had to be disposed of. It contained sensitive documents relating to the *Seeadler* project and command orders in respect of Operation *Paukenschlag*.

Just then he was startled by the sound of a muffled bang directly above him. The boat rocked, and he realised the deck gun had fired its first round. He rapidly scanned the room for other personal effects. Lying on his berth was his uniform tunic, *kleiner Dienstanzug* as the tailors called it. He struggled out of his leather topcoat, and was about to don the tunic. Then his eye was drawn to the shiny Iron Cross First Class pinned to the breast pocket. With fumbling fingers, he released the pin fastener and removed it. Then he probed the lower pockets, pulling out his Knight's Cross with Oak Leaves, and wrapping it in its red, black and white neck ribbon. He clenched his fist around it, closing his eyes for a second and taking a deep breath. He wondered what would become of him in the coming hours, or minutes even.

The stirring U-boat sailor's song *U-Bootsfahrer Lied* now began to resonate loudly through the boat's speaker system, no doubt the *funker's* attempt to boost morale just one last time.

'...*Ob Sturm uns bedroht hoch vom Norden, ob Heimweh im Herzen auch glüht; wir sind Kameraden geworden...*' bellowed the patriotic male choir to an accompaniment of relentless crackling.

Another thud as a second shot was unleashed above and the boat swayed again.

His senses once again under control, Max grabbed a small knife from the wardroom cabinet and hastily cut a small slit in the lining of his tunic. He removed the neck ribbon from the Knight's Cross and then thrust the two medals through the hole he'd made. There was a clunk as he felt them fall to the bottom of the void beyond. He pulled the jacket on over his thick woollen jumper, driving his arms down into the sleeves. With the four brass buttons secured, he quickly donned his leather sea coat. It was time to go, and at least he would stay warm, whatever happened to him.

With his black cap firmly on his head and briefcase in hand, now weighted down by several cans of tinned fruit, he glanced around the wardroom for the last time before hurrying aft. He was surprised to see so many of the crew still below as he climbed the ladder to the bridge, and paused when he reached the hatch above the control room. The men beneath him sensed his presence, and stopped to salute. He returned the gesture, and carried on climbing.

The deck gun thundered again as he emerged from the hatch and he heard the shell whine away towards its target. Hahn and Faust were crouching behind the bridge screen monitoring the fall of shot through their binoculars.

The destroyer was much closer now and Max knew it wouldn't be long before her gunners found their mark. He didn't have to wait long, The Royal Navy's initial response screamed overhead as he took up position next to Hahn. The shell plunged into the sea some twenty metres beyond the submarine.

'They'll be scoring hits any time, and we'll soon be in range of their lighter armament,' Hahn panted. 'Look, I need you to come with me.'

He took Max by the arm and led him to the rear of the bridge.

Another shell from the British warship crashed into the water, closer this time, sending a foaming white plume high into the air. The boat swayed again as the U-boat men responded. Hahn ducked under the rail of the *wintergarten* platform and descended the small ladder to the deck casing. He looked up and gestured to Max to follow him.

Once both men were safe on the casing, Hahn made his way along the side of the conning tower until they were out of sight of the approaching destroyer. A crewman was waiting for them. He was holding the end of a mooring line that looped down to a rubber dinghy. The raft bobbed around in the water, gently nudging the side of the submarine.

Hahn nodded towards the briefcase. 'Dump that case Max, and get in that dinghy... now.'

'Are you crazy, Werner? I'm not going to abandon you now. What about the rest of the crew, aren't you getting them off?'

'Look Max, we don't have time for this. Bruno tells me the crew are refusing to leave until I do. They want to do their bit stalling the *Tommis* until we can scuttle the boat. Ernst says the scuttling charge packs may be damp, so we might have to rely on some other method.'

'Then *Kapitänleutnant* Hahn, I will stay too, leaving is not an option I'm afraid.'

'This is not a time for honour Max. You're more important alive; you know why. So you have to go... *now*! I promised Von Thalberg I would ensure your safety.'

Max stared coldly at Hahn, struggling for something worthwhile to say, but he couldn't think of anything. He knew why his colleague was doing this, and he would have probably done exactly the same. The loss of Friedmann, another U-boat ace, would be a huge blow to the Reich. At least he had a chance if he was taken into captivity, a chance to escape. Then there was the small matter of just *being* there. He should never have been on the boat in the first place. His CO, Admiral Von Thalberg, had relented and eventually let him go. The admirals at the High Command in Berlin would be incensed when they discovered what had happened, not to mention the Führer himself! God help Von Thalberg when the British commenced their mocking of Hitler, with news of their latest victory against the *Ubootwaffe*. The expedition was spiralling towards disaster, whatever happened to him.

Another explosion rocked the boat violently. Acrid smoke began to curl its way around the conning tower, concealing the carnage at its source and masking the tortured screams of wounded and dying crewmen. Hahn edged forward and peered around the curved side of the tower. Max followed him. Hahn gasped as he edged back behind cover. 'They've scored a direct hit on the other side of the tower.'

He raised his voice to make himself heard. 'Look, you've got to get off now.' He pushed Max backwards, the flat of his hand pressed hard against the young ace's chest. Max resisted, sweeping Hahn's had away. The two men stood for a second, glaring into each other's eyes; so close that Max could almost sense the warmth of Hahn's breath on his face. Then he felt the briefcase being wrenched out of his hand. Hahn swung his arm back, summoning all his strength, and launched the leather *tasche* into the swirling surf.

'I can't do it Werner, I just can't go. My place is here.'

Hahn raised his arm again before Max could react. The force then applied to his chest threw him off balance and he stumbled backwards, falling helplessly towards the icy water that he thought would consume him. Instead, he landed on rubber. The dinghy buckled under him, allowing a quantity of water to slop over the side and soak him. Max felt the sudden chill as it was absorbed by his clothing and heaved himself upright. Pulses of spray peppered his face as he struggled to steady himself against the rise and fall of the little raft. The crewman had released the mooring rope and he realised he was drifting backwards, away from the stricken submarine. He raised an arm in hopeless protestation, then let it drop limply to his side as if in acceptance of the hopeless situation he found himself now in.

Hahn was still standing on the casing offering up a smart salute. He then scurried around the side of the conning tower and disappeared.

Max recovered his cap from the water that slopped around his feet. He returned it to his head and lifted his hand to the peak, returning the salute briefly and licking the salty moisture from his lips.

The two opposing vessels were now exchanging fire with their smaller calibre weapons. Max could clearly make out the dull cadence of the U-boat's secondary armament as it blasted away towards the destroyer. Tracer flashed low across the water and then back again as the British unleashed their powerful Oerlikon cannons against the submarine. A column of black smoke still drifted upwards from U-500's conning tower, but it was evident that the deck gun was still fully operational. The weapon fired and recoiled, sending a projectile into a wave crest just ahead of the destroyer's bow. The warship was now turning in a fast tight manoeuvre, trailing a long curving wake; Max presumed this manoeuvre was intended to allow more of its armament to be brought into action. He was right, the Oerlikon canon mounted amidships now entered the fray, spewing another stream of tracer across the submarine's aft decking and ploughing up the water to his left. The close fall of shot sent Max instinctively diving for cover behind the sides of the dinghy... not that he believed rubber and air would stop any of the British projectiles!

The raft continued to drift away at an angle of forty-five degrees from the submarine. Such was his position that he was now able to get a clear view of the deck gun. He could just make out Hahn and others clustered around it. At their feet was a pile of corpses. A large, smoking hole had appeared in the conning tower's port side and a human chain consisting of crewmen and officers was now passing ammunition through the gaping cavity towards the gun. There, it was eagerly awaited by the boat's commander and his gun crew. Max couldn't see the young 2WO and assumed Kessel and his men would have been killed or wounded when the British shell exploded close to their position.

As he crouched behind the sides of his raft, endeavouring to make sense of the scene before him, the destroyer's Oerlikons began to strike their target with deadly accuracy. Tracer raked the forward deck of the U-boat, tearing into the metal plates and reducing them to razor-like shards of shrapnel. The rounds stitched their way along the submarine's deck and around the feet of the German crewmen. Max saw them crumple amidst the smoke and debris. His view was temporarily obscured, but then, as the wind did its work, a scene of horror greeted him. The pile of corpses heaped around the smouldering gun was now two or three deep, Hahn presumably amongst them. No one was standing; the deck gun had been silenced.

The U-boat itself was lying deeper in the water now. Max wondered if the efforts to scuttle the vessel were at last beginning to take effect. Whatever the case, U-500 was taking a pounding from the destroyer's guns. There was no sign of life now on the bridge, and clearly the flak gun mounted there had also been silenced.

As he scanned the blackened hulk for signs of life he detected the whine of another four-inch shell hurtling towards him. Once again, he dropped to the bottom of the raft just as another loud explosion rocked the submarine's casing, this time aft of the conning tower. The steel framework fitted for the *Seeadler* trial spiralled skywards and disintegrated, crashing back into the sea with a synchronicity that reminded him of a flock of seabirds diving for food. Thick smoke now billowed upward like a grubby cotton shirt blowing in the wind. It seemed to be emanating from the torn and twisted decking plates above the aft torpedo room. There followed without warning a series of loud explosions. Fingers of flame erupted through the dense screen of darkening grey as the hull of the U-boat lifted out of the water. The stern section broke away, sinking briefly then bobbing up again to the surface, before finally disappearing through a slick of burning oil. The remainder of the submarine followed, sliding silently backwards, water draining like a water feature from its exposed vents. The malevolent union of sea and war had claimed another victim as U-500 and fifty good men were finally consumed by the waves.

Max stared incredulously as the oily sea recovered from the disturbance to resume its slow, perpetual rise and fall. A spiral of slowly dissipating smoke still hung over the spot, providing a dark canopy over the debris that floated amongst a carpet of thick oil. In places, short bursts of flame leapt skyward, resembling the crater of an awakening volcano. Most conspicuous, however, was the silence; no more gunfire, no cries from the dying, just the sound of the sea whispering and humming to the accompaniment of the wind.

Max slid down into the sanctuary of his raft and closed his eyes tight. He struggled to grasp what had just happened, unable to beat back the tears that had begun to track their way down the side of his nose. He wiped them away with a shaky hand and, with a faltering voice, quietly recited the words of the short sailor's prayer that his grandfather had taught him as a boy.

Chapter Twelve

'Good morning, sir.' An anxious-faced British Naval Officer, no more than twenty years old and dressed in a thick duffel coat, peered down at Max. He was leaning cautiously over the side of a whaler that had gently come alongside the German's dinghy. From the whiteness of his knuckles one could conclude that he didn't seem entirely comfortable negotiating the Atlantic swell in such a small boat. 'Commander Todd requests the pleasure of your company aboard His Majesty's Ship *Wareham*.'

Max glared back from his waterlogged raft. Hunched with knees drawn up to his chin and shivering, more from shock than cold, he struggled to find the words to respond. A gloved hand was extended down towards him.

'I'm afraid you don't really have much of a choice sir. Here, take my hand.'

Max couldn't disagree. He grudgingly took the hand, and was unceremoniously hauled out of the dinghy and into the long wooden boat. An older rating moved forward and, once Max was seated, he was subjected to a cursory search.

'Sorry about all this, would hate you to shoot us all. Sure you'd do the same.' The young officer perched himself on the thwart next to Max, his pale lips expanding into a grin. Max was told to remain seated as the whaler slowly carved its way through the dark film of oil left by the U-boat. All eyes were scanning the debris in the vain

128

hope that someone may have survived. Satisfied that they had done what they could, the bow was turned back towards the looming grey hull of the British warship. The Englishman leant across and offered his prisoner a cigarette. Up until now Max hadn't uttered a word, so he spoke slowly, unsure of his ability to speak English.

'My... name's... Sub Lieutenant... Kenneth... Wells... RNVR. That's Royal... Naval...Volunteer... Reserve, in case you were wondering. Can... I... ask... your... name... sir?'

'*Korvettenkapitän* Max Friedmann, *Kriegsmarine Ubootwaffe*.' Max took the cigarette and toyed with it.

'Thank you, sir. That would be the equivalent to our commander rank I believe.'

'You believe correctly, Sub Lieutenant,' said Max in perfect English.

'Your English is very good sir, if you don't mind me saying.'

Max accepted a light for the cigarette and looked away towards the approaching harr that he'd hoped would offer sanctuary to him and his countrymen. He exhaled blue smoke through his nostrils.

'Thank you Sub Lieutenant Wells, so is yours.'

The rating pulling on an oar behind Wells gave his colleague a sideways grin. Wells blushed. He'd got the message, and the remainder of the short journey was completed in silence.

With the whaler pitching against the destroyer's side, Max struggled to gain a foothold on the climb net suspended from the deck. His arms and legs felt like jelly, as if a sudden fatigue had consumed him. With some assistance from his captors, he at last clambered over the rail.

Standing close by, intent on witnessing his arrival, were a number of ratings, some still wearing white flash hoods from the recent encounter. They looked on with interest as Max regained his composure and stood dignified but uneasy by the rail. He now felt isolated, like a species of wild animal not seen before.

Intent on avoiding eye contact with the expressionless group of men, his gaze fell upon a line of corpses, all covered by tarpaulins, that lay upon the deck in front of him. He took a few steps towards them and recognised the *Kriegsmarine* issue boots extending beyond the black sheets. An arm lay uncovered at one end of the row. Upon the sodden, oil stained sleeve, he could just make out the faded insignia of an *obermaschinist* – chief mechanician 1st class.

Max stood smartly to attention and saluted. Wells appeared beside him. 'We've found a couple of your men that *are* still alive sir. They're in a shocking state I'm afraid, but we'll certainly do all we can for them.'

Max nodded in silent acknowledgement as he stared at the twelve inert pairs of feet. Wells called across to a senior rating, also dressed in a duffel coat and wearing a battered steel helmet.

'Take this officer down to see the old man will you, Grainger?' then to Max, 'Welcome aboard sir, if you'd like to follow this man, Commander Todd, our CO would like to meet you.'

Max followed the helmeted figure to a nearby bulkhead door. After a few steps, he turned and called out to Wells. 'Thank you Sub Lieutenant Wells, you've been most gracious. Forgive me for my reaction earlier.'

'Don't think of it sir, I quite understand.'

Once through the doorway, Max was led along a narrow corridor towards the captain's day cabin. The warmth inside the ship surged through him and he felt his spirits begin to rise a little, if indeed that was possible. The rating stopped at a varnished wooden door and knocked. A gruff voice called out from within, 'Come.' Grainger opened the door and ushered Max in. He then followed and closed the door behind him, stiffly taking up position in front of it.

Sitting by a small desk at the foot of a neatly made-up bunk sat an officer in his mid-forties. Dark curly hair, still damp from the wind and spray, receded from his deeply furrowed brow. In his left hand he clutched a glowing briarwood pipe, from which sweet-smelling blue smoke twisted its way upward. The officer eased himself out of his chair. He was taller and stockier than Max, the buttons on his tunic straining against both his well-fed torso and the thick woollen jumper he was wearing. A sleeved arm adorned with three gold rings shot out. 'Commander Bill Todd, I'm the CO on *Wareham*.' He grasped the German's hand firmly. 'I'm so sorry about your crew. They fought gallantly.'

'*Korvettenkapitän* Max Friedmann. Thank you for your kind words Commander. That is war I'm afraid, there are winners and losers. On this occasion, I have to concede that you are the winner.'

'Please sit down *Korvettenkapitän*.' Todd indicated to another small chair. 'Can I get you some cocoa or something? You must be frightfully cold.'

'Thank you, that would be most welcome,' said Max politely.

'Before we do anything, we need to take any personal property from you. Admiralty instructions I'm afraid.' Todd tapped the copy of the Admiralty Instruction C.B 3074, titled *Treatment and Handling Of Prisoners Of War In Ships Effecting Capture*, that lay on his desk.

'Could I ask you to remove your coat and tunic, and hand them to Grainger here?' Max complied and watched nervously as the garments were checked and pockets emptied. A small pile of belongings built up on the desk. A torn photograph of his parents, the empty green pack of Eckstein cigarettes, a *Deutsche Reichsbahn* ticket from Berlin to Kiel, a handkerchief and a couple of pens.

'We'll have to retain these,' said Todd as he removed the U-boat War Badge and Spanish Cross in Bronze from Max's tunic. 'There appears to be an impression here, left by another decoration on your jacket. Looks to me like an Iron Cross. Can I ask where that decoration is now?'

'I left it aboard the U-boat, on another jacket,' Max lied as he observed Grainger run his hands over the lining of the leather sea coat.

'I see, shame,' said Todd as he handed the tunic back to Max. 'Well we'll leave the buttonhole ribbon,' he said, pointing to the red, white and black of the Iron Cross Second Class, 'but the rest we'll bag up and keep safe. You'll get the items back at some stage, no doubt.'

Max slowly slid his arms back into the sleeves of his tunic, hoping the two medals secreted in the lining didn't give the game away with a tell-tale chink of metal on metal.

The search continued as Grainger found Max's wallet and some coins in his trouser pockets. Then it was the turn of his boots and socks before he was invited to sit down again. The items were placed in a bag and labelled with Max's name and rank. Grainger then left the cabin, bag in hand, directed to bring up two mugs of cocoa from the galley.

Todd sat down and re-lit his pipe. He studied Max for a few seconds before speaking. 'What's an officer of your renown doing playing second fiddle on a U-boat out here in the middle of the Atlantic?'

Max's eyes narrowed in disbelief. 'I beg your pardon Commander, second fiddle?'

Todd leant back in his chair and grinned. 'You heard me *Korvettenkapitän*. You're regarded as a fast emerging U-boat ace, tipped to far exceed the achievements of your contemporaries. Your reputation goes before you, even amongst your enemies. I've read about your triumphant tour of Berlin in that open-topped Mercedes.' His eyes remained fixed on Max who sat expressionless, apparently unaffected by Todd's impromptu summary of his career.

'What was it, three tankers and the merchant cruiser *Narborough*, all in thirty-six hours? That's a lot of tonnage. Your boat did some serious damage in the Irish Sea that day... April wasn't it, this year? They say you were closing in on Kretchmer's total rather quickly. I'm honoured indeed.'

Max remained silent for a moment. 'You seem to be very well-informed Commander, but you will forgive me if I refrain from discussing details of German military operations with you.'

'Yes, yes, of course, let's change the subject. How's that leg wound coming along? I noticed you were walking with a slight limp when you came in just now.'

Max responded with an uneasy smile. 'I'm fine Commander,

thank you for your concern.' He'd been ruffled by the Englishman's level of knowledge of his background, and it had come as a complete surprise.

Their conversation was interrupted by a knock on the door. Grainger then entered with two mugs of cocoa on a tray. He placed them on the table and awaited further instructions. 'You can leave us now, Grainger,' said Todd. 'Just wait outside the door will you?'

Once he'd left, the interrogation resumed. 'Our chaps in Naval Intelligence were putting the word about that you'd been taken off active duty. Nasty injury they said. So I'm surprised to have found you all these miles out here, serving on a submarine again.'

'It is no secret that we have submarines patrolling out here all the time. I am just one officer, like any other, doing his job.'

'But that's just it, you're not are you?'

Todd inclined across his desk, thrusting his pipe out accusingly and causing the dying embers in the bowl to redden. 'You're an *ace*, a *korvettenkapitän*. You weren't in command of that U-boat were you? There aren't too many *korvettenkapitäns* commanding U-boats are there?'

'You are misinformed, Commander. There are a number of officers of my rank commanding U-boats.'

Todd leant over to where Max had left his cap on his bunk. He picked it up and held it aloft. 'But U-boat *captains* have white tops to their caps don't they? It's an unwritten rule is it not? The only officer I saw on *your* submarine with a white top to his cap was the courageous chap commanding the deck gun in the final moments of our little spat. So you were on board for some other reason, weren't you?'

Max had no intention of rising to the bait. 'Look, I have nothing to say Commander, I believe the Geneva Convention requires…'

'Yes, yes, you only have to give your name, rank and number. But it's fascinating isn't it? We find a long-range U-boat, type nine I believe, in the middle of nowhere with some weird contraption fitted to the deck. When we get closer for a shufty, all hell breaks loose and the entire crew sacrifices themselves to prevent us getting

133

too good a view. Then to add to the mystery we find you, hale and hearty, bobbing around on your own in a dinghy; the only surviving officer. It's all a bit odd don't you think?'

Max smiled. 'You know what they say Commander; strange things happen at sea.'

Todd slumped back, defeated. There was no way Friedmann was going to spill the beans to him. Perhaps the interrogators at the London Cage would have more luck. 'I suppose there's no mileage in asking what that contraption on the submarine's aft casing was?' He was struggling now.

Max deliberately ignored the question, drained his mug and got up. He picked up his cap and smiled. 'How do you say it... no mileage at all Commander.' Then after a pause, 'I would appreciate it if you would allow me to visit my two fellow survivors. Then I would like to get some rest.'

'I can certainly offer you some comfortable quarters, but the visit to the men in the sick bay is not possible I'm afraid. *Paragraph 7A* in this document forbids it, sorry.'

'As you wish, Commander. I trust they will be afforded the very best of care?'

'The very best, *Korvettenkapitän*.'

'May I ask one further question?'

'Fire away.'

'Where exactly are we headed?'

'Well, that would normally be confidential, but I don't suppose it will be long before you find out. Normally we'd drop you off at Liverpool, but I'm afraid we've been redeployed... to Scapa Flow in the Orkneys. I'm sure you know where Scapa is, your chaps have already paid a visit, back in '39.'

'Yes Commander. I know where Scapa Flow is located. That would be about two days sailing would it not?'

'Something like that. Perhaps a little longer dependant on the weather.'

Todd summoned Grainger and directed that Max be taken to a

berth where he could get some sleep. Grainger nodded. 'Yes, sir. Sorry to be the bearer of bad news sir, but one of the jerry prisoners in the sickbay has just died, sir.'

Todd turned to Max, glum faced. 'I'm very sorry.'

'Thank you Commander, I'm sure your medical staff did their best.' He turned to leave. Todd watched him go, then called out.

'*Korvettenkapitän* Friedmann.'

Max turned. 'Yes, Commander.'

'How is it that you have such a good command of English?'

'I have an aunt who lives in Scotland. I used to visit her with my family.'

Todd's expression changed to one of comprehension. 'Did you spend much time there?'

'Yes, when I was young, always during the summer holidays.'

'I see, thank you.'

Todd sat for a while, reflecting on his conversation with the German submariner. He was a cool customer alright. Every bit the calibre of officer he would have expected. Dignified, controlled, professional. He tapped the ash from his pipe into the bin by his desk and got up. With cap in hand and duffel coat under his arm, he left his cabin, heading for the radio shack.

The duty telegraphist sat hunched over his equipment, absorbed in a CS Forrester novel and unaware of Todd's appearance in the doorway. The captain tipped the book back towards the shocked young seaman, tilting his head slightly so that he could read its title.

'Umm, *Ship Of the Line*, eh? I hope Horatio Hornblower has more success inspiring you than I have, Evans. Now send this signal to the Admiralty, there's a good chap.'

Evans slammed the book shut without bothering to mark his page. 'Yes sir. Right away, sir.'

With the news of *Wareham's* successful attack on the U-boat and Friedmann's subsequent capture being relayed to his masters, Todd returned to the bridge. The first lieutenant was awaiting relief and the captain had promised to provide it. Whilst they sheltered from the wind behind the bridge screen, he briefed his colleague on the conversation he'd had with the German.

'Quite a catch, eh number one?' he concluded as he relit his pipe. Then, left alone with his thoughts, he panned his binoculars across the darkening horizon, still wondering what his celebrity prisoner had been up to, all those miles out in the Atlantic. All the while, the elderly destroyer headed eastward at twenty knots, scything through a roughening sea.

Below, Max lay on his bunk in the officers' quarters, oblivious to the worsening weather. He dozed to the rhythm of the ship's turbines and the distant vibration of the officers' crockery. He'd checked his tunic before retiring, and his prized medals had still been there in the lining. Not quite believing his luck he wondered when, if ever, he'd get to wear them again. He closed his eyes, but sleep was not on his mind. There was little doubt that fatigue would soon consume him, but for now there was plenty to think about. The final minutes of U-500 played out in his head again and again. He wondered whether he should have sailed with Hahn in the first place. The political backlash would be unimaginable. Ernst Von Thalberg was a good man. The head of *BdU* Special Operations had been good to him during his recovery from the injury, but he now feared for the ageing Bavarian's career, and possibly his life.

His thoughts turned to happier times as he tried to block out the unthinkable. Eyes half-open under heavy lids he focussed sleepily on the panelling above him, recalling the high, heather-clad peaks that towered above Glendaig, and the good times he'd spent with his family during those long summer holidays in the thirties. Memories of those halcyon days in the Highlands only provided temporary respite though, before the stark reality of his current situation again crowded his thoughts. He imagined himself seated in a cold bare room. Another man in khaki uniform faced him across a battered old table. Voices echoed around his head; questions, endless questions. His conversation with Todd had been child's play compared to what was to come. He closed his eyes again and this time drifted into unconsciousness.

Chapter Thirteen

The approaching growl of a motorcycle prompted the young *Luftwaffe* conscript to lean out from the sanctuary of his brightly-painted sentry box. Water dripped from the rim of his helmet as he stepped into sleet-laden winter rain. A solitary motorcyclist, clad in a substantial greatcoat and large owl-like goggles, pulled up at the barrier. Behind him, a soft topped Opel staff car slowed to a halt.

A short conversation ensued between outrider and sentry before the latter hastily raised the wooden barrier. He then stood smartly to attention as the staff car swept past. It carried two officers, one in naval uniform, the other in *Wehrmacht* grey. Fluttering proudly from the bonnet was the pennant of *Vizeadmiral* Karl Dönitz, officer commanding the *Ubootwaffe*.

Major Hans Bauer peered dreamily through the window of the shiny black limousine. A relentless trickle of raindrops obscured his view as they sped away from the southern access gate to Kerlin-Bastard Airfield. Through the wet glass and fug from his cigar he managed a brief glimpse of one of the large Focke-Wulf Condor maritime reconnaissance aircraft that operated from the base near Lorient. Sitting forlornly on its concrete hard standing, the four-engined monster was the same type as that in which he'd just arrived from Gatow.

It had been a long flight from the *Luftwaffe's* prestigious base in

Berlin, and Bauer was content to be back on the ground. He'd always detested flying, and this had been his worst experience yet.

The thirty-year-old from Saxony was self-assured, mildly arrogant, and truly Aryan in appearance. He was a career intelligence officer, respected by Admiral Canaris, the head of the *Abwher*, and instrumental in the reorganisation of the German intelligence organisation in 1938. His companion, Udo Prehn, on the other hand was a somewhat introverted character, small in stature and with a nervous disposition. *Kapitänleutnant* Prehn had commenced his naval career between the wars. He was an academic, and well-connected within the intelligence community in Berlin.

The two *Abwher* officers had been dispatched the previous night from their comfortable, centrally-heated offices overlooking the *Tirpitzufer*. They'd received very little notice, and even less information about their deployment. It had, however, been made clear that it was vitally important they attended a meeting at the headquarters of the *Ubootwaffe*, or *BdU* as it was commonly known in naval parlance.

Prehn had, in fact, been provided with a solitary clue as to why the meeting had been called. Canaris himself had asked him the previous day to research reports of the possible capture of a German naval officer from a U-boat in the North Atlantic on 21st December. Otherwise, they'd been kept well and truly in the dark.

So what was so important that necessitated the dispatch of two senior intelligence officers from the capital, in the early hours, and the day before the Christmas celebrations reached their peak? Whatever the reason, they were here now speeding through the drab Brittany countryside in a *Kriegsmarine* staff car, en route to Dönitz's headquarters at Kernével.

Their driver had assured them that journey's end was less than an hour's drive away, and Prehn now contemplated whether or not his naval comrades could be persuaded to open up the well-stocked wine cellar at the Villa Kerillon.

They were soon rumbling through the old streets of Ploemeur, almost deserted this early in the morning except for the odd hardy soul, head down, battling against the driving sleet. There followed a dash along another hedge-lined country road before finally they reached the urban sprawl of Lorient, port city and now home-base of the Second U-boat Flotilla.

It was apparent from the outset that this was an important military centre. Army and naval traffic could be seen in abundance as the staff car cruised along between grubby shuttered tenements, now long overdue for significant maintenance. As they waited at a crossroads for a convoy of dapple-green Opel trucks to pass in front of them, the gelid waters of the Ter River could be glimpsed between the passing vehicles. The Ter was a considerable-sized inlet that, together with the Scorf River, formed the greater part of Lorient's harbour. Crossing hastily behind the last of the trucks they were now skirting a beach to their left. This was an affluent residential neighbourhood, but the substantial bourgeois properties of the previous century were now sharing their beachside location with a more ominous form of architecture: concrete pill boxes, anti-tank ditches and an impressive array of anti-aircraft weaponry now lined their route into Kernével.

In contrast their destination, the Villa Kerillon, was an imposing château-like structure. Its steeply-pitched roof, tall balconied windows and grand staircase to the main door made it a residence clearly befitting an officer of Dönitz's standing.

As their driver opened the rear door with a deferential click of the heels, a naval officer tripped down the steps to greet them. He was highly decorated, with the Knight's Cross suspended around his neck and an equally impressive cluster of assorted metalwork suspended from his tunic. He provided the two visitors with a brief salute before extending a welcoming hand.

'*Korvettenkapitän* Klaus Förster, *Konteradmiral* Von Thalberg's staff officer. Good you could come. Please follow me.'

Förster was a slightly built man with intense dark eyes and

thinning hair, swept back across a forehead crisscrossed with deep furrows. Prehn was also drawn to his rather prominent ears as he followed his host up the steps to the main doorway.

Inside, the full opulence of the villa became apparent. High ceilings, ornate panelling and a magnificent spiral staircase that wound its way up to the upper floors. A large Christmas tree stood in the hallway, and although spartanly decorated, it did at least offer some Christmas cheer.

Förster ushered Prehn and Bauer into an equally impressive sitting room, where they were invited to sit whilst he arranged some refreshment. The two visitors were then left alone to admire their surroundings.

Prehn was particularly interested in a series of side tables, their tops adorned with tiles, each depicting heraldic style crests. He was examining one of the tables when a voice boomed across the room from the doorway.

'I hope you had a pleasant journey gentlemen, I must thank you for coming so quickly.'

Konteradmiral Ernst Von Thalberg strolled into the room, hands stuffed into his trouser pockets. Grey-haired and in his mid-fifties, he was the product of the Bavarian aristocracy, connected to the House of Wittelsbach; a dynasty which had provided the Kings and Dukes of Bavaria for centuries. He was also a veteran of the old *Kaiserliche Marine*, having served on the massive dreadnoughts of the Grand Fleet. For a number of years the suave, affable aristocrat had been a close and trusted confidante of Admiral Karl Dönitz, and was now his Head of Special Operations. He gestured towards the colourful tiled tables. 'Those are the insignia of the boats based here in Lorient. The Second Flotilla operates from the new bunkers across the harbour from here. You can see them clearly from the front of the villa.' He shook hands with the *Abwher* men just as Förster re-entered the room.

'Coffee is on its way,' he announced.

Bauer and Prehn were directed to a couple of sumptuous leather armchairs. As they took their seats Von Thalberg took up position in front of the fireplace.

'Welcome to Villa Kerillon gentlemen, or more affectionately; the *Chateau Des Sardines* as we like to call it!' He warmed his hands before the crackling flames 'So, who has my old friend Admiral Canaris sent to assist us?'

Prehn spoke first. He appeared nervous, blinking repeatedly, his slicked-back hair glistening under the light of the chandeliers. '*Kapitänleutnant* Udo Prehn, sir. I'm currently with *Abwher* section 1-M Naval Intelligence. We have responsibility for collection of intelligence relating to British mainland naval establishments. Before that I was working with the *Etappendienst.*'

'Ah the secret naval supply system from the last war, eh?'

'That's right sir, the system was reactivated back in '39. I was engaged in work to supply our U-boats from interned merchant ships in neutral ports.'

'And how about you, Major Bauer?'

'I'm attached to *Amtsgruppe Ausland*. My role is liaison with *OKW* and the chiefs of staff. Requests for *Abwher* support for foreign missions are normally channelled through my department, sir.'

'So we're in good hands then,' said Von Thalberg with a smile.

Introductions over, the Admiral reclined into an armchair. 'Well gentlemen, let me explain why I have requested your urgent assistance. Firstly I must make it clear that any discussions here today are to be treated as secret. They are not to be discussed with anyone, and that includes the occupants of 76-78 *Tirpitzufer*. Any documentary records relating to these proceedings, or any activity related to them, must not to be removed from this building. Is that understood?'

The two *Abwher* men nodded before exchanging puzzled glances. Von Thalberg continued; 'This is by decree of *Vizeadmiral* Dönitz, with the full support of the *generaladmiral* commanding *Marinegruppenkommando West.*'

'I assume then, our superiors in Berlin have not been consulted regarding the subject of our discussions,' said Prehn.

'You assume correctly, *Kapitänleutnant*,' Von Thalberg snapped. 'Only Canaris himself has been briefed regarding this matter.'

Prehn remained straight-faced and silent, acknowledging the level of secrecy involved. The Admiral's dark piercing eyes remained fixed upon him.

'I understand you can brief us regarding the capture of a German naval officer following the sinking of one of our U-boats two days ago?'

'Yes, sir. *B-Deinst* in Berlin have intercepted transmissions from the British warship *Wareham*, operating at grid AL27, northwest of Ireland. It seems they have sunk a U-boat at that location and have captured a German naval officer of senior rank. We believe the U-boat concerned was U-500, commanded by *Kapitänleutnant* Werner Hahn, although we don't know if *he* was the officer referred to in the British signal.'

'Why U-500?'

'A transmission was received by *BdU* from U-500 an hour before the British sent their signal. In it, they stated that they were being attacked by a British warship and were preparing to scuttle. The position they gave was almost identical to that given by the British.'

'You are well informed, we did indeed receive such a message. And this warship – *Wareham* – is heading for Scapa Flow, is that right?'

'So it would seem, sir.'

Von Thalberg reflected on what he'd been told. 'And do you think this information is credible? Could the British be attempting to fool us? They may be mindful that we have deciphered their signals code.'

'I'm confident that the location is correct, sir.'

He went on to explain how the *Kriegsmarine* code breakers at the naval signals intelligence service had deciphered earlier Royal Navy transmissions from *HMS Wareham*. 'Wareham has been redeployed to Scapa Flow to join the destroyer screen protecting the British Home Fleet. She is due to arrive there sometime late tomorrow afternoon.'

Von Thalberg massaged his chin before turning his attention to Förster. 'Enlighten our friends here as to who *we* believe this so called prisoner is, Klaus.'

Förster handed his colleagues several sheets of paper, together with a photograph of an exuberant looking naval officer being driven in an open-topped Mercedes through a city street lined by an excited crowd. '*Korvettenkapitän* Max Friedmann, you've no doubt heard of him?'

'Of course,' said Prehn, 'surely it's not him... I thought he'd been taken off operational duty following his injury?'

'Yes, you're right,' said Förster. 'He was working here with Admiral Von Thalberg, doing the job I'm doing now. You have a summary before you of his naval service to date. I'm sure you will agree that it is most impressive.'

The Admiral looked up. 'Dönitz wanted us to set up a small group to look at the possibilities of increasing the level of proactive operations by the U-boat flotillas. Friedmann and I have been working on one such operation, codenamed *Paukenschlag*. It involves the initial dispatch of five of our ocean-going type nine boats to the east coast of the United States. The initial phase of the operation will be followed by others in due course. Their orders are to inflict a heavy blow against coastal shipping, operating along the eastern seaboard of the United States. This strike against the merchant fleet of our new enemy will effectively be our first blow; a statement of intent, gentlemen. I have also directed that the harbour of New York City be penetrated, and shipping at anchor be attacked, thereby delivering a clear message to the American public; that they are by no means safe from offensive operations by the Reich.'

Bauer grinned. 'Interesting choice of name, Operation *Drumbeat*. I'm sure the drums will be beating in Berlin, if the plan succeeds!'

'When is this operation to begin?' Prehn asked.

'It has already begun,' said Förster. 'The first boat sailed on the eighteenth. Another leaves today, and a third tomorrow. Then two more, U-130 and U-109, leave on the twenty-seventh of this month.'

'...And Friedmann. Where does he fit into this?'

'Initially there were to be six boats involved. Admiral Dönitz had asked for twelve, but the bureaucrats in Berlin wanted six for the Mediterranean. Then one of the boats dropped out with technical problems; that was the official story to keep OKM off our backs. In fact the sixth boat was being replaced by another. It's been fitted out in Kiel with experimental equipment that remains top secret. The equipment has been in the development phase for months, and this was to be its first operational trial. The project is known as Seeadler and I'm afraid that is all you need to know for now, gentlemen.'

Von Thalberg took up the briefing. 'I feel I must now speak candidly. Korvettenkapitän Friedmann never really took to a land-based deployment. He accepted that he had to refrain from sea duty after he was wounded, but as his health improved he started to get itchy feet. He made the case to me initially, and then to Admiral Dönitz, that he should return to his previous role and be given a new U-boat command. We resisted this request because Berlin, and more importantly the Führer himself, directed otherwise. Now that Prien and Shepke have been killed, and Kretchmer captured, it is considered vital by the political elite that for the purposes of morale, and of course the propaganda machine, Friedmann is kept safely out of harm's way. Yet as an officer with combat experience, I empathise with Friedmann's view, as does Admiral Dönitz and Generaladmiral Saalwächter in Paris. Friedmann's father and Saalwächter were well acquainted during the last war. There is almost a family bond between them.'

Von Thalberg returned to the fireplace, and lit a cigar. 'Friedmann was understandably disappointed when his request for operational command was turned down. He still had some way to go before he was physically fit enough to resume sea duties, and he knew it. So when we decided to send those boats over to America, and especially U-500 with its new technology fitted, Friedmann came up with the idea that he should sail with them, as a one off, thereby boosting the morale of the *Paukenschlag* crews and affording him the opportunity, on behalf of *BdU*, to witness the *Seeadler* trials. We saw this as a reasonable compromise; on the understanding he resumed his duties here afterwards. Dönitz went to Paris back in November for a series of meetings at the headquarters of *Marinegruppenkommando West*. During his visit, he managed to persuade *Generaladmiral* Saalwächter that it was a reasonably safe venture for Friedmann to take part in. The Americans are, after all, never going to be much of a threat to our boats, certainly not for the time being.'

'But the British and Canadians would be, surely?' Prehn interjected.

'Of course, but for the most part U-500 would be operating out of range of the British. I personally instructed *Kapitänleutnant* Hahn to refrain from any hazardous activity whilst operating within range of British Naval units. Clearly things have gone a little wrong along the way.'

'So how can we help?' asked Bauer. It seemed a more politic choice of words than "how can we save your backside?"

'I would have thought that was obvious,' Von Thalberg replied. 'I want you to get him back for me.'

Bauer shifted his gaze towards Förster, but was met with the blankest of responses. Then came an anxious glance in Prehn's direction, expecting a similar reaction on his colleague's face to that of his own. His judgement had been spot on; his colleague was clearly struggling to take in the Admiral's request.

'How do you suggest we achieve that exactly?' Bauer asked, shifting position in his chair to a more attentive posture.

'That's surely your area of expertise Major?' Von Thalberg's expression remained blank.

'One thing is for sure, *Korvettenkapitän* Friedmann is… how shall I put it… a *significant* prize for both us and the British. Max is a highly decorated U-boat commander and hero of the *Kriegsmarine*. What's more, he is privy to incredibly sensitive information; quite frankly one of the most important advances in weapons technology we have ever seen, a breakthrough which could affect the outcome of the war. If the British extract this information from him it would be disastrous, especially if they turned the technology on us!' He inspected the glowing end of his cigar, and returned it to his mouth.

'Of course, if they were to announce to the world that another German U-boat ace had been captured, that in itself would be bad enough in terms of propaganda. Last but not least we must not forget that Friedmann is like a son to Saalwächter, and he is not best pleased that the apple of his eye is currently languishing on a British warship. So gentlemen, the options are simple. We either leave him to his fate, whereupon the morale of not only the navy but also of our civilian population will no doubt be significantly lowered. Equally, if he talks, we may have lost a golden opportunity to bring this war to an early conclusion… in our favour.' The old Admiral puffed on his cigar again, blowing exhaled smoke up towards the ceiling. 'Then of course, there's the distinct likelihood that the Führer, when he gets to hear of this, will arrange for myself and several other senior figures in the *Kriegsmarine* to be placed in front of a firing squad!'

'…Not to mention compromising Operation *Paukenschlag,* and the safety of the men engaged in it,' Förster added, checking his watch.

'Exactly,' said Von Thalberg. 'The other option is to get him back. If we succeed in doing so, all our problems will go away. No one would ever be the wiser. It is my belief that the British will not be so keen to boast of their success if the prize has been snatched from under their noses! In fact, it is highly likely that they will ensure the whole affair is kept very much under wraps. That is certainly my hope. So gentlemen… will you help me to facilitate his breakout?'

'Put like that, I do not see we have much choice,' said Bauer. 'How long do we have to plan this so called *breakout* sir?'

'Thirty-six hours,' Von Thalberg replied curtly.

Quiet descended on the room as the *Abwher* officers glared at the Admiral with incredulity. Förster broke the silence. 'Please do excuse me; I think it is time I checked on the refreshments.'

He made his way across to the large panelled door at the end of the room and threw it open. He was greeted with a scene better suited to a comedy production on the stage. The void left by the open door was filled by a plump figure dressed in a white tunic. He was stooped, his intention clear. Förster could see the redness to his left ear, the tell-tale sign that it had been pressed firmly against the door. The steward was carrying a large silver tray loaded with cups and a coffee pot. Startled, he stepped back and stood to attention. Förster exploded. 'Schaube! How long have you been listening there?'

'I wasn't listening sir, I was… errr… just wanting to be sure you were still there. I've been rather a long time with the refreshments, sir.'

'Did you overhear what was being said in here?' Von Thalberg barked as he joined Förster in the doorway.

'No sir, of course not. I'm so sorry, sir.'

'Bring the tray in here and leave it on the table, then get back to your duties Schaube. If I hear that you have repeated *anything*, anything at all that may have originated from this meeting, I will shoot you myself, is that clear?'

'Yes of course, sir.'

'Now get out, before I change my mind and have you shot anyway.'

Schaube shuffled across to the door, his fleshy cheeks flushed from the dressing-down. He turned, gave a small bow and closed the door behind him.

Von Thalberg turned to Förster. 'Speak to him again after this meeting. I want him to be under no illusion as to his fate if he breathes a word out of place.'

'Of course sir, be assured he'll say nothing once I have finished with him.'

Förster poured coffee into the four cups, allowing Von Thalberg to continue the discussion.

'I know this is a big ask of you, gentlemen. Correct me if I'm wrong, Prehn; the British will be seeking to interrogate Friedmann at the first opportunity, correct?'

'Yes, correct sir.'

'And would I be correct in assuming that this would not be conducted at Scapa Flow, yes?'

Prehn nodded. 'We must assume that the British know who they've captured. Secondly, they may have some idea that U-500 was fitted with new technology. Is that feasible do you think?'

The Admiral frowned, as if unsure. 'Additional equipment had been fitted to the casing, yes. The question is whether they got close enough whilst our boat was on the surface, to get a good look at it. We can only hope that they didn't succeed in getting on board.'

'*BdU* received a brief signal from U-500 to confirm that they were under attack and scuttling the boat. We have no further information,' Förster added.

'Let us then assume the British know who they have captured, and they *have* had a glimpse of the *Seeadl*er equipment,' said Prehn. 'It is my guess they will want to transfer Friedmann to London, to what they call the "London Cage".'

'It sounds like something out of the dark ages,' said Förster, grimacing.

'It's actually a grand mansion in Kensington, a rather affluent district of London,' Prehn continued. 'The British have a unit called the *PWIS* – Prisoner of War Interrogation Section. We understand they run a number of so called *cages* around Britain, but the Kensington address is believed to be the centre of operations. And that, in my opinion, is where Friedmann, their big prize, will be taken.'

'If you are right, then what sort of time scale are we looking at?' Von Thalberg asked.

'Well,' said Prehn, 'if he arrives at Scapa Flow tomorrow, he'll be transferred to the custody of the senior naval officer. He in turn will need to arrange an escort to London. His options are flying or train. It's far too far by road. Normally it's train, and even that's a very long journey indeed! I wouldn't rule out the flying option though.'

'Perhaps I can help with this,' said Förster. 'Our meteorological office is predicting some extreme weather arriving over Scotland during the next forty-eight hours or so. There's a deep depression sitting to the west of the Hebrides, feeding heavy snow across the northern half of the country. The weather signals from one of our boats operating to the east of the Pentland Firth confirm that there's one hell of a storm brewing.'

'Good,' said Prehn. 'That'll hopefully keep the aircraft on the ground. It may even prevent the transfer of prisoners across the Firth to pick up the train south. With Christmas so near, and the weather so bad, I would expect that Friedmann will remain at Scapa Flow for a few days. We'll need to make urgent contact with our man over there and try to confirm this.'

'This is all just a theory,' Bauer interjected. 'We haven't even got the slightest notion of a plan yet. What if you've got it all wrong, Udo?'

Prehn looked across at Von Thalberg. 'Then you'd better find yourself a blindfold, Admiral,' he said glumly.

Chapter Fourteen

Tuesday 23rd December
Scottish Highlands

'Oh don't leave me just yet James.' The young woman extended a freckled arm from beneath the crumpled sheet that shrouded her nakedness. She smiled seductively at him as he sat on the edge of the bed pulling on his trousers. 'Come on, my train's not until six. We've still got plenty of time.'

Her bed partner looked back at her over his pale scrawny shoulder. His build was slight, and his torso reflected it. 'It's nearly twelve for God's sake!' he protested. 'There's something I need to do downstairs, then I'll be back.'

He got up and reached for his shirt. Then, with his braces snapped back over his shoulders and his receding dark hair smoothed back into place, he made for the door. 'Beth...'

'Yes, James.' She raised herself up on one elbow, allowing her long auburn hair to tumble about her shoulders. He said nothing, but tossed a packet of cigarettes onto the bed in front of her. Then he was off down the stairs, two at a time.

It was sleeting outside, tiny white flecks being tossed about on a cutting northerly breeze. James wrapped the heavy herringbone fabric of his overcoat about his shivering form. He hurried away from the small stone cottage towards the ramshackle workshop that doubled as a garage. Once inside, he pulled the heavy doors shut and skirted around the side of his slush spattered Morris eight.

Stretching along the wall behind the red and black car was a wooden work bench littered with rusting tools. He crouched down to remove the several jerry cans that were stored underneath. Once these were out of the way, several large stones were extracted from the lichen-encrusted wall beyond. Secreted in the void was a dark tan leather case. James carefully pulled it free and set it down on the bench. He snapped open the catches and pushed back the lid to reveal the neatly packed components of a radio transmitter. Next, he pulled up an old stool, perching himself upon it so that he could prepare the apparatus for use. Then with the headphones clamped to his ears and the Morse code tapper ready beneath his slender fingers, he waited. His watch showed twelve o'clock exactly. Seconds later the machine hummed and burst into life, emitting a relentless stream of "dits" and "dahs".

James stared at the dials in front of him as he absorbed the information flowing into his ears. Once the machine had fallen silent, he sent his reply, working the tapper with the speed and confidence of a seasoned operator. It was one of a number of skills he'd learnt at the *Abwehrschule* near Brandenburg. The coded conversation between James and his handler, Hans Bauer, lasted five minutes, after which he hurriedly returned the case to its hiding place in the wall.

The sleet was turning to snow now, dusting the driveway that climbed up from the main road below. Through the trees Loch Ness looked bleak, it's stony water whipped into white-crested wavelets that rushed across towards the opposite shore. James returned to the warmth of the cottage and made his way upstairs.

Beth was waiting, smoking a cigarette. She patted the pillow next to her. 'Shall we carry on where we left off, darling?'

The little man ignored her and sat down heavily on the chair in the corner of the room. 'Tell me what happens when prisoners are brought in to Scapa. How are they processed?'

The smile faded from Beth's face. 'You mean *German* prisoners?'

'Of course I mean *German* prisoners. What happens to them?'

Beth shook her head. 'We haven't had many brought in, I don't really know…'

'You must have some bloody idea woman, you work for the King's bloody Harbourmaster don't you?' His demeanour had changed, it was threatening now and it frightened her. She felt compelled to say something constructive.

'I suppose they'd keep hold of them temporarily, probably on one of the depot ships, then farm them out to interrogation centres or camps.'

James looked down at the dark double-breasted jacket hanging from the back of his chair. The sleeves bore the blue sleeve insignia of a Wren third officer. He threw the jacket across at Beth. 'Get dressed now. You'll have to catch an earlier train back to Thurso. I need you to do some digging for me and that won't happen if the weather worsens and you can't get back across to Lyness.'

Beth climbed out of bed using her jacket to protect her modesty. James lit a cigarette and watched her get dressed.

'Two destroyers are due to arrive at Scapa late tomorrow, the *Wareham* and the *Voracity*. *Wareham* will be carrying at least one German prisoner, a *Korvettenkapitän* Max Friedmann. I need to know exactly what your superiors intend doing with him, and I need to know quickly, understand?'

Beth was fumbling with her tie. 'For God's sake James, you promised me there'd be no more of this. If they catch me, they'll probably hang me… is that what you want?'

James leapt out of the chair and pushed her back onto the bed, her cheeks squeezed together between his fingers. As he applied more pressure, she winced with pain. He drew himself close to her, so close that she could feel his spittle landing on her face. 'What happens to you, Beth, is of little consequence to me. We're not lovers, we're business partners. That was the arrangement wasn't it, eh?'

He released her and returned to his chair whilst she massaged her reddened cheeks.

'We agreed didn't we, after that night in Inverness. You provide me with the information I need and I compensate you handsomely in cash… Oh, and I ensure our little affair doesn't become public knowledge so that hubby of yours, working hard down in Liverpool, is none the wiser.'

Beth pulled on her jacket and fastened the buttons. 'This is the last time James, I mean it.'

He followed her out of the room grinning. 'We'll see, when you run out of nylons, or when you crave the physical attentions of a man.'

She stopped on the stairs and turned to him. 'I could easily turn you in, you know that don't you?'

He sneered. 'I don't' think that'll ever happen… do you? Just remember, if I go down, no one will care, but you… what about that posh little family of yours down in Oxfordshire? Daughter cheating on her husband with an enemy spy… hanged for treason… the disgrace of it!' She glared at him, but said nothing, then continued down the stairs.

Not a word was uttered between them as they headed into Inverness. James parked his grubby Morris outside the station and escorted her to the ticket office.

She returned to him, ticket in hand. 'The train goes at two. It'll get me into Thurso before six, so I should be in time to get on something across the firth.'

They walked to the platform where her train, formed of soot-blackened coaches behind an ancient looking locomotive, stood ready to depart.

James thrust an envelope into her hand. 'Get yourself something nice for Christmas,' he instructed, his hawk-like features bereft of any compassion. 'Remember, I'll be ringing the number you gave me at midday tomorrow. I need to know what's going to happen to this man Friedmann, understand?'

She nodded as she stuffed the envelope into her bag and turned towards the train. 'I'll call you tomorrow.' She walked away without looking back, fading into the swirling cloud of steam that hung across the platform.

'Beth.' She turned, wiping away a tear. 'Happy Christmas,' he called after her, but his expression was devoid of any seasonal cheer.

Once Beth's train had clattered out into the murk, its last coach finally disappearing from sight, James ambled back to the ticket office. He asked the clerk behind the glass screen if he had any timetables.

'Where're you heading for?' came the gruff reply.

'Have you got anything for the line up north to Thurso and down to Perth?' James asked, stamping his feet against the cold.

'Och, the services these days are all over the place,' said the dour-looking clerk. 'Longer trains, specials, military stuff, it's all over the bloody place, bears no resemblance to what's published.'

'Can I take one anyway? I'm working all over you see, just useful to know where I can catch the train from.'

'I suppose I can let you have an old one. Company's a wee bit touchy about timetables and maps... frightened of German parachutists getting hold of 'em, I s'pose.'

He let out a sharp cough as he reached beneath his desk. A 1939 LMS timetable then appeared under the glass. 'Treat it with a pinch of salt mind, I have warned you,' said the clerk.

James thumbed through the book. Inside the front cover were maps of the LMS network with a specific section for the Highlands. He smiled to himself and stuffed the little book into his pocket.

Snow was lying on the footpaths along Academy Street. Pedestrians shuffled along, hats pulled down, collars turned up, avoiding the grey slush being thrown up by passing vehicles. This was the third Christmas of the war and the glum expressions on their frozen faces reflected the nation's mood.

James ducked into a dingy-looking bar not a hundred yards from the station. The tiny lounge was full of khaki uniforms, crowded together several-deep amidst a haze of cigarette smoke. The sound of glass chinking against glass provided a faint accompaniment to the cacophony of voices and laughter.

James found a free stool at one end of the bar. After a considerable wait he managed to order himself a whisky and waited, cash in hand, for its eventual delivery. He caught the eye of the customer standing next to him; a young sailor, clearly the worse for wear, who was also trying to catch the barman's attention.

'What are you having?' James asked, as he paid for the drink that had just been placed in front of him.

The sailor tried to focus on his new acquaintance. 'I am wanting a pint of your best beer,' he slurred in a strong foreign accent. 'Thank you so very much.'

As the barman slid a pint mug of heavy bitter across the slop-soaked counter, James held out his hand. 'James Chisholm, how do you do?'

The sailor grasped his hand, and shook it vigorously. 'Jan Bielawski, from Warsaw. Very pleased to meet you, sir.'

'So you're Polish then, serving with the Royal Navy, eh?'

'No sir, Polish Navy. I arrive two days ago at the Scapa Flow base with my ship, the *ORP Pilsudski,* attached to Polish Destroyer Squadron.' He pulled the rough woollen garrison cap from his head and pointed to the embroidered name around the rim. 'Now I go to Greenock to join *new* ship.' Bielawski placed his cap on the greatcoat that lay folded across the kit bag at his feet. The Pole was a convivial fellow, apparently oblivious to the fact that *walls have ears*! James put it down to his apparent youth, and of course the influence of drink!

Their conversation continued, hampered at times by language difficulties and a crosswind of loud conversations that filled the small space. Bielawski, now struggling with the effects of the alcohol, was attempting to explain his life story to his companion. James nodded from time to time, outwardly displaying genuine interest in his new friend's ramblings.

'And your ship... to whom does the name refer?' James asked.

'Ah yes, Józef Piłsudski, he was a great statesman, creator of modern Polish Navy.'

'I see, a national hero then… another drink Jan?'

'Yes perhaps, but first I must pee.' He chuckled to himself, for no apparent reason it seemed, whilst his glazed eyes roamed the bar, seeking out a viable route to the toilets. Then, target in sight, he slid off his stool and stumbled into the crowd.

James waited until his swaying form was out of sight, then, checking that no one was paying him any attention, he scooped up the young man's kitbag, greatcoat and dark blue cap. Having quickly drained his glass, he hurried out into the late-afternoon chill.

It was a short walk back to the station and the sanctuary of the car. He tipped his rain-soaked fedora down over his eyes, wishing to avoid any inquisitive looks from passers-by, and hurried along the pavement, kitbag over his shoulder, cap and greatcoat under his arm.

Forty minutes later he was back at Castle Brae Cottage, soaking up the warmth of the peat fire and sipping a whisky. He thumbed through the timetable he'd obtained from the ticket clerk. It had been a piece of cake, and he couldn't believe his luck. *They'll never win this bloody war if they can't keep their mouths shut,* he thought, all the while studying the timings between the stations south from Inverness to Perth.

He placed the little book down on the flickering hearth and went over to the small dresser by the door. From the drawer, he pulled out two Bartholomew's maps; sheet 21, Moray and The Black Isle and sheet 15, covering Lochaber. Both were a little frayed, damage sustained from constant use during his walking expeditions during the mid-thirties. He spread them out across the small pine table that stood in the corner of the room. Then, turning to the Moray sheet, he traced the railway line out of Inverness with his index finger. The line to Aberdeen branched away to the east, whilst the line to the south curled away across the bleak expanse of Drumossie Moor. Just to the south of the B9006 road was the tiny station of the same name, remotely situated close to the famous battlefield of Culloden where Bonnie Prince Charlie had famously been defeated, ironically by a German, back in 1746.

The station stood close to the massive Culloden Viaduct, an impressive sweeping structure that carried the railway across the wide floodplain of the River Nairn. At 598 metres long, with twenty-eight spans, it was the longest viaduct in Scotland; a masterpiece of bridge building by the Victorian Railway engineer Murdoch Patterson.

He tapped his finger on the little station. This would be where Friedmann would be liberated… *if* the opportunity arose, of course! His finger strayed to a small yellow-coloured road that ran underneath the southern end of the viaduct and then hugged the railway line down to Daviot where it joined the A9 road to the south. Close by, the B851 snaked its way westward across country towards Fort Augustus and Loch Ness. His attention now turned to the Lochaber map. Picking up the same road into Fort Augustus, he ran his finger onto the main Fort William to Inverness road that ran along the northern shore of Loch Ness. It was this route, further east, that Castle Brae Cottage looked down upon from its lofty position at the end of a rough track.

James had decided that any rendezvous point with a submarine should be somewhere along the west coast. Generally, the Atlantic seaboard of mainland Scotland was remote and rugged, its continuity interrupted by the mouths of numerous deep-sea lochs, any one of which could offer a temporary haven to a visiting U-boat.

The east coast on the other hand would prove to be a far more dangerous prospect, long open stretches of beach bordering the busy North Sea, vigorously patrolled by the Royal Navy and RAF.

He then traced the main route west from Glenmoriston, the A887. From the Kyle of Lochalsh where the road reached the sea, his eyes followed the coast to the north and south. They eventually settled on a finger of blue that carved its way inland towards the mountains of Knoydart.

Loch Coinneach, deep, secluded and dotted with small islands, certainly had potential as a rendezvous point. But there was something else that caught his eye, something that rendered the location perfect. A narrow road ran along the northern shoreline, linking the few isolated communities that continued to thrive in this barren, inhospitable terrain. The road eventually passed through the larger village of Camuscraig before snaking its way up through the mountains to join the main road near Invershiel.

It was indeed perfect. Next, he studied the string of islands that lay off shore. One of them, *Eilean Ceann-Cinnidh*, seemed quite large. It sheltered what appeared to be a sandy cove, above which the road ran particularly close by. The only settlement in the vicinity was Glendaig, just a church and a few scattered properties. He picked up a pencil and ringed the location, then retrieved his glass, a smile creeping across his face. Tomorrow he would take a look, early though; it would take him around an hour to drive over there. Then he'd go out to Culloden and check out the little station and its environs.

The old clock in the hall whirred and clunked, then struck the hour... eight o'clock. He went to the hall and pulled on his jacket, then picked up a torch and headed out to the workshop, and his wireless set...

The little Morris rocked gently as the icy wind from the northwest buffeted its red and black bodywork. The windows rattled as the cold air crept in anywhere it could. James sat hunched behind the steering wheel, admiring the panorama before him. Wind-tossed gulls soared gracefully above the ash grey tract of Loch Coinneach, their white plumage vivid against the dark mountains of Knoydart that loomed beyond. This was as remote as it could get, just as he'd envisaged it, perfect for the rendezvous.

He'd only passed half a dozen vehicles on the drive from Loch Ness, and they'd all been on the main road from Invermoriston. So far he'd not seen a soul since he turned left at Invershiel; not even in Camuscraig.

He started the engine and turned the car around, retracing his route through Camuscraig. It was just after ten o'clock on Wednesday morning. He'd been up since six planning, preparing, and hoping that Beth would not let him down. It had occurred to him early on that the plan couldn't succeed unless he had the assistance of someone who knew Friedmann personally. If the U-boat man was to be transferred south by rail then there was every chance he'd be one of a number of prisoners being escorted. He may even be wearing civilian clothing. No… someone had to be landed to assist him, he couldn't do it all alone. He knew the powers that be within *BdU* wouldn't be keen to place another man at risk, but there was no option, and he'd relayed his concerns to them during his scheduled transmission the previous night.

It wasn't far off midday when James pulled into the little car park behind the railway station at Drumossie Moor. He'd already toured the lane that ran from Daviot along to the viaduct, and had stopped to inspect the towering embankment that inclined steeply from the railway line at its southern end. Then he'd timed himself on the drive up to the railway station. It had taken him past the prehistoric Clava cairns and the giant boulder next to the Inverness road, reputed to be the place from which the Hanoverian Duke of Cumberland observed the progress of the famous battle against the clans.

He'd found himself alone as he climbed out of the car, so he'd strolled nonchalantly onto the platform through an open gate beside the station building. Not surprisingly, it too was deserted. At its southern end there stood a small signal box, inside of which he could sense movement. The distant sound of a series of bell chimes drifted across from the box, presumably from the communications instrument therein.

Then, as he turned to leave, he was taken aback to find his path obstructed by an elderly porter, white haired and sporting a bushy, untamed moustache. The old man was leaning on a large broom, his face expressionless. 'Can I help you laddie?'

'I was wondering when the next train to Aviemore was?' James gestured towards the viaduct.

'Not til' after five, the next one. You'd have a wee bit of a wait I'm afraid.'

'That's alright. I'll just have to drive on this occasion.'

'Aye, that's probably your best bet.' The porter was clearly a man of few words, having immediately returned to his sweeping duties, and not wishing to prolong the conversation. James, happy to oblige, left him to it and made his way back to the car.

It was a short drive back to Inverness and, conscious that he'd left it a little late to call Beth, he pulled up at a wayside telephone kiosk. With the telephone number of her lodgings scrawled on a scrap of paper in front of him, he called up the operator. His call was duly connected, and answered by a stern sounding woman with a strong Orcadian brogue.

'Hello, Lyness 211.'

'Could I speak to Beth Willoughby please, I'm a friend of hers.'

'Please hold the line, I'll try to locate her.'

There was no emotion in her voice, just formality of the kind that he would have expected from a news reader on the wireless. The sounds of someone walking on stairs could be heard from the earpiece, thereafter a protracted silence, and then more footsteps followed by Beth's breathless voice. 'Hello, is that you James?'

'Aye it is, I couldn't call earlier. Can you talk?'

'Yes, I can.'

'Good. Do you have any information for me?'

Beth's voice lowered to a whisper. 'The ships you spoke about, they arrived yesterday evening. There were two prisoners from a submarine, the U-500. One is that chap Friedmann, and the other a seaman, who's quite poorly. The rest of the crew didn't survive.'

'Do you know what they intend doing with Friedmann?'

Again, she spoke in low tones. 'They're keeping him on board the depot ship *Dunleven Castle* until the 31st, then taking him across

161

to Thurso for a train to Glasgow, and then on to London I believe. There are some other prisoners being escorted with him, *Luftwaffe* men shot down near Wick, and some other U-boat survivors from another sinking, apparently.'

'Why the wait? That's seven days away.'

'Well, it's Christmas I suppose, and the weather's closed in up here, it's expected to be foul for a number of days. I heard this morning the railway line beyond Georgemas Junction is blocked by snow already.'

'I see, and what about the train, will it be a normal service or what?'

'The train's a special, been laid on for military personnel from up here and down at Invergordon. I suppose they've scheduled it for then because the railway system will be under less pressure over the new-year period.'

'Umm, I suppose so. Do you have the exact timings of this train?'

'I can probably find out a little closer to the date. You know how flexible everything seems to be these days.'

'Flexible or not, I need to know, understand? I'll be in touch.'

'Alright, I'll be in during the evenings from now on, I'm working day shifts over Christmas.'

'Then I'll call on the 28th for an update, you should know more by then.'

'Just make it after tea, say seven o'clock.'

'Seven o'clock it is. Make sure you have the information.'

He replaced the receiver and returned to the car, then sat for a minute, reflecting on the information Beth had just imparted. Incredibly, it was all going according to plan. All he needed now was the assistance he'd requested to arrive on time.

Chapter Fifteen

Wednesday 24th December
Villa Kerillon

The meeting the previous day had concluded with an impassioned plea from Admiral Von Thalberg; a solution to the problem relating to the capture of Max Friedmann had to be found at all costs. Förster had then escorted the *Abwher* men next door to the Villa Margaret, where they'd been shown to their rooms and given the opportunity to freshen up.

Prehn had taken a bath. He was gazing out across the harbour when Förster knocked on his door. He delayed his response for a few seconds, mesmerized by the relentless procession of wind-feathered wavelets progressing across the harbour; broad brushstrokes of white on grey. His attention was now focussed on a solitary U-boat. It had just emerged from the massive concrete pens in the distance and was heading out to the sea, its pencil-thin hull rising and falling as it carved its way through the incoming tide.

Förster had taken his visitors back to Villa Kerillon, where they'd trooped through the kitchen to a pair of armoured doors. Prehn had remarked that they'd seemed strangely out of place in such a functional room. Förster hadn't replied, he just heaved them open and led the visitors down some steps to the nerve centre of the *BdU*; *Berlin*, as those individuals working within the bunker had affectionately called it. They would spend the next thirty-two hours

163

in this subterranean world, snatching the odd hour of sleep whenever they could.

The self-contained operations complex, 10,000 square feet of wood-panelled reinforced concrete bunker, had been completed by the Organisation *Todt* earlier that year. Now the bunker's fourteen rooms were a constant hive of activity, where Dönitz's signals staff processed incoming radio traffic, decrypts and intelligence reports.

Large maps adorned the walls, used to plot the positions of U-boats at sea and the slow lumbering convoys they were hunting. It was an impressive place, tightly managed, where Dönitz, "the Lion" could himself interact with his officers and men, and drive the U-boat war forward in his own indomitable way.

Prehn leant forward onto one of the mapping tables, across which numerous charts and documents had been strewn. He'd removed his tunic and had rolled up his shirt sleeves. The air conditioning in the bunker was efficient but the heat from the electrical equipment crammed into the windowless rooms generated considerable warmth. 'I think we've done all we can,' he said, returning to the vertical before arching his aching back.

Förster sat back in his chair and sighed. 'We seem to have achieved a great deal in a short time, it's down to the individuals on the ground now, and it could still go seriously wrong. We need a fair amount of luck to pull this off.'

Bauer then walked in with a sheet of paper in his hand. 'Signal just in from U-114. Von Bramsdorf is making ready for sea. He'll leave Bergen in the early hours, and expects to be at the designated grid reference on time on the 28th, weather permitting.'

'Good, Hans. All we can do now is wait and hope the British don't get impatient.' Förster glanced up at the clock on the wall. 'Nearly nine o'clock, the Admiral will be in for a briefing shortly, he's due to speak to Dönitz in Germany later tonight.'

The head of the *Ubootwaffe* was spending Christmas at home with his wife. He'd asked to be kept fully briefed as to how the plan was developing.

'Do you think Dönitz is fully on board with this operation?' Bauer asked.

'He has reluctantly agreed,' Förster replied, 'but it will be Von Thalberg who reaps the whirlwind if all this goes wrong! Dönitz has close ties to the Führer, and I'm sure he sees himself as Grand Admiral at some stage. He won't want to scupper his chances. My guess is, both he and Saalwächter will want to distance themselves from any disaster.'

'Perhaps we too should distance ourselves, or we might need more than one blindfold!' Prehn tried to make light of the situation, but his joke fell flat.

Admiral Von Thalberg walked in on their silence, a pensive expression etched on his face. 'Happy Christmas, gentlemen. My, the atmosphere seems heavy in here. This does not bode well. I do hope you have a plan for me, yes?'

'We do, sir,' Förster replied. 'And we actually think it might work, if the British play along.'

'Why so glum then?'

'Oh it's nothing, Udo's sense of humour, that's all.'

'I see.'

The Admiral sat attentively on one of the chairs arranged around the table and lit a cigar. 'You'd better explain to me how it will work then, *Korvettenkapitän*. I'll then endeavour to put the *vizeadmiral* out of his misery.'

Förster had assumed the role of spokesman for the group, and got to his feet. 'My colleagues made contact with our agent in Scotland last night. He is known by the codename *Phoebus*. He initially needed some time to speak with his contact at Scapa Flow, but in the meantime he's been looking at potential pick-up points along the west coast where a U-boat can safely operate close to the shore. He now thinks he has found a suitable location.'

The Admiral rose from his chair and leant over the chart on the table. He studied the point on the map that Förster was tapping with his finger. 'Loch Coinneach? Why there?'

'It's a deep-water sea loch sir, accessible from the Sound of Sleat that runs through here, between the Isle of Skye and the mainland. The area is extremely remote, so a U-boat could enter the loch at night with little chance of being seen. If necessary, there is sufficient depth throughout the loch for the boat to run submerged.' He slid his finger across the map. 'As you can see here, there is a narrow road along the shoreline. It links these isolated villages along the loch side with the main road from the west to the east, and on to Inverness.'

Von Thalberg leant over the map again. He pointed to the location where the road skirting Loch Coinneach was closest to the water. 'There is a cove here, perhaps a good point for a pick-up?'

'Our thoughts exactly,' said Prehn. 'The boat can get in close to the shore, and this small group of islands along here will be a useful navigating aid.'

'What about this small village nearby, how do you say it…? *Glendaig*. Is it likely there would be any interference from the residents? It's not at all far from the proposed rendezvous point.'

Förster reassured him. 'It's no more than a group of fishermen's cottages, sir. They'll either be drunk and unconscious, celebrating the New Year, or tucked up in bed when any planned transfer takes place. Whatever, I'm sure they won't be a problem for us.'

Von Thalberg nodded. 'Alright, so my next question is how do we release Friedmann from the grips of his captors and get him across to this remote loch?'

'I have to advise you sir, that the details are still being worked on by Agent *Phoebus*. He transmitted to us late this afternoon having discovered that Friedmann, and we now know it's him, is currently being held on a depot ship called the *Dunleven Castle*. The agent's contact states that two prisoners were captured from the U-500. Friedmann, and another badly injured crewman. The remaining crew members perished.'

'That is a great shame, Hahn was a good man. He had great promise.'

'Of course sir, but for now we must concern ourselves with Friedmann.'

'Fair enough, do go on.'

Förster continued the briefing. 'The good news is, they intend to keep Friedman on the depot ship until the thirty-first of this month. Apparently the weather is terrible at present. The depression that's causing it has settled just to the west of Cape Wrath, here, producing high winds and snow. There has also been disruption on the railway line to Thurso; drifting snow apparently. It seems the British have given up trying to beat the weather and have settled in for Christmas. There's no air activity reported at present, and they seem understandably unwilling to use smaller boats to ferry personnel across the Pentland Firth, here, with the weather being so bad.'

'So the good lord has provided us with some breathing space,' said Von Thalberg, relief spreading across his face.

'So it would seem,' Förster replied with a hint of a grin.

'The British Navy intends to transfer their prisoner by boat to the mainland, sometime during the thirty-first. He will then be taken by train down to London, we assume overnight. We are also told that there will be other German prisoners on the train; some *Luftwaffe* fliers and several U-boat survivors. *Phoebus* intends to snatch Friedmann from the train when it passes near Inverness, then drive him across to the rendezvous point with the U-boat.'

'How exactly is he going to be *snatched* from under the noses of the British, on a train packed with their troops?'

'That's what is still being worked on, sir. *Phoebus* has asked that this element of the operation be left to him. He has, however, requested that we provide him with an assistant... someone who knows Max Friedmann.'

'An assistant?' The Admiral fanned the remnants of cigar smoke away from his eyes. 'Why does he need an assistant for God's sake, and how on earth are we going to find someone who will fit the bill at this late stage?'

'We've already found someone, sir,' Prehn announced with a sense of pride.

'And who exactly is this someone?'

'*Oberleutnant Zur See* Jürgen Reiniger. He's the first watch officer on U-114, currently operating out of Bergen in Norway.'

'So how does he satisfy the requirements of this Mr *Phoebus*?' Von Thalberg returned to his chair and lit another cigar.

Prehn crossed the room and handed the Admiral a yellowing folder with Reiniger's name scrawled across the label on the front. He opened it and studied the black and white photograph pinned to the papers. Prehn then explained their choice of assistant.

'*Oberleutnant* Reiniger is personally acquainted with Max Friedmann. In fact he saved his life back in 1932.'

The Admiral looked up, his attention assured. 'Really? Tell me more.'

'You will recall the *Niobe* incident in July of that year?'

'I certainly do. *Niobe* was a three-masted barque, a training ship, sunk in a squall if I'm not mistaken. In fact I knew one of the crew members who was killed in the accident.'

'You are correct sir, *Niobe* was built originally in 1913 in Denmark. She was bought by our navy in 1922 to replace the officer training ships seized by our enemies as war reparations. Tragically, during a cruise in the Baltic near Fehmarn Island on 26th July that year, a sudden squall caused her to capsize. It had been a hot day and all the hatches and portholes were open. She went down in minutes, taking many of her crew with her, together with twenty-seven cadets from the officer cadet crew *Thirty-Two*.' He went on, 'Friedmann had been rendered unconscious by falling debris from the deck. He was found in the water by his fellow cadet, Jürgen Reiniger, who managed to keep him afloat until they were rescued by the crew of the freighter *Theresia L M Russ*.'

'Well well, some story, so the two men know each other well, yes?'

'Yes sir, they remained good friends during their initial officer training, but their paths have not crossed for some time so I'm led to believe.'

Von Thalberg studied the photograph. The young man portrayed was wearing his dress uniform. He was powerfully built, dark haired and with gleaming eyes; eyes in which there lurked a sense of mischief. 'What does *Phoebus* want his assistant to do?' he asked.

'It seems the agent has a good idea as to how he intends to facilitate the *korvettenkapitän's* release,' said Prehn. 'To carry out his plan, he will need the help of a second man; someone who Friedmann knows personally. He feels such a contingency is necessary so that the rescue is not jeopardised by Friedmann refusing to comply with the instructions of a stranger. It is also likely other prisoners will be transferred south at the same time. *Phoebus* needs someone to be on that train who will know Friedmann instantly.'

'And Reiniger, is he an officer of the calibre we need him to be for this operation?'

Förster joined the conversation. 'You will see from the file there Admiral that Reiniger is certainly a colourful character. He served on the destroyer *Curt Beitzen* from thirty-eight to forty, was decorated following the second battle of Narvik, then began his U-boat training with his current Commanding Officer, Felix Von Bramsdorf. They both attended the U-boat Commanders course at Memel, then he was posted to the 24th Training Flotilla. He worked his way up to the rank of 1WO, and always hit it off with the men... but unfortunately not always his superiors. I believe he is known affectionately by his current crew as *Leutnant Kopfschmerzen*, as he has a habit of banging his head on the bulkhead hatches.'

'Umm, not surprising he suffers from headaches,' said Von Thalberg, smiling. 'He does look to be a big man from this photograph. I would have expected an officer with this length of service to have had a command of his own by now.'

Förster nodded before continuing. 'He was due for promotion back in January. However, he apparently had a very public disagreement with his then commanding officer as to whether they should pick up survivors from a Dutch freighter they'd torpedoed. It almost came to blows, we understand. His promotion was stopped and he was transferred to Von Bramsdorf's boat in June. They've been operating out of Bergen since then. The two men get on well and make a good team. U-114 has enjoyed considerable success during recent patrols.'

'Are you sure we can trust this man Reiniger to do what he is told? From what you say, he seems to be something of a loose cannon.'

'We have no choice, sir,' Förster explained. 'He's the only suitable candidate in terms of availability.'

'Very well, and this man *Phoebus*… are we happy he can carry this off? The last thing I want is Friedmann dead.'

'I have every confidence in agent *Phoebus* sir,' said Bauer, who'd been sitting quietly at the end of the table. He was clearly irritated by the Admiral's question. 'He has been extremely effective during the last year. You need to look no further than his success at infiltrating the highest level of command at Scapa Flow. He also has reliable sources within the seaplane base at Invergordon.'

'He has indeed done well,' said Von Thalberg.

'You may also recall, Admiral, that the British moved their Home Fleet from Scapa Flow shortly after the outbreak of war. Their temporary base was known as *Port A*. It was *Phoebus* who quickly identified this location to be Loch Ewe. Several U-boats were deployed to patrol the mouth of the loch in October '39, but the British had moved their capital ships back to Scapa Flow before our boats arrived. *Phoebus* had even supplied details of the *almost* non-existent anti-submarine defences at Loch Ewe. There was potential here for an even greater strike than that perpetrated by Prien against the Royal Oak.'

Von Thalberg raised a conciliatory hand. 'I think you have persuaded me, Major. I take it Reiniger will be put ashore and met by *Phoebus*?'

'That's correct, sir,' Förster confirmed. 'U-114 will make the rendezvous at 2300 hours on the 29th December. This will give some time for *Phoebus* to brief Reiniger and prepare him for his role in the operation on the 31st.'

'And is Reiniger aware of the adventure he is about to embark upon?'

'No, not yet sir, Von Bramsdorf was ordered to prepare his boat for sea earlier today. He has been given sealed orders and briefed by his flotilla commander that he is to take up station north of the Butt of Lewis by midnight on the 28th, whereupon he will receive a further signal from *BdU*.'

'When will he leave Bergen?'

'We have just received word from Norway that U-114 has been fully provisioned and will be departing sometime after midnight.' Prehn held the recently received signal aloft.

'Well, I thank you gentlemen, you have worked hard. I will now go and speak with *Vizeadmiral* Dönitz and hope he agrees with the plan. Ideally, I'd like to have been able to provide him with more detail as to Friedmann's removal from the train, but I suppose we have to go with what we've got.' He got up and stubbed the remains of his cigar into an ashtray nearby. 'I do have one other question for you before I go.'

'Yes sir?' Förster looked across at his boss enquiringly.

'Would it be feasible to release all the prisoners on that train? It seems a shame to leave them to their fate, does it not?'

Förster nodded. 'Yes it does sir. It's just too much of a risk. Timing is of the essence here, we can't afford to wait around and potentially lose Friedmann in the process of liberating half a dozen lower ranks. It seems harsh, but that's the way it is I'm afraid.'

Von Thalberg grunted his acceptance of Förster's explanation and ambled out of the room, hands in pockets, Reiniger's personal file tucked under his arm.

As the three planners busied themselves clearing the map table, a smartly dressed rating bearing the sleeve insignia of a telegraphist entered the room. He carried a tray of sandwiches and a pot of coffee and placed them on the table. Having accepted Prehn's thanks, he marched smartly out.

Förster and his colleagues sat around the table devouring the meal in silence. Bauer eventually sat back in his chair and rested his feet on the mapping table. He took a large slug of coffee from the mug he was cradling between both hands, and glanced up at the clock on the wall. 'He's been talking for thirty minutes now,' he declared.

'It's hardly surprising, there's a lot at stake here,' Förster replied.

'They're hardly going to reject the plan, are they?' said Prehn. 'They've got more to lose than most!'

Their conversation was interrupted by the sound of rapid footsteps on the concrete floor outside the room. Von Thalberg marched into the room grim faced. He dropped the Reiniger file on the table and poured himself a mug of coffee. The three officers pushed back their chairs and stood in respectful silence, expressions of grim anticipation present on their tired faces.

Von Thalberg sat down heavily, coffee in hand. His face was blank. Slowly, his frown melted into a grin. 'The operation is to go ahead, gentlemen. Dönitz is a little concerned that the critical element of the plan currently lacks the necessary detail for him to be confident of success, but like me he knows we have little option but to go with it.' He looked across at the three officers in turn, and then said, 'I recall Friedrich Schlegel once wrote… "In life every great enterprise begins with and takes its first forward step in faith." Faith is what is needed during the coming days. If we fail, I am finished gentlemen. Don't let it fail.' Then he sat in silence blowing gently into his coffee to cool it.

Förster made towards the doorway, pausing by Von Thalberg's chair. 'I'll arrange for an immediate signal to be sent to Agent *Phoebus* and the flotilla commander at Bergen to inform them of the decision.' He turned to walk out.

'Yes of course, and Förster?' Admiral Von Thalberg called after his staff officer.

'Yes, Sir.'

'Wish them good luck and God's speed from me.'

'Yes, of course sir.'

2 0 0 9

Chapter Sixteen

Neil had become restless as the hardness of the metal seat began to numb his backside. He stood up stiffly and hastily folded the copy of the *Ross-shire Journal* he'd bought at the bookstall. It wasn't easy concentrating on the contents of the paper when your backside was aching! The arrivals screen on the wall opposite told him that the evening flight from Gatwick had landed at last.

A small group of car-hire representatives had begun to muster around the glass doors to the baggage hall, a sure sign that an influx of arriving passengers was imminent. To his right, the departures area of the terminal was empty. The last outbound flight had departed sometime earlier. Only the girl who'd sold him the paper was still engaged in anything useful; tidying the piles of tabloids that had remained unsold during the day. This was the last inbound flight to Inverness that evening, so hopefully the passengers would be through promptly.

Neil's interest shifted to a couple of middle-aged men who'd just walked into the arrivals area. They were dressed smartly in kilts and carried a small board advertising the fact that they were representatives of a prestigious local hotel. He opened the paper again and browsed through an article about an underage drinking problem in Tain, but it wasn't holding him. Boredom had set in, and he folded it up again.

The swish of the automatic doors distracted the little group of meeters and greeters as passengers from the flight began to stream into the hall. The clock on the arrivals board was showing 21.45. It had been a long day.

Fortunately the wait was a short one. Two men, both in their early forties, appeared from the baggage hall pulling small cases on wheels. On reaching the arrivals area they stopped and looked around, as if expecting someone to be meeting them. Neil sensed immediately that these two lost souls were his German visitors. There was something different about them, distinctly non-British!

As he approached the pair, the shorter of the two, immaculately dressed in an expensive grey suit, stepped forward with outstretched hand. 'You must be Inspector Neil Strachan?' he asked in perfect English, and with just a hint of an accent. He was of average height and build with tightly-cropped sandy coloured hair. A pair of expensive-looking rimless spectacles sat high on his nose. *Unassuming sort of a fellow,* Neil thought.

'That's right, and you must be Matthias Fuchs?'

'Oh please call me Matt, everyone else does.' He turned, and gestured towards his companion. 'This is Tomas Zeigler. He's with the *Volksbund Deutsche Kriegsgräberfürsorge*. It's our version of your Commonwealth War Graves Commission.'

'Pleased to meet you, Tomas. Welcome to Inverness.'

'Thank you,' Zeigler replied. His flat, once broken nose and deep-set eyes gave him the appearance of a retired prize fighter. However, Neil doubted whether he'd ever entered a boxing ring in his life. Zeigler also spoke English fluently, and Neil instantly warmed to the two Germans. He initially sensed an air of efficient formality about them, but this soon melted away as he led them across the car park with a promise of a single malt or two when they reached their hotel.

The early conversation in the car revolved mainly around the Germans' journey from Rostock where Fuchs was based at the *Deutsche Marineamt*, the German Naval Office. He'd met up with

Zeigler in Cologne, the latter apparently having travelled by train from Kassel, where the *Volksbund* office was located. The two had then travelled on to London to connect with the Inverness flight.

'You've certainly had a long day,' said Neil, having heard of their adventures across Germany.

'Yes we have,' said Zeigler. 'And I am now looking forward to a glass of your scotch whisky.'

Neil stopped at the junction with the A96. As he waited for the traffic to clear, Fuchs, who'd been peering out across the darkened Scottish countryside, was the first to get down to business. 'So you think you have found the remains of *Korvettenkapitän* Max Friedmann, our missing U-boat ace?'

Neil checked his mirror and pulled away. 'Well it's beginning to look that way, especially if we take into account the medals we have found with the remains.'

'That's good. It certainly fits with my theory. It will be satisfying to finally solve the mystery of his disappearance. Did you read the piece in my book on Friedmann?'

'Yes, very interesting, in fact I read the whole book. Some of the characters you've included certainly had colourful lives.'

'Ah yes, but no more so than your own naval heroes I think. It is the *colourful* characters who come to the fore in times of war I believe?'

'Yes, I suppose they do. Your book deals with Friedmann's military service in some depth, but what about his earlier life, do you know much about that?'

'Umm, what can I tell you about the young Max Friedmann? I have to say, it's been rather difficult researching this element of his past.' He inhaled deeply before continuing. 'The Friedmanns were a tragic family. There were no living relatives left to talk to when I was researching the book. At least none that I know of. What I do know is that he was born in 1914 in Konstanz, in the south of Germany. I believe it was his mother who came from that area. His grandfather on his father's side, Gerhard, was a vice admiral in the

Imperial German Navy of the Great War, and his father Karl-Heinz, an only child, was also a naval officer. He too served in the Great War with the likes of Alfred Saalwächter and Karl Dönitz; both prominent admirals in the last conflict.'

'It seems Friedmann had an impressive naval pedigree then?'

'Oh yes. The young Max was always out in boats, often with his grandfather at the *Kaiserlicher* Yacht Club in Kiel, close to where they lived. You can understand why he joined the navy!'

'So he lived in Kiel from an early age. Kiel's in the north isn't it... some way from Konstanz where he was born.'

'Well, his father was based in Kiel, and of course it was the paternal family home. Karl-Heinz was killed at the Battle of Jutland, serving on the cruiser *Rostock*. The family stayed on in Kiel and the grandparents helped bring the boys up.'

'And Friedmann had a brother who was killed early in the war, is that right?'

'Yes, his name was Otto. He was a little older than Max. Otto was tragically killed when his ship, the *Blucher*, was sunk in Oslofjord in 1940.'

They were now driving along Milburn Road towards the city centre. There was a light drizzle in the air and the windscreen wipers swept the screen intermittently. 'So what happened to the rest of the family?' Neil asked as he pulled up at a red light under the Eastgate Centre.

'Well, the mother became involved with an old friend of her husband's; a man called Bruno Treiber. He was a submariner in the First War. It was most probably Treiber who sparked Max's interest in the *Ubootwaffe*. They married sometime in '39. Then there was a big row apparently, about a year afterwards, whilst Max was home on leave. The word was that Max suspected Treiber, who was a gambler and drinker, of preying on his mother's wealth. Max apparently stormed out of the house and never returned. Tragically, his mother was killed during an allied bombing raid on Kiel in 1943.'

'So he never saw his mother again?'

'It would appear not. Treiber survived and became an alcoholic. He died in the early sixties.'

'What happened to the grandparents?'

'Oh, died of old age I presume.'

Neil turned into the car park of the large modern hotel on Bank Street where the Germans had booked their rooms. It was a popular location for tourists and locals alike, a number of whom were heading across the car park towards the entrance to the restaurant. Across the road, light from the six-storey building shimmered on the fast-flowing waters of the nearby River Ness. 'Here we are,' he announced. 'Journey's end.'

'Thank God for that,' said a relieved Zeigler from the back seat.

Neil escorted the men into the reception having agreed to stay on for a night cap. Leaving his companions with the young woman at the desk, he had strolled into the cosily-lit lounge bar, allowing them to complete their check-in formalities. He selected a bay near the window and, as instructed, ordered three large malts; the Glen Orrin, his personal favourite. He was savouring the first mouthful as Fuchs and Zeigler at last joined him. They settled onto the adjoining couch and lifted their glasses.

'*Prost Inspector*! I think I will like Inverness and its whisky very much,' said Zeigler. 'In fact I must bring my wife here sometime, as long as the shopping is good!'

Neil smiled. 'I'm sure she'll find plenty to spend her money on.' He was eager to steer the conversation back to the case in hand. 'I assume you'll be wanting to return the remains to Germany at some stage?'

'Not necessarily,' said Zeigler, sloshing the golden liquid around his glass. 'Firstly, we need to establish who this character is, beyond all doubt if we can. Of course we would normally work closely with surviving relatives, but as you have heard, if these remains are those of Max Friedmann, then there appear to be none still living that we know of to consult with.'

'Are you happy that you've exhausted all your lines of enquiry as far as family is concerned then?'

Zeigler nodded. 'Yes we think so. I have a close contact who works with an organisation called the *Deutsche Dienststelle*. They are based in Berlin, and maintain records of German military personnel killed in action or held as prisoners of war. They also maintain extensive war graves data. The *Volksbund* work very closely with them, as you can imagine.'

'I see,' said Neil. He took another sip from his glass. 'How comprehensive are these records?'

'Extremely comprehensive, for example, they hold over two million personal files on German naval personnel alone. My colleague, Felix Ostermann, at the *WASt* as we know it, has done some extensive research for us before we left Germany. I believe we have located all there is to know about *Korvettenkapitän* Friedmann.'

'I have also completed a considerable amount of research of my own,' Fuchs added, retrieving a thick file of papers from his briefcase. He dropped it on the table. 'If there's anything to know about this man, then we've got it here. In fact I'm still reading it!'

'Good, that's reassuring to hear,' said Neil. 'So Tomas, going back to the interment of these remains. How do you see this being taken forward, once we've completed our investigation?'

Zeigler sat forward, and placed his glass on the table. 'Once we're happy that we have conclusively identified the remains, we will seek the approval of the British authorities to arrange burial. It may be locally, or at a designated cemetery. It is my job to facilitate this and record the process on behalf of the relevant German agencies. In the circumstances, I do not see that there is anything to be gained by removing the remains to Germany, if they are indeed those of Max Friedmann.'

Neil opened the folder. The first page of notes detailed Friedmann's antecedents. Although in German, Neil recognised the date of birth, parents' names, Karl-Heinz and Katharina Friedmann. There was an address recorded of 16 Fraunhoferstraße, Ravensberg, a district of Kiel. No doubt the family home at some stage.

He turned the page as he sipped his whisky. The next sheet, typed in bold font and in English, outlined Friedmann's service in the navy...

Joined the Reichsmarine – April 1932.
Survived the Niobe sinking July 26th 1932 – During his officer training he was one of the few survivors when the sailing school ship tragically sank in the Baltic sea during a freak accident.

Career Progression

15 Aug 1932	*Offiziersanwärter*	*18yrs.*
1 Jan 1934	*Fähnrich zur See*	*19yrs.*
1 Sep 1935	*Oberfähnrich zur See*	*21yrs.*
1 Sep1936	*Leutnant zur See*	*22yrs.*
1 Mar 1938	*Oberleutnant zur See*	*24yrs.*
10 Mar 1940	*Kapitänleutnant*	*26yrs.*
29 Jul 1941	*Korvettenkapitän*	*27yrs.*

Decorations

6 Jun 1939	*Spanish Cross in Bronze without Swords.*
9 Nov 1939	*U-boat War Badge 1939.*
17 Dec 1939	*Iron Cross 2nd Class.*
17 Dec 1939	*Iron Cross 1st Class.*
4 Dec 1940	*Knight's Cross.*
1 Sep 1941	*Knight's Cross with Oak Leaves.*

Notes

Joined the Ubootwaffe 1936, having initially served as a junior officer on the pre-dreadnought – Schleswig-Holstein.

Saw service during the Spanish Civil War, Autumn 1937-38.

Completed 9 combat patrols – Total of 28 ships sunk – 176,000 tons. Included in the aces league.

(Most successful Commander – Korvettenkapitän Otto Kretchmer – 273,000 tons at 30 yrs. old).

Nov 1939 – 1ˢᵗ Combat Patrol – Sank 4 merchants and destroyer escort – 41000 tons – awarded Iron Crosses first and second class simultaneously.

Oct 1940 – 6ᵗʰ Combat Patrol – 6 vessels sunk (incl. 2 corvettes) 58,000 tons – awarded Knight's Cross.

8th April 1941 – 9ᵗʰ Combat patrol – Irish Sea – HMS Narborough (armed merchant cruiser – 12,000 tons) sunk – off UK west coast. Same patrol – further three tankers sunk. total 37,000 tons.
U-boat attacked by British aircraft (wounded in upper-right thigh). Earned the nickname 'Irish Max'.

2nd July 1941 – Transferred, following long spell in hospital, to BDU Ops Kernével, Lorient – promoted to korvettenkapitän in Special Ops Section.

Awarded oak leaves to Knight's Cross in the September 1941.

Neil placed the file on the table. 'Some career,' he said emitting a low whistle. 'And recorded in English too.'

'That's for you,' said Fuchs. 'Just a summary of some of his highlights.'

'Thanks for that, Matt. I have to say, I got the impression you were undecided as to Friedmann's eventual fate. The book seems somewhat inconclusive.'

'Yes, I know. You are referring of course to the suicide theory. I don't really subscribe to that, if I'm honest. I have no evidence to the contrary though, only my own thoughts. You understand I had to be objective in the book.'

'So what do you *really* think happened to him?'

'I think he was captured by your Royal Navy and for some reason the whole thing was hushed up. As I said on our way here, your discovery of these remains seem to support this version of events, and if this *is* him then the mystery deepens, as he appears to have got himself shot by someone. The question is, why... did he escape, or what? Then there's the obvious lack of response from the German side. The willingness of senior figures in the German Navy to accept the suicide theory leads me to suspect that a similar cover-up was perpetrated by my own countrymen... that's what *I* think'.

Neil drained his glass. 'Enthralling... I could carry on chatting all night, but it's getting late. I'm sure you must be tired after your journey, so we'll continue this discussion tomorrow. I'll pick you up around nine, is that okay?'

The Germans rose as Neil picked up his car keys. Fuchs shook his hand again. 'That will be fine. We look forward to tomorrow. Good night and thank you for the lift.'

Neil stepped out into light rain. He marched across to the unmarked police car he'd been using and slid into the driving seat. The journey back to police headquarters took less than ten minutes, as the dampened streets were all but deserted. Only a few late revellers heading for home from city centre restaurants followed him back towards the A9.

Having swapped cars, it wasn't long before he was standing at his front door, fumbling with his keys. Cat was lying on the sofa watching an old black and white movie. Tam lay coiled at her feet, one open eye the only sign of life. 'Did you meet the German guys?' she asked as Neil patted his dog.

'Aye, I did. Nice pair of fellas they were too.'

'Do you think they can help you with this case over in Glendaig?'

'I hope so,' Neil replied pulling off a shoe. 'I just have a feeling that finding this skeleton is just going to open up one big can of worms!'

'What do you mean, *can of worms*?'

'Well, if this German guy's suspicions are true, then we're looking at a bloody great cover up, and at the highest level, both in this country and his.' He pulled the other shoe off, and sunk into the sofa. 'And you know what? I'm inclined to agree with him.'

Cat looked at him enquiringly. 'Why's that then?'

'Call it an historian's intuition,' and he closed his eyes.

Chapter Seventeen

The two Germans had been waiting patiently for Neil in the foyer of the hotel. He'd arrived five minutes early and had then managed to avoid the morning traffic by threading his way through the back streets to the police headquarters. The three men were now sitting in Brodie's office drinking coffee. The overnight rain had long since cleared and now strong sunlight streamed through the half turned window blinds. Neil had introduced them to his boss, but the conversation had been cut short when the DCI had offered his apologies and hurried out, apparently late for a meeting to discuss "adjustments" in resourcing levels within CID.

Fuchs examined the contents of the various exhibits bags. 'These are, without doubt, authentic decorations,' he confirmed. 'The sleeve rings, or *ärmelstreifen* as we call them, are also genuine examples of those worn by a *korvettenkapitän* at the time.'

He ferreted around in his bag and produced a small black and white photograph, torn across one corner. It had been taken on a narrow beach in front of a large brick-built mansion where a group of young men in naval uniform stood smiling in the sunshine. In the centre of the group was an officer leaning heavily on a crutch. He handed it to Neil. 'This is probably the last known photo of Max Friedmann. It was taken outside the Villa Kerillon, Admiral Dönitz's headquarters at Kernével, near Lorient. As you now know, Friedmann was badly wounded in April 1941 and spent two months in hospital. On his discharge, he was posted to *BdU* Operations at Kernével, where he became staff officer to *Konteradmiral* Ernst Von Thalberg, the mastermind of the Special Operations Section.'

'And who are these other people in the photo?' Neil enquired.

They're all non-commissioned staff who were working within *BdU,* in the U-boat command bunker. It was an impressive complex, built under the villa you see here.' He tapped his finger on one of the men in the photograph. 'This fellow here, wearing the white tunic, was a steward, his name was Gottfried Schaube. I borrowed this photograph from his widow. You can imagine, every member of *BdU* would have wanted their photograph taken with an ace like Friedmann. It's likely that he was wearing the very medals here that we have in front of us, *and* of course the jacket which these *ärmelstreifen* come from.'

Neil held the photograph up to the light, studying it with interest. He picked up the folder containing Friedmann's service record that Fuchs had given him the night before and read through it again. 'So I assume this is the Spanish Cross in bronze without swords?' he asked, pointing to the decoration worn under the eagle motif on the right side of Friedmann's tunic.

'That's correct, for outstanding service during the Spanish Civil War between 1936 and 39. And this one, on the opposite side of the jacket, is the U-boat war badge of 1939, awarded usually after two war patrols.'

'So where are these decorations now, I wonder?' Neil rubbed his chin as he pondered over his own question.

'That's anyone's guess,' said Fuchs with a shrug. 'If he was taken prisoner as I suspect he was, then *all* his medals and insignia would have been seized by his captors; that's a fact. How he managed to retain the two other crosses is a mystery, one that works *against* my theory I'm afraid.'

'Yes, I recall Dr Miller explaining that to me too. There's something else that doesn't make sense.'

'What's that?' Fuchs asked.

'Well, in this photograph the Knight's Cross is being worn around the neck, as it should be, and the Iron Cross is being worn on the left side of the tunic, between the second and third buttons.'

'...As it should.'

'That's right. So, if our man was wearing these decorations, as per this photo, and his jacket has just rotted away over time, then why did we find the crosses *together* next to his right thigh?'

'I don't know, perhaps they were just thrown in the grave with him.'

'Or perhaps they were in his pocket?' said Zeigler, eager to contribute.

'Strange though, I admit,' said Fuchs, shaking his head.

He flipped the photograph over for Neil to see. Scrawled on the back in pencil were the words; *Kernével, Frankreich, 10. September 1941 mit unserem helden Korvettenkapitän Max Friedmann.* 'It says, Kernével, France 10th September 1941, with our hero Commander Max Friedmann.' He handed the photograph back to Neil.

'Schaube's widow also gave me his diary after he died. She'd heard that I was writing a book about the U-boat Aces and thought that it would be of interest to me. When I read through it I found an intriguing entry on 23rd December 1941. It seems Schaube was on duty throughout that day, assisting with the preparations for the villa's Christmas festivities.' He turned the pages in his file, and finally stopped at a photocopy of the page of a diary. It was boldly headed: *23 December 1941.* Under the date were some hastily written notes in pencil.

'He says here he was ordered to take refreshments to Dönitz's sitting room during that morning. He was delayed, having been tasked by his petty officer to unload a delivery of wine. So when he arrived with his tray, he listened at the door to establish whether there was anyone still inside the sitting room. He goes on to explain that he overheard a discussion between Admiral Von Thalberg, his staff officer Klaus Förster, and two other officers who he believed were attached to the *Abwher*. The *Abwher*, if you weren't aware, was the German military intelligence organisation during the war.'

'Yes, I've read about them, and their shady goings on!'

Fuchs continued to run his finger over the text without looking up. 'Yes, they were indeed *shady*, but spying is a shady profession, no?' He quickly moved on; 'It says here that Von Thalberg was talking about Friedmann *languishing* on a British warship, and opportunities to bring the war to an early end. He goes on to say that the Admiral was fearful that if the Führer learnt of this *he*, Von Thalberg, would be shot. Then he uses the words *breakout*, and *thirty-six hours*. The entry then becomes garbled.'

'What else does he say?' Neil was hoping for more revelations.

'He says that he was caught by Förster, when the latter unexpectedly opened the door, and was given a severe rebuke for listening to their conversation. He goes on to mention that Von Thalberg even threatened to shoot him!'

Neil sat back and folded his arms. 'Interesting, if true.'

Fuchs raised finger as if to indicate that there was more to come. 'Later in the day, Schaube makes an entry here stating that Förster visited him in his quarters and warned him never to breath a word of what he'd heard. He says the consequences were to be at best a transfer to the Russian Front, and at worst a firing squad. Not surprisingly, Schaube never spoke of the incident again.'

Neil got up and went over to the window. He adjusted the angle of the blind so as to shut out the shaft of sunlight that was now streaming across the room and into his eyes. 'Strange, he made such an entry in his diary after being threatened with a firing squad! But if true, then surely this information tends to discredit the suicide theory?'

Fuchs shook his head. 'Not really I'm afraid. My historian colleagues were certainly interested to hear of the contents of the diary but they argue, understandably, that it comes from only one source. Like you, they question its authenticity. The information is garbled and lacking in detail, and of course the claims cannot be corroborated. For example, there's no official record of Friedmann ever being taken into captivity by the British.'

'So looking at it from another angle, what evidence is there that Friedmann committed suicide then?'

'There's a letter in existence from Von Thalberg to Dönitz in which he discusses Friedmann's fragile mental state, possibly brought on by combat fatigue and frustration with his new desk job. He even mentions that Friedmann was, in his view, *suicidal*. Förster, in *his* diary, also mentions a night out in Lorient with Friedmann in early December. The entry states that Friedmann, whilst drunk, spoke of depression and a wish to end his life.'

'Compelling stuff, eh?' said Neil.

'Personally, I think not,' said Fuchs, tidying his papers. 'I believe the word *convenient* would be more appropriate.' He rested his hands on the closed folder, fingers tightly interlocked. 'Let me explain.' He paused for a second before continuing, his dark eyes now fixed on Neil. 'You see I actually tend to believe the steward's account. Consider this... December 7th 1941; the USA enters the war after the Japanese attack on Pearl Harbor. Admiral Dönitz, freed from any constraints regarding the targeting of American shipping, decides to send a pack of U-boats to strike the Americans on their own doorstep. He calls it Operation *Paukenschlag*, or *Drumbeat* in English. Six type-nine ocean-going U-boats are initially allocated to the operation but one, U-128, drops out due to technical problems. The first boat leaves on 18th December, the last on 27th December. The operation is a total success, over 150,000 tons of shipping sunk. Are you with me so far?'

'Yes, go on.'

'Now, Friedmann leaves Lorient on 14th December. We know this as he is recorded as being a passenger on board a routine flight from Kerlin-Bastard Airfield near Lorient, bound for Berlin. From here the trail goes cold.'

Neil looked at him bemusedly. 'So how does he become a prisoner of the British, if he's supposedly in Berlin?'

'Please, hear me out Neil. Friedmann mentions in passing, to a fellow officer travelling to Berlin on that flight, that he is on home leave, visiting his mother in Kiel.'

'How do you know that?

'Because I traced the officer he spoke to from the flight manifest that had miraculously survived. There are ways and means you know, and, well, luckily he was still alive. The guys at the *WASt* certainly have their uses!'

Neil looked confused again. 'Didn't you mention last night that Friedmann had fallen out with his mother and her new husband?'

'Absolutely right, back in 1940. So unless they'd made up, which is highly unlikely as we've no record of him being granted home leave since the row, he was going to Kiel for something else.'

'I hear what you're saying, but don't you think this is all rather tentative? He may have been visiting friends, or possibly other members of the family. Perhaps he wasn't going to Kiel at all; perhaps he said it just to keep people off his back.'

'Yes, perhaps, but isn't it also a coincidence that the U-500, a type-nine U-boat similar to those heading for America, departed Kiel on 17th December, apparently for a patrol to the south of Iceland?'

Neil was not convinced. 'So what evidence is there to connect that with Max Friedmann's disappearance?'

A smirk now crept across the German's face. 'U-500 had been undergoing a refit for several weeks, clearly under a veil of secrecy. I can find no documentation whatsoever or any witness testimony as to what was going on in respect of this boat. She was sunk by a British destroyer in the North Atlantic on 21st December 1941. All hands were lost when the boat apparently exploded, having been subjected to sustained gunfire during a surface engagement. The captain of the destroyer, a man called Todd, submitted a comprehensive action report to, amongst others, the Secretary of the Admiralty and the Commander In Chief Western Approaches. In it he mentions that the U-500 had some form of metallic framework mounted on the casing to the rear of the conning tower. Such was the level of resistance offered by the U-boat's crew, and the subsequent retaliatory action by the British, that the boat exploded and sank before he could get a closer look. Secondly, he mentions that *two* survivors were taken on board. *Matrose* Emil Schmidt and *Obermachinist* Joachim Voller. Voller apparently died almost immediately, Schmidt survived, and went on to five years' captivity in Canada, where he remained until he died in 1981.'

'Fascinating stuff. So how does all this help us?' said Neil.

'Well, the action report, the formal report of the event submitted to the Admiralty dated 21st January 1942, mentions *two* survivors. The captain's entry in the ship's log, made at the time of the sinking, mentions *three*. One of the names, the middle one in the list recorded initially, was erased by an ink spill! The figure *three*, against Voller's name, was subsequently struck through and the figure *two* substituted.'

'Perhaps the captain just made a mistake in the record. He may have been given incorrect data initially regarding the number of survivors. The ink spill could have been an accident, surely?'

'My, Neil, you are not easily convinced eh? I simply don't believe that mistakes were made or ink was spilt! The log entry was made some time after the action. Todd would have been sure of his facts by then. No, there were definitely three survivors logged initially. I think the captain of the British warship was, at some stage, directed to lose a survivor from his records, and that survivor was most probably Max Friedmann!'

There was a protracted silence. Then Neil rocked forward in his seat. 'Like I said, this is all very interesting, but also very much circumstantial. Only this man, Schaube, provides any corroboration to this theory. And why would the British authorities ensure that the capture of such an important prize was covered up so quickly, and so thoroughly?'

'Simply because they *lose* him Neil... he escapes. Can you imagine the implications? You British have always boasted that no German ever managed to escape from this island during World War Two. I would suggest that the escape of such a high-profile figure would have provoked a political storm. Heads would have rolled, public morale would have been affected and there must also have been a fear that *my* countrymen would take great pleasure in advertising the fact, thus creating an even greater hero in Friedmann than before! No, it would have been best to keep it all quiet, deny it had ever happened, especially when the German side had miraculously remained silent too! Mr Churchill must have been overjoyed. He would've had no idea that in some quarters within the German U-boat Command it had been considered best policy to bury the whole affair too!'

'I see where you're coming from,' Neil murmured. 'So by escaping, but then disappearing, and never returning to Germany, neither side could afford to say anything for fear of the repercussions.'

'Exactly,' Fuchs replied with a contented nod.

'Are you are also inferring, then, that the documents suggesting that he may have taken his own life were false?'

'Not false in themselves, just containing a series of lies. The officer who travelled with Friedmann to Berlin recalled that he was very cheerful and, how do you say it… the life and soul of the party. This does not match exactly the assessment of Von Thalberg and Förster, whose written comments, incidentally, were made in early 1942, nearly a month after he disappeared. As I said, most convenient.'

'Fair point,' Neil conceded. 'What about the crew of the destroyer, have you managed to trace any of them?

'Yes, I did identify three crewmen still living when I was doing my research. One was suffering from dementia, and the other two recalled a couple of German sailors being rescued, but not any details of their rank or condition. They never saw them apparently as they were working below decks.'

Fuchs unravelled his hands and gently patted the file in front of him. 'So there you have it, Neil. Now I'd like to see the remains myself. I think by doing so I can finally put all the other theories to rest.'

'Yes, of course,' Neil replied. 'I hope you're right. There's not much to see though, it's a pretty average skeleton in my view.'

'I sincerely hope not, Neil.'

'What do you mean, you *hope not*?'

'All will become clear when I see the bones, trust me.'

Neil looked across at Zeigler, as if seeking some sort of clarification from him on the subject. 'Don't ask me,' he said, raising his hands defensively.

Neil called the mortuary and spoke to Dr Carnie's assistant, then placed the phone receiver back on the cradle. 'Yes, it's okay for us to go across and have a look. I'm afraid he's still waiting for the test results though.'

Fuchs smiled. 'If I'm right, we won't need test results!'

Fifteen minutes later the three men were marching through the swing doors to the mortuary. Carnie, dressed in his greens and short rubber boots, greeted them with his customary enthusiasm. 'Welcome to my world once again Neil.'

Neil grinned, and gestured towards his companions. 'This is *Kapitänleutnant* Matthias Fuchs, with the German Navy and Tomas Zeigler, who's with the German War Graves Commission.'

'Pleased to meet you gentlemen, welcome to Scotland. So, you've come to view our mysterious skeleton... or perhaps I should say *your* skeleton!' He chuckled in response to his little joke, then turned and gestured to his visitors. 'Please do come with me.' He led them between the examination tables, past the corpse of an elderly male whose chest cavity had been unceremoniously exposed by peeling back the outer layers of skin and muscle. Zeigler winced and looked the other way as he brought up the rear. 'My assistant, Jack has laid the bones out for you over here,' said Carnie. They rounded a corner into another small room. Sure enough, laid out on a stainless steel table were the remains recovered from Glendaig. Jack was busy arranging the last of the small bones in the feet.

Fuchs made directly for the side of the table from which he could examine the skeleton's right side. He picked up the long, yellowing femur at one end and caressed it with his free hand. His companions looked on in silence, a little perplexed. Carnie broke the silence. 'Nice example of a femur that. He was a good strong example of a man in his prime.'

Fuchs turned on him, disbelief present in his eyes, and an anxious expression on his face. 'That's just it, Herr Doctor; he wasn't. Did you find any evidence of damage to the kneecap or insertion of a pin into this bone? I am no expert, but it doesn't look like it to me.'

Carnie's demeanour quickly changed to match that of the German's; there was an air of formality about him now. He took the bone from Fuchs and examined it. 'No, this femur is undamaged,' he confirmed. 'There's no evidence of pinning here.'

'Then these are not the remains of *Korvettenkapitän* Max Friedmann. God only knows who *this* man is.'

Neil wiped a hand across his brow, stunned by Fuchs' announcement. 'I assume this is something to do with the wound he received on his last patrol. Is that what you are saying?'

Fuchs was now examining the knee bones. 'Yes, that's what I'm saying Neil. Friedmann was on the bridge of his boat when it surfaced in the Irish Sea to recharge its batteries in April 1941. The boat was attacked by a British aircraft; he was struck in the knee and upper-right thigh by shrapnel fragments. The knee and thigh bones were badly damaged; in fact there was talk of him losing his leg.'

'Surely this was a little early for surgery of this nature?' said Carnie. 'The use of intramedullary rods wasn't pioneered until after the war as I recall. I would have thought that treatment of such injuries would have been limited to traction or plastering in those days.'

'Not so Doctor, a German surgeon called Gerhard Küntscher first developed the use of rods or pins, whatever you call them, to treat fractures to the long bones. He first used the device in 1939, ironically at the department of surgery at the University of Kiel. Initially the German military disapproved of the technique, but they had a change of mind, introducing it widely in 1942. Soldiers would recover in less time you see, and then they could be returned to the front much more quickly.'

'Well, you learn something every day,' conceded Carnie, leaning on his knuckles.

'So how did Friedmann get the new pin, if the military initially disapproved of the procedure?' Neil asked.

Fuchs shrugged. 'Friends of friends I suppose. He was a willing guinea pig, and it came with the promise he could return to sea duties quickly. One of Küntscher's associates agreed to travel to the military hospital in Lorient to do the surgery.'

'Why on earth didn't you mention this leg pin before? We could have ruled Friedmann out much earlier.' Neil struggled to mask his irritation.

'Because I only read his medical notes last night,' Fuchs replied defensively. 'Felix Ostermann sent me all these papers from Friedmann's personal file. Many of them I hadn't seen before as they'd been misfiled. I only received them the day before I left, and have been working my way through them as quickly as I can.'

'I can vouch for that,' said Zeigler. 'He hasn't stopped reading since we left Germany!'

'I knew about the injury and the hospitalisation, but not exactly how they treated him. Felix has since taken possession of a batch of patients' records from the German military hospital in Lorient. WASt have taken some time to catalogue them, and came across Friedmann's name. Felix knew I had an interest and sent copies to me. I looked up Küntscher on my laptop last night because I was unsure about the dates involved. Then I suppose I was convinced that you'd found Friedmann's remains, what with the medals and uniform fragments. I knew we were coming here today and thought the identification would just be a formality, so thought I would wait before…'

'…Throwing a spanner in the works,' Neil interjected. Fuchs looked bewildered. Neil shook his head and sighed.

Chapter Eighteen

'Jesus Christ Neil, I thought you were well on your way to getting a result with this job. Now I discover we're back to square one, and you haven't a bloody clue whose remains we've dug up.' Brodie, having just returned from a long and fractious meeting with Human Resources, was in no mood for shocks and hadn't taken the news at all well.

Neil peered through the glass door panel towards the two Germans who were sitting in the general office out of earshot. 'I know it's frustrating sir, but we're convinced this guy Friedmann remains a main player in this enquiry. We're still confident the clothing and personal effects found with the remains are his.'

'Then I don't bloody care much for your choice of *main player*. I was hoping the *main player* was the poor bugger buried on a beach with a hole in his head!'

'Okay, okay, I take your point, can you just let me have a little more time on this please? I'm sure I can still get a result.'

Brodie ran an agitated finger around the inside of his shirt collar. 'Look Neil, I've got a pile of stuff here that needs a DI's attention.' He brought his fist down onto the stack of folders lying on the edge of his desk. The force was such that air expelled from within the pile caused several sheets of paper lying close by to flutter down onto the floor. Neil stooped to pick them up.

'The end of the month sir, give me until then and I'll draw things to a close. It is a suspicious death enquiry after all.'

'It's a bloody *old* suspicious death enquiry, and it's getting older every day. It's as well for you Neil, that our supercilious bloody fiscal and his boss in the Crown Office seem obsessed by this job. You can have until the end of the month, not a day later, okay? Then some other bloody historian, not one employed by the Chief Constable, can take over the enquiry and *you*, Neil, can take some of this shite off my desk.'

'I'm indebted to you, Alex,' said Neil in a half whisper.

Brodie looked up, trying to suppress a grin. 'Don't push it DI Strachan, now get back to your German chums and try to discover who put a hole in that skeleton's head. And if you can't do that, a name for him would be a bloody good start.'

Neil returned to his desk having poured himself a cup of water from the machine nearby. 'Big boss giving you a hard time?' Fuchs grinned.

'Oh, he has a point. We've got plenty of work on at the moment. As always we're short-staffed and here I am working on a sixty-eight-year-old murder mystery that's unlikely to be solved. In fact, it's even more unlikely to be solved since your promulgation at the mortuary!'

'So, what now Neil?' Zeigler asked.

'I'm going to take you out for a drive to Fort George. It's a bit like a castle. I need to speak to someone there about escaped prisoners of war. Then we'll run over to Glendaig and I'll show you where the remains were found.'

'Sounds good,' said Zeigler, trying to remain upbeat. 'Perhaps we get to see some of the famous Scottish scenery, yes?'

The easterly wind was still tugging at their jackets as they passed through the main gate at Fort George. Neil could see big Jim Morrison emerging from the door of the museum as they approached along the driveway. He waved when he saw Neil and made his way across the immaculately manicured lawn to meet them.

'Sorry Neil, I've been meaning to give you a call. I'm glad you dropped by because I might have some news for you.'

Following introductions, they were once again herded along between the old barrack blocks to the café in the heart of the fort. Over coffee, Jim answered questions from the Germans regarding the history of the fort. Neil maintained a diplomatic silence until he sensed a natural break in the conversation.

'You mentioned you may have some news for me, Jim,' he prompted.

'Aye Neil, I have. We checked the regimental records for the period you were interested in; nothing at all that would possibly be of use to you, I'm afraid. However, I did speak to one of my old soldier pals who comes in regularly to help out in the museum. He's getting on now, but feels he's being useful making the tea and suchlike.'

Neil was impatient to get to the point. 'Aye, and what did he say, Jim?'

'Well, he was with the Seaforths during the war, stationed here in late 1941. He recalls being turfed out late one night to assist the police setting up checkpoints in the area. They were told that there'd been an incident along at Culloden, a *POW* was on the run and it was believed he was still in the area, east of Inverness. It must have been some search, because he remembers being deployed in company strength, and all night long.'

'Yet there's no trace of this in the local military records, isn't that odd?'

'Well we don't hold every record maintained by the regiment. Perhaps it was noted elsewhere.'

'Does this chap recall whether the prisoner was ever found?'

'He doesn't know. They were deployed over a period of a couple of days in all, but heard nothing. Not surprising perhaps, seeing that he was a young private, just having completed basic training.'

'And does he remember exactly when this was?'

'Oh yes, he'll never forget, it was Hogmanay!'

Fuchs seemed excited. 'The timeline fits, if Friedmann was held for a few days at Scapa Flow. That's where *HMS Wareham*, the ship that I believe rescued Friedmann, was heading. I discovered during my research that she had received orders to join the destroyer screen for the British Home Fleet. Records show she arrived at Scapa Flow on the 24th of December.'

'It's hardly conclusive, is it?' said Neil dismissively. 'Is it worth me speaking to this old soldier, Jim?'

'Wouldn't have thought so,' he replied. 'I think I extracted all the info I could from him.'

Having finished their drinks they headed for the main gate, leaving Morrison waving from the door of the café. 'It's a bit of a drive to Glendaig,' said Neil, as they reached the car. 'We'll stop off on the way for something to eat.'

Having interrupted their journey for lunch at the hotel at Invermoriston, Neil re-joined the lonely road westward. As the A887 climbed away from Loch Ness, the dense woodland skirting the road gave way to a bleak moorland landscape ringed by distant hills. Dark shadows of fast-moving clouds tracked across the heather-clad slopes, blotting out the afternoon sun. The weather had remained settled all day and visibility was particularly good.

The Germans gazed out of the car windows, clearly enjoying the changing vistas that emerged around every bend in the road. The local man had hoped that the Five Sisters would be fully visible as they zigzagged their way up the steep and narrow road from Glen Shiel. He was rewarded when he reached the top, the summit ridge with its five peaks being completely free of cloud. Small pockets of snow still clung to the rock in the more sheltered corries and glistening ribbon-like burns snaked their way down the range's south face. Neil stopped in a lay-by for a minute or two so that his passengers could admire the magnificent view then, conscious of the time, he hurried on towards Loch Coinneach, and ultimately Glendaig.

A blue Ford Galaxy stood in the lay-by across from the beach. It was accompanied by a shiny black Volkswagen Golf, parked close behind it; Neil sensed *press*. He was soon to be proved correct. As they wound their way down to the beach, a young woman with straw-blonde hair hurriedly approached them.

'DI Strachan, how fortunate.' Annie Dunbar clattered to a halt on the shingle, blocking the policeman's way. Her cameraman and sound engineer formed a little queue behind her, as if knowing their place in the media pecking order. She waved a microphone in her right hand. 'I'm doing a piece about the Glendaig skeleton on *Highlands Tonight*, Inspector. I don't suppose I could get a few comments from you?'

'Aye, of course Annie.' He turned to his companions.

'This is Miss Annie Dunbar, one of our local TV presenters. These gentlemen are colleagues from Germany.'

'Germany indeed! So the theory still revolves around the remains being a wartime German sailor?' She turned to her colleagues who were setting themselves up to film the conversation. Once they'd confirmed they were ready, she turned back to Neil.

'Detective Inspector Strachan, are you any closer to identifying the remains that were found on the beach here on 24th May?'

Neil stood stiffly, hands clasped firmly to his front. 'We *are* making progress with the enquiry but, as you know, the remains appear to have been buried here for some considerable time. We're currently conducting tests to establish exactly how long.'

'There has been some speculation that the bones are those of a wartime German sailor; can you confirm this, Inspector?'

'That is one line of enquiry we are following up. We are being assisted by the German authorities in an effort to confirm whether this is the case. However, at this stage we are keeping an open mind.'

'And are you still treating this as a murder enquiry? It seems a little strange if the remains have been here since World War Two.'

The furry microphone was thrust in his direction once again. 'The remains have been fully examined and we believe cause of death was a single gunshot wound. Until we're clear as to the circumstances here, bearing in mind no actual combat activity occurred on British soil, the procurator fiscal has directed that this matter be treated as a suspicious death. We therefore intend to do all in our power to identify these remains and discover what happened on this beach, so that justice can be done if at all possible.'

'Thank you, Inspector.'

'Thank *you*,' Neil replied, relieved that the ordeal was over. Although trained in media relations he was always wary of speaking to TV reporters, fearful of the "low-baller" question, or providing a response that may come back at some stage to haunt him.

As the TV crew made their way back to the road, Neil and his companions walked across to the grave site. Blue and white police tape still fluttered in the immediate vicinity, although the forensic team had by now completed their investigation. The indentations of the graves were still clear to see.

'Why two graves, I wonder?' said Fuchs, his eyes fixed on the disturbed shingle.

'All I can think is that one was not needed, because the body was taken elsewhere for some reason,' said Neil. 'You never know, it may have contained the remains of Max Friedmann at some stage, and if that's the case God knows where they are now!'

'Perhaps the second corpse, if there was one, turned out not to be dead or was spared perhaps, or might have even recovered sufficiently not to be buried,' Zeigler suggested.

'Anything's possible,' Fuchs agreed. 'Whatever happened, the graves were dug in a hurry, they were fairly shallow.'

Neil walked away to the point just above the high-water mark where the spent cartridge had been found. He tapped his foot on the shingle. 'The search team found a single cartridge case about here. I'm told by the experts that it was an example of a nine millimetre parabellum round, lead core, developed in Germany early in the war.'

'Interesting,' said Fuchs. 'Could it possibly have been from the gun that killed our man?'

'Very possibly. But there again it could have been any one of a number of rounds that may've have been fired. It's almost too good to be true, finding it, but having said that, very few people tramp over this beach and it was found above the high-tide mark.'

Zeigler stood, hands in pockets, staring out across the loch. 'You know, I think *this*, or perhaps I should say *an* individual came here intending to be picked up, or to depart himself, in a boat. He was probably disturbed by someone, who shot him, before burying him over there.'

'I'm sure you're not far from to the truth,' Neil agreed. 'But who was in that second grave? And why dig two? And *who* shot *whom* in order to escape? Is it possible Friedmann fired the shot before escaping?'

'Then why was the deceased possibly wearing Friedmann's uniform, and where did the fragments of British battledress come from? I've never seen any photos of Friedmann wearing the captured uniform,' said Fuchs. He shook his head and walked away along the water's edge, trying to apply some logic to the mystery. Neil turned to Zeigler.

'Let's assume that Friedmann escaped from this beach, having shot whoever tried to stop him. Perhaps he left the corpse dressed in his tunic to give the impression that it was him, especially if it was found some time later.'

Zeigler nodded. 'The fact is, Friedmann never reappeared. Whatever vessel picked him up may have been sunk. I wonder if any of the recorded U-boat sinkings around the end of 1941 corresponds to our timeline.'

He called to Fuchs to return to them. As he stumbled back along the beach, Neil asked, 'Do you have access to records relating to the dates and locations of U-boats sunk during the war?'

'On my laptop, sure,' Fuchs replied.

'Can you check, and let me know if any U-boats went down anywhere near here around 31st December 1941, or very early in 1942?'

'Of course, I'll get onto it as soon as I return to the hotel.'

The three men climbed back up to the road and returned to the car.

'Is there a local church around here?' Zeigler asked. 'Only, it may be a more practical option for the remains to be interred here, if possible.'

'St Columba's, the parish church at Glendaig is just along the road there; would you like to have a look?'

'That would be most helpful,' said Zeigler from the back seat.

Neil pulled back onto the road and headed east. The peaks of Stac Coinneach Dubh and Beinn Caisteal stood proudly together in the early summer sunshine, stubborn wisps of thin cloud grasping their summits like a witch's fingers. It had turned out to be a perfect day for anyone visiting the region; clear, warm, light, no haze and a breeze to keep the midges at bay. Neil pointed out two red deer stags grazing by the side of the road, their young antlers just beginning to take on a majestic prominence. The animals raised their heads lazily when the car sped past but, unperturbed, returned to their grassy meal as the threat quickly diminished.

As usual, the car park was empty when Neil drew up close to the church. The faded invitation to the craft sale still hung from the sign by the red gate. As they entered the churchyard Zeigler halted and spun around. He sniffed the air, and nodded gently, as if in agreement with some unseen companion. 'This is a very peaceful place,' he said. 'I think it would be a most suitable final resting place for one of our countrymen.' He walked around the church, leaving the path as it turned towards the door and continuing to the end of the building before disappearing out of sight along the west wall.

When Neil and Fuchs caught up he was slowly patrolling amongst the lines of headstones, hands clasped behind his back, deep in thought. 'Perhaps somewhere under those trees at the back of the cemetery would be acceptable,' he called out, acknowledging the presence of the other two men.

'And what exactly is it that would be *acceptable* to you?' The voice came from the opposite end of the church. The Reverend Mackay was marching across the grass towards Zeigler. Neil hurried to catch up.

'Hello Duncan, may I introduce you to Tomas Zeigler, with the German War Graves Commission and Matthias Fuchs who's an officer in the German Navy.'

'Oh, I see, pleased to meet you gentlemen.'

'We were just discussing the interment of the remains found on the beach. At some stage they'll be released. Tomas will be arranging burial in due course and was wondering whether a suitable plot could be made available here.'

'Ah yes, I'm sure that would be possible, and have you finally established that the remains are indeed those of a German serviceman?'

'Well, we're leaning towards that conclusion.'

'I'll take it that means you haven't, Inspector. And what if the poor soul remains unidentified?'

Neil coloured briefly. 'Well at some stage we will have to make a decision that he is indeed a German serviceman based upon the evidence, such as the personal effects found with him.'

Zeigler interjected. 'If we can't name him conclusively then we will mark his grave with a stone referring to him only as *Ein Deutscher Soldat.* Unfortunately, as is the case in many British and American cemeteries, many of our soldiers, sailors and airmen lay in graves marked in this way.'

'It seems so impersonal,' said the minister, shaking his head. He turned to Neil. 'I do hope you are successful in identifying the remains, Inspector. I'd hate to think of someone lying in this place referred to only as *a German soldier!*'

'We'll certainly give it our all,' Neil assured him.

'Good, now Mr Zeigler, you must explain how you arrange such burials. I find the whole process intriguing. I see no immediate problem accommodating you. Perhaps you could show me where you were thinking he should be laid to rest.' MacKay ushered Zeigler away towards the tree-lined northern boundary of the graveyard, leaving Neil and Fuchs to themselves.

'Are there any other military graves here?' Fuchs asked.

'It depends what you mean by military grave. I'm not aware of there being any war graves as such. The only one I've seen with military connections is around here.' Neil led Fuchs to the other side of the church, intending to show him Dugald Matheson's grave.

As they stood under the dancing branches of the birch tree, Neil spoke first. 'He was the son of the minister who lived here during the war. Not killed in action. Apparently the result of an accident locally, something I've not got to the bottom of as yet.'

'Umm,' Fuchs murmured. 'Such a waste of a young life.'

Then, as they passed the monument to Dugald's parents Fuchs stopped suddenly. 'How interesting. This is certainly a coincidence,' he said, pointing at the large granite cross.

'What's that?' Neil enquired as he appeared from behind him.

'*Kreuzlingen*, Switzerland.'

'Yes I know, it's unusual to see a place like that on a gravestone in these parts.'

'No it's not that. Do you remember I told you Max Friedmann was born in Konstanz in southern Germany?'

'Yes I do.'

'Well you could argue that Kreuzlingen is a district of Konstanz. This lady and Max Friedmann appear to have been born in the same town, albeit twenty-four years apart!'

'Forgive my ignorance; aren't the two places in different countries?' said Neil.

'Yes they are,' Fuchs explained. 'Konstanz is located at the north-western end of the *Bodensee*. You would call it Lake Constance in English. The Rhine river flows through the lake and then through the city of Konstanz, pretty much dividing it in half. The German-Swiss border generally follows the line of the river, and passes through the city itself. The greater part falls in Germany, but the districts to the south are in Switzerland. Kreuzlingen is one of those districts, effectively a suburb of Konstanz.'

There was just a hint of excitement in Neil's voice as he patted the cross gently. 'Well, well, the links to this man Friedmann just keep on popping up, don't they?'

It was nearly 8pm when Neil got home. There was a good couple of hours' daylight remaining at this time of year, so he dropped his jacket on the armchair and wandered into the garden carrying a cold bottle of beer. Having wiped off a garden chair, he sat down and sipped from the bottle. Tam barked, prompting Neil to throw the tennis ball he'd deposited at his master's feet. Neil obliged, and then sat back gazing skyward. Feathery ribbons of high cloud now drifted slowly overhead, their ragged edges bathed in a pink hue from the setting sun. He closed his eyes, relishing a few moments of relaxation; then his mobile phone began to vibrate, followed by its familiar musical ringtone. He leaned to one side and retrieved the phone from deep within his trouser pocket.

'Hello, Neil Strachan.' He immediately recognised the accent at the other end of the phone.

'Hello Neil, Matt here. I checked the records of U-boat sinkings from the last day of December, '41. Bad news I'm afraid. There was nothing that day.'

'What about the first couple of days of '42?'

'Nothing. The first recorded sinking is the eighth. Four U-boats were lost during the month of January that year; two in the Mediterranean and two in the North Atlantic. The location of one of the sinkings in the Atlantic was specific, the other was not.'

'Not conclusive then,' said Neil.

'Not really,' Fuchs replied. 'I'll do some more digging though, and I'll be in touch.'

1 9 4 1

Chapter Nineteen

The deep low-pressure system circulating around the north of Scotland had stalled as expected. Driving snow and storm conditions now battered the remote country around the far north of the British Isles. Howling gales and mountainous seas maintained their relentless onslaught against the ancient cliffs that stood guard along the Atlantic coast of the northern Hebrides. Even the normally resilient islanders had retreated into the peaty warmth of their dreary little cottages as the ferocious storms lashed their isolated crofting communities.

Off the west coast of the Isle of Lewis, the towering crests of giant breakers plummeted into deep troughs of swirling grey. Spray, whipped up by the wind, blew asunder amongst a descending curtain of snow as the odd seabird hung in the air, tossed about mercilessly in the gale.

Two miles out from the shiny gneiss-formed cliffs, a periscope cut through the surface, trailing a ragged white wake. Heading south beneath the heaving Atlantic cauldron, U-114 hummed along on battery power, relatively unaffected by the raging storm above.

In his cramped berth the boat's commander, *Kapitänleutnant* Felix Von Bramsdorf, sat pensively at his desk thumbing through a small leather-bound photograph album. The thirty-four-year-old aristocrat paused as he came across a snap of an attractive woman, not that much younger than himself, her blonde hair whipped about her face in a strong breeze. She was seated nervously on the edge of a castellated stone rampart, her arms wrapped around a very young boy, also blonde haired, who sported a broad grin.

The photograph had been taken that summer at the family seat; Schloss Bramsdorf in western Saxony. The baroque style fortress, perched on a rocky pedestal and overlooking a vast lake, had been the home of countless generations of the Von Bramsdorf dynasty. He, his wife Mathilde and son Wilhelm lived in an apartment at the castle which was currently occupied by his mother and father. The Count Von Bramsdorf had once been a respected general in the Kaiser's army. His wife, the Countess, was a formidable woman, not dissimilar in appearance to Britain's Queen Mary of Teck.

Von Bramsdorf's contemplation of the picture was cut short by a knock on the bulkhead. The cheerful face of the boat's cipher officer appeared around the curtain. 'Signal from *BdU* sir. It's marked top secret, to be read only by the commanding officer.' He thrust the paperwork into Von Bramsdorf's hand, and then withdrew behind the curtain.

The captain closed the photo album and placed it on his desk. He unlocked the small cabinet next to his desk with a key that hung with his dog tag around his neck. Then, having retrieved the commanding officer's personal cipher book, he busied himself decoding the signal. When he at last scanned the text, his eyes narrowed as he digested the brief content.

Lassen sie den hirsch frei gehen. 2300hrs, 29 Dezember… Let the deer go free.

It was the code he'd been told to expect, authorising him to read the sealed orders he'd been given back at Bergen. When he'd asked what the message had meant, he'd been told by the flotilla commander that all would be revealed when he opened his orders.

He reached into the open locker and took out a large manila envelope, sealed and stamped *Geheimnis* – secret. Placing it gently on his desk, he tore off the flap and removed the documents from within. Each was stamped in red – *Nach dem ablesen zerstören sie* – destroy after reading. The content was brief, and took only minutes to digest.

'*Reiniger*, why?' he mouthed to himself as he returned the papers to the envelope and gazed down at the photograph album lying on the desk. He opened it again and sat for a few seconds as Mathilde and Wilhelm smiled up at him. Then, with the envelope safely locked away, he grabbed his cap and adjusted the cravat at his neck. Without further ado, he slipped out from behind the curtain and headed for the control room. Thirty seconds later, he was leaning over the chart table with the navigating officer.

'We need to be here no later than 2300 hours tonight, Obermeyer. Can we do it in this weather?' He tapped the jagged sided inlet on the map that indicated the position of Loch Coinneach.

The navigator walked his dividers across the chart and made a calculation on his note pad. 'It'll be a struggle at this speed sir, but on the surface at full speed we should make it.'

'*Should* is not good enough *Leutnant*. We must get there on time. I have agreed to run submerged, to give the crew some respite from the surface conditions and to prevent any further seasickness on the scale we saw last night. However, if needs must, then we will surface.'

He turned to the 1WO, who was wrapped around the handles of the search periscope, scanning the scene above them for potential threats. '*Oberleutnant* Reiniger, what's it looking like up there?'

The first watch officer, Jürgen Reiniger, remained firmly attached to the rubber eye-guards. 'Nothing doing sir, just heavy seas and snow… lots of snow.'

'Fine,' said Von Bramsdorf, pushing his cap back to reveal strands of blonde hair stuck to his high, glistening forehead.

'Jürgen, surface the boat, then hand over to Obermeyer and join me in my quarters.'

'*Jawohl, Herr Kaleun*,' Reiniger responded, with an element of bewilderment at the captain's sudden decision to surface. He snapped the periscope handles back into place and manoeuvred his bulk from around the smooth steel column. The twenty-nine-year-old from Bremerhaven was tall and powerful, a keen sportsman from an early age and champion boxer within the *Kriegsmarine*. His nose bore the tell-tale signs of the sport; broken several times and now a tad crooked, testament to the many bouts he'd fought since his youth.

He barked out a string of orders as he watched his captain withdraw through the bulkhead hatch. A sense of unease washed through him but he couldn't pinpoint exactly why. Perhaps it was the anxiety he'd perceived in Felix Bramsdorf's weather-beaten face. It wasn't something he'd detected that often in his long-time friend and colleague.

With the boat on the surface and the watch crew deployed to the bridge, Reiniger made his way gingerly along the walkway to Von Bramsdorf's tiny berth. He lurched left and right as the boat rolled unceasingly, but as always his sturdy sea legs never let him down. He steadied himself by the flimsy swaying curtain and called out; 'May I come in sir?'

'Yes, come in Jürgen,' came the terse reply.

As he entered, Von Bramsdorf was pouring out two glasses of schnapps. He handed his second in command one of the glasses and gestured to him to sit down on the bunk. 'I'm sorry to have kept you in the dark about our current deployment, Jürgen. As you know, I was instructed to make ready for sea with very little notice. I can tell you now that my initial orders were to set a course for a location to the north-west of Lewis and there await a further signal. I now have that signal in my hand, sent just now, for my eyes only.'

He handed the decrypted signal to Reiniger. '*Let the deer go free*?' What is that supposed to mean?'

Von Bramsdorf unlocked the cupboard and removed the envelope stamped "secret". 'I think you'd better read this, as it specifically involves you.'

Reiniger read the text in silence. He massaged his chin through the embryonic beard that obscured his angular jaw. Then he raised his eyes, a look of bewilderment carved into his pale features. 'I am being sent ashore to liaise with some agent called *Phoebus*? Am I having a bad dream here, Felix?'

'I was hoping you might be able to tell *me*,' protested Von Bramsdorf with a straight face. 'I doubt they've plucked your name out of the air.'

Reiniger's eyes dropped once more to the sheet of paper he was holding. 'We are to proceed to this map reference on Loch Coinneach at 2300hrs tonight, then I'm to be put ashore once this agent *Phoebus* has made contact with us. I'm to introduce myself with the words: *Are the herring plentiful in these parts?* to which he will respond *I don't know, I prefer to hunt the deer.*' He read on: *You, (Officer commanding U-114) will then depart and patrol to the north of Canna, returning to RVP – Loch Coinneach, at midnight on 31ˢᵗ December…*' His voice dropped off. 'What the hell is this all about? Am I reading this correctly? I am to spend *two* days in the company of some agent on the British mainland, my God.'

'I was told that we'd been personally selected for a most important task before we left Bergen,' said Von Bramsdorf. 'Our orders were relayed directly from Dönitz's office. I had no idea what it involved.'

Reiniger read on, focussing on the chilling words at the foot of the signal…

…Remain on station Loch Coinneach for thirty minutes <u>only</u>.
Following signal will confirm presence of shore party – <u>The Drumbeater is</u>
<u>ready for collection</u>.
If no signal received by 0031hours, you will depart immediately and proceed
to Bergen.

'Signal confirming presence of shore party… Would I be right in assuming from that wording, we are to collect someone…? Or is it referring to me? And who is this *Drumbeater*?'

Von Bramsdorf shrugged and took a sip his schnapps. 'I don't know, that's the truth. I think it's best we just do as we are told and I'm sure all will become clear.' The CO was dutifully accepting his orders without question, as Reiniger would have expected.

'That's all very well Felix, but you're not the poor bastard who's been selected to go ashore and play at being a spy. I never joined the *Kriegsmarine* to do that.'

The captain smiled. 'Remember what I always say; variety prevents complacency, Jürgen. Besides, you may get that second Iron Cross, possibly something better!' He raised his glass. 'Prost! Here's to the *Drumbeater*… whoever he or she is!'

Reiniger drained his glass with a flick of the head. 'I'm not happy about this Felix, not happy at all.'

Von Bramsdorf poured him another schnapps, then fixed him with a solemn stare. 'Yours is not to reason why, Jürgen. Orders are orders.' The stern visage then melted away. 'I know this must have come as a shock to you, my friend. I wouldn't normally offer you a second schnapps whilst on watch, so think yourself lucky, eh?' He perched himself on the desk, and once again fixed Reiniger in his sights. 'Tell me Jürgen, are you sure you cannot think of a reason why you have been selected for this task?'

'I have absolutely no idea. I speak a little English that's all.'

'Very well. Best you get back to the control room. It goes without saying, don't mention this to anyone. I'll brief the crew later.' Von Bramsdorf stuffed the secret order into its envelope, and dropped it into the waste bin next to the desk.

Reiniger finished his drink and got to his feet. 'Thank you sir, I will of course do my duty, whatever that duty is.' As he slipped around the curtain, he just caught a glimpse of the captain touching the flame from his lighter to the torn edge of the envelope.

Von Bramsdorf shuffled around a further ninety degrees, arms loosely draped over the handles of the periscope. Through the eyepiece he

214

could see little more than sea water splashing against the lens. He looked away and blinked as he checked his watch. It was 2100hrs, and U-114 was submerged again. They had made good time since receiving the orders to proceed to Loch Coinneach. The cruise south along the west coasts of the Isles of Lewis and Harris had been challenging but uneventful. The submarine had been tossed about like a twig in a torrent, plummeting into cavernous foaming troughs, before rising again, carried along on the next mountainous wave crest.

The watch crew, clad in oilskins and harnessed to the rails by safety straps, had borne the brunt of the Atlantic's fury. Down below their crewmates had held onto anything they could, praying that the storm would abate. A grim cocktail of sea water and vomit swilled around their feet, resulting in an unbearable fetidness that was now causing the most experienced seamen to gag.

The navigator had suggested they sneak through the Sound of Harris, a narrow and turbulent stretch of water between the island of that name and its neighbouring North Uist. It was a treacherous channel to navigate in such conditions, but Obermeyer had done a good job and they'd slipped through around midday, at periscope depth. The sheltered waters of the Little Minch had provided some considerable respite from the battering and they'd progressed slowly along the west coast of Skye running submerged, but now with time to spare.

'Navigator, confirm our position.' The boat's commander took another peek into the periscope eyepiece.

Obermeyer called across from the chart table; 'The Point of Sleat is abeam of us on the port side sir. Mallaig will be away to starboard.'

Von Bramsdorf turned away from the periscope. 'Can't see much up there, just darkness. Maintain current speed and heading.'

The U-boat slipped quietly into the Sound of Sleat heading north at eight knots. To their left was the barren coastline of the Isle of Skye and to their right, the Scottish mainland.

Von Bramsdorf called out to the *funkobergefreiter* in the hydrophone shack; 'Hydrophones. Any contacts on the surface?'

'Nothing at all sir, weather must be keeping the *Tommis* indoors.' The tension was relieved briefly as a trickle of nervous laughter resonated around the control room

'Umm, don't bank on it.'

Von Bramsdorf joined Obermeyer by the chart table. 'Advise me when we reach the mouth of Loch Coinneach, then if all is well, we'll surface.' He turned to Reiniger. 'Best you go and prepare yourself to go ashore, Jürgen.'

'Yes, sir.' The big man swung through the hatchway and disappeared.

Quietness descended over the occupants of the control room. The captain had briefed the crew as to the nature of their mission. They were all acutely aware that they were in a dangerous place, enemy territory surrounded them on all sides and, if detected, there was little chance of survival. The weather and the sea were now their only allies.

After nearly forty minutes, Obermeyer called out; 'Mouth of Loch Coinneach should be off our starboard bow now sir.'

'Thank you, navigator.' Von Bramsdorf returned to the periscope and after a complete revolution, snapped the handles up. The metal column sank downward into its housing with a protracted hiss.

'Hydrophones, anything?'

'Still nothing, sir.'

'Good, surface the boat.'

U-114 emerged slowly from the sanctuary of the Sound's tenebrous depths. First the bow, then the conning tower quietly rising through the fast-running swell.

Von Bramsdorf was quick to reach the bridge. Clad in oilskins and thick gloves, he was relieved to feel the chill of the night air gripping his cheeks. The warm, sweet stench of vomit quickly cleared from his nostrils as he took in a deep lungful of salty air. Now he felt human again.

The night was black as pitch; no moon only snow, large flakes colliding with his eyelids like frozen needles. He could just make out the mouth of Loch Coinneach, guarded on either side by massive granite bastions that rose up into the darkness. Surf broke violently against their glistening cliffs like ragged white claws reaching up from an abyss.

He flicked opened the voice tube. 'Fifteen degrees starboard rudder, ahead one third.' His watch now said ten o'clock.

'Fifteen of starboard rudder now on sir,' came the confirmation from the control room.

The M.A.N marine diesels had now engaged and their comforting throb drifted up from below as the bow swung slowly around and headed into the forbidding glacial jaws of Loch Coinneach. However the sound of the submarine's engines, far from providing comfort, soon added to Von Bramsdorf's sense of anxiety, echoing off the rocky sides of the loch and amplifying their slow steady beat. He could feel the gentle thud of his heartbeat as he leant heavily against the bridge rail, his tired eyes straining into his binoculars. If they were heard, or worse, spotted now, they'd be nothing less than rats in a trap.

Reiniger appeared beside him, diverting his attention momentarily from the dark chasm ahead. 'Are you going ashore like that? I thought you'd want to be a little less conspicuous,' said Von Bramsdorf.

Reiniger was wearing his leather sea coat, upon which the epaulettes of an *oberleutnant zur see* adorned the shoulders. Under the coat he wore his tunic and a thick polo-neck jumper. His uniform cap was planted firmly on his head. 'I'm not a spy and I do not intend to get shot as one. I've got some other clothes in the bag, should I need them, but I intend to go ashore as a German naval officer, nothing less.'

'Do you have a sidearm?'

'Yes of course, Felix. But I have little intention of using it!'

Von Bramsdorf grinned and looked away, amused by his colleague's sense of chivalry. Reiniger was a good and courageous officer, but the uncertainty and secrecy surrounding the mysterious task ahead of him was clearly eating him up inside.

It was not long before the sides of the loch began to open out in front of them. The captain called down to the control room: 'Five degrees left rudder, ahead slow.'

The engine tone became softer, and the boat noticeably slowed. The bow turned slightly. 'Midships.'

The submarine was now running along the northern side of the loch. The watch crew peered out into what amounted to emptiness, hoping to spot the small islet of Eilean Ceann-Cinnidh, behind which was the beach onto which Reiniger would land. A further ten minutes passed, then Von Bramsdorf spotted it materialising gradually from the darkness, a small island topped with spindly trees, bigger than the other rocky islets they had passed earlier. He turned to Reiniger. 'Best you get down onto the casing and prepare to launch the dinghy. Take an extra man with you to the beach, as insurance.'

'Aye sir, will do.' He turned and swung onto the ladder from the *wintergarten* platform.

Von Bramsdorf called after him; 'Jürgen, good luck, see you in forty-eight hours.'

Reiniger raised a hand in acknowledgement and disappeared quickly down the ladder. His captain returned to the task in hand; the island was now abeam of them on the port side. He called down to the control room; 'Depth under keel?'

'Forty metres sir,' came the reply from Obermeyer.

'Good, all stop… man the flak gun.'

'All stop, sir. Sending up the gun crew, sir.'

The engine noise died away and all was quiet. Only the lapping of water against metal and the whispers of the men preparing the dinghy on the casing below pierced the silence. Von Bramsdorf surveyed the shoreline through his binoculars. Behind him, the twenty millimetre flak canon was cranked around towards the beach and cocked by a nervous young rating.

Nothing, just darkness. Were they in the right place? The luminous dial on his watch said two minutes to eleven. He panned the binoculars around for a second time, and on this occasion there *was* something; a brief flash of light from the shoreline. His glasses swung back and there it was again, a steady on-off torch beam from the beach. He leant over the side of the conning tower and called to Reiniger, his voice hushed; 'Can you see it, Jürgen?'

'Yes sir, we're launching the dinghy now.'

There was a faint *thwack* as the rubber boat hit the water, then a crewman climbed in, positioning himself with the oars. Reiniger was next, followed by another rating carrying a Schmeisser machine pistol. The crowded little boat then manoeuvred away towards the light.

It was about a hundred metres to the beach. Reiniger looked back as the long silhouette of the submarine faded into the murk. His attention reverted to the route ahead, prompting him to remove the Walther P38 automatic from his pocket and flick off the safety catch. The crewman followed his lead and cocked the Schmeisser, somewhere behind his left ear.

As they approached the shoreline more detail became clear; a rocky beach, dusted by snow, sloping gently upwards from the water's edge. Dark foliage grew along the western side and then the terrain rose steeply behind. As the oars sloshed through the water, Reiniger stared into the night wide-eyed, blinking away the snowflakes that were still falling steadily and searching for the man they called *Phoebus*.

It seemed to have taken an age to reach the beach, but in fact it took only a few minutes. As the dinghy grounded itself upon the pebbles the oarsman leapt out into the shallow water to steady the craft. Reiniger emerged next, somehow managing to keep his boots dry. The remaining crewman threw him the small bag that he'd taken with him. As he caught it clumsily under one arm, he heard a voice further up the beach.

'Good evening to you... and right on time too!'

The man's voice had a soft Scottish accent, and was closely followed by the emergence of a dark figure; slightly built, no more than five feet six tall. His arms were raised as if in a state of surrender, but he didn't appear the slightest bit nervous. 'Don't worry, I left the gun in the car.'

Reiniger tracked the man's approach, his pistol aimed at him from an extended arm. He could hear his heart pounding against his chest. 'Are the herring plentiful in these parts?' He blurted the words out in heavily accented English.

'Oh I don't know,' said the man, almost blithesomely. 'I prefer to hunt the deer.'

Reiniger lowered his pistol, sensing that the Schmeisser was still levelled at the man's chest. He could see him clearly now. He was no more than forty, had fairish hair and what appeared to be a smudge of a moustache under his nose. The man cautiously lowered one arm and extended it in greeting. Reiniger grasped the open hand. He now saw that his host to be was wearing a thick tweed suit, complete with waistcoat and glinting watch chain.

'Welcome to Scotland *Oberleutnant* Reiniger, pleased to meet you. I'm *Phoebus*.' This time the words were in fluent German.

Reiniger picked up his bag and turned to the crewmen. 'Go,' he ordered, 'now.'

The two men didn't need telling twice. They leapt back into the boat, the gun carrier having pushed it backwards into the shallows. The steady cyclic sound of paddle strokes then retreated into the snow-laden night.

Chapter Twenty

Phoebus placed a comforting arm around Reiniger's shoulder as they walked up the beach. 'Best we get you out of this uniform, or neither of us will survive for long,' he remarked, shaking his head in disbelief.

'Spying is not something I have much experience of,' Reiniger replied. 'I assume you'll be explaining to me exactly what form of spying I'm to be engaged in?'

The Scotsman laughed. 'No, you're way off mark. You're not going to be doing any spying old son, that's what I'm here for. By the way, do you mind if I call you Jürgen?'

'Not at all. So what do I call you?'

'*Phoebus*,' came the curt reply. 'That'll do fine.'

'Umm, strange choice of name for an *Abwher* agent, and would you consider yourself to be a *radiant* character?'

'I'm sorry, you've lost me.'

Reiniger grinned. '*Phoebus*, in Greek mythology, an epithet of the god Apollo, means literally, *the radiant one.*'

'Ah, a student of ancient Greece, Jürgen, then I certainly hope I can live up to my name.' He paused to catch his breath. 'So why the interest in Greek mythology?'

'I travelled to Greece before the war… I was fascinated by the antiquities there. I suppose it prompted me to read about their culture, if only to understand the significance of what I was looking at.'

Their conversation was placed on hold whilst they scrambled up the slope to the narrow road above. There, *Phoebus'* slush splattered Morris Eight awaited them, parked in the lay-by hewn from the adjacent hillside.

Reiniger was of the opinion that the car had definitely seen better days. Its black bodywork was dented in places and the passenger side door, which appeared to be a contrasting red colour, sported a deep longitudinal scratch. He walked around the vehicle and tapped one of the headlamps mounted beside the bonnet.

'Wouldn't have thought you'd need these up here,' he joked, referring to the bulky blackout filter fixed to the headlamp. *Phoebus* reached inside and emerged with a long gabardine raincoat.

'Rules are rules I'm afraid, even up here, and to flout them would certainly be a mistake! Here, best you put this on.' He slid the raincoat across the bonnet and climbed into the driver's seat.

As they pulled away and headed west along the twisting road that hugged the coastline, Reiniger glanced across to where the submarine had been. He thought he saw it turning away and heading out of the loch, but he couldn't be sure. Whatever the case, it would now be well on its way towards the open sea, and relative safety.

'Must have been a choppy ride in,' said *Phoebus*, breaking the silence.

'Yes, I've had better trips. So are you going to tell me why I'm here?'

'In good time my friend. Best we get home first, don't you think?' He glanced across at Reiniger, sensing his apprehension. 'I can assure you all will become clear… and for the record, I'm about as unhappy about having you here as you are being here. So I certainly intend to make sure that your visit is a short one. That alright with you old son?'

'That suits me fine,' Reiniger retorted.

'Still, nothing wrong with getting to know each other a little. Where do you hail from, Jürgen?'

'Hail from?'

'Sorry… *come* from, live?'

'Oh, I see… Bremerhaven.'

'Do you have family there?'

'Father and two sisters, my mother died some time ago.'

'Are you close to your father and sisters?'

'Yes, I like to think so, but I don't see much of them these days. What about you?'

'I was born near Dumfries, down in the Lowlands. My father was a local school teacher down there. I'm ashamed to admit he was something of a bully. We never saw eye to eye when I was growing up.' He laughed, and shook his head.

'Was he cruel to you?'

'The old bastard threatened to throw me down the well behind the school house once.'

'That's terrible. Do you keep in touch with any of your family?'

'I'm afraid I haven't seen any of my immediate family for several years. I've tended to move around a bit… and I'm sure they haven't missed me.'

Reiniger could sense the bitterness in his voice. 'So, how did a Scotsman end up working for the *Abwher*?'

'Ah, that's a long story, perhaps for another time.' *Phoebus* clearly did not wish to dwell on his own life history.

There was another period of silence, a lengthy one this time. The two men peered into the darkness ahead, both engrossed in their own thoughts. All the while, the stumpy little wipers did their inefficient best to clear the windscreen of wet snow. To make things worse, the visibility afforded by the masked headlamps was at best minimal, prompting Reiniger to hope to God that they wouldn't meet anything coming the other way.

It was close to midnight when they entered Camuscraig. A row of tiny fishermen's cottages lined the village street, their windows darkened, their occupants presumably tucked up cosily in bed.

Reiniger sensed himself dozing off, a state no doubt brought on by the warmth and motion of the car, but he was far from having lapsed into sleep. Every turn and bump in the road succeeded in jarring him back to full consciousness. Then, during one such momentary catnap whilst they passed the church on the outskirts of the village, he felt the vehicle swerve to the right and skid to a halt.

'Stay here,' the agent snapped, and got out of the car.

A bicycle lay in the middle of the road, it's slowly revolving rear wheel half covering the body of the youth who'd been riding it. Reiniger watched anxiously from his open window as *Phoebus* lifted the frame of the machine off the boy and helped him to sit up. He yelped in pain as he moved and clutched at his left knee.

Just then, Reiniger became aware of another motor car heading towards them from the opposite direction. As it approached, the slits of light from its own hooded headlamps provided a faint pool of illumination on the road ahead of it. The small black Austin Ten eased to a halt next to *Phoebus'* vehicle. He looked across as the three occupants, a man in khaki military uniform and two young women, jumped out. They ran back towards the agent who was still speaking to the stricken cyclist.

Reiniger sank lower in his seat and pulled the collar of the raincoat up around his neck. He heard voices in the dark; Scottish accents, a woman asking, 'Are you alright Lachlan, what happened?'

What happened next was wholly unexpected. There was a sharp tap on the roof, directly above Reiniger's head. The German turned instinctively to see where the noise had originated from. A tall man of similar build to himself, peered in at him. He was wearing British military battledress and a khaki Tam O'Shanter pulled low over his head, to which was affixed the stag's head insignia of the Seaforth Highlanders.

'Are you not concerned that a man's been injured back there, mister?'

Reiniger recoiled as the sweet aroma of digested alcohol reached his nostrils. 'I'm sorry,' he said, lost for any other suitable words within his limited vocabulary. The Scotsman swayed and leant on the car roof to steady himself.

'Are you bloody foreign?' he enquired, trying to focus on Reiniger's darkened features. Reiniger again struggled to think of something to say. Then a woman appeared at the car door and placed a hand on the man's shoulder.

'Come away Dugald, you're drunk, leave the poor man alone.' Then to Reiniger, she said, 'I'm sorry about my brother, he's a little the worse for wear I'm afraid.'

Reiniger raised a hand in acknowledgement, but remained silent. The woman was extremely attractive and in her early twenties.

'I'm going nowhere, Ursel; I want to know why this fella's keepin' himself hidden away in here.'

He leaned into the car and looked about. He then withdrew suddenly. 'Jesus Christ, that's a bloody German cap on the back seat. Get out of the car you bastard.'

'For God's sake Dugald, don't be silly,' Ursel protested, pulling him back by the arm. 'You can't see straight.'

Reiniger felt for the gun in his pocket, but there was no need. *Phoebus* had heard the commotion and had returned to the car. He swung the drunken soldier away by the arm, sending him crashing into a nearby hedge. Then he leapt into the car and started the engine, ignoring the protestation of the Scotsman's female companion. *Phoebus* and his protégé sped away, lights now extinguished, and disappeared into the night.

Ursel Matheson supported her brother by the arm as he clambered out of the hedge. Once he was upright again, she brushed the leaves off his uniform. 'Are you alright?' she enquired. 'Are you sure that it was a German cap you saw? You know there are all manner of foreign troops over here these days.'

'It was bloody German alright, there was a bloody eagle on that cap.'

The other woman joined them, having finally managed to get

the injured cyclist moving again. 'What on earth happened just now?' she enquired.

Isobel Grant had grown into a strikingly attractive young woman. She'd retained her mane of luxuriant dark hair since childhood, and now her gleaming dark eyes gazed out anxiously from beneath its fringe.

'Dugald thinks the man in the car was German,' said Ursel in a mocking tone.

'I don't *think*, I *know*,' Dugald muttered, apparently experiencing some difficulty in forming his words. 'I'm going to speak to Davie MacAllister... now.' He staggered off along the road, heading towards the village policeman's house.

'He's going to get himself into all sorts of bother,' said Ursel, squeezing Isobel's arm. 'I'll go and look after him. Can you get Lachlan home?'

'Aye, of course, leave him to me,' Isobel replied, adjusting her scarf.

'Mr Matheson, I understand what you're telling me. And how long ago did all this happen?' PC MacAllister was clearly irritated by the late-night intrusion. He wrapped his dressing gown tightly around him as the night's chill invaded the hallway of his cottage.

'About ten, fifteen minutes ago,' Dugald responded, his voice raised.

'And you say there was a *German* military cap on the back seat of the car?'

'Aye, that's exactly what I'm saying, Constable,' Dugald slurred.

MacAllister turned to Ursel. 'Did you see this so-called cap, Miss Matheson?'

No, I'm afraid not Davie. I'm sure Dugald must be mistaken, he's had a lot to drink tonight. But it was strange the way they made off like that, I suppose.'

'How do you mean *strange*, Miss?'

'Well this chap pushed Dugald into the hedge, got into the car and drove off with the lights off. I suppose he must have been thinking my brother was spoiling for a fight.'

'I see, and where has your brother been tonight?'

'I can bloody well answer for myself you know,' Dugald protested. 'I've been at a regimental dinner in Inverness, if you must know.' He swayed precariously and took hold of the door frame for support.

'And did you manage to read the car's number plate, sir?'

'No, the bloody thing went off too quickly, and with the lights off like she just told you.'

'Well Mr Matheson, there's not much I can do tonight. They'll be long gone by now. I'll make a note of the men's descriptions, then I'll speak to the inspector at Inverness and let him know what has happened. In the meantime, I suggest you get yourselves home and get some sleep.' The descriptions provided by the pair were frustratingly vague, an observation that the constable was eager to share.

'Y'know, Constable MacAllister, I'm not at all sure you're taking me seriously. Be it on your head if I'm proved to be right.' Dugald pointed an accusing finger in the policeman's direction, working hard to keep his arm raised, his eyelids drooped heavily over the bloodshot spheres beneath.

MacAllister was losing patience. 'I think it best you go home now young man, otherwise you may live to regret the consequences yourself.'

Ursel took the hint, and steered her brother away.

'I take it young Lachie Macdonald is alright?' MacAllister enquired. 'I'll go and see him tomorrow.'

Ursel smiled back. 'Aye, he seems alright, just a few bruises that's all. My cousin Isobel has taken him home.'

'Good, now away home with you both, and if you see any parachutists on the way give me a call in the morning.' Ursel waved as she led her intoxicated brother back to the car.

Isobel was standing hunched against the biting wind when Ursel and Dugald joined her. She was waiting outside the terraced fisherman's cottage that fifteen-year-old Lachlan Macdonald shared with his elderly grandmother. She clambered into the back seat of the car and brushed the snow from her coat. 'I think he'll live,' she declared. 'Best we get on our way the now.'

'Wait!' Dugald fumbled with the door catch and threw it open. He climbed out and staggered across to Lachlan's front door, rapping on it repeatedly until it finally opened. Lachlan stood nervously framed in the doorway, nursing his bruised arm.

'Macdonald, listen to me. If you see that bloody car again, the one that just ran you off the road, I want you to call me at Glendaig Manse, d'you understand?'

Lachlan was not going to argue. 'Aye, Mr Matheson, I'll do that sir. I'd be needing to use the public telephone though.'

'Yes, yes, you do that.' He stuffed his hand into his pocket and handed the youth some coins. 'Here, use these to call. I'll make it worth your while laddie, so keep your eyes well-peeled.'

'You can count on me, sir.'

'Good lad, now you get yourself away to bed. I'll be waiting to hear from you.'

Dugald turned and zigzagged his way back to the car. He poked his head in through the open door and grinned. 'I'll get the bastard if he comes back along here, you mark my words.' Then he tumbled onto the front seat. Ursel leant across him and closed the door. 'You're in no state to *get* anybody Dugald, so shut up and keep quiet until I get you home.'

Phoebus and Reiniger had reached the main road by the time the Mathesons had concluded their conversation with the policeman. They were now speeding across the wilderness east of Glenshiel, avoiding the patches of snow which were creeping ominously across the frozen road. Reiniger glanced over his shoulder. 'Can't see anything behind us,' he said.

'It's not what's behind us that worries me, it's what's ahead of us,' *Phoebus* replied, struggling to keep the centre line of the road in sight.

'What do you mean?'

'Well if the snow doesn't block the road further on, there's a distinct possibility the police will... if the occupants of that car have reported seeing your cap on the back seat. Bloody cyclist. And I can't believe I left it there on the seat.'

'I'm sorry, I should've thought... but surely the police won't accept the word of a man that drunk?'

The agent glanced across at him. 'I hope for both our sakes you're right. The two women weren't drunk though.'

The road seemed to go on forever, the soft white glow of the newly deposited snow contrasting sharply with the inky blackness of the road surface that still remained uncovered.

They passed a junction to their right. There was no signpost. 'Where does that road go to?' Reiniger asked, just to make conversation.

'Down to Glengarry. They've removed the fingerpost so as to confuse you chaps if and when you invade.'

Reiniger smiled. 'I think our glorious Führer's given up on that idea, at least for the time being.'

The conditions eased a little as they descended into Glenmoriston Forest. The unrelenting splashes of snow on the windscreen then ceased completely. *Phoebus* allowed the car's speed to drop off. 'If they're going to be waiting for us, it'll be down here, where we meet the main road along to Inverness.'

He pulled into the side of the road just outside Invermoriston village. 'Stay here,' he said for the second time that evening, and climbed out of the car. Reiniger watched him as he jogged away towards the village.

At least ten minutes elapsed before *Phoebus* returned. 'All clear,' he said as he slid into the driver's seat.

They turned left at the junction further down the road and now headed along the side of Loch Ness. The moonless night robbed Reiniger of any view of the famous expanse of water that snaked its way through the Great Glen. Only the dim outline of the pines lining the road could be made out in the light from the car's ineffective headlamps.

After several miles, *Phoebus* turned off the road onto a gravel track that climbed steeply up the hillside beside the loch. A crumbling wooden post stood by the main road. Its arm bore the name *Castle Brae Cottage*.

At the top of the track was a small stone cottage with dormer windows peeking out from a steeply angled roof. A large wooden workshop, its double doors wide open, stood close by and it was into this structure that *Phoebus* drove the car. He then closed and padlocked the double doors and led his visitor to the front door.

Reiniger had retrieved his bag and cap from the car's back seat. He stood by the workshop doors for a moment, taking in his surroundings.

'Home sweet home,' said *Phoebus*, waiting at the front door.

A peaty aroma greeted Reiniger as he stepped into the hallway. It was a smell he'd not come across before, but assumed it originated from the embers of the open fire that still crackled in the small sitting room. *Phoebus* closed the door and turned on the light. 'Your room is at the top of the stairs. There's some spare clothes in the wardrobe. Put them on and get rid of that uniform. We'll store it in the woodshed for the time being.'

Reiniger slowly climbed the stairs. The flaking white treads creaked under his weight. He was beginning to feel weary now, and yearned for a comfortable bed and a good night's sleep.

His allotted room was plain, yet comfortably furnished. A single bed, covered by a large red overhanging quilt stood in one corner. A bedside table with a lamp, a wooden wardrobe and an old chair were the only other items of furniture. Stacked neatly on the chair was a pile of coarse grey blankets. The walls were bare, recently whitewashed from the pristine state of them. The only wall-hanging was a small watercolour of a stone cottage overlooking a loch, which hung above the bed. Reiniger tested the mattress with his fist whilst he gazed up at the painting. The bed was firm and freshly made up. He could smell the clean linen; a far cry from his berth on the stinking U-boat.

He removed the Walther pistol from his pocket and slid it under the pillow. One couldn't be too careful in these circumstances. In the wardrobe was a surprisingly varied collection of clothing. He selected a pair of dark flannels and a blue fisherman's jersey and, having changed, made his way downstairs again.

The sitting room was dimly lit, but his host had been busy attending to the fire, as it now roared within the soot-stained stone hearth. The light from the flickering flames danced around the room, firing shadows across the uneven walls. *Phoebus* was setting a small round table in the corner.

'Make yourself at home,' he said, retreating into the tiny kitchen. Reiniger sat down on the battered leather sofa that stood in front of the hearth. He stared into the flames, thinking of his comrades who were still braving the harsh Atlantic weather off the coast of Skye.

'Get this down you.' *Phoebus* thrust a large glass of malt whisky under his nose. 'I've got some broth heating on the stove. It'll be ready in no time.' He raised his glass. '*Slàinte mhath*! Or perhaps you'd prefer *prost*!'

Reiniger raised his glass, sniffed the fumes rising from within it, and took a slug of the contents. '*Prost*,' he said. '*Now* will you tell me why I'm here?'

Phoebus slumped into an equally battered armchair on the other side of the room. 'Of course I will, but it's too late to discuss the details tonight. I'll explain in depth tomorrow… or perhaps I should say, later today!' he sipped from his glass, a long measured sip as if he intended to keep his guest in suspense.

'I believe you know a man called Max Friedmann. He's currently a *korvettenkapitän* in the *Ubootwaffe*.'

Reiniger seemed surprised that Friedmann's name had been

mentioned. Max was the last person he'd expected to be connected to his current adventure. 'Yes I know him, but haven't seen him in a good while. He's become quite the national hero in Germany.'

'How did you get to know him?' *Phoebus* asked.

'We were good friends for a time, just after we joined the *Kriegsmarine*.' He pursed his lips, privately reminiscing about their early days in the navy together. 'I don't remember when our paths last crossed. It must have been three years or more.'

Phoebus sloshed his whisky around his glass. 'Well Jürgen, your old chum has got himself captured by the British and you, my friend, are going to help him escape… with a little help from me, of course.'

Reiniger stared at him, wide-eyed and silent. Then at last he spoke. 'I assume you must be joking,' he said, followed up with a nervous cough.

Phoebus grinned as he lifted his glass to his mouth. 'I've never been more serious in my life, old son.'

Chapter Twenty-One

Monday 30th December

Phoebus had resolutely refused to discuss any further details of the plan to free Max Friedmann that night. The two men had consumed their broth in silence and soon after, Reiniger had gone to bed. His mind was awash with speculation as to what dangers the next few days would bring, but the whisky and the warmth of the blankets wrapped around him had done their work, and he'd quickly lapsed into unconsciousness.

The following morning dawned cold and grey. A thin crust of ice clung to the glass inside the window. Reiniger lay for a while, dreading the unwelcome transition from bed to room-temperature that his body was about to make. It was as he'd expected; the room was icy cold, and the process of dressing was completed as speedily as possible.

As he descended the stairs the warmth of the sitting room rose to meet him. His host was sitting at the table eating from a steaming bowl of porridge. 'Sit down, I'll get you some,' he said cheerfully as Reiniger entered the room. 'How did you sleep?'

'Well, thanks. At least the room wasn't pitching up and down like I'm used to!'

Phoebus poured his companion a mug of tea from the pot on the table. He got up and went to the kitchen, returning a few seconds later with another bowl of porridge. He placed it before Reiniger, who sampled it with caution. His features contorted momentarily, indicating that the oaty concoction was never going to feature amongst his favourite foods. 'Keep at it man, it's an acquired taste but it'll do you the power of good,' *Phoebus* reassured him. Reiniger just nodded and reluctantly slid another spoonful into his mouth.

'Right, down to business,' said *Phoebus*. 'I expect you'll be wanting to know how we're going to remove Friedmann from the clutches of the enemy, eh?'

'You have my full attention,' said Reiniger, his facial expression switching rapidly to one of expectation. 'Firstly, I'd like to know why he is a prisoner of the British... how did it happen?'

Phoebus shrugged. 'I don't know all the details myself, but I understand he was captured when they sank one of your U-boats somewhere out in the Atlantic. I believe it was back on the twenty-first of this month. The submarine was apparently engaged on some sort of secret mission, and carrying new weapons technology that was to be used in action for the first time.'

'Is that why he was on the boat, to oversee the trial of this so called new weapon? The last I heard was that he was recovering from injuries sustained on his last mission, when he sank a number of ships in the Irish Sea.'

'Evidently he'd recovered, at least sufficiently to take part in this latest venture. What I do know is that Admirals Von Thalberg and Dönitz, your masters in *BdU*, want him back very badly. Whether it's because of the knowledge he's privy to, or whether there is some other political motive involved, I don't know. Perhaps both theories have some relevance.'

'Everyone back home knew Friedmann had become a tool of the Reich,' said Reiniger. 'He was being exploited by Hitler and his cronies to promote their propaganda war. They wouldn't have risked losing him now, especially during a period when he was at his most useful. No, I fear the Admirals have acted alone, without the Führer's knowledge, and are now bitterly regretting their decision. I knew Max well; he wouldn't have taken too kindly to his role as a propaganda icon, he would've wanted to be back at sea as soon as possible, doing what he loves. Now it appears *we've* got to pick up the pieces.' He sighed heavily. 'So why *me*, why am *I* here?'

Phoebus scooped up a last spoonful of porridge. 'Because you were in the right place at the right time. My plan requires two people to facilitate the escape. One to *stop* the train that'll be carrying Friedmann to London, and one to be *on* the train... someone who knows him by sight and can pick him out from the contingent of POW's travelling with him. And when we do locate him, we want him to trust his liberator without question. We don't have time for arguments as to whether he will comply with our instructions or not. *You* were considered to be our best bet; a personal friend who could be delivered to me within the very limited time-span set out for this operation.'

'I see, so this plan involves springing him from a train, right under the *Tommis* noses... by *me* I suppose?'

Phoebus went to a cupboard behind the table. From it he produced a rolled-up map and spread it out across the table. He pointed to the long finger of blue marked *Loch Ness*. 'We're here; half way along the loch, just to the west of Urquhart Castle.' He looked up. 'Tomorrow afternoon at 1.35pm a train will leave Thurso, up here on the north coast, for London. It will be carrying a large contingent of allied service personnel from Scapa Flow Naval Base. In addition there will a number of *Luftwaffe* and *Kriegsmarine* prisoners of war on board, heading for the various interrogation centres in England. We don't know how many. Amongst them will be Max Friedmann who, if we don't get to him first, will, according to my contact, be transferred to the centre known as the "London Cage". I'm told that Friedmann will be travelling at the rear of the train, in a compartment with two military policemen, both of whom will be carrying side arms. There may also be another escort patrolling in the corridor outside the compartment. I'm assuming they will be wanting to keep the prisoners isolated from the other passengers, so there shouldn't be anyone else present in the corridor... the MPs will no doubt make sure of that. I also believe the other prisoners will be held in separate compartments within the same coach.'

'How do you know all this?' Reiniger asked, shaking his head in disbelief.

'Let's just say I have a friend on the inside, an attractive little *Wren* working in the King's Harbourmaster's Office in Lyness. She's worked all over the base at Scapa, the communications centre at Wee Fea, depot ships, you name it. She's a bit of a good time girl. Men tend to regard her as a bit of a catch, so much so, that's she's now got lots of friends in lots of places.'

'Can you trust her?'

'Oh, completely. She's a good Catholic girl, married to a poor unsuspecting chap working down at the Western Approaches Command Centre in Liverpool. She'd never want him to know about the little... how shall I put it... liaisons that *we* enjoy when she stops off in Inverness on her way down to visit hubby. She wanted out last time I saw her, but I told her that would be unwise for the time being. Besides, I keep her well supplied with nylons, cigarettes and cash, for which she's always grateful.' He tugged at his ear lobe. 'Then of course, if the military authorities at Scapa Flow ever learnt of her treachery, I assume she'd hang! That would be such a pity. So I suppose you could say I own her for the time being.' He turned his attention back to the map.

'You really are a cold-hearted bastard aren't you?' Reiniger, glared at the little man. *Phoebus* glanced back, unmoved. His piercing, unblinking eyes darted from side to side, as if studying every tiny blemish on Reiniger's face.

'Needs must old son, needs must.' He threw his head back and laughed. 'What is it they say? All's fair in love and war.'

The German felt a shiver run through him. This was not a man to turn your back on.

A solemn expression had now returned to the Scotsman's face. 'So, now you know about my love life, let's get back to more important things. This train will arrive at Dingwall, a little to the north of here, at around 6.35pm. We'll be waiting, and you will board the train here. It will take on water, and then depart at 6.50pm. You then have until eight o'clock to locate Friedmann and secure him.'

'What happens at eight o'clock?'

'I stop the train at Culloden Viaduct or, to be precise, at the small station just before it, just here… Drumossie.' He pointed to the map. A red dot indicated Drumossie Moor station, located on remote moorland at the western end of the massive stone viaduct. The twenty-eight spans of the viaduct were symbolised in bold black with small v-shaped ramparts. Underneath, the River Nairn, a meandering line of bright blue, flowed northwards through a wide valley to the Moray Firth.

'And how exactly are you going to stop the train? By lying across the track?'

'Nothing so dramatic, old son. I intend to enlist the help of the signalman at the station. You will have *only* one minute from when the train stops to get off. I don't want the signalmen further along the line to start questioning the delay. Anyway, that's my problem. So all you and Friedmann need to do is hop off the train, wait until it's gone, and then make your way across the viaduct. Get yourselves down the embankment at the east end, to the road, and I'll pick you up in the car there.'

'But surely if you're going to be at the station yourself, you can pick us up there?' Reiniger seemed confused.

'I could. In fact the part of the train you'll hopefully be in will indeed overhang the station. But just in case I encounter any problems, I'd rather you make your own way from the station to the place I described. I feel it would be safer to start our journey west from there. Trust me, Jürgen.'

'Alright, you know best I suppose.'

'Believe me, I most certainly do. So, then we wend our way along the back roads through here to Loch Ness and across to Glendaig, where your boys will hopefully be waiting in their submarine. They've been ordered to pick you up at midnight, and wait for only thirty minutes, which means time is of the essence. So, any questions?'

'Yes, how exactly do I deal with the three escorts without drawing attention to myself for heaven's sake?'

'Well, I would expect you to be using a little of your own initiative during this stage of the proceedings. It's impossible to formulate too rigid a plan, but this might be useful.' He went over to the armchair and pushed it aside. Stooping down, and with a muffled grunt, he lifted a dusty flagstone from the floor. He leaned into the void underneath and retrieved an object wrapped in an oily cloth. Having placed it on the table, he carefully unwrapped the cloth. The dull metallic barrel of a Walther P38 pistol emerged from the wrapping. In essence, it was a similar model to the one Reiniger had brought with him from the U-boat; standard military issue, but this example was different. It had a long cylindrical attachment screwed to the barrel. Reiniger picked it up and ran his hand over the smooth steel extension.

'What on earth is this?' he asked.

'It's called a suppressor. Designed to eliminate muzzle flash and reduce sonic pressure when the gun is discharged.'

'Which means…?'

'…Which means you can kill people *quietly*. That's what it means. Some individuals call them silencers, but that's a bit of a misnomer as they don't actually silence the weapon.'

'I've never heard of such a thing before,' said Reiniger, still caressing the so-called suppressor.

'Oh they've been around for some time. Not the sort of equipment the German military use on a day to day basis, but they have been issued to panzer units on the eastern front, predominantly for night patrols.'

'I see, and I'm supposed to use this against Max's escorts, just kill them in cold blood?'

'Well, if they're dead, they're not going to give you any problems are they?'

Reiniger chewed his lip thoughtfully. 'Yesterday I was just a naval officer,' he mused. 'Today, it would appear I'm a spy, and now a cold-blooded killer.'

'Spare me the morality speech,' said *Phoebus* derisively. 'You and your chums in the *Ubootwaffe* kill hundreds of merchant seamen every month with your guns and torpedoes, what's the difference?'

'At least they have a chance.'

'Well these escorts will be armed as well, so they *will* have a chance, and if you don't act quickly enough it'll be you that's dead, and possibly Friedmann too. Does that satisfy your sense of conscience?'

Reiniger didn't reply. He'd released the magazine from the stock of the Walther and was checking the number of rounds stacked therein. 'A full magazine of eight and one in the breach. That should suffice,' said *Phoebus*, arms folded.

'And what am I to wear when I'm on this train? I assume *Kriegsmarine* uniform is out of the question?'

'I'm glad you mentioned that,' replied *Phoebus* with a grin. 'I've got you a naval cap and greatcoat upstairs. You can wear your own uniform trousers and boots, no one will notice the difference in the dark.'

'Royal Navy issue?'

'No, Polish Navy. More appropriate for someone with your accent, don't you think?'

'How on earth did you get hold of them?'

'Oh I got talking to a nice young laddie in a bar in Inverness the other night. Jan Bielawski was his name. Anyway, he was so drunk by the end of our session, he didn't much care what was going on. So I borrowed his kitbag, coat and cap whilst he was away for a pee. It's probably worth you knowing that he was serving on a Polish ship that had come into Scapa, attached to the Polish Destroyer Squadron. He'd been posted, and was travelling down to Greenock to join another ship there. So that's your cover story for the evening. I've got some of his personal effects so you can fill your pockets with them; Polish coins, photos from home, you know the sort of thing.' He studied the German wide-eyed, expectantly. 'Any other questions?'

'Not for the time being,' said Reiniger, 'but I'm sure I'll think of something before tomorrow night.'

'Good, I'll put these dishes away, and then I need to pop out for a couple of hours. I have to meet up with one of my contacts at the railway works in Inverness. Can you sort that flagstone out by the armchair?'

Reiniger obliged, leaving *Phoebus* to collect the empty porridge bowls. He'd just turned to enter the kitchen when there was a loud rap on the front door. He spun around and pointed to the cupboard under the stairs. 'Get in there, quick, and take that bloody gun with you.'

Reiniger pushed the armchair back into place and grabbed the pistol and map before disappearing into the cupboard. *Phoebus* waited until he was out of sight, then opened the front door. Reiniger could hear the conversation clearly from his musty hiding place.

'Good morning Constable, what can I do for you?'

'Morning sir, we're just following up on some information received last night that a couple of Germans were sighted out on the west coast. Apparently two men in a red and black Morris Eight ran a cyclist off the road.'

'I see, not more reports of fifth columnists. You must be fed up with all this paranoia?'

'Aye, that we are sir, we're getting several reports a week of spies and parachutists, but I'm sure you understand we have to follow up each and every report.'

'Of course. Over in the west you say... So how can I help?'

'Well sir, the locals tell us you've been seen driving a red and black vehicle of the same make, is that correct?'

'Aye, I have one in the workshop over there, but I can assure you gentlemen that I was nowhere near the west coast last night. I was tucked up in front of the fire with a mug of cocoa listening to the light programme on the wireless.'

'All the same sir, can we have a look at the car please?'

'Of course, follow me.'

Reiniger listened, his heart pounding, as the footsteps faded away. His left thumb rested on the safety catch of the Walther, praying he wouldn't need to use it. Minutes seemed like hours. Then he heard voices approaching from afar.

'Sorry to have troubled you sir, thanks for your time.'

'That's quite alright, Constable. Good morning to you both.'

'And you sir. Just for the record, can I have a name please?'

'Of course, it's Chisholm, James Chisholm.'

'Thank you, and would be you working around these parts?'

'Aye, I'm doing some scientific work for the War Office up at Ullapool, can't say a lot more than that I'm afraid.'

'Your secret's safe with us sir, good day to you.'

The sound of a car engine replaced the voices, followed by the crunch of tyres crushing loose stone as the policemen drove back along the track. The front door slammed, and moments later the cupboard door was thrown open.

'Christ, I don't need too many visits like that. All because of your bloody cap.'

It was the first time Reiniger had seen *Phoebus* flustered. He emerged from the darkness, blinking, and brushing himself down. 'Sorry,' he said. 'Do you think they suspected anything?'

'No, I don't think they even considered for a minute that the information was genuine. They kept referring to their informant as a drunken buffoon. Says it all doesn't it? Still, they had a good look round the car. Luckily there was no damage to speak of.'

'So should I be calling you *James* then, or perhaps *Jakob* in our language?'

Phoebus turned on him. 'I thought I'd made it clear that my name is unimportant as far as you're concerned.'

'Alright, sorry I mentioned it. So what now?'

Phoebus placed a large piece of peat on the flagging fire. 'I'm off to Inverness to see my contact about the train schedule tomorrow night. You keep your head down. Don't answer the door, and if necessary slip out the back and into the woods behind the workshop.' He picked up his jacket and stuffed a packet of cigarettes in his pocket.

'I'll see you later then *James*,' Reiniger called after him, not being able to resist a little joke.

Phoebus looked over his shoulder and scowled. 'This is not a time for jokes *Oberleutnant*. Your time would be better spent rehearsing your cover story. Now stay out of sight until I return.' He slammed the door behind him, leaving the German to wallow in his embarrassment.

2 0 0 9

Chapter Twenty-Two

Cadha the collie was nowhere to be seen when Neil opened the old gate and strolled up the path to Mary Galbraith's cottage.

He knocked several times and listened for any sound from within. Nearly a minute elapsed before he heard the sound of shuffling the other side of the door. The swollen wood flexed and resisted as the old door was tugged from the inside. Then it sprung open with a protracted squeal.

Mary supported herself against the door frame, weary from the exertion. 'Oh it's you again Inspector. What can I do for you this time?'

'I was wondering if I could come in for a moment? I just have a couple of questions to ask.'

'Aye, of course.' The old woman turned and shuffled away, disappearing into the shadowy interior of the cottage. Neil followed her and stood in silence as she slowly lowered herself into the same old wing-backed chair. She indicated to him to sit and he complied, perching himself on the edge of the leather sofa.

'Well, what is it you want to know, laddie?'

Neil glanced over to the old photo on the dresser that had attracted his attention during his first visit. 'That old photo over there, the one of your parents and the Grants. Can I have another look at it?'

'If you must, but I cannae think why you're so intrigued by such an old snap.'

Neil returned to the sofa, photo in hand. He studied it closely for a few seconds, then looked over at the old lady. 'I believe one side of this photograph has been cut off,' he said accusingly. 'This girl, Isobel Grant, is looking up at someone taller than her, someone standing close by. Why would that person have been cut out of the picture do you think?'

'I really don't know what you're talking about Inspector. It's a very old photograph, given to me by my cousin David many years ago. As I said before, I wasn't there, so I don't know who was present at the time of its taking.'

'It must be a relatively important photo to still be displayed in your home all these years later.'

'It is, I think it's a particularly bonny picture of my mother and father, if you must know.'

'Can I take it out of the frame for a second?'

'If you must.'

Neil released the clips to the rear of the frame and removed the backing card. The photograph fell onto his lap. He picked it up and turned it over. Written across the back were the words: *Aunt Liz, Uncle Torquil and Muireall with Mother, Father and Iso...* It should have read *Isobel*, but the last three letters were missing, obviously cut off. Under the row of names, a date had been scrawled: *26.12.43.*

'Part of this photo has definitely been cut off. There was someone else in the picture, and they've been removed.' He was unashamedly pursuing the point, but getting anything other than a denial of any knowledge from Mary just wasn't going to happen.

Mary fidgeted around in her chair, and glared at Neil. 'Well whoever else was in that photo is unknown to me. I have no idea who it was, and I don't believe we will ever know all these years later. Are you accusing me of keeping secrets Inspector?'

Her tremor had now become noticeably more pronounced, and Neil didn't want to push his luck. 'Of course not Mary, I was just hoping you could tell me who the missing person was, that's all.'

Mary nodded, acknowledging his climb down and at the same time exhibiting a degree of relief. An awkward silence followed, interrupted only when the front door opened and a man in his mid-sixties walked in. Cadha also appeared from nowhere and made straight for the policeman, sniffing busily at his trousers and shoes.

'She can smell my own dog,' Neil concluded in an attempt to lighten the atmosphere.

Mary ignored his comment. 'This is my son, Iain,' she announced with a frown.

Neil got up and introduced himself. Iain Galbraith was small and wiry, almost bald, and without doubt the source of a faint aroma of fish that had begun to permeate through the cottage. He appeared to Neil to be one of those individuals who struggled to raise a sense of humour; a dour Highlander, no doubt the product of a strict and insular upbringing.

'I thought my mother had provided you with answers to all your questions?' he declared as he removed his battered old leather jacket and hung it on a hook behind the door.

'Aye, she has, but you know what policemen are like. They'll always think of another one to ask.'

'Well hopefully you won't be thinking up any more once you've left here today, Inspector. My mother doesn't need all this at her age. Surely you can see she's not in the best of health?'

'I can assure you I will not trouble you for a moment longer than necessary Mr Galbraith. I was just asking your mother if she had any idea who may have been in this photograph originally. Someone seems to have been cut out of the picture at some stage.'

'I have absolutely no idea what you're on about Inspector. Was someone cut out of that photo Ma?'

'I've just told him, I wasn't there when it was taken. I had no idea that it had been cut,' said Mary.

'There you are then Inspector. Neither of us can help you I'm afraid.'

'Fair enough,' Neil conceded. 'I assume you'll remember the minister who officiated here during the war, Callum Matheson?'

'Aye, I knew him very well,' said Mary. 'What about him?'

'His wife Anna, she was Swiss I believe?'

'Yes, I think she was, but she met Callum when he had a living in Edinburgh.'

'Do you happen to remember her maiden name?'

'Och, what sort of question is that?' Mary growled with a look of disdain. Then just as quickly, her tone softened. 'I did know, once, but I cannae recall it, not now. I'm afraid age is playing havoc with my memory.'

'Don't worry. I'm sure I can find out. What about the name Max Friedmann, does that mean anything to you?'

Mary stared intently at Neil, but said nothing, as if buying herself some time. For a second he thought she was going to respond in the positive. But then she shook her head. 'No, who's he?' she replied, her face blank.

'He was a German naval officer during the war. We thought initially the remains on the beach were his, but we've ruled that out now. We are also considering the theory that he may have escaped from captivity at the end of 1941, and was picked up from the beach where the remains were found. I've recently discovered that this man Friedmann and Anna Matheson, the local minister's wife, came from the same area around the city of Konstanz on the border of Germany and Switzerland. You see, I think this man has links to this area, but I can't prove it just yet.'

'I see,' said Mary, 'well I've never heard of this Max Friedmann. Perhaps it's just a coincidence he and Anna came from the same area.'

'Perhaps, but I don't think so.'

Iain Galbraith was standing behind his mother's chair, his hands firmly grasping the wings either side of Mary's head. 'Have you asked all your questions now Inspector? Only we're about to have our lunch.'

'Yes of course, I'm about done for now, I'll leave you both in peace.'

Neil patted Cadha on the head and stood up. Iain escorted him to the door and opened it. As Neil stood at the doorway, he turned. 'Sorry,' he said. 'Just one other thing.' He grimaced, more as a humorous gesture than an expression of genuine guilt at asking yet another question. Mary was levering herself out of the chair with the aid of her walking stick. She looked up.

'Yes Inspector.' Iain sighed, his annoyance plain to see. 'Can we make this quick please?'

'Do you remember Dugald Matheson, the minister's son?'

Mary's eyes narrowed. 'Aye, of course, what about him?'

'I visited his grave the other day. It appears he died around the same time Max Friedmann went missing. When was it…?' Neil seemed to have difficulty recalling the date.

'It was New Year's Day, 1942, I'll never forget it,' Mary interjected.

'That's right, *tragically taken* the wording on the stone said. You didn't mention him when I asked you about the local folk who'd been lost during the war. Can I ask why?'

'I thought you were asking about the men who'd been killed in action, Inspector. Dugald Matheson was killed in an accident here in Glendaig.'

'So what happened to him Mary?'

The tremor was noticeable again now as Mary leaned heavily on her stick. She winced momentarily. 'Dugald was an avid hunter. He loved stalking the deer. It was tradition for him to accompany Donald Grant, my uncle, and his son David when they went out stalking on the first day of the New Year. They went out as usual, up Beinn Caisteal on that terrible day. David apparently tripped whilst carrying a loaded rifle and shot Dugald through the back. The bullet passed through his heart as I recall, and he died instantly.' She looked away, visibly upset, before continuing.

'I remember them carrying his body back from the hill.' Then she raised a shaking hand to her face, and sat down heavily. 'He was a difficult boy, Dugald. Some found him hard to get along with, but he didn't deserve that.'

'And did the authorities at the time accept the explanation that it was an accident?'

'Aye, of course, the police and the fiscal were informed immediately.'

'Okay, thank you,' said Neil, 'now I *will* leave you in peace.' He bade Iain goodbye, and ambled through the door, escorted by the ever-loyal Cadha.

Mary called after him; 'Inspector?'

'Yes Mary?' He was back in a flash.

'It was *Eichel*... Anna Matheson's maiden name. I've just remembered.'

Neil hovered in the doorway. 'Eichel, did you say?'

'Yes, I remember seeing the name written in a photograph album once. There was a photo of her parents and sister somewhere in the mountains in Switzerland.'

'Your memory is not as bad as you make it out to be, Mary!'

The old lady's expression remained solemn. 'It's an unusual name I suppose.'

'And did any of the Eichels, other than Anna, ever come to Glendaig?'

Mary considered her answer. 'The sister came on occasions. Her name was Katharina, if I remember correctly.'

'Well, thanks again,' said Neil, and he disappeared into the late morning sunshine, a satisfied smile creeping across his face.

The signal bars on Neil's mobile phone had flat lined. He grumbled to himself as he marched down the track, directing a series of maledictive utterances towards his mobile phone provider. On reaching the road through the village, he crossed to the telephone kiosk next to the property called Burnside. Once inside, he found himself pleasantly surprised to find it in working order. There was even a phone directory on the shelf; out of date of course, and almost consumed within the trifid-like grip of the ivy which had invaded the little red structure.

He scooped some coins out of his pocket and called the office.

250

Firstly, to check whether he'd been left any messages, but more importantly, to ask whether Brodie had been enquiring as to his whereabouts. As he chatted with the detective sergeant in the office he peered nonchalantly through the kiosk's murky glass panels. Away to his left he was surprised to see Mary Galbraith scurrying down the track, admittedly with the support of her walking stick, but at a rate of knots he would have considered her incapable of several minutes earlier. She turned left at the metalled road and crossed the bridge before disappearing through the gate of Lochview, Murdo Stuart's cottage.

Neil finished his conversation, relieved that Brodie hadn't been seen all day. He slipped out of the kiosk and returned to his car, parked close by. Once inside, and keeping one eye on the rear view mirror, he unwrapped the garage-bought sandwich he'd purchased during a fuel stop at Camuscraig Stores. Ten minutes passed, then Mary reappeared, retracing her route back up the track towards the farm, and home.

Neil finished his snack and emerged from the car, brushing crumbs from his suit jacket. Less than three minutes later he was standing at the front door of Lochview.

Ursula Stuart opened the door. 'Inspector Strachan, you'll be after speaking to Murdo, no doubt.'

'Aye, Mrs Stuart, if he's in.'

'Come in Inspector, he's in the garden.'

Ursula led him through the house and out through the French doors from the sitting room. 'Murdo, this is Inspector Strachan from Inverness. He wants to ask you some questions about the bones they've found down on the beach.'

Murdo Stuart was seated on a wooden bench on the patio. He looked up from the newspaper he was reading. 'Hello Inspector, I was expecting a call from you. I hope you don't think I killed that poor devil on the beach?'

Murdo was a still a big man, although the frailty of advanced age had replaced the bulk of earlier years. His head was all but bald, heavily tanned and encircled by a thin trace of snowy white hair. An equally white goatee beard clung to his chin, neatly trimmed to perfection.

Neil shook hands and sat down next to him. Ursula stood supportively, one hand on her husband's shoulder. Neil angled his position so that he faced Murdo directly.

'I learnt a lot from your wife the other day Mr Stuart, but I still need to ask you a few questions I'm afraid.'

'Fire away,' Murdo replied as he folded his paper.

'Your wife tells me you've lived in and around Glendaig all your life. So you no doubt recall life here during the war, yes?'

'Unfortunately, just like it was yesterday.'

'Good, so do you remember any events which occurred here, that you'd consider to have been unusual? Perhaps something that would give me a clue as to what went on down on that beach. I'm thinking particularly around late 1941 or early 1942.'

Murdo scratched at his beard, then looked up at his wife. 'I'm sorry,' he said. 'I think the war passed us by for the most part. Life here has always been reasonably uneventful.'

Ursula interrupted. 'Please excuse me Inspector, I'm in the middle of some baking. I'll leave you to it if you don't mind.'

Neil gestured his approval, and as she disappeared into the house, he continued with his questions. 'Okay, what do you remember about Dugald Matheson's untimely death. I'm sure you remember that?'

Murdo looked away for a second, gathering his thoughts, as if re-living the event. 'Of course I remember, but that was a tragic accident, nothing to do with what went on down on that beach, surely?'

'I'm told young David Grant shot him, is that right?'

'Aye, but as I just said, it was an accident for Christ's sake. Young Davie never got over it. He just tripped, that was all.'

'But you weren't there, were you?'

'No, but Donald and Davie told me what happened. I believed

them. Why are you asking these questions after all this time?'

'Well we've found one man with a bullet wound on the beach, and I now discover that a second sustains a fatal bullet wound around the same time, and just over a mile away. It all seems such a coincidence… two shooting fatalities around the same time, and in such a quiet place as this. So I'm just trying to establish the facts, that's all. You seem to have been deeply affected by Dugald's death?'

'It was a shock, of course it was. Dugald was not a pleasant man. I had little time for him if I'm honest. He was brash and arrogant, the result of his public school education no doubt, because his parents were very nice, gentle people. No, if anything I was more concerned for Davie Grant and his family. Davie was my best friend in those days.'

'Mary Galbraith told me about Dugald's reputation earlier.' Neil felt the time was right to introduce Murdo's recent visitor to the conversation.

'Aye, Mary knew them too. She would have known what Dugald was like.'

'Do you know Mary well? I noticed she was leaving here just before I arrived?'

'Aye, we're acquaintances. She dropped by with her lottery money. I get her a ticket when we go across to the shop at Camuscraig to get ours.'

'I think you've been a little more than acquaintances over the years, dear.' Ursula appeared through the French doors and prodded her husband with a finger.

'Aye, alright, we had a bit of a fling back in 1940 or thereabouts. It never came to anything. She met her husband John the year after. We still speak from time to time, but that's about it.'

He looked up and glared at his wife as she picked up her gardening gloves from a chair nearby and disappeared again.

'So, Mr Stuart.' Neil leaned forward, clasping his hands together between his thighs. 'Other than Mary, is there anyone else you keep in touch with, anyone who lived here during the war?'

'No, no, they've all gone now I believe.'

'What about Isobel Grant, Davie's sister?'

'I have nae seen her for years and years. Christ, for all I know she's dead too. Why do you mention her?'

'No reason, Mary mentioned her that's all. What about the name Max Friedmann; does that name mean anything to you?'

Murdo grunted and folded his arms. Neil sensed that he was becoming irritated by the flow of questions. 'Nothing at all, and who the hell's he?'

'Just a name that's come up during the investigation. We thought he may be the man whose remains were found on the beach.'

'Well, I can say with some certainty that I've never heard that name in all my life, Inspector.'

'Thank you for your time Mr Stuart, I'll leave it there for now.'

'Leave it there *for now*. Jesus man, am I to be interrogated again?'

Neil patted him on the arm. 'I can assure you it's not an interrogation. You and Mary are the sole remaining Glendaig residents from that time. Your memories of life in and around the village back then are crucial to my investigation. I'm just seeking your assistance, that's all.'

'Alright, I suppose that's fine by me,' Murdo muttered, gazing into the middle distance, his mind clearly in a different place.

Ursula returned from the end of the garden just as Neil was reassuring the old man. She saw him to the door and, once out of Murdo's earshot, seemed eager to speak.

'I know my husband comes across as a wee bit grumpy at times, Inspector. He finds the ageing process difficult to deal with. He's got a heart condition you see, and isn't supposed to get himself upset about things, but he just can't help himself.'

'I'll do my best to go easy on him, Mrs Stuart. You never know, I may well be able to spare him the worry of a further *interrogation*.' He laughed, and Ursula followed suit.

'Have a safe trip back to the big city,' she called after him, and the front door closed with a thud.

Chapter Twenty-Three

'So, what do we have here…? Nine millimetre parabellum, type 08mE. German wartime origin. Pre-1944 black casing.'

Brodie was perched on the corner of Neil's desk reading the ballistics report that had just arrived.

'That's right. Apparently, the Germans developed the 08mE in an effort to conserve lead. The round had an iron core encased in lead. The jackets were always black up until 1944, when the copper jacket was reintroduced.'

'Doesn't look like I needed to spend out on a ballistics analysis the way you're talking, I'm impressed.' He handed the plastic evidence bag back to Neil. 'They all look the bloody same to me.'

'At least the boffins *we* use agree with the boffins at the Imperial War Museum,' said Neil.

'Aye, I suppose so. How are things going then? Do we even know who the bloody victim is yet? Seems to me you know more about the round that killed him than the poor bugger himself!'

'I'm still working on it sir. I've been back to Glendaig to speak to a couple of the elderly residents who lived there during the war; a Mary Galbraith and her friend Murdo Stuart.'

'Have they been able to shed any light on any of this?' Brodie asked, still scanning the ballistics report.

'Not much, but they have given up a few interesting morsels. Personally, I believe they know a lot more than they're letting on.'

'Best you keep the pressure up then. Don't forget you've only got twenty-one days to get to the bottom of this!'

Neil was just about to reply when the phone rang on his desk. He picked it up. 'Excuse me if I take this, sir.'

'Aye, fine.' Brodie slid off the desk top and sauntered back to his office, unaware of the significance of the phone call that had just interrupted their conversation.

'Hello, DI Strachan. Can I help you?'

'Hello Mr Strachan. My name's Robert Durward, I live over in Camuscraig.'

Camuscraig… this must be something to do with the Glendaig enquiry… surely?

'How can I help you, Mr Durward?'

'It's more a case of how I can help you, Inspector. My Grandfather, David MacAllister, was the village policeman here during the war. We heard about the remains that were found on the beach over at Glendaig and all the talk of German spies landing there, so we thought we'd have a look through his old notebooks to see if they threw up anything of interest.'

Notebooks…? Could this be treasure trove… finally the key to this mystery! No, steady on Neil, don't get carried away.

'…I see… and did they, Mr Durward?'

'Aye they did, and the notes have also prompted my mother to remember a few things too.'

'Look, I think it would be best if I came over straight away and had a look at these notebooks, is that okay?'

'Fine, and I'll make sure my mother is here too.'

'Excellent, what's your address?'

'12 Kirk Brae, just on the left as you enter the village from the Kyle Road.'

'I'll be there before two, see you then.'

Neil finished scrawling down the address, ripped the sticky note from his pad, and then grabbed his jacket. He poked his head into Brodie's office as he passed.

'You'll never guess, that phone call was from the grandson of the village constable at Camuscraig during the war. He's only kept hold of his grandfather's old pocket books. Can you believe that? And it appears his mother may have some useful information, too.'

'Best you get over there and see what's what then.' The muffled reply originated from behind a pile of expense claims.

It was ten minutes before two when Neil arrived outside the neat little seventies' semi on the outskirts of Camuscraig. It was one of a number of new builds from that era, a project intended to encourage the locals to stay in the area and buy a place of their own. Kirk Brae climbed up behind the village providing its residents with panoramic views across the Sound of Sleat and across to Skye. The narrow road stopped short of the ruins of an old church, left to decay during the worst years of the clearances, and now a playground for local children.

Robert Durward opened the blue front door. He was in his late fifties, almost bald, with a drinker's nose and cheeks crisscrossed by broken veins. He ushered his visitor into the cosy sitting room where his mother Elspie was sitting on the sofa by the window.

Introductions completed, Robert produced a small leather suitcase, adequate perhaps for a weekend away but nothing more. He placed it gently down next to the chair where Neil was sitting, and returned to his armchair. 'The notebook you'll be interested in is the first one in the stack,' said Durward as he lowered himself into the chair.

Neil flicked open the rusty catches and opened the lid. It contained dusty, long-forgotten artefacts that reflected thirty years of service to the crown. Buttons inscribed with the crest of the old Inverness-shire Constabulary, whistle chain, handcuffs and a truncheon. A pair of motorcycle gauntlets, the leather cracked with age, lay under the half-dozen or so pocket books that were neatly stacked in one corner of the case. Lying loose amongst the other items were the silver numerals that once would have adorned the high-necked collar of the constable's tunic.

However, it was the little stack of notebooks that excited Neil the most. Bound in yellowing string, their stippled black covers were now frayed and their pages faded, but these little books were the crown jewels within that battered old case. Neil fumbled with the string, releasing the first book from its fetters. Once free, he rapidly turned the pages, marvelling at the neatness of the handwriting and the detail recorded. The contents of some pocket books he'd seen recently, especially those of younger officers, left a lot to be desired in terms of brevity and legibility!

He paused on a page dated *Monday 30th December 1941*. In the margin, MacAllister had noted the time *12.30am*. Then the following entry:

Mr Dugald Matheson of the Manse, Glendaig, and sister Ursel Matheson personally attended Camuscraig Police Office. They reported that Lachlan MacDonald, resident of Bothan Nan Greag, Camuscraig, had been thrown from his pedal cycle due to the reckless driving of a male in possession of a dark coloured Morris Eight motor car. Registration number unknown. Male described as fair-haired, mid-thirties wearing tweed suit. Second male, dark hair, thirty years wearing raincoat fastened to the neck. Mr Matheson reported seeing what he believed to be a dark-coloured uniform cap on the back seat of the motor car. He believed this was of a type worn by the German armed forces. When he challenged the male in the passenger seat, the driver returned to the vehicle and pushed him to the ground. Both men made off in the vehicle, in the direction of Glenshiel. Miss Matheson did not see the garment, but confirms the assault.

Miss Matheson reported that Lachlan MacDonald was uninjured and had been taken home to his grandmother.

Mr Matheson was very drunk and at times abusive. He was sent home in the company of his sister. I am not convinced regarding the accuracy of Mr Matheson's account due to his state of intoxication.

Then he made a further entry timed at *12.45am,* when he noted that he had informed an Inspector Fleming at Inverness Police Headquarters of the sighting.

'Well,well,' Neil concluded, thumbing through the following pages.

'I remember my father being very angry with Dugald,' said Elspie, who until now had remained silent. 'I'd woken up, disturbed by the banging on the door, and I heard the conversation. I couldn't fail to, the voices were so very loud. I think Pops was about to arrest him. Miss Matheson seemed to be very much embarrassed by the whole affair.'

'Thank you Mrs Durward, anything you can remember after all this time is really helpful.' Neil beamed at the sprightly old lady, who'd impressed him from the outset. She was smartly dressed in a tweed skirt and twin set, her grey hair was neatly cut in a bob, and stylish rimless spectacles rested upon her nose. She was wearing well for a woman in her late eighties.

He returned to the notes. There was a brief entry later on the 30th recording a visit to Lachlan MacDonald, who had apparently made a full recovery. Then two pages further on came another revelation! *Wednesday 1st January 1942 at 8.30 am.*

…Patrolled coast road from Camuscraig to Kinloch Coinneach in search of escaped German POW, missing from Inverness area. Spoke to residents of Glendaig and Invertulloch. No reports or sightings of any person fitting given description.

…Damn, no description of the POW had been recorded in the book. 'Elspie,' said Neil with a sense of urgency. 'Do you remember your father searching for this escaped German? It's really important.'

'I do, now you mention it,' the old lady replied. 'Pops never believed he would come near here. I think the extent of his search reflected that view. If Pops thought something was a waste of time, he never spent much time pursuing it.'

'Yes, I see what you mean,' Neil agreed. 'The next timed entry records him taking refreshments at home at 10.35am. He must have just taken a quick drive to Invertulloch and back. Tell me, do you remember *how* he was told that there was an escaped POW on the loose?'

'Me? Och no, I expect they telephoned him from Inverness, or perhaps the Kyle, I don't remember. What I do remember, as if it were yesterday, is the call from the Reverend Matheson later that day wishing to report the terrible news about his son. I took the call you see.'

Neil flipped over the page in the notebook; Elspie was right. There was a short entry at 4.02 pm recording Callum Matheson's call. MacAllister then called his Inspector to inform him of the incident and departed for the Manse at 4.10pm. His next entry was timed at 5.18pm, and he recorded his visit in some detail:

Attended Glendaig Manse following the report of the accidental shooting of Mr Dugald Iain Matheson aged twenty-six years. Son of Revd and Mrs Anna Matheson. Dr Alpin Macrae in attendance who had confirmed death and probable cause. Evidence of single gunshot wound to the back. Mr Donald Grant of Seal Cottage, Glendaig Estate Stalker (also present) states that deceased had been present on Beinn Caisteal during a deerstalking expedition when Grant's son, Mr David Grant aged seventeen years also of Seal Cottage, Glendaig, was responsible for the shot that killed Dugald Matheson. States that he (David) was following the deceased at a point below the summit crag when the accidental shooting occurred. Grant slipped on wet moss and, as the loaded rifle he was carrying hit the ground, it discharged, hitting Mr Matheson in the back and killing him instantly. The incident was also witnessed by a Mr Murchadh Stuart aged nineteen years, a ghillie of Taigh na Beinne Croft, Invertulloch...

Neil read the line again, *Murchadh Stuart*, he couldn't believe it. The Gaelic name, meaning *sea warrior*, was often shortened to *Murdo!* So the old stalker was lying; he *was* present when Dugald Matheson was shot.

Neil read on...

...The time of the shooting was reported as around midday. The body was carried back to the Manse and laid out in the scullery, after which Dr Alpin Macrae was summonsed to attend.

I have since examined the body at the Manse, accompanied by the doctor.

I saw a single wound to the back as reported, together with an exit wound to the upper chest. There were no other indications of violence on the body.

Some evidence of early rigor mortis was present in the limbs. Dr Macrae confirmed that this would be consistent with the reported time of death.

The deceased's clothing was present, and left to be collected with the body. The rifle, BSA Lee Enfield .303 sporting model No 4c remains at Seal Cottage, to be collected by myself. Informed the family that I would be submitting a report to the Procurator Fiscal through my superiors, and arrangements regarding collection of the body for post-mortem examination would be communicated to them soonest.

Neil looked up again. Durward and his mother sat pensively, awaiting his assessment of the notes. 'Does that help you, Inspector?' asked Robert.

'Aye, it certainly does, sorry if I appeared engrossed.'

'Don't worry about that Inspector, we thought the books would interest you.'

Neil flipped the pages. The next entry at 5.50pm recorded a conversation with David Grant and Murchadh Stuart at Seal Cottage that same evening, together with the seizure of the rifle. He stopped again on *6th January 1942*, having come across another entry relating to Glendaig. At 11.10pm MacAllister had made a note recording a visit to Glendaig Estate, following a report of poachers seen in the grounds of the big house. The Laird's wife, Lady Lillian Macleod, had been the informant. However, it was his comment after visiting the estate that caught Neil's eye…

11.25pm. Stopped to speak to two men in possession of a Dennis thirty hundredweight goods vehicle on the Glendaig to Camuscraig Road. They were known to me; David Grant and Murchadh Stuart. Both stated that they had been playing cards with friends in Camuscraig and were returning home. Had stopped to relieve themselves. Not believed connected to incident on Glendaig Estate. Allowed to go on their way.

The following day, the 7th January, MacAllister recorded that he'd attended Dugald Matheson's funeral at Glendaig Church. He timed the entry at 10.00 am. There was certainly useful information lurking within these pages; perhaps something he'd missed. 'Can I hold on to these books for a while?' Neil asked.

'Aye of course, Inspector. Keep them for as long as you like.' Durward seemed eager to oblige.

'Before I go, is there anything else, anything at all that you remember that might help me, Elspie?'

'No Inspector, my memory's not what it used to be, I'm afraid.'

Neil got up to leave, notebooks in hand. 'Not at all, you've both been a great help. It's a shame I can't speak to Lachlan Macdonald. He's the only other person who'd have possibly remembered the incident with the so-called Germans.'

Elspie smiled. 'Well what's to stop you, Inspector? He lives up the road at Ruthven House, the old people's home. He's not exactly the full shilling, if you take my meaning. In fact he never was, but you never know, you might glean something from him.' She saw the shock in the policeman's face and quietly, inside, was bursting with pride that she, Elspie Durward, still possessed something of value that others wanted, be it only the knowledge of an elderly widow!

Ruthven House was not an attractive building. Its sharp symmetrical lines and flat roof were typical of a 1970's design, but the gardens were well kept with an abundance of colourful shrubs planted in borders around newly-mown lawns. A brass plate on the oak panelled front door announced:

RUTHVEN HOUSE RESIDENTIAL CARE FOR THE ELDERLY
Founded 2001
PROP. Mrs Shona Stevenson-Weir SRN
All Facilities

Once inside, there could be no mistaking the purpose of the establishment. Elderly folk of both genders sat quietly in high-backed chairs, some with heads slumped, their frail bodies hidden under colourful woollen blankets, perhaps dreaming of some happier world that had long since gone.

A care assistant in a shiny nylon apron scuttled past with a tray of half-eaten sandwiches. She directed Neil to the office along the corridor where Mrs Shona Stevenson-Weir could be found.

The *prop* turned out to be exactly what he might have expected, brassy and bottle-blonde, her plump body squeezed into a grey suit that, to Neil's reckoning, was at least a size too small.

'And what can we do for Her Majesty's Constabulary?' she gushed from behind her cluttered desk. Her accent was Glaswegian, but in a decidedly modified form. Neil suppressed a grin and wondered whether she'd developed the accent to fit the name, or vice versa.

'I was wondering if I could have a word with Mr Lachlan Macdonald? I believe he's a resident here.'

'Well no, and yes officer,' came the perplexing reply, accompanied by a distinct smirk. After a pause, presumably to allow her witticism to be fully absorbed, she continued. '*No*, you can't speak to him *now*, because he's rather poorly at present. It's the flu you know, goes round these establishments like wildfire… Oh, and *yes*, he is a resident here.' She sat staring glibly, waiting for his response.

Neil had immediately assessed the woman to be of the "highly irritating" mould. He produced a business card and laid it on the desk with some force. 'Perhaps then, you could give me a call when *no*, he's not so poorly and *yes*, I can see him because I need to speak to him in connection with a murder enquiry. I assume he's sufficiently *compos mentis* to speak to me?' He glared back, playing the *prop* at her own game.

She sensed his irritation, and reacted with a dismissive twitch. 'Aye, he's *compos mentis,* to use your phraseology, Inspector. I should warn you that he is, to put it delicately, a simple soul. He experienced learning difficulties from an early age you see. He has no family now, so I'd have to insist that a member of my staff was present when you speak to him.'

'That would be fine, Mrs Stevenson-Weir, just give me a call please as soon as he's well enough to talk to me.'

Neil then made a hasty exit, leaving the faint aroma of urine and the abrasive Mrs Shona Stevenson-Weir SRN behind the rose-draped front door.

1 9 4 1

Chapter Twenty-Four

'The cap suits you. Does it fit alright?' *Phoebus* could sense the level of anxiety present in his German companion and tried his best to lighten the atmosphere a little. 'My young friend Jan told me the name on the cap band relates to the chap who founded the modern Polish Navy... you'd do well to remember that, just in case you're asked!'

Reiniger sat next to him in the front passenger seat of the Morris. He looked strangely vulnerable; his large frame hunched, his arms tightly folded. Bielawski's heavy naval greatcoat was fastened high to his neck, with the collar pulled up about his ears. He pulled the rough woollen garrison cap from his head and examined it briefly. The cap band was made of heavy gauge wool, upon which the name of the destroyer *ORP Pilsudski* had been embroidered, *not* to German standards he mused proudly. Above the ship's name was the Polish Naval insignia; a silver eagle sitting astride a gold anchor.

'Very interesting,' Reiniger remarked, before returning it to his head. 'But I'll be happier when I get back into my own uniform.'

The two men sat quietly for a while, absorbed in their own respective thoughts and fears. Snow was falling steadily again; large flakes now, like leaves gliding to earth on an autumn breeze. It melted as it floated onto the car's hot bonnet and trickled slowly down to the running boards like strands of silver thread.

Ahead, through the snow-dappled darkness, the roof of the Victorian station building was quickly disappearing under a coating of white. A few hunched figures, hats tipped forward, scurried across the sparkling forecourt making for the warmth of the ticket office.

Phoebus started the engine and moved forward, following the wheel tracks of the few cars that had recently delivered the more affluent travellers to the station. It was a winter scene that had been repeated year in, year out since the railway station serving the little town of Dingwall had been built in 1862. Only the mode of transport parked on the station forecourt would have differed since the horse-drawn era.

He pulled up short of the ticket office door, and looked at his watch. 'Six twenty,' he murmured. 'You'd better make a move. The train's due in at any time.'

Reiniger adjusted his headgear and opened the car door. As he eased himself out into the freezing night, *Phoebus* leant across from his seat. 'You'd better take this.' He handed Reiniger a ticket. LMS Third class single from Dingwall to Glasgow. 'Remember, you're transferring to a ship at Greenock if you're asked. Have you got my P38 with you?'

Reiniger stuffed his hand into the pocket of the greatcoat and felt the icy steel barrel of the Walther pistol. He'd detached the silencer earlier and placed it in his trouser pocket. The very thought of using a firearm on a train full of British servicemen terrified him, but it was too late now, and not the time to question tactics. 'Yes, I've got everything. Just make sure you look after *my* kit.'

'Don't worry, it's safe in the boot. You'll soon be back in that smelly leather coat of yours and riding the ocean wave. Good luck then, see you on the road beneath the viaduct.'

Phoebus pulled the door closed and drove slowly away, passing around the poignant little memorial to the Seaforth Highlanders of the previous war. He glanced into his rear view mirror and watched as the lonely figure of Jürgen Reiniger hurried into the station.

Well here goes… The young German submariner joined the small group of passengers seeking shelter in the ticket office. There were more people travelling than he would have expected on New Year's Eve. Some waited at the little oval window to purchase tickets, mainly soldiers wearing khaki bonnets and heavy greatcoats, but a couple of young women with children also stood patiently in the line.

Reiniger bypassed the queue and made for the door to the platform. An ageing porter with a humourless expression stood in his way. Dressed smartly in black cap and overcoat, with lapel patches confirming he was an employee of the London, Midland and Scottish Railway, the old railwayman exuded an air of authority.

'Ticket please laddie,' he boomed as Reiniger appeared before him. He carefully inspected the ticket that *Phoebus* had purchased earlier, then studied Reiniger for a second, as if to question the young man's motive for travelling on this of all days. 'Over the footbridge, next train on the other platform.'

Reiniger gave a nod of acknowledgement and returned the ticket to his pocket. He emerged onto the platform, mostly free of snow thanks to the elegant glass canopy that stood above it. There were a number of people milling about, mostly civilians waiting for a northbound train from Inverness.

Across the tracks on the island platform a number of military men stood in the cold. They stamped their feet to keep warm, whilst leaning on kit bags or smoking cigarettes. Reiniger crossed the footbridge taking the steps two at a time. He remembered *Phoebus'* briefing about the POW's being carried in the last coach, so he sauntered casually along the platform, through the group of shivering khaki-clad passengers, and took up position so as not to attract any attention or conversation.

His watch showed six thirty-eight. The train was late. Reiniger stared expectantly into the darkness beyond the platform, his heart pounding, his mouth tinder box dry.

At six forty a shrill whistle drifted in on the northerly breeze, accompanied by the faint rhythmic chug of an approaching locomotive. A minute or so later, a blurred shape emerged through the swirling snow, its wheels obscured by a veil of steam that drifted up into moonless night. A grubby simmering locomotive, known affectionately by railwaymen at the time as the *Black Five*, coasted into the station, slowing as it did so. Reiniger felt its warmth surge through him as the overworked monster, bearing the grimy nameplate *Ayrshire Yeomanry*, glided past. The canvas air-raid hood draped over the cab hid the crew from sight, but not the glow of the firebox that flickered eerily through the gaps in the dark material. Behind the locomotive, a long rake of equally grubby maroon-coloured passenger coaches screeched to a halt. Doors flew open and a surge of khaki and black-coated servicemen flowed onto the platform, clustering around the little WVS refreshments trolley that had appeared from nowhere.

At the south end of the platform, the engine crew busied themselves positioning the long trunk of the water crane above the locomotive's tender. The train was indeed much longer than Reiniger had expected; no doubt a symptom of the immense pressure on the railways at the time. He thought he'd positioned himself ideally for the trailing coaches, but he now had to walk for some distance back along the train before realising the coach that he needed to get into was standing out of reach, beyond the platform.

He walked as far as he could, stopping only once to glance back. He was reassured to see a number of men still queuing at the refreshments trolley, and even more relieved to be alone. Fortunately, none of the chilled souls waiting to join the train wished to venture so far back to the rear coaches.

Having positioned himself near an open door he waited, intending to remain isolated from the other passengers for as long as possible. Then a man's voice boomed out in the distance; 'This train for Perth, Stirling, Carlisle, Crewe and London Euston. Change at Perth for Edinburgh and Glasgow…' His broad Scottish accent then became lost momentarily, drowned out by a blast of steam from the locomotive. Reiniger then thought he heard the words '*All aboard please*' flow from the invisible announcer's powerful lungs. Coated figures flowed back onto the train and doors slammed shut. He too made for the open doorway at the end of the penultimate coach and, having taken a deep breath, climbed in, turning to close the door behind him.

He made towards the last coach, soon finding himself at one end of a narrow corridor. Immersed in a fug of cigarette smoke, twenty or so servicemen stood packed against each other in the narrow space, some standing, some leaning awkwardly against kit bags. They seemed cheerful enough and chatted loudly, apparently undaunted by the lack of seating. The half a dozen or so compartments that opened onto the dingy passageway were closed off to prying eyes. Their doors were firmly closed and window blinds lowered to comply with the air raid restrictions.

Reiniger now turned his attention to the last coach. He gingerly made his way through the jovial crowd and then into a connecting passage, eventually finding himself alone in a small vestibule. Either side of him was an external door. A third door provided access to a toilet. He opened the door to the toilet and looked inside. It was empty. Closing it again, he peered around the edge of the polished wooden end partition of the first seating compartment. The corridor was clear except for two military policemen, smartly turned out in their red-topped caps and blancoed webbing. Both were carrying side arms. This was a concern; he was expecting just one escort in the corridor, not two! *Was the second man one of the pair expected to be inside the compartment, just out for a smoke perhaps?* 'Damn,' he mumbled under his breath.

It didn't take long for him to be noticed. The two redcaps, now aware of his presence, both turned to face him. One of the men, a corporal with a steely expression, marched up the corridor towards him. At the same time, the train lurched and moved forward, causing the corporal to lose his balance momentarily.

'I'm afraid this carriage is off limits son,' growled the NCO from beneath the near-vertical peak of his cap. Reiniger raised an apologetic hand, in which he clutched a pack of woodbines. 'Sorry,' he said. 'Light please?' The corporal relaxed a little, and produced a silver lighter from his trouser pocket. His gaze fell on Reiniger's cap band.

'*ORP Pilsudski…* what's that then, son?'

'Polish destroyer,' Reiniger replied as he raised the end of his cigarette to the lighter being held in the corporal's hairy fist.

'Oh right, good for you son… comin' over 'ere and continuing the fight. I'm sure we'll kick Jerry out of Poland before you know it.' He leant towards Reiniger, his eyes darting about as if about to impart a secret. 'You'll be pleased to know, we've got a group of Jerry prisoners in here. Those bastards who prowl around in those bloody U-boats, sinkin' our boys on the convoy runs. One of the buggers is a bit special see. That's why we've got to keep this area clear. So I'm afraid you're goin' to have to run along now mate.'

Reiniger nodded, acknowledging the corporal's disclosure. 'Thank you so very much,' he said, almost in a whisper, trying hard to disguise his own accent.

Puffing heavily on his glowing cigarette, he made his way back to join the hordes in the next coach. With the now steady *clickety-clack* of the wheels under his feet and the drone of multiple conversations in the background, Reiniger stared out through the darkened glass, desperately trying to formulate a plan. He could see nothing, just the odd featureless shape beyond the window from which his own reflection stared back at him.

The train then slowed, and passed through a small deserted station. "Beauly" he heard someone announce further along the corridor. He glanced at his watch again just as a weary-looking naval officer emerged from his darkened den further down the coach and shuffled past to the toilet. It was seven fifteen. He had forty-five minutes to come up with something. The officer returned, swaying to the motion of the train and still fumbling with his flies. He smiled fleetingly before disappearing back into his compartment and sliding the door back into place.

As Reiniger struggled to think of a way to release his old friend from the clutches of his enemy, a distant voice in the back of his head was warning him that *any* plan would be suicidal. This was a non-starter, this ridiculous mission, instigated by a couple of admirals; relics of the last Great War who merely wished to protect their own miserable arses from the political fallout.

He checked his reflection in the window again, at the same time recalling Max Friedmann's waxen unconscious face that day in July, '32. He'd swum across to him from the relative safety of some floating wooden debris; a makeshift raft that had been his sanctuary since the *Niobe* had slipped beneath the icy Baltic Sea. Max's head had been bobbing up and down lifelessly, his body supported by the air trapped in his tattered uniform. He hadn't left him then, and he knew he couldn't now, but Max owed him big time and he wouldn't let him forget it!

The train was slowing again. It clattered over a metal bridge and began to negotiate a tight curve. Metal ground against metal as the train's bogies negotiated the tight turn. Then it came to a standstill. Reiniger rested his head against the window and listened to the rhythmic thud of his heartbeat. He still couldn't see much, but the snow was more in evidence now, flying past the window carried on the stiff wind; a tattered rush of white fading into the darkness. It was now seven forty. Fear was building somewhere deep within him. His stomach tightened into a nervous cramp, as it did when the boat was being depth charged. The next twenty minutes would determine his destiny. In fact these may be his last minutes on earth, perhaps Max's too, but at least *he* had no idea of what was coming.

He looked at his watch again. Still the train stood motionless in the snow. A soldier standing to his right sighed. 'It's always like this around Inverness. I dinnae know what they're bloody playing at, there can't be many trains coming oot the bloody station this time of night, and I'm bloody sure it's no' an air raid. Even the Jerries can't be arsed coming across here in this weather!'

'Why do we stop then?' Reiniger asked.

'Och, God knows,' said the soldier. 'It's a busy station here, and there's a bloody great engine shed just along the way. We'll bypass the station, but we always get held up regardless.' As he spoke the train moved off again. The murky shapes of buildings came into view as it snaked its way through Inverness, clattering across the web of different tracks at the mouth of the station.

'Looks like we're on our way again mate,' said the soldier standing next to him. 'Next stop Perth. Best you make yourself comfy for a couple of hours.' Reiniger smiled, but remained silent.

The train gained some speed and appeared to be running around a gentle left-hand curve. Seven forty-four. He hoped that agent *Phoebus* was doing his bit further along the line. A rush of air then buffeted the coach, startling him momentarily, as another train passed by, this one headed by two locomotives. There followed a repetitive clanking of metal wheels as an endless column of tarpaulin-draped wagons trundled slowly by. 'That's probably what we've been waiting for,' said the soldier, as if to reassert his reputation as an armchair expert on railway operation.

Phoebus had arrived outside the little station at Drumossie Moor at precisely seven thirty. He'd parked the Morris in the station yard and was now standing on the station platform. He looked left and right, checking there was no one about. The only significant sound was that of the strengthening wind whistling through the telegraph wires high above his head.

He turned towards the little signal box set back from the southbound platform. Inside, he could make out an orange glow. A wisp of pale smoke rose vertically from the stove pipe at the rear before being blown asunder by the icy wind. *Phoebus* approached the box slowly, taking care not to announce his presence from the crunch of his boots on the snow-crusted platform. He quietly ascended the wooden steps and gently turned the door knob. In his right hand, he firmly grasped the butt of his Walther PPK automatic pistol. With a deep intake of breath he threw the old door open. The signalman, Jack Ritchie, was in the process of shovelling a spadeful of coal into his stove.

He straightened up, startled, and then saw the gun. 'Who the hell are you?' he mumbled from behind the pipe clenched between his teeth.

'You don't need to know who I am mister signalman. You just need to know that this gun is loaded, and if you so much as blink when I have advised you not to, I will have no hesitation in ending your life prematurely... understand?'

'Aye, I do,' said Ritchie, raising his hands voluntarily. He had experienced many unusual events since joining the Highland Railway at the age of fifteen, but this certainly eclipsed them all.

'What is your name please, mister signalman?'

'Jack... Jack Ritchie.'

'Good. Now Jack, tell me, are there any other staff working on the station tonight?'

'None,' said Jack, trembling. 'Nothing is due to stop here after seven this evening, so they've gone home.'

'That's good. What about northbound trains that don't stop here, are there any due?'

'Well yes, there's a northbound munitions train due shortly.'

'That's fine. I want you to see it through normally. Then you have a southbound passenger, correct?'

'Aye, a special through to Perth and on to London.' He glanced up at the wall clock, 'It'll be through here around eight o'clock.'

'Good, because I want you to stop that train for a couple of minutes; before it crosses the viaduct. You can do that, I assume?'

'Aye, of course. There's a signal down the way protecting the viaduct. Can I ask why?'

'Well as you ask. Someone wants to get off here, that's all. I'm afraid I can't tell you any more than that.'

The telegraph bell suddenly rang out, a signal from Ritchie's colleague down the line at Tomatin, heralding the approach of the northbound munitions train. *Phoebus* gestured to Ritchie to go about his business as usual. Then, several minutes later, the double-headed Thurso-bound freight train thundered past shaking the panels of the little wooden cabin.

Phoebus sat on the floor out of sight, his pistol still very much in evidence and aimed at Ritchie's back. The signalman did as he was told, waving nervously to the train's guard who returned the gesture from the doorway of the trailing brake van. Once the van's tail light had faded into the distance, another flurry of bell codes rang out. Ritchie acknowledged these with his normal quiet efficiency.

'Should be getting notification of the southbound special shortly,' he announced without looking at his visitor. Then, as if on cue, a series of four bells rang out, this time to warn of the approaching passenger train from Inverness. The clock on the wall showed seven fifty-five. Ritchie approached his signal levers. He raised his old cloth cap and smoothed back the curly white hair that lay compressed beneath. 'I need to pull off the home signal back down the line to warn the driver that he can proceed.'

'Just do what you have to, I'm not interested in the technicalities,' said *Phoebus* calmly, still sitting on the floor with pistol raised. Ritchie carried on, pulling back one of the heavy steel levers.

'I need you to hold the train this side of the viaduct until one minute past eight. No earlier, no later. Then I'll be away, understand?'

Ritchie nodded, his mouth as dry as sandpaper. 'It'll be with us in a few minutes. I've left the starter signal that protects the viaduct *on*, so he should stop there.'

'Good,' said *Phoebus*, 'everything's going to plan then.'

Chapter Twenty-Five

Whilst *Phoebus* was checking the time on the signal box clock, Reiniger had been doing the same. He had just five minutes to make his move. It was looking very much like he was going to have to take drastic action to get into the compartment where he hoped he'd find Max Friedmann.

He looked back along the corridor in which he was standing. The level of conversation had died away, most of his travelling companions now dozing against their kitbags, so he made his way quietly back through the coach connector, sensing the motion of the train beneath him and the now steady clatter of the wheels. As he emerged into the last coach, he unexpectedly came face to face with the military police corporal.

'I thought I asked you to stay out of this coach,' the corporal snarled, his tobacco-laden breath drifting into the German's nostrils.

'Toilet please,' said Reiniger, pointing to the door.

'Well that's just where I'm goin' son, so best you join the queue.'

The corporal opened the door and was about to enter. Reiniger allowed himself a momentary glance over his shoulder. The other redcap was only partially in view, staring out through the blackened glass at nothing in particular and totally unaware of Reiniger's presence.

The corporal was half inside the small toilet when he made his move. With his Walther grasped tightly in his clammy hand, he careered into the toilet behind the big military policemen, resulting in the latter lurching forward towards the partition wall. Startled by the attack, the corporal tried to turn and face his assailant, but his vain attempt at protestation was answered by the butt of the Walther crashing down on his skull like a steel hammer. He only managed a muffled grunt and dropped like a stone, cap skewed across his head at an unseemly angle. A trickle of dark red blood appeared from beneath his dark hair line and gathered pace as it tracked down the side of his nose. Reiniger, shaking now as adrenalin surged through him, closed the door gently. The altercation had clearly not been heard by the second redcap who remained by the window, still peering into the night.

Reiniger heaved the unconscious man up onto the toilet seat where he sat limp, head slumped forward. Strands of blood from his head wound hung semi-clotted and string-like before splashing onto the urine-soaked floor. Reiniger hurriedly retrieved the silencer from his trouser pocket and screwed it to the muzzle of the Walther. He checked his watch, seven fifty-six. With the door open slightly, he could just make out the second redcap standing alone by the window. He slipped out into the corridor and closed the toilet door gently then, with pistol out of sight behind his back, he approached his second target.

'Your friend, sick, in toilet,' he announced, pointing to the toilet door.

'What d'yer mean, sick?' said the redcap, staring firstly towards the toilet door and then back at Reiniger

'He very sick, me Polish, no good English,' said Reiniger.

'Bloody hell, what are you doing here anyway?' questioned the redcap as he marched towards the end of the coach and the toilet. Reiniger followed, checking over his shoulder again. The train was slowing and he sensed they were negotiating another curve in the line, this time a gradual sweep to the right. The soldier went to open the toilet door just as the Walther crashed down on his skull with equal force to that which had neutralised his colleague. The man crumpled without letting out a sound. Reiniger caught his body as he fell and dragged him backwards along the short passage to the external doorway. Leaving the inert body on the floor, he lowered the door window, recoiling as the biting wind stung his face. Squinting against the driving snow he leant out, grabbed the door handle and, using all his strength against the slipstream, threw open the door. He then heaved the redcap's body across to the void and, with a last surge of effort, eased him out into the snowy night. The body landed heavily on the trackside ballast, arms and legs flailing about like a tailor's dummy, and then he was gone, left to live or die in the freezing wilderness that was Drumossie Moor.

Reiniger closed the door and wiped the sweat from his forehead with the back of his hand. He panted rapidly in an effort to recover quickly from the physical exertion required to expel the redcap's body.

The train now slowed significantly. The wheels squealed as the brakes were applied. Seven fifty-eight. It was now or never. Thank God no one had heard anything so far. With the Walther cocked and held just behind him at arm's length, he made his way steadily along the corridor, stopping at the first compartment to try to get a glimpse around the sides of the window blinds. He could just get sight of the occupant sitting closet to the window. Another redcap, damn!

At that moment the train lurched again as the locomotive accelerated, taking up the slack in the long string of coaches. The jolt resulted in the compartment door sliding back just enough to reveal the interior. Reiniger registered the scene and moved on quickly: four *Tommis* and two German prisoners – *Kriegsmarine*, low ranking officers. The door clicked shut as one of the escorts reached up to secure it.

The next compartment was, as far as he could see, empty and in darkness. He moved on to the third; the one outside of which the two redcaps had been loitering. Dim light framed the edges of the blinds in this one, a good sign.

The train was crawling along now, hardly moving. He looked ahead of him towards the end of the corridor… four more compartments. There was no time to keep looking. He threw open the sliding door. Sitting by the window at the other end of the compartment was his old friend Max Friedmann, still wearing his crumpled naval uniform with its faded gold *ärmelstreifen* and Iron Cross buttonhole ribbon. His black cap lay on the roof rack above him, neatly stacked atop his leather sea coat. He looked pale and tired as he sat arms tightly folded, dozing, his head tilted forward.

The sound of the door opening awakened him and he looked up, attempting to focus on the apparent interloper. Two military policemen sat opposite him. One, a sergeant, leapt to his feet, his hand dropping to the flap buckle on the white canvas holster that hung from his webbing. 'What the bloody hell do you think you're playing at? Get out of here now sailor boy, this coach is off limits.'

Reiniger raised his left hand in a conciliatory gesture. 'Sorry, sorry, Polish, not understand.'

The sergeant, now believing the threat to have diminished somewhat, raised his hand from the holster, and pointed towards Reiniger menacingly. 'Out now,' he bawled, 'before you end up well and truly in the shit.'

Reiniger backed off, left arm still raised. The redcap private grinned and turned back to the book he was reading. Reiniger backed into the open doorway. He looked across at Friedmann who by now had recognised him and was staring back with incredulity, his mouth open, unable to speak.

The sergeant took his eyes off Reiniger for an instant and turned to his companion. 'Where the bloody hell are those two out there, go and…'

He never finished the sentence. As the train screeched to a halt, the Walther delivered two rounds into his torso, the only sound from the shots were the two puffs as the silencer did its job. The shots propelled the sergeant backwards onto the seat, leaving Reiniger's line of sight to the second escort clear. Two more puffs, and he too slumped sideways across the seat, a look of disbelief frozen in his now lifeless eyes. His book dropped to the floor, the open pages sprayed with his blood.

'Hello Max, we meet again at last.' It may have seemed a humorous form of greeting, but Reiniger never intended it to be. He launched himself forward and grabbed at Friedmann's sleeve. 'Quick, we've got less than a minute,' he whispered as he dragged his friend out of his seat.

In the confusion, Friedmann left his belongings on the luggage rack and stumbled out of the compartment, allowing himself one last look back at the two blood-spattered bodies lying motionless across the seat.

Reiniger quietly closed the compartment door and led the way back along the corridor, Walther poised to deal with anyone who crossed their path. Miraculously, no one did.

With the external door open, he pushed Friedmann out into the winter chill. The length of the train was such that the last four coaches were, as expected, overhanging the station itself. The drop was considerable on the track side, and Friedmann landed on the snow covered ballast with a low grunt. He crouched down instinctively, wondering what to do next. Reiniger followed him, reaching up from the lowest of the two step boards to gently close the door. As he joined his friend on the track, the locomotive let forth a great blast of steam followed by a series of shorter rapid expulsions. The couplings on the coaches clanked as the locomotive took up the strain and the train eased forward.

Reiniger grabbed Max and ushered him forward. Struggling to catch their breath, they trotted alongside the train as it gathered pace. Thankfully, the blinds on the windows were fastened in the down position and only the faintest chink of light could be seen, halo-like around the periphery of the window frames.

Finally, the last coach drew clear of them leaving the two men alone, exposed, and fighting for breath. Fortunately, they were now clear of the station and any danger that it may have posed. The steady rhythm of the train's wheels slowly diminished as the last coach was consumed by the darkness and the whine of the wind returned to their ears.

Reiniger stumbled towards a lineside telegraph pole and sunk down next to it, thankful of the support against his back. Max, his injured leg causing him considerable discomfort, did likewise.

Reiniger turned to his old comrade and grinned. 'Well, we did it,' he panted.

'We've certainly done something,' Max replied, also gasping for breath. He repositioned his aching leg. 'Perhaps you'd like to tell me what the hell's going on and why you, of all people, have just helped me escape from that train?'

Phoebus had been watching Ritchie closely as the large black locomotive drifted past the signal box. Luckily there had been no visual communication between the signalman and the train crew as the blackout hood had been fastened securely over the cab. When the train finally screeched to a halt the signalman had stood, hands clasped around the starting signal lever, awaiting the agent's instruction to pull it back to the *off* position. *Phoebus* had been checking his watch, and just a few seconds after one minute past eight, he had called, '*Now*, pull it now.'

Ritchie had heaved it back and the train had responded quickly, resuming its journey across the long sweep of Culloden viaduct and away into the night. He returned the signal lever to it's *on* position and stepped away from the frame… 'I need to inform the signalman at Tomatin that the train is out of my section,' said Ritchie.

'Just do it then,' said *Phoebus*. Whilst the signalman tapped out the "section clear" code on the little wooden cased instrument *Phoebus* asked, 'When is the next train due through here?'

'Not until tomorrow morning,' Ritchie replied.

'Good, now come with me.'

Phoebus steered Ritchie through the door and out into the snow. With a series of gentle prods from the pistol, he shepherded the old railwayman along the platform towards the station building. He then threw open the door marked *Gentlemen's Toilet* and pushed Ritchie inside, guiding him into one of the small cubicles.

'Turn around and face the wall,' he said quietly. Ritchie obliged, terrified that he was about to be executed. He could feel hot urine trickling down his leg as he stood shaking, and contemplating how his wife would cope without him. But instead of a gunshot he became aware of his hands being tied behind his back, and then his head was jerked back as a gag was applied to his mouth. *Phoebus* turned Ritchie around and sat him down roughly onto the toilet seat. He then busied himself securing the signalman's legs to the pedestal itself. A further bond was applied from his wrists to the cistern pipe that rose directly behind the toilet, then *Phoebus* stood back and examined his work.

'Sorry about this old man, I'm afraid it's necessary to give us a bit of a head start. Try to sit still and I'm sure your colleagues will find you in the morning.' Ritchie's response was to mumble something incomprehensible from behind the gag. *Phoebus* patted him on the arm. 'Thanks for all the help, really appreciate it,' and he slipped back through the door to the platform.

The two Germans hadn't seen the activity on the station platform. They'd been resting briefly whilst *Phoebus* had dealt with the signalman. Reiniger had now briefed Max on the sequence of events that had culminated in his escape. The latter had in turn summarised the importance of the mission he'd been on, and the secrecy that had surrounded the *Seeadler* project. Reiniger was quiet now. He'd stopped panting and was trying to take it all in. He glanced at his watch again as he'd been doing constantly throughout the evening. It was just before ten past eight.

'Come on Max, let's go. Not far now.'

Max groaned as he pulled himself up. 'God, this country's cold.' He folded his arms, burying his frozen hands under his armpits. 'You could have waited for me to get my coat.'

'Stop complaining Max, and follow me.'

Reiniger led the way onto the imposing viaduct. The ballast

shifted noisily under their feet as they braved the icy cross wind that stabbed at their numbed faces. Max limped along behind, struggling to keep up with his fitter companion. It took a good ten minutes to traverse the twenty-eight spans of the viaduct. Once they'd made it to the southern end of the curving red brick parapet they stopped and allowed themselves a backwards glance. The temperature continued to fall steadily, as did the snow.

'We need to get down to the road,' said Reiniger as he started to descend the steep rocky slope beyond the viaduct. Max followed cautiously, feeling his way over the loose rock with his hands. The darkness echoed with the sound of falling scree as the two men slipped and tumbled down the slope.

Then, without warning, Reiniger lost his balance. He fell forward and rolled several times before steadying himself with grazed hands. The Walther he'd been carrying was gone. He thought he could hear the pistol as it skipped away down the steep slope, metal ringing out on stone. 'No time to retrieve it now,' he muttered to himself and carried on towards the road, thirty feet below him.

After what seemed like an eternity, they reached the narrow metalled road that ran beneath the viaduct. Reiniger brushed away the grit that clung to his bloodied hands and looked left and right along the lane. Nothing; just the dull grey line of the roadway as it hugged the course of the River Nairn on its journey northwards towards the sea.

It was a matter of waiting, hoping *Phoebus* wouldn't leave them freezing in the dark for too long. They slipped out of sight behind one of the viaduct's massive piers and crouched against the damp stonework, shivering uncontrollably. A solitary owl taunted them by repeatedly announcing its presence from the woodland nearby. Eventually, when the nocturnal raptor's monotonous call had finally died away, their only other companion was the wind whining between the viaduct's towering arches.

Max leant against the pier wall, hands thrust deep into his pockets. 'So who is this man we're waiting for?'

'He's some sort of agent, uses the codename *Phoebus*.'

'Is he German?'

'No, he says he's Scottish, from near a place called Dumfries.'

'Have you asked him his name?'

Reiniger stared back at him through the darkness. 'Of course I've asked him his name. Waste of time though. He wouldn't tell me, not surprisingly I suppose.' There was a pause, then he said, 'He did use the name James Chisholm yesterday, when speaking to some policemen who came knocking on his door, but obviously that was just a cover too. The only thing he's ever told me about himself is that his father was a school teacher and threatened to throw him down the well behind his school house, not very fatherly, eh?' They stood in silence again, listening to the wind. 'Shouldn't be long now,' said Reiniger between shivers.

As it happened, only ten minutes had passed before the distant purr of a motor car's engine drifted across the river towards them. The sound was closely followed by the glimmer of light from the two shielded headlamps. *Phoebus'* Morris Eight pulled up directly under the viaduct. The front passenger door flew open and a voice called out; 'Hello, anyone there?'

Reiniger emerged from the shadows first, followed by Max. They jogged across to the car, keen to get out of the cold. Max slid into the front seat next to the grinning *Phoebus*. Reiniger turned up the collar his Polish greatcoat and allowed himself one last glance up towards the towering viaduct before climbing in himself.

With the doors closed, the agent accelerated away, travelling the short distance to a junction where he turned right. Having completed the manoeuvre and gained speed along a relatively straight section of road, he turned his attention towards Max. 'Good evening *Herr Korvettenkapitän*, pleased to meet you at last!'

'I believe I'm to call you *Phoebus*,' Max replied, staring ahead through the windscreen.

'I'd prefer it that way if you don't mind. Our paths will only cross for a relatively short period of time, so please do bear with me.'

'Fair enough, *Phoebus* it is then.'

'Good, now you can relax for a wee while. I intend to travel across to the west coast along the quieter roads. He glanced into his rear view mirror at Reiniger, who was lounging on the back seat. 'All went well on the train, I hope?'

'Well we're here in one piece, aren't we?' Reiniger replied from the darkness. 'I'm afraid there are two dead *Tommis* on that train, and another in the toilet with a hole in his skull.'

'So there were only three escorts as expected?' *Phoebus* enquired.

'No, I'm afraid not. There was a fourth in the corridor. I threw him out of the train some way back.'

'My, you have been busy *Leutnant* Reiniger. You can never trust a Polish sailor not to start a fight, it seems.'

'Well one thing's for sure,' said Max. 'When the British discover what has happened, they'll be crawling all over this country, baying for blood. I only wish my escape hadn't involved so much violence. We're going to end up swinging from a noose if they catch up with us!'

'Don't worry,' said *Phoebus*. He checked the luminous face of his watch. 'In just under three hours you'll both be tucked up on one of your submarines heading back to the Fatherland.'

'Sounds like the perfect end to an awful day,' said Reiniger from the darkness. 'But I'd feel happier if you put your foot down, just in case.'

'Where exactly *are* we heading for?' asked Max.

Phoebus looked across at Max and grinned. 'You speak as if you have knowledge of the Highlands, Herr *Korvettenkapitän*.'

'I have visited Scotland on a number of occasions before the war.'

'I see. Well, we'll be rendezvousing with the U-boat a little to the west of a tiny village called Glendaig on Loch Coinneach. I'd be surprised if you'd heard of it.'

Max didn't reply. He closed his eyes, allowing the brief knowing smile to fade from his lips.

Chapter Twenty-Six

The narrow country road hugged the course of the railway line for a couple of miles. They sped along at a pace that Reiniger considered a little too fast for the conditions, but then he had asked his driver to put his foot down! He could see nothing out of the window; just the cloud of powdered snow swirling up from around the rear wheels. There were few signs of life along this remote river valley, just the odd farm worker's cottage standing by the roadside, dim light visible around the edges of firmly pulled curtains.

At Craggie they turned onto the A9, the main Inverness to Perth Road. The road was empty for the short distance to the turning for Fort Augustus. Then it was westward again, along another minor route, twisting and turning between small lochans and low hills.

The warmth of the car had begun to permeate through Max's snow-sodden uniform. The drone of the engine and absence of conversation lulled him into a restless state of slumber, interrupted frequently by the sharp bends and unevenness of the road. It was slumber nonetheless, and his subconscious began to generate comforting images of past celebrations, when the New Year had been welcomed by family and friends at his grandparents' home in Kiel. In his mind's eye he could see himself, beer stein in hand, his other arm draped around his brother Otto's shoulder. They stood with others, clustered around their grandfather's *Feurich* piano, listening to their mother playing beautifully as always.

His eyes blinked open suddenly as Reiniger spoke from the back seat. 'I lost that damned pistol back there, sorry.' He sounded fearful of the response he might receive.

'You won't need it,' said *Phoebus* reassuringly. 'Anyway, I have this,' and held up the Walther PPK he'd secreted next to his seat. 'Your own pistol is in the boot with your other things, so we've got plenty of firepower if we need it!' He laughed. 'I'm hoping we won't!'

'I would've thought you'd be less than impressed that I'd lost your magic silencer, or suppressor, whatever you like to call it.'

'These things happen when you're under pressure, Jürgen. Forget about it. I'd never had cause to use it anyway.' The conversation died once more and in response, Max's eyelids slowly descended again.

They were now running along the western side of Loch Mhor. It was nine fifteen. All appeared to be going without a hitch. It was almost too good to be true! Reiniger sank back onto the firm leather seat that spanned the back of the car and closed his eyes. He tried to relax but inside he was still wound up like a spring. There was no way he could sleep, so he stared out of the window into the darkness, his breath misting the cold glass each time he exhaled. Somewhere out there was Loch Ness, but he couldn't see it.

The small settlement of Fort Augustus lay ahead of them along General Wade's old military road. In the village they turned onto the main route that ran back along the western side of Loch Ness. For the first time during their journey they encountered signs of life. Several couples hunched together, their arms linked, walked quickly through the village. There was an urgency in their pace, a clear desire to reach their destination before their clothing became saturated by the snow that clung to their shoulders. Reiniger imagined they'd be hurrying to a local inn, or for drinks with friends, a ritual that would be played out throughout war-ravaged Europe that night. He too looked forward to a tot of schnapps with Von Bramsdorf once they were safely back on board U-114. A smile crept across his lips as the scenario played out in his head; the clanking of glasses, relieved faces and the throb of the diesels.

His dream was short-lived as he sensed the car slowing rapidly. *Phoebus* called out from the front; 'Get down out of sight – now!'

Max woke with a start. His tired eyes focussed on a figure standing in the road some way ahead, waving his arms furiously. Beyond him, parked half on the verge, stood a drab coloured Austin staff car. It was definitely military as the rear was marked with unit insignia. Two other figures stood nearby, a mixture of exhaled breath and cigarette smoke hanging about them in the chill air.

Phoebus pulled up well short of the staff car. He slipped the Walther into his pocket and got out, leaving the driver's door open. As he approached the figure in the road, he could see that he was wearing army battledress.

'Hello mate, can you help? I think the bleedin' clutch as gone.' The soldier, a private, was evidently worried, and not a native of the Highlands.

'I'm not much of a mechanic I'm afraid,' said *Phoebus*, his finger curled firmly round the trigger of the pistol inside his pocket.

'Oh no mate, there's not much that can be done here. I need to use the TK along at Invermoriston to call the duty officer at Fort George. Hopefully he'll be able to get us picked up. Hey, you're not going that way are you?'

'No, sorry old son, I'm turning off towards Glen Shiel at Invermoriston.'

'Bugger. Well if you could drop me by the phone box, that would be fine.'

'I'll do better than that, I'll even bring you back. You tell your mates and I'll go and bring the car along.'

'Well thanks mister, you're a gem.' He winked at *Phoebus* playfully. 'Hey, they're not bloody mates, they're officers. I'm supposed to be taking them to some bleedin' do at the officers' mess over at the Fort. They've definitely got the arse with me, they have!'

Phoebus walked purposefully back to the Morris and climbed in.

He watched as the young private returned to the staff car and spoke with his passengers. 'Right, get out now you two and lose yourselves in amongst those trees over there… and take all your stuff with you from in here.'

The Germans didn't need telling twice. Their doors were eased open, just enough to squeeze out. Having gently closed them again they crouched low and headed up the verge, disappearing out of sight between the towering pines that embraced the mountainside.

'I'll be back shortly,' *Phoebus* had reassured them as they slipped out into the cold. He then drove forward slowly to collect the soldier, before speeding off towards Invermoriston.

Reiniger sat awkwardly, propped against a tree trunk, and scanned the dark canopy of trees that creaked and groaned above him. The forest resounded with the sounds of wild animals as they called one another from the rocky slopes above. He shivered and sunk his chin into the collar of Jan Bielawski's greatcoat. In the distance they could just make out the chattering voices of the two British officers as they stood smoking by their stricken staff car. They may have been foes, but such was the eeriness of their hiding place that their presence was strangely reassuring to the two fugitives.

Minutes ticked by that seemed like hours to the two frozen Germans. Two cars and a military truck had driven past in the direction of Inverness, but nothing had come the other way. The luminous dial on Max's watch now showed nine forty-five. Concern was beginning to creep in. 'How long is the drive to the rendezvous point, Jürgen?' Max asked.

'If we get going again soon, we should still make it alright. It's about an hour and a half from here,' said Reiniger, having made a quick mental calculation based on his earlier journey over the route.

'Umm, that's if nothing else goes wrong.'

'We'll just have to hope it doesn't then, Max.'

It was ten past ten before the slits of light from *Phoebus'* headlamps re-emerged through the curtain of snow. He stopped by the staff car and muffled voices could be heard as pleasantries were exchanged. Then the car moved forward to a point adjacent to the Germans' hiding place. It swept around in a wide arc before coming to rest facing in the same direction it had just come from. *Phoebus* got out and seemed to walk about slowly in small circles, changing directions every couple of seconds.

'What's he playing at?' Reiniger whispered to his companion from the tree line.

'He seems to be looking for something,' said Max, equally baffled by the agent's actions.

Phoebus' hushed voice then drifted softly across to them. Hardly audible above the wind. 'Come out slowly to the rear of the car, then get in the back using the driver's-side door.'

They did as they were told, sliding through the narrowest of gaps to gain access to the back seat. Once safely inside they stayed low, their faces pressed hard against the pleasant-smelling leather of the front seats. A few seconds later, *Phoebus* climbed in and started the engine.

'Stay down there,' he warned as he selected first gear. The car moved off and sped up as higher gears were quickly selected. They were on their way again. A minute or so elapsed, then, 'You can get up now,' said *Phoebus*.

Their two heads appeared simultaneously and looked around. They were driving in darkness again, following the same tree-lined road as before. Nothing else was visible, just the dim pools of light from the headlamps gliding along ahead of the bonnet.

'What was all the walking around in circles about?' Reiniger asked.

'I told the *Tommis* I'd dropped my father's lighter when I got out of the car. You'd have thought they'd have offered to help me look ·for it, but they didn't. Ungrateful buggers. Still, it gave me an excuse to come back and pick you up.'

'Who were they?' said Max, making himself more comfortable.

'Oh, they were on their way over to some shindig in Inverness.

I couldn't shut that driver fellow up. He told me he was from Kent, and that the officers were attached to the Special Training Centre for combined operations at Inverailort House. The British call them *commandos* apparently. Still, our *Abwher* colleagues will be interested in that! You know, they have posters up all over the place, telling people that *careless talk costs lives*. I'm not so sure that idiot has seen any of them yet!'

They'd reached the sleepy village of Invermoriston, and *Phoebus* swung left onto the Glen Shiel road. As they sped past the village school, he called out; 'We've got an hour and a half, it'll be a bit tight. Still, the submarine has been ordered to remain on station off the beach for thirty minutes.'

Silence descended again as they hurried west through the lonely moorland wilderness. The minute hand on Reiniger's watch seemed to be revolving at twice the normal speed, so he stopped looking at it and closed his eyes. They *were* making good progress and thankfully the road was empty for the most part.

Ten miles further on, two pinpricks of light appeared in the distance. As the unidentified vehicle approached, the three occupants, tensed up; mouths dried, hearts pounded. The oncoming car sped by just as they passed the Cluanie Inn, its dark shape receding into the night. Sighs of relief drifted around the car from its now paranoid inhabitants.

'We'll be turning off shortly,' said *Phoebus*. 'The worst will then be behind us.'

The mountains closed in as they reached Glen Shiel. The lonely road swept left, then right, carried over swirling torrents by old stone bridges, crumbling structures that had carried this road since the days of the Jacobite rebellion.

At last, through the snow splashed windscreen the little granite lodge at Shiel Bridge came into view. It was here that the Camuscraig Road forked to the left. *Phoebus* hardly braked as he took the turn. They were on the home run; the *Tommis* had little chance of catching up with them now.

Their rate of progress slowed considerably as the little car struggled up the steep gradient. The road zigzagged dramatically as it snaked higher and higher above the floor of the Glen. The time was just before eleven fifteen.

By the time the Morris had climbed to the top of Glen Shiel's southern rim, huge sticky snowflakes were colliding with the partially-misted windscreen at a relentless rate. The wipers swung to and fro, scything through the build-up of ice, but they appeared to be losing the battle. Only when the car's nose dipped, commencing its descent down the steep side of Gleann Craig, did the onslaught abate. Ahead was the darkened village of Camuscraig, the only sign of life being the pale smoke rising from some of the settlement's chimneys. The inhabitants of the little fishing community would no doubt be huddled in front of their peat fires sipping whisky, or the fiery product of their age-old stills. With the approach of midnight young and old would come together, either in their cottages, or at the village inn. They were preparing, as always, to celebrate the coming of the New Year; their appetite for Hogmanay undiminished by wartime austerity measures.

The occupants of the grubby little Morris were preoccupied with other matters though. They headed into the village, still travelling a little faster than perhaps they should. The sound of the car's engine now echoed back off the walls of the cottages that huddled along the narrow street.

At the Inn the door stood open, allowing light from inside to flood across the snow. A young couple lingered outside, shaking the white powder from their long coats, too distracted by the welcome from inside to pay any attention to the car that sped past.

Phoebus slowed now to negotiate the bend at the end of the street. In the upstairs window of the last cottage, a threadbare curtain swept back to reveal the dark scrawny silhouette of a young man. The Germans didn't see him, but their driver did. He drove on, unaware of the fateful sequence of events that had just been triggered.

Lachlan Macdonald stepped back from the exposed window and into the shadows. His grandmother appeared in the doorway of the small bedroom. 'Lachie, pull that curtain back or we'll have Sandy Macrae banging on our door.' She was referring to the village ARP warden, a temperamental old fellow who seemed convinced that Camuscraig was a priority target for Hitler's *Luftwaffe*!

Lachlan let the curtain drop back into place and pondered over what he'd just seen. He pushed past his grandmother and trotted downstairs to the front door, grabbing his duffel coat on the way. He slipped out into the deserted street and turned right towards the village store and telephone kiosk. The kiosk offered some respite from the cold and, having closed the door behind him, he felt around for the coins that Dugald Matheson had given him two days earlier. They were still there, deep in his trouser pocket, partially wrapped in his handkerchief. Clutching them in his free hand, he picked up the receiver. He pushed the coins into the slot with nervous fingers, and waited. After a lengthy wait, the local operator's weary voice drifted into his ear. He pushed button *A* and spoke. 'Glendaig six four three please.'

The voice at the other end seemed surprised. 'Is that you Lachlan Macdonald?'

'Aye Morag, it is.'

'What in heaven's name are you doing out at this time of night… and on Hogmanay too! You're lucky I've answered.'

'Just connect me please Morag, and hurry.'

There was another short delay before Dugald Matheson's slurred voice came on the line. 'Hello, Glendaig Manse.'

'Is that Mr Dugald Matheson?' Lachlan asked nervously.

'Aye. Who's this?'

'Lachlan Macdonald here Mr Matheson.'

'Oh, hello Lachlan, what is it?'

'I believe I've just seen that car again Mr Matheson. You know, the Morris that knocked me off my bicycle.' His statement was met with a period of silence.

'Are you absolutely sure, Lachlan?'

'Aye sir, I'm reasonably sure. The sides seemed to be a different colour to the roof, like before.'

'Did you see who was in it?'

'No sir. It was too dark, sorry.'

'No bother Lachlan, when was this?'

'Ten minutes ago. It was heading your way.'

'Good lad, well done Lachlan. I'll make this worth your while if I find them.'

The phone went dead. Lachlan stepped out of the kiosk and blinked as the first snowflake drifted into his eyes. He dropped his head and trudged back along the street, feeling rather pleased with himself.

Phoebus and his companions were now well on their way towards Glendaig. It wasn't a great distance as the crow flew, but the course of the road was far from straight, twisting and turning as it followed the numerous inlets that incised the rocky coastline. The dark expanse of Loch Coinneach stretched away to their right, almost invisible, like an endless void fading into the night sky. It was twelve minutes to midnight, and they would need that time to get to the rendezvous point. It was looking good; they were going to make it, and dead on time.

The three pairs of eyes desperately searched the Loch hoping, praying, that they would catch a glimpse of the U-boat, but the dips in the road and the cluster of small islets hugging the shoreline made it nigh on impossible to distinguish between submarine and rock. The weather seemed to be improving though; the snowflakes settling on the windscreen were reducing in number and light from the emerging moon was beginning to highlight the contours of the breaking cloud.

They were very close to the beach now. The road climbed steadily to a blind summit, and as they coasted over the brow the jagged mass of Eilean Ceann Cinnidh at last came into view. At the same time, the moon broke fully through the low cloud, bathing the loch in a ghostly pale glow. A long finger of moonlight crept across the glistening water, illuminating the foamy crests of the incoming tide. Then as they watched, a long dark shape glided into view. It passed slowly from right to left, briefly highlighted against the moonlit water. A long curving wake fanned out behind it, fading back into the darkness.

U-114 had arrived to take them home.

2 0 0 9

Chapter Twenty-Seven

'There's a call for you over here, sir.' The young detective constable held the telephone handset aloft, his hand clamped over the mouthpiece. 'It's a Mrs Stevenson-Weir from Ruthven House Residential Home in Camuscraig.'

'Can you transfer it over here, Dan?' Neil asked from behind his computer screen. A thumbs up gesture heralded the imminent pleasure of a conversation with the less than delightful *prop* of Ruthven House.

'Hello Mrs Stevenson-Weir, what can I do for you?'

'You wanted to speak to Mr Macdonald, Inspector?' came the terse reply. She'd adopted the most refined of Glaswegian accents. Neil had never heard the like before.

'Aye, I did. Has he recovered from the flu now?'

'He has indeed Inspector, so please feel free to pop in at any time.'

'Thank you, I haven't got much on today so I'll be over this afternoon if that's okay?'

'We'll have the kettle on.'

'Thanks, shall we say two o'clock?'

'Two it is. Bye for now, Inspector.'

The phone went dead, leaving Neil staring at the handset, bewildered by Mrs Stevenson-Weir's apparent willingness to assist him with his enquiry… and offer him tea!

He logged off from the force intranet screen and headed for the office door. 'I'll be over at Camuscraig if DCI Brodie wants me.'

His young colleague raised a hand without looking up from his pile of papers. He knew that it would be highly unlikely on a Saturday; Brodie would be up the road sipping single malt in the clubhouse at Culcabock.

Neil had achieved one of his best ever runs over to Camuscraig that day. It would've been even quicker, had he not found himself stuck for a time behind a heavily-laden people-carrier packed to the gunnels with French tourists and their luggage.

He pulled up at Ruthven House ten minutes early, so he killed a few minutes reading through Davie MacAllister's pocket book again. Having refreshed his knowledge of the incident involving Lachlan Macdonald, he made his way slowly up to the front door.

'Welcome back to Ruthven House, Inspector.' Mrs Stevenson-Weir greeted him in the foyer as if he were a fee-paying relative. 'Mr Macdonald is sitting in the rose garden. Would you like to speak to him there?'

'That would be fine, is he expecting me?'

'Aye, he is.' She patted the sleeve of his jacket. 'He's a little nervous for some reason. I've told him you won't be dragging him off in handcuffs.' She chortled, more to herself than anyone else, her substantial cleavage wobbling violently as she did so.

'Did you want to join us? I recall you wanted someone to be present when I spoke to him.'

'I spoke with him this morning, Inspector. He intimated to me that he'd rather speak to you alone. I did reassure him that you were a very nice young man, so no need for a chaperone, as long as he was happy with the arrangement.'

'In that case, I'll find my own way,' said Neil with a cursory smile.

'Well you'll find him just over there by the *buff beauty*.'

He looked puzzled. '*Buff beauty*?'

'It's a *rose* Inspector, beautiful apricot blooms, very hardy. Did you think we were providing our residents with some sort of raunchy entertainment?' There was another chuckle from somewhere behind her lipstick-stained dentures, then she concluded the display with a deep snort.

'Tea or coffee?' she asked.

'Tea would be great, thanks.' He only hoped that she didn't snort into the tea!

'Well you go along and have a chat with old Mr Macdonald and I'll get Ailee to bring your tea over. Just remember he is quite frail, and a wee bit slow… if you get my meaning.' She spun around and scuttled off, like an ageing model parading proudly along a catwalk.

Neil found Lachlan Macdonald sitting on a wooden bench, gazing dreamily out across the blue-green waters of the Sound of Sleat. A tartan rug had been wrapped about his knees, no doubt to protect his lower limbs from the keen breeze that blew across the hillside. The stems of the *buff beauty* rustled behind him sending a cascade of pale orange petals fluttering down onto the lush green lawn.

Both age and ill health had taken their toll of the old man. His wiry frame lurked somewhere within the pale blue shirt and red cardigan that he was wearing. The flu had sallowed his bony features, but his hearing seemed unimpaired. He heard the approaching footsteps and looked around. The few strands of white hair that still graced his scalp whipped about in the breeze, somehow reminiscent of arcing cables.

Neil sat down next to him and extended a hand. Lachlan took it and shook it feebly. Having commented on the weather and the pleasant surroundings, Neil gently steered the conversation around to the events that had prompted his visit. 'I was wondering whether you'd be happy to speak to me about an incident that happened in the village when you were a boy?'

'Aye, I can do that,' said Lachlan, his voice faltering. 'You want to know what happened when those men made me fall off my cycle, eh?'

'That's right Mr Macdonald, I believe it was quite late at night just before Hogmanay in 1941?'

'Aye son, that's right. I was riding home from my Auntie Jean's…

been there for my tea y'see. I used to take eggs over to her on a Sunday.'

'Can you tell me what happened exactly?'

'Och, I cannae mind now, I just fell off, that's all.' He turned his head away, distracted by a pair of seagulls wheeling and shrieking overhead.

'I was told that you fell off trying to avoid a car that was speeding through the village, a car possibly containing some Germans. Is that right?'

The old man looked back, his eyes moist from the effect of the wind. He studied Neil for a second. 'Who told you that?' he asked.

Neil pulled out Davie MacAllister's pocket book. 'It's all in here,' he said. 'PC MacAllister, the village policeman. He recorded what happened.'

'But Davie wasn't there, how could he have done?'

'Dugald Matheson told him all about it. Do you remember him?'

'Aye, for sure. He was killed the day after Hogmanay.'

Neil read the constable's notes to Macdonald. Then he asked; 'Did Davie come to see you about the incident?'

'Aye, he did.'

'What did he say he was going to do to find the car?'

'He said he'd told the boys in Inverness, but that was it. He just wanted to know if I was alright. I said I was, and he told me to take care in the future. And that was that.'

The chinking sound of china being carried on a tray interrupted their conversation. Neil looked round to see Ailee, a petite but podgy teenager, approaching warily across the lawn. She carefully placed the tray on the bench between the two men, having first been at pains to state the obvious. 'Your tea, gentlemen.' With a timid smile she retreated, the swishing sound of her plastic apron diminishing gradually as she headed back to the kitchen.

Neil handed Lachlan one of the cups. 'You seem unwilling to talk about the incident Lachlan, why would that be?'

The old man raised the cup to his lips. He sipped his tea then, with a shaky hand, lowered it again. All the while, he observed Neil through suspicious eyes. 'Why is all this so important now? It was such a long time ago.'

'Well Lachlan, did you know that we'd found a skeleton buried on the beach along by Glendaig?'

'Aye, of course, I do watch the news you know. But what's that got to do with me?'

'Because we think he might have been a German naval officer, and that he'd been buried on that beach since the war. Dugald Matheson seems to have believed that the men who caused you to fall off your bicycle had a German military cap in the back of their car. If this was true, the two incidents might be linked.'

Lachlan looked down at his feet, both of which were now poking out from the blanket. 'Rubbish,' he declared.

Neil sipped his tea. 'Why do you think its rubbish, Lachlan?'

'Because Mr Matheson was drunk that night. He was probably seeing things.'

'Well, I have a feeling he wasn't mistaken, strange as it may sound. Look, don't you think it's time we laid this poor chap to rest with some dignity, and perhaps let his family know that he's been found? That's all I'm trying to achieve here.'

'So you're no' interested in who killed him then?'

'Of course I am, but I'm under no illusions as to the difficulties we face finding that person, if indeed we can after all these years. So surely it can't do any harm telling me what you know. At least I can then make a decision as to whether the two incidents are linked.'

Lachlan looked away again and mumbled, 'I can't.'

'What do you mean Lachlan?'

'I mean I can't. I promised.'

'Promised who?'

Lachlan looked back. There were tears present in his eyes. 'Mr Grant.'

Neil was getting somewhere now. 'Would you be referring to Donald Grant, the stalker on the Glendaig Estate?'

'Aye, that's him.' Lachlan suddenly looked vulnerable. He gave Neil a sideways glance, as if fearful of what was to come next.

'Donald died a long time ago, Lachlan,' Neil reassured him. 'I think you've kept your promise long enough.'

'Is that right? Donald died. I never knew.' He shook his head and sighed, his relief clear to see. 'He threatened to tell the Laird if I ever opened my mouth about the men in that car.'

'Tell the laird what, Lachlan?'

There was a pause. 'That I'd been poaching on his land, that's what. I know the old man, Sir Brodric, is dead, but the estate is still in the family isn't it?'

'So I believe, yes, but you don't have to worry about that now. To use your words; it was a long time ago.' He placed a hand on Lachlan's shoulder. 'Look, I'll make you a promise: that you'll never get into trouble over *any* poaching you did all those years back. How does that sound?' Neil couldn't believe what he was saying.

'So I can trust you then?'

'You *can* trust me, Lachlan.'

'Alright then.' He paused for thought again. 'Are you sure old Donald's dead?'

'Aye, I'm sure.'

Having at last freed the old man from his fear-induced vow of silence, Neil sensed that Lachlan would begin to open up. He was right. Lachlan Macdonald began to talk. He was without doubt a man desperate to share his story, a story that many would have considered insignificant, but to Lachlan it meant everything. To him, the events of that December in 1941 and the days that followed seemed like yesterday. They had burned into his memory, like stars shining through the fog of an otherwise unremarkable life.

He started to explain what had happened on the night of the 29th of December, when he'd fallen off his bicycle, and how Isobel Grant had been so kind to him. Then, he recalled Dugald's visit and his request that he be told if the car ever returned to the area.

'Did you ever see inside the car or speak to the men, Lachlan?'

'No, but I heard Mr Matheson giving them what for!'

'And *did* you see the car again?' Neil held his breath.

'Aye, of course, it came through the village on Hogmanay. I was listening to the wireless with my granny. It must have been sometime after eleven. We were waiting for midnight, see. Then we'd have a wee dram, like we did every year. Granny asked me to go up to her room and fetch down her shawl. I could nae find it at first, because it was dark I suppose. Anyway, I heard this motor car coming up the street. It was unusual to hear a car that late at night, and especially one travelling so fast, so I pulled back the curtain and looked out. The thing flew by; I knew it was a Morris; I'd seen one on a cigarette card only the week before. I could just make out that this one had different colour sides, red I think, like the one that knocked me off my bicycle.'

'And did you see who was in it on that occasion?'

'Och no, it was far too dark… and too quick.'

'Of course, so what did you do next?'

'Well, I'd promised Mr Matheson that if I ever saw the car again, I'd call him. He actually gave me some coins to make the telephone call, so that's what I did, from the phone box up the street.'

'What did he say?'

'He was very happy. I think he was drunk mind, but less so than on the Sunday. He thanked me for the information, and told me he'd make it worth my while. Then said he was going to find them.'

'Did you ever hear what happened, whether he found them or not?'

'No I heard nothing, until two days later, when word went around that Mr Matheson had been killed whilst out stalking with Mr Grant. And before you ask, I never saw that car again either.'

'What about Donald Grant, how did he become involved with you?'

Lachlan bit into a hobnob biscuit. He considered the question whilst he ate. 'I was mending some fishing net on the beach down there. It must've been a few days after Dugald Matheson died. He stopped in his lorry, then he marched down to see me on the beach and made it quite clear how much trouble I'd be in if I ever mentioned the car or the men again. I remember what he said to this day; "Ye'll get yir heid in yir hauns an yir lugs ti pley wi." It was something my granny used to come out with, you're probably too young to remember such sayings.'

Neil hadn't heard of the phrase before, but had no problem deciphering it. '*You'll get your head in your hands and your ears to play with*. Sounds a bit gruesome to me.'

'Aye, and he meant it too, believe me. He was a big man, Donald Grant. Folk were feared of him. Yet I cannae mind how he'd got involved in the whole affair. It was always a mystery to me.'

'And did anyone else ever come and talk to you about the car, or the men?'

'Never, and I never breathed a word about them to this day.'

Lachlan's attention returned to the sparkling waters of the sound as he followed the progress of a small yacht. It was forging its way south, its shiny blue hull labouring under billowing sails. Trailing behind was a small black dinghy, bobbing and weaving in the larger vessel's wake. 'I spent much of my life out there you know, fishing for herring with my cousins, whatever the weather. Aye, it seems like yesterday.'

He was locked into another world, and Neil understood why he wanted to remain there. Life must have been hard, but communities were close knit. They were resilient people who worked and played hard, untouched by the complexities of the current century. He got up and gathered the cups together on the tray. 'I'll leave you to enjoy the view Lachlan. Thank you for telling me about the men in the car, you've been very helpful.'

Lachlan looked up. 'Just be sure to get that poor devil back to his family, that's all I ask.'

'I'll do my best Lachlan, you can count on that.'

Neil walked back across the lawn carrying the tray. He paused at the top of the gentle slope and looked back, admiring the view. Lachlan hadn't moved and was sitting quietly amongst the thorny

306

limbs of Mrs Stevenson-Weir's *buff beauty*. He was still out there on the sound with his cousins, doing what he'd always done.

'Was Mr Macdonald helpful at all?' Mrs Stevenson-Weir took the tray from him when he reached the French doors to the residents' lounge.

'Yes he was, thank you very much. I won't be needing to trouble him again though. Thanks for the tea.'

He skirted around the building and climbed into his car, sitting for a while and pondering over what he'd been told. He'd been expecting a far more challenging conversation with Lachlan but, to his surprise, things had gone well and he'd had no issue with the credibility of the old man's account. He felt confident that the enquiry was moving forward. It was now becoming clear that there *had* been some form of clandestine military activity in the area, most probably involving the German Navy and some of the locals. However, the satisfaction of moving forward was short-lived. Neil's sense of reality re-emerged from somewhere deep inside him… *For Christ's sake*, he thought. *I've got remains that I can't identify, a second grave with its contents missing, that's if there were any contents. I have no real motive and certainly no suspects…* Then there was Dugald Matheson, whose death was supposedly the result of an accident, but his instinct was telling him otherwise. Nothing was adding up and he urgently needed a break!

He waited at the bottom of the hill for a tractor to pass, then turned right. The road took him past the war memorial; a kilted highlander, his rifle held up to celebrate victory. The statue stood on a grassy promontory, the remains of a former raised beach that had been eroded away by the cold peaty waters of the Sound of Sleat.

Further along, the village street was bordered on either side by brightly-painted cottages. Neil pulled up abruptly and glanced across to his right. The cottage at the end of the row still bore the name *Bothan Nan Greag*. It had been from the flaking upstairs window of this property that Lachlan Macdonald had watched the mysterious Morris Eight rush past, sixty-eight years earlier.

307

Chapter Twenty-Eight

Monday 15ᵗʰ June

Sunday had been a welcome distraction from the enquiry. Neil was acutely aware that the clock was ticking on this one, and Brodie was monitoring the hour hand with intense interest. He hadn't necessarily been aware of it and certainly wouldn't admit to it, but his frustration at getting nowhere and the stress that came with it were certainly taking their toll.

There was now pressure on him to get a result, predominantly because he was the new boy on the team but equally because *he* himself now had an acute desire to discover what had happened all those years ago. He needed at least *some* of the answers to the growing catalogue of questions that this case now posed. He was confident that the answers were probably out there… or was he? One thing was for sure; the prospect of handing Brodie the case papers, with a recommendation on the crime report that the matter be *filed as undetected*, was not giving him a warm feeling. It never did. Such an endorsement was always considered an admission of failure by any conscientious detective.

The walk along the beach at Nairn had helped him clear his mind. They'd strolled arm in arm for over two miles. Tam had been happy beachcombing, running to and fro then circling the couple, busily herding his pack. At the same time, he'd not missed any opportunity to harass the resting seagulls or pull the legs off of a dead crab.

Neil had looked on contentedly as Cat ran across the glistening expanse of beach, spaniel in hot pursuit, then squealed with delight as the dog caught up with her, spraying her jeans and wellington boots with sea water and sand.

But that was yesterday. He was now on his way back to Glendaig once again, this time to see Murdo Stuart. The time had come to challenge the ex-stalker's account of the circumstances surrounding Dugald Matheson's death, and his assertion that he wasn't present at the time of the accident.

The days had been warm of late and the skies above the Highlands had been free of all but the thinnest ribbons of cirrus cloud. Wind-dried heather blanketed the ancient peaks, a breathtaking panorama set against an azure sky. Their summits were visible for miles, unusually free of the misty cloud that often clung to their highest slopes.

To his right, Loch Coinneach sparkled under the late morning sun. The small islands that lay offshore rose up from the tranquil water, green and grey against a background of shimmering blue. He sped past the beach on which the whole saga had begun, deserted like it had been for centuries, the flapping lengths of police tape now gone.

Minutes later and he was entering Glendaig, passing the old sign that bore the same name, bent over and rusting at one corner, leaning backwards against the grassy bank. The damage had no doubt been due to a collision of sorts, but how one could collide with a sign halfway up a near-vertical embankment had always been a source of amusement for Neil when he'd entered the village.

The Reverend Mackay was outside the Manse pushing an antiquated motor mower over the hardy tufted grass that surrounded his home. All seemed as it should be in Glendaig on such a beautiful morning, but in less than five minutes that would all change.

Neil decided to park outside Siobhan Stuart's cottage. He then took the short walk over the little bridge and along towards

Lochview. As he approached the little cottage, he felt sure that he could smell the faint aroma of smoke. Not wood or coal smoke, but that which often seeped endlessly from the glowing core of a garden bonfire.

He knocked repeatedly on the front door but there was no reply, so he made his way around the side of the house and past the garage. The door was up and the Ford Escort was missing, raising the speculation that his visit had been mistimed. Once in the garden to the rear of the house, he headed for the little column of smoke rising from behind a giant rhododendron bush.

As he negotiated his way around the leafy shrub, he came upon a scene that he found both confusing and concerning in equal measure. Murdo Stuart stood with Mary Galbraith next to an old oil drum. Murdo was selecting items from a box that Mary was holding and feeding them into the rusting container.

Neil quickened his step, a sense of urgency rising within him.

'Can you stop that please,' he called out, pointing with an outstretched arm as he approached. He broke into a jog as he got nearer, reaching the pair just as another item fluttered down into the smouldering brazier. Neil reached into the drum and quickly retrieved what appeared to be a letter, its edges scorched by the heat but mercifully not yet burnt.

'What on earth are you doing?' he demanded, glaring at the couple.

Mary looked distinctly uncomfortable. 'They're just old letters and photos, things I don't need any more, Inspector.'

'Well perhaps I'd better be the judge of that Mary, can I see what's in the box please?'

'And what authority do you have to seize these documents?' she snapped.

'The authority of a warrant if need be Mary. So what is it to be? Hand them over now, or I can always make a phone call and arrange the paperwork.'

He held his breath, hoping the bluff had succeeded. There was no way he'd get a phone signal in Murdo's garden! Mary's eyes narrowed. She glared at Neil, weighing up her options, then Murdo intervened.

'Come on Mary, give him the box. You heard him, he'll get hold of it one way or another.'

Mary glanced across at him, angry that he hadn't supported her stance on the matter. There was hesitation, as if she was considering her position further. Then with an air of defeat, she handed the box over. Neil took it, trying to hide his sense of relief.

'Thank you Mary, now what do we have in here?'

A brief examination of the contents of the box revealed an assortment of letters, envelopes and old photographs. He pulled out a handwritten letter and read it. The document looked to be the work of a child. It was dated 15th October 1985, written to Mary and signed *Diana*. The content focussed on a sweater that Mary had knitted for Diana's birthday. The latter had written to thank the old lady for her kindness. 'Who's Diana?' Neil asked.

'Isobel Grant's granddaughter,' Mary answered curtly, her arms folded tightly against the chill breeze that was now agitating the leaves on the shrubs. He delved into the box again as if it were some sort of lucky dip, and brought out another old letter. This one, dated 1982, was from Isobel Grant herself, chatting about this and that. Neil searched the page eagerly hoping to find an address, but there was none, just the date.

'You won't find anything of interest in there Inspector, believe me.' Murdo stood with his hands thrust deep into his trouser pockets, his cheeks flushed red from the heat of the fire.

'Like I said, I'll need to be the judge of that. I assume all this belongs to you, Mary?'

'Aye, they're all mine.'

'So why burn them and why come here to do it?'

'Och, they're from a time gone by, I don't look at them anymore and Iain won't want them. I knew Murdo had the brazier, so I asked him if I could burn them.'

'So what's wrong with the wheelie bin?'

'Nothing, I just wanted to destroy them, they're private, not that you seem to care.'

Neil didn't react, but managed a disbelieving grin. Murdo walked over to the garden bench and sat down. 'What brings you out here then Inspector? I'm sure it wasn't to stop us burning rubbish.'

'I need to go over some of the things we discussed during my last visit. Is that okay?'

'Of course, perhaps we'd best go inside then.'

'Well I'll be off then, Murdo.' Mary turned to leave.

'Alright lassie, I'll see you later.' Murdo patted her arm reassuringly.

As she brushed past him, Neil said, 'I'll get these back to you as soon as I can, Mary.'

She turned and frowned. 'You might as well throw them in the bin Inspector, finish what we'd started. They're just painful memories now, that's all they are.'

Neil followed Murdo through the French doors and into the sitting room. Murdo went across to a table, upon which stood a variety of bottles. 'A dram, Inspector?'

'No thanks Murdo, I've got a long drive ahead of me.'

Murdo poured himself a straight whisky and sank into one of the leather armchairs. 'So what is it that you wanted to speak to me about?'

Neil pulled out Davie MacAllister's pocket book and tapped the black cover with his finger. 'This belonged to the village constable at Camuscraig, Davie MacAllister. Remember him, Murdo?'

'Aye, I do that. Lazy bugger as I recall.'

'Well not so lazy that he failed to make a full entry in here regarding Dugald Matheson's untimely death.'

'I see.' Murdo's ruddy cheeks took on an even deeper hue. 'What does it say?'

'It *says* that you were present when Dugald was shot during that stalking expedition on New Year's Day in 1942. That surely seems to be at odds with your version of events.'

Murdo fidgeted around in his chair and took a lengthy slug from his glass. 'He was obviously mistaken, wasn't listening to what he was being told.'

'No Murdo, he seems quite clear in his understanding that *you* were present. Even noted down your address. Time for some straight talking, eh Murdo?'

'Alright, alright,' avowed the old man, running a stumpy finger through the grooves etched in the crystal glass. 'I said I was there to help my wee pal Davie Grant confirm his story, so to speak. You know… so there was no likelihood of him getting into trouble, like. Donald told me they needed an independent witness because the police might not have believed his account of what happened, but in reality I wasn't there, I swear.'

'So let me get this straight, Murdo. You agreed to corroborate the Grants' version of events relating to Dugald's death, by stating that you *were* present when the accident occurred, but in truth you *weren't* actually present when he was killed?'

'Aye that's correct, Inspector.'

'And was Dugald actually killed on a stalking expedition, or were the circumstances distinctly different. For example, was he involved in some form of altercation with some German sailors, or suchlike?'

Murdo became even more agitated. 'Look, I wasn't there. I was just trying to help them out. I know there was some sort of argument and the gun went off, but as far as I know it was during the stalking trip. I only know what Donald and Davie told me.'

'Argument? What sort of argument are you referring to?'

'I was never told. They said it was best I didn't know and just keep to the version they had given me.' He looked across at Neil, concern etched on his face. His breathing had become laboured and he ran the palm of his hand across his chest.

'Are you alright, Murdo?' Neil asked.

'Aye, aye, I'm just a little bit uptight with all this.'

'Okay, I'll be on my way in a minute. Just answer me this. Why not tell me this from the outset? Why worry about corroborating their story after all these years, they're all dead now as far as I'm aware.'

'I know,' Murdo panted. 'I didn't know these records had survived, did I? I just wanted to distance myself from the whole affair. And Mary agreed never to mention that I'd been treated as a witness. I'm sorry, but whatever happened to Dugald Matheson is as much of a mystery to me as it is to you.'

'Alright Murdo. I see from the constable's pocket book that he had reason to speak to you and David Grant five days later. It was late at night, you were both having a pee by the roadside, next to a Dennis thirty hundredweight truck... remember that?'

'No, sorry Inspector, I don't. We'd probably been over to Camuscraig to the dancing or something like that. We were probably pissed at the time... No drink drive laws in those days!' He attempted to laugh but winced instead. 'Are you done, Inspector? It's just that I'm feeling a bit off colour.'

'Yes of course Murdo, are you sure you'll be okay?'

At that moment the sound of a car could be heard pulling up outside the garage. A door slammed and several seconds later Ursula Stuart walked through the French doors. 'My, my Inspector, you must have fallen in love with the place.' Then, when she saw her husband, her jovial demeanour faded quickly away. 'Have you had another angina attack Murdo?'

'Just a wee one dear, don't fuss for Christ's sake.'

'I'm going to get your medication. I'm afraid this conversation has come to an end, Inspector.'

Neil got up to leave. 'I think we're just about done Mrs Stuart.' He then turned to Murdo; 'You take care and don't worry. I'll try not to trouble you again.'

'Is that a promise?' asked Murdo.

'Oh, I can never promise,' Neil replied with a smile. 'I'll just do my best, that's all.'

Ursula scurried back into the room with a bottle of tablets, the concern on her face clear to see. 'Are you still here, Inspector?'

'Just going,' he confirmed. 'I'll see myself out.' He picked up the box of photographs and disappeared through the French doors, suitably rebuked.

The journey home had seemed longer than usual. The last shafts of sunlight had finally disappeared behind the distant peaks to the west, their red embers fading into a perfect dusk sky.

Neil turned away from the window and switched on the lamp in the corner of the dining room. He returned to the long oak table that dominated the small room and lowered himself onto one of the leather-cushioned chairs. He reached for the can of McEwans bitter that stood before him on the table and eased the ring pull back, releasing a hiss from within.

Scattered on the table in front of him were all the documents and photos from the box he'd acquired earlier. There must have been around forty or so items in all: photographs, letters, empty envelopes and Christmas cards.

He examined each one in turn whilst he sipped the cold beer, all the while stroking Tam with his free hand. A number of the letters were signed by Isobel Grant, others by Ursel Matheson or Mary's sister Muireall. There was nothing particularly interesting within their content; just general news and conversation as one would expect. The envelopes were empty, stacked separately and addressed in block capitals. Their postmarks were almost illegible, so no clues there.

He was contemplating which letter belonged to which envelope when the front door opened. Cat walked in looking resplendent in a cream tracksuit. She'd been to an exercise class in town and had stayed on for a drink at the gym with friends. She appeared behind Neil and curled her arms around his neck, her long blonde hair falling onto his shoulders.

'What's all this then?' she asked before planting a kiss on the top of his head. He explained how he'd found Murdo and Mary attempting to burn the contents of the box.

'There must be something here to give me a clue,' he said, raising his hand from the dog to stroke the side of his girlfriend's face.

'You sound a wee bit desperate honey. Have you looked through all this stuff yet?' Cat was enjoying having her face caressed.

'Yes, I am, and no, I've just had a quick look, then stopped to get a beer.'

'Got your priorities right then. Wait till I get a glass of red and I'll join you. Two heads are always better than one so they say.' She disappeared into the kitchen, followed by the dog. Neil examined another photo, then dropped it onto the pile, shaking his head.

Tam reappeared, munching noisily on a biscuit, followed by Cat with a large glass of Merlot. She pulled out the chair next to Neil and sat down. 'Let's have a look see,' she said, cradling the wine glass in her palm. With her free hand, she reorganised the documents into separate piles: correspondence, envelopes and photographs.

'Tidy-minded as always,' commented Neil as he looked on with some amusement.

'I do love old photos,' said Cat, ignoring his jibe and placing the pile of black and white images in front of her. 'Let's look at these first. You can glean so much from them… the fashions of the time, changes to the environment, personal relationships…'

'You reckon you can tell how someone gets on with someone else, just from a photo?'

'Aye, of course, in some instances you can.' She rummaged through the glossy old photos with a forefinger, pushing away the top copies. 'Take this one for example.' She picked up a black and white print. It depicted a family group posing against the backdrop of a dry stone wall. On the left was a short stocky man in his late forties. He had light-coloured hair and wire-framed spectacles. Interestingly, he was wearing the long black cassock of a priest. Next to him was an elegant, dark-haired woman, perhaps a little younger than the priest but taller. She was wearing a figure-hugging summer frock decorated with a vivid floral print. Both she and the priest seemed dwarfed by the tall young man, about twenty, standing to her left. He was athletically built with wiry hair, similar in colour to the priest's, and smartly turned out in a tweed jacket and kilt. His beefy hands were clasped together in front of him as if to conceal his impressive sporran from view. His face was expressionless, devoid of any hint of a smile as he stood gazing directly at the camera lens. To *his* left was the attractive looking young woman Neil had seen in the photograph at Mary Galbraith's cottage, but this picture had been taken when she was some years younger, perhaps in her mid-teens. There was no mistaking the shiny dark hair tumbling about her shoulders, the equally dark eyes and fine attractive features. Isobel Grant was also gazing at the camera, arms held to her front in formal pose.

Neil took the photo from Cat. 'The young woman's called Isobel Grant. I've seen a photo of her before. I assume the priest is Callum Matheson, her uncle and next to him that must be his wife, Anna. Good looking woman, eh?' He handed it back to her and continued his commentary. 'She was Swiss, according to her gravestone.'

'Umm. It's the younger pair that interest me,' said Cat. 'Look at the body language; she's standing some distance from him, unnaturally so. If he's a friend or relative, she's clearly uncomfortable in his company. Do you know who *he* is?'

'Aye, I see what you mean. I've got a feeling he must be Dugald Matheson, but I haven't seen a photo of him so can't be sure.' He turned the photo over, but there was nothing to give him a clue on the reverse.

Cat had moved on through the pile. She held up another group photo, grainier than the image they'd just been looking at. The picture was of a group of youngsters; some were teenagers, some perhaps a little younger. They were posing on a beach with two women. It was a windy day, and strands of their hair had been blown across their faces, partially concealing them from the photographer.

'Well if I'm not mistaken, she's related to *her*… sisters I'd say.' Cat pointed to the slightly younger version of Anna Matheson, and then to the other woman in the group. 'And there's that girl Isobel again, she's even younger in this snap.'

Neil turned the photo over, hoping that there might be some sort of caption on this occasion. He was lucky. Someone had scrawled in pencil…

July 1930, on the beach by Castle Coinneach with Katharina and the boys.

'Ah, now this is interesting. Anna had a sister, Katharina. From the caption here, these two laddies would appear to be her sons.' Neil held the photo up close. 'I wonder where this was taken exactly.'

'Who knows, but I'm sure you could find it if you wanted to.' Cat tapped the photo with a slender finger 'And there's *Mr Happy* again, on the end there, looking as miserable as sin.' She pointed to a tall sullen-looking youth, clearly a reluctant participant in the photograph. 'That other photo, when he's wearing the kilt, it must have been taken a good few years later, five or more, I'd say.'

She sipped from her wine glass, watching Neil sort through the remaining photos. He picked up another, this time of two men, the younger one in army uniform. They were standing by the door of a shiny black motor car parked outside the door of a stone cottage. 'This is him again, in uniform this time, and I know that cottage, I've been inside. The local post woman in Glendaig lives there now.' Someone had also written on the reverse of the crumpled image…

Lt Dugald Matheson 6th Seaforths with Uncle Donald Nov 1939. On leave from officer training.

'This confirms it then, so it *is* Dugald Matheson in those other photos. And this fellow here must be Donald Grant.'

Grant was also a big man, his stubbly fair hair receding to reveal an expansive brow. A sparse beard clung to his jowly lower jaw, hardly visible at first sight. Neil estimated both Dugald and his uncle to be well over six feet in height. 'No wonder he put the fear of Christ into Lachlan Macdonald,' he muttered to himself, then tapped the image of Dugald, and took another sip of beer. 'So you and Isobel weren't the best of friends, eh… interesting.'

'Well this'll interest you even more,' said Cat as she pushed another photograph towards him. He picked it up and examined it, then turned it over. The note on the reverse read…

Isobel 15, Mary 14, and Max 21 Beinn Caisteal. May 1935.

Neil's eyes focussed on the name *Max*, like beams from a powerful searchlight. He flipped the photo back to examine the picture again. There was Isobel again, this time wearing dungarees. Her hair was tied back into short pigtails. She was standing on a steep heathery slope, gazing down towards a shimmering loch some distance below her. Standing nearby, but slightly further down the slope was another girl, petite, with dark bobbed hair and with a slightly hooked nose. Neil recognised her immediately as a young Mary Galbraith. However, it was the third figure in the photo, a young man standing behind Mary, which really caught his attention. The man, probably in his early twenties, was well-groomed with dark slicked-back hair. He was well-built, and wore a loose cotton shirt and matching trousers that billowed in the wind.

Cat leant across to look at the photo. 'I'm sure he's one of those boys posing with his mother in the 1930 photo, you know, the one that had *Katharina and the boys* written on the back.'

Neil grunted in acknowledgement, but there was another photo that he really wanted to compare to the one in front of him. Jumping up and almost toppling his chair in the process, he rushed out of the room. Tam, disturbed from his slumbers by his master's hasty exit, followed close behind. Cat raised her glass and wondered what on earth had triggered he partner's urgent departure. She listened as he moved around upstairs, eagerly awaiting his return, and hopefully an explanation!

Seconds later he thundered back down the stairs and reappeared carrying a hardback book, Matthias Fuchs's book, *Leading The Wolfpacks*. He returned to his seat and flicked rapidly through the glossy pages. When he reached chapter six he stopped and tapped heavily on the image that occupied most of the page. 'That's him,' he gasped, still panting from his excursion upstairs. 'That's bloody well him, Max Friedmann!'

Cat said nothing. She spun the book around and calmly compared the picture of the handsome-looking naval officer wearing the Knight's Cross with the photo in front of them. Neil looked on expectantly, willing her to say something. Then, after a few seconds silence, she said, 'Yes, I agree that's him, that's your German.'

Neil examined the 1930 photo again, concentrating on the youth standing next to Katharina. 'I didn't recognise him in this one, it's too grainy, and I suppose he was just a boy in this photo.'

'Well it's definitely him in this one,' said Cat pointing to the picture taken on the mountainside.

'Well, well, so Mary Galbraith *did* know Max Friedmann before the war… and so did this woman Isobel Grant.' Neil had a glint in his eye.

'Not only that,' said Cat, 'it would appear that he's related to the local minister's wife and is a cousin of your *Mr Happy*, Dugald Matheson.'

Neil returned to the window and stared out across the garden, reflecting upon his newly-acquired knowledge. Then he turned back to Cat, who was still examining the items on the table. 'It all makes sense now, Anna Matheson's place of birth being so close to Max Friedmann's. I need to go back and see Mary Galbraith and her friend Murdo Stuart tomorrow, before they concoct some story to explain this away.'

'I'm not so sure they can,' Cat replied. 'It's all here in black and white.'

'Aye, but all the same, questions need to be asked without delay. The bloody clock's still ticking on this job and I need to make some headway soon.'

He stooped, gently brushing the hair away from Cat's neck and planted a kiss on the exposed flesh. 'You're not just a pretty face, are you?' He kissed her again.

'I'm glad you appreciate me, perhaps I'd better stick around then.'

'I wouldn't want anything else, Cat.'

'Are you sure about that Neil? Only I keep dropping hints about making this living together thing more permanent, but I never get a straight answer. Perhaps you'd prefer it to be just the two of you.'

She gestured towards Tam who was lying on his back, stretched out on the sofa. Neil walked over to the dog and rubbed his chest. 'What do you think wee boy, shall we let her move in with us *permanently*?' Tam opened one eye, and his tail started to thump repeatedly on the leather cushion. 'Looks like the answer's a resounding *yes*,' said Neil, reaching into the drinks cabinet. He pulled out a bottle of single malt. 'Shall we have a wee dram to celebrate?'

Chapter Twenty-Nine

The overgrown driveway from the coast road led away beneath a dense canopy of Caledonian pines. The heavy boughs way above Neil's head creaked to the accompaniment of the wind, and the distant voices of the forest's wildlife now echoed all around him. He shivered, not because it was cold but because of his surroundings. Did he really want to venture up that track? Tam, however, unfazed by the eerie woodland sounds, ran on ahead darting left and right across the stony path, seeking out any ground-level wildlife.

Neil had been keen to get back to Glendaig to see Mary Galbraith. He'd driven up to Rowan Cottage only to have found her out. Cadha's incessant barking from somewhere deep within the property seemed to confirm her absence, as normally the boisterous collie would have been promptly rebuked, so he'd decided to take his own dog for a walk and at the same time attempt to locate the beach where the two Swiss sisters had picnicked with their children eighty years before.

The ordnance survey map of the area indicated that there were a string of small coves hugging the shoreline of Loch Coinneach close to Glendaig. The largest was accessible from the old track that led to Castle Coinneach, the imposing ruin that stood between the coast road and the loch.

The approach to the castle, darkened by creaking pines and

heralded by the cries of unseen rooks, was certainly not a place for the faint-hearted. Neil, having established that his mind was playing tricks on him, now sensed a presence behind him as he progressed through the avenue of trees. He felt the hair on the back of his neck rise and glanced nervously over his shoulder. Was there something there? In his mind's eye he sensed an apparition observing him from the shadows between the trees, an ancient warrior clad in armour and mounted upon a white charger. He imagined the giant horse scuffing at the gravel, ejecting pulses of condensed breath from flared nostrils whilst its heavy metal barding clanked against its muscular flanks. For a second the vision persisted, as the animal reluctantly stood its ground agitated, wide-eyed. Then, as quickly as the image had manifested itself it faded away, back into Neil's subconscious. He felt another shiver run through him and quickened his step, calling on Tam to come to heel.

As the track meandered to the right, the crumbling gatehouse of the castle came into view. The imposing grey stone structure, part-obscured by a veiny network of ivy, remained largely intact. Behind it, the long-abandoned keep towered above the crumbling perimeter wall. A pathway diverged to the right, leading around the lofty ramparts and down towards the beach. Neil paused to study the faded coat of arms carved into the stonework above the gateway. Centuries of inclement weather had eroded the intricate heraldic emblem but he could just make out the outline of a shield, surmounted by the visored helmet of a medieval knight. The shield was simple, bisected by an inverted chevron and decorated with three axes; unbeknown to him, the arms of *Black Kenneth*, Earl of Knoydart.

A sudden flapping of wings from inside the fortress startled him and he walked on, not wishing to linger for too long. He was now aware of a more intense light source flooding the path ahead, sunshine at last and hopefully some respite from the jumpiness that had possessed him for the previous twenty minutes.

Fifty yards further on, and the trees gave way to provide a

panorama of Loch Coinneach, sparkling blue in the late morning sunshine. A steep bank dropped away to the sandy beach beyond, accessible from a narrow winding path. Tam had already found his way down to the beach and was now running around wildly in all directions churning up the virgin sand.

Relieved to be on the beach, Neil strolled across to the water's edge. He pulled the old black and white print from the pocket of his jacket and studied it again, lifting his sunglasses periodically to compare the scenery behind the little family group with his current surroundings. He changed position, then turned and retreated across the beach to a point not far from where the path had emerged onto the sand. The points of reference all matched now, the conical peak in the distance, the large boulder away to his left. Yes, this was the spot where they'd mustered all those years ago, so that one of their group, whoever he or she was, could take the picture. Hardly anything had changed. The rowan trees at the far end of the beach were much bigger now, but that was about all.

It was a glimpse into the past, there being few places left in the modern world where time had stalled in this fashion. The experience invoked a range of emotions unlike any other. For a historian, it was the ultimate dream, returning to a time that now existed only in books and memories. But here he was, living the dream, experiencing the world as the Eichel sisters knew it, unchanged and real.

He headed for the shoreline again, picking up a length of driftwood on the way and hurling it into the clear water for Tam to chase. The spaniel crashed into the shallows, sending up a plume of spray. He re-emerged with the bleached grey branch and dropped it at his master's feet, then shook himself violently. Neil picked it up and launched it again, then stood smiling, watching Tam hurtle off along the beach in pursuit.

Neil's engrossment with his dog's activities was interrupted by the sound of footsteps in the waterlogged sand behind him. He turned to see Ursula Stuart standing behind him, dark jeans stuffed into blue wellington boots, hands stuffed into the pockets of her long cardigan. Her grey hair had been ruffled by the wind. Her cheeks were pallid, the colour of porridge.

'I thought I would find you here, Mr Strachan. I saw your car parked up at the end of the track.'

'I didn't know you'd seen the MG before Ursula?'

'I haven't, but word gets about quickly around here.'

'So it appears,' said Neil, amused at the efficiency of Glendaig's "jungle drums". 'I thought I'd bring the dog down here for a walk, it's a hidden gem this beach, is it not?'

'Aye, you're right, it is. I used to bring the children down here when they were wee. We had some wonderful times back then.'

'It seems the locals have been bringing their children here for generations…' Neil handed Ursula the black and white photograph.

'How did you get hold of this?' She seemed surprised and was looking up at him, puzzlement etched across her face.

'I rescued it during my last visit to your cottage, from a box, the contents of which, your husband and Mary Galbraith were in the process of burning.'

'Och, he said nothing of it to me, he can be a bloody fool sometimes.' She shook her head. 'But he's essentially a good man, Inspector, he's never done anyone any harm, and he's worked hard all his life. I just don't know what's got into him lately. He seems anxious about something, but when I try to get him to talk about it he just gets angry and tells me to leave him alone.'

Neil threw the stick for Tam again. 'I'm afraid he's not being entirely honest with me, Ursula. You know I'm going to have to speak to him again?'

'Is that why you're here today?'

'Not specifically, no. I came to see Mary, but she's out.'

'Oh I see. Well she's home now. I took her to the supermarket over at the Kyle. If you don't mind, I'd rather you left Murdo alone at the moment, Inspector. I'm afraid he's not very well at all.'

'I'm sorry to hear that. Is it the angina playing up?'

'It's connected to that. You see, Murdo has suffered a number of heart attacks. The doctors say his heart is becoming progressively weaker, and it's essential he's not subjected to any stressful situations… as if that's going to happen! I'm afraid all these questions are certainly not helping.'

'I do understand Ursula, and I'll do my best not to trouble him.'

Ursula seemed unconvinced. 'Look, if I can provide the answers to any of your questions, I'd be happy to. If it means you'll promise to leave Murdo alone.'

Neil gave her a sideways glance, allowing him time to mull over her proposal. 'I was under the impression you knew nothing of life in Glendaig before your association with Murdo.'

Ursula nodded. 'Aye, that's true enough, but I don't go around with my eyes shut, Inspector.'

'Shall we walk back?' Neil suggested, suddenly intrigued by Ursula's newfound willingness to assist him. Led by Tam, they began the steep ascent back to the castle ruins.

'So, *do* you know anything about the goings on here over the Hogmanay period in 1941? Certainly something was occurring. I know there was possibly a German prisoner of war on the run in the area because the local constable was out searching for him. Then Dugald Matheson ends up dead, in what I would consider to be less than straightforward circumstances.'

She looked down towards her feet, as she turned a corner in the path. 'What I told you before was true, Inspector. I didn't come here for the first time until 1943, so I have no first-hand knowledge of any *goings on* as you call them, but that's not to say there weren't any. I sense something went on here that seems to have had an effect on everyone's life in this community… something to do with Dugald's death. I've tried to find out over the years but have failed miserably. This was a strong community in those days. The old folk looked after each other, they had a sense of kinship and duty to their own, not like today. Whatever secrets were kept were kept well. Loyalty meant something then, you see.'

'Murdo and Mary have certainly signed up to that bond of loyalty in a big way,' added Neil, a little out of breath.

'Aye, they have. I've no doubt they know more than they're letting on, but they will never let friends and family down, not even after all these years. Murdo just tells me it's best I don't know.'

Neil stopped in his tracks. 'Ursula, this is still a murder enquiry, however old. I believe the answer lies within this community, so I have to ask questions of those who can provide the answers, and that includes Murdo.'

'I understand, but this is a very old murder enquiry, isn't it? Wouldn't it be better to let history remain just that? Who's really going to concern themselves about all this, certainly after so many years?'

'I'm afraid the law doesn't work like that, Ursula. We have to find out whose remains were buried along the road there, and we're duty bound to investigate what happened to him. What if he'd been a relative of yours?' He held out his hand to assist Ursula over a fallen tree trunk.

'Point taken, I suppose,' she conceded.

'Can I ask you a couple more questions?'

'You can, but I don't know whether I can answer them.'

'What was the relationship between Dugald Matheson and Isobel Grant?'

'They were cousins. Dugald's father Callum, the local minister, and Isobel's mother Morag were brother and sister. I never met Dugald... but you already know that.'

'So can you tell me who's who in this photo?'

He stopped and produced the photograph taken on the beach again. Ursula leant across. She extended an arthritic finger. 'This is Isobel Grant here, and next to her is Anna Matheson, Dugald's mother. Then there's Ursel, Dugald's sister, and then Dugald himself.'

'Ursel's a strange name,' Neil interjected.

'I believe it has Swiss origins. Anna was from that part of the world.'

'Ah yes, that make sense, so who's this then?'

'Well that would be Anna's sister Katharina. She lived somewhere in Germany I'm told, but came here regularly for holidays during the thirties. I seem to recall she was killed sometime during the war... I assume these are her two boys.' She pondered for a second... 'The youngest was killed in the war. I don't know what became of the other laddie.'

'Do you remember the boys' names at all?'

'Och, no, sorry.'

Neil tapped his finger on the photo, drawing her attention to Max. 'For a while, I thought it was his remains that were buried on the beach.' There was a silence whilst Neil studied her reaction.

'Never!' Ursula looked genuinely shocked. 'But I take it, from what you say, they're not then?'

'No, apparently not, it's all a bit confusing I'm afraid. I can't really go into too much detail for the time being.'

He changed the subject, conscious that Ursula was cogitating silently over what he'd just told her. 'Do you know what Katharina's married name was?'

Ursula blinked and looked up. 'No, I've no idea. Murdo might know.'

'Okay, these other two girls, I think this one is Mary Galbraith and...'

'That's Muireall, Mary's sister. She was a nice girl, I met her several times. They were McSweens then, of course.'

They had started walking again, heading back into the dark woodland that encompassed the castle. 'I wish I'd spoken to you before,' said Neil. 'It would've saved me a lot of time.' He walked on for a few yards, then stopped. 'I asked Murdo the other day whether he'd heard of someone called Max Friedmann. He said he hadn't.'

Ursula pursed her lips and shrugged. Neil was studying her again. 'Actually, I already know Katharina's married name... it was Friedmann. You see, Max Friedmann was her son.'

328

Ursula shrugged again. 'Personally that's news to me, perhaps Murdo too, but I wouldn't be surprised if he *did* know.'

'Oh I'm sure he knows, Ursula. Tell me, how do *you* know so much about this photo?'

'I suppose I didn't explain when you first showed it to me. Murdo took it when he was eight years old, bless him. He had one of those Box Brownie cameras. I think one of the grandchildren have it now. He took photos of everyone and everything. That's his copy if it was in that box.'

'So why was he taking photos of the Matheson's then?'

'Well, he went to school with the Matheson children… and the McSweens come to that. They were a wee bit older than him, but he still got invited to all the children's picnics. I think Anna had bit of a soft spot for him.'

'I think that answers my earlier question then. Murdo clearly knew Max Friedmann and his mother, he's taken a photo of them!'

Ursula blushed. 'So it seems Inspector, so it seems.'

They'd almost reached the road by now, and Tam was reattached to his lead. 'Where are you off to now?' Ursula folded her arms against the breeze, and rubbed them through her cardigan.

'I thought I'd drop in on Mary for a quick chat.'

'I see. Look, I know you're going to keep on digging but like I said, I don't want Murdo hounded for answers. I'm worried about his health, and I fear that any more pressure will finish him off. I know he's innocent of any wrongdoing, as is Mary. If you want to know what happened back then I suggest you go and see Isobel Grant.'

'Is she still alive then?' Neil gave her a piercing look.

'As far as I'm aware, I've no reason to believe she's dead.' Ursula seemed surprised by his question.

'So do you know where I might find her?'

'Good God no. We lost contact with her when she left the village in the late seventies. But you should be able to find her surely; that's what policemen do don't they?' She smiled briefly.

Neil ignored her joke. 'Why did she leave the village?'

'I don't really know. It was all a bit strange. This journalist started snooping around asking about life in the village during the war, just like you've been doing. Murdo was getting a bit jumpy about it all. I haven't seen him like that since... funnily enough, not until you appeared on the scene. Well, he ended up having words with Isobel over something, I don't know what exactly; he refused to say. It must have been just after he'd spoken to the journalist fellow, and I'm sure the row was something to do with him.'

'How do you know they had words? Did Murdo tell you?'

'I saw them. I was visiting the big house, Glendaig House. To get to it, I had to cycle past Isobel's cottage. Her husband was deputy stalker on the estate, you see. They were provided with a cottage in those days. Well, Isobel was at the door having a slanging match with Murdo. I went over to intervene but she had slammed the door in his face. I asked him what had happened but he refused to discuss it and stormed off, so I knocked on Isobel's door and she was as cagey as Murdo. She told me to ask him. I never got to the bottom of it. Next thing I hear is that her man is retiring and they're leaving the village. Again, I never found out where.'

'Did you not try and find out?'

I asked Mary, but she said she didn't know. Personally I think she did, but had clearly been told to keep her mouth shut. I also asked Ursel.'

'Was she still living in the village then?'

'Not living exactly. Her parents moved to Skye View Cottage, across the way from us, when Callum retired as minister... 1955 I think it was. Callum died in the mid-sixties and Anna stayed on until her own death in 1979, the same year Isobel moved away. Ursel kept the cottage on as a holiday home until 1990, when they sold it to the current owners, the Rolands. Ursel and her husband Bill went to live in Inverness. They both died a few years back.

'So what did Ursel say?'

'She was about as unforthcoming as Mary. She was always great friends with Isobel, but things weren't the same with Ursel after Isobel and Murdo's argument.'

'Was there anyone else you could've asked?'

'Not really, Donald was still alive but suffering from dementia by then. He died the following year. Morag died the same year as Anna, and David had moved away. Let's be honest, I wasn't *that* close to Isobel, I wasn't going to go to the ends of the earth to find her. She certainly didn't endear herself to me when I asked her about row with Murdo.'

'Tell me, did Isobel have any children?'

'Aye, one daughter, Jeanne. She must be in her sixties by now. And before you ask, I haven't kept up with her either.'

'What about Isobel's husband? Tell me about him.'

'Nothing much to tell, really. His name was Robert, we always called him Robbie. He was a nice chap, a man of few words, a little older than Isobel perhaps. He'd been working on the estate as a ghillie long before I came on the scene in 1943. He ended up as Murdo's deputy when Murdo became head stalker.'

'What was Isobel's married name, do you remember?'

'Funnily enough, it was the same as her maiden name – Grant. That's why I remember it!'

'Umm, bit of a coincidence that?'

'Aye, I suppose, but *you* must know Inspector, it's not that uncommon around here. So many highland folk share the same name. We must all be interbred somewhere down the line.' She laughed, expecting him to follow suit, but she only got a brief smile.

'Aye, you're right there, and they lived on the estate you say?'

'When he became deputy stalker, that's right. Before that they rented a small bothy up at the Mains. The McSweens' place.'

'Okay, one last question. This journalist who came sniffing around, what do you recall about him?'

'Nothing much. He was a freelance from down south. I never actually spoke to him myself.'

'But Murdo might know more about him?'

'Perhaps.'

'Look, you've been really helpful Ursula, but I think you know that I'm going to have to speak to Murdo again, particularly about the photos I took from the box.'

'What do you mean *photos*? Is there more than one that supposedly incriminates my husband?'

Neil hesitated. He then showed her the other image taken on Beinn Caisteal in 1935. 'This was taken of Max five years *after* the shot on the beach. He's posing with Isobel and Mary up on the mountain over there. Now that I know Murdo took the first photo, I'm convinced he must have come into contact with Friedmann more than once when he was here during the early thirties. He has lied to me Ursula, and I firmly believe he knows more about the mysterious Max Friedmann than he's letting on.'

'I see,' said Ursula, a little embarrassed that her husband had been branded a liar. 'Well he's never mentioned the name Max Friedmann to me. Can you give us a few days, and I'll call you when I feel he's up to answering some more questions… if you really must speak to him.'

Neil pulled out a business card from his wallet. He wrote his mobile number on the back. 'I'll steer clear of him for now Ursula, but I can't wait forever. Please call me in a few days.'

'Fair enough Inspector, and I'll let you know if I think of anything else. Perhaps Mary can answer some of your questions about the photos?'

'I certainly believe she can Ursula, and I'm on my way up to see her now.' Ursula climbed into to her Ford Escort, and with a limp wave of the hand she drove away, creating a cloud of dust in her wake.

Chapter Thirty

Having loaded a weary Tam into the MG, Neil set off for Rowan Cottage. As he turned onto the track leading up to Glendaig Mains his progress was unexpectedly obstructed by a large blue tractor being driven by Tom Buchanan. Neil pulled over to allow the monster to pass and acknowledged the gesture of thanks from the young farmer. He then sat for a few seconds, observing the small white cottage ahead of him and to the right. There was no sign of life, other than the presence of a small red pickup parked at one end of the property, skilfully manoeuvred between an old boat trailer and a collection of rusting oil drums.

He continued along the track, drawing to a halt outside Rowan Cottage. His arrival was advertised by an excited Cadha, who appeared out of nowhere, barking madly and performing pirouettes. The series of frenzied rotations continued as Neil climbed out of the MG. Inside the little car Tam shook and whimpered with excitement, eager to be released so that he could make his acquaintance with the collie. Realising that he was going nowhere when his master locked the driver's door and headed for the gate, he slumped back onto his seat, disappointed.

As Neil stepped into the garden the front door opened, and Iain Galbraith filled the frame, hands in pockets as he tracked his visitor's progress up the path. 'Hello Iain, is your mother in?' Neil smiled as he approached the door, trying to avoid the still-rotating collie.

'Aye,' came the clipped reply. A brief standoff then developed at the doorway as Iain fixed the policeman with a long, distrusting gaze.

The impasse was broken when Neil asked, 'Do you mind if I come in then? I need to speak with her.'

A woman's voice called out from within, 'For heaven's sake let the man in Iain.'

Iain stepped aside without speaking, allowing Neil to pass by. Once inside, the door clunked shut and the summer sunshine that had flooded into the cottage through the open void was again snuffed out. The interior beyond was returned to the melancholic space that Neil remembered from his previous visit. A shaft of dusty sunlight pierced the gloom through the tiny window and fell upon the seated figure of Mary Galbraith, illuminating her like a biblical figure in an old master's oil painting. She sat primly, hands clasped on her lap as before, and slowly turned her head towards Neil.

'I thought you'd be back once you'd seen the contents of that box.'

'Umm, I think we need to have a wee chat about those photos, Mary.'

Iain stood by the doorway, immersed in shadow. 'You know you don't have to answer any more of these damned questions Ma.' Then he turned to Neil. 'She's not a bloody suspect... is she?'

Before Neil could reply, Mary barked at her son; 'Just go and do something useful Iain. You're not helping. The man's got to do his job.' Iain scowled and snatched his waxed jacket from the back of a nearby chair. He stormed out of the door, half-slamming it behind him. His gravelly voice could be heard admonishing Cadha before fading into the distance.

'I'm sorry about him Inspector, can I get you some tea or something?'

'Aye, that would be nice Mary.'

The old lady levered herself up from her armchair and shuffled across to the kitchen area at the far end of the cottage. Having filled the kettle, she called across; 'So what have you discovered from the box of photographs?'

Neil joined her as she stood waiting for the kettle to boil. He pulled out the photograph of Max with Isobel and her on the mountainside and handed it to her. 'This is the man I asked you about last time I was here, Max Friedmann, and this is you... am I right?'

'Indeed you are, Inspector.' She turned it over. 'Aye, that's right, spring 1935. It had been a bonnie spring that year as I recall. Max had come over to visit his aunt for the last time before he attended his officer training course in the navy. We never saw him again, such a terrible shame.'

'You mean *Aunt* Anna Matheson, the minister's wife?'

'Aye, Max was Anna's sister's laddie.'

'So what do you think happened to him... or perhaps you know for sure?'

She shook her head. 'Anna said he'd gone missing during the war. I assume from what she said he'd been lost at sea somewhere. He served on those awful U-boats you see, not many of their crews survived the war. Perhaps I shouldn't be concerned, they were the enemy after all, but life's more complex than that... for some folk.'

'Yes, I can see that can be the case. So you're saying you never saw him again after May 1935?'

Mary filled the teapot with boiling water. She shook her head again. 'That's right, I never saw him again after that visit.'

'Surely Anna Matheson was provided with more specific information than that, regarding his fate I mean... from her sister perhaps?'

'Not really, she lost contact with her sister Katharina during the early part of the war.' She frowned. 'Not surprisingly, would you not agree? Their parents in Switzerland were in a similar position to Anna's. They were given very little information at the time, it was all a bit of a mystery. Max's younger brother Otto was also killed early in the war. Like I said, I know they were on the *other* side so to speak, but it was so tragic. They were such nice boys when they were young.'

'Yes, I knew about Otto. So you're saying Max disappeared off the face of the earth, and that was accepted by all concerned?'

Mary handed Neil a cup of tea. Then she returned to her chair, the sound of her walking stick tapping on the flagstones to mark her slow rate of progress. Neil followed and took a seat on the old leather sofa. 'You must understand Inspector, that many men went missing on both sides during the war, and they remained just that, *missing*. People accepted that this was the case. As time went on, families came to terms with the fact that there was never to be any final closure. Max was just one of many who apparently fell into that category.'

'Okay, so going back to this photo. This is you, with Max and Isobel Grant, yes?'

'Aye, that's right. Ursel took it up on the hill away yonder.'

'He seemed to get on well with you all, and vice versa?'

'He certainly did. He was a handsome young man, a real gentleman. We were just young lassies, at that stage of our lives when young men were becoming interesting. Having said that, he was over twenty in that photo, far too old for us. Didn't stop us having a crush on him though.' She chuckled briefly, before sipping her tea.

Mary returned her cup to its saucer, before looking up again. 'There was another photo of Max and his family in that box. Murdo took it on the beach down by the castle when the family were over on holiday. It was taken a good few years before the one you have there.'

Neil rose from the chair and removed the copy of Murdo's photo from his trouser pocket. He leant across and handed it to Mary. 'You mean this one?'

Aye, that's the one. Heavens, we all look young there don't we?' She handed it back, the slight tremor again evident in her spidery hand. 'So I expect you're going to ask me why I didn't tell you all this before?' She briefly caught Neil's eye before looking away, a gesture that appeared to confirm her genuine embarrassment.

'Well yes, I *was* coming to that.'

'It seems silly I suppose, but when those remains were found

336

on the beach and you came to the village asking questions about Max Friedmann… well we were scared. We thought the remains were his and if that was the case, then who knows, you may have suspected *us* of something.'

'By *us*, I gather you mean Murdo Stuart and yourself?'

'Aye, of course. Murdo knew him when they were young.'

'And that's why you were having that little bonfire the other day, to destroy any evidence of your association with Friedmann?'

'We didn't make too good a job of it, did we Inspector?'

Neil shook his head, registering his disappointment in her. She looked away towards the stone hearth, her demeanour resembling that of a naughty pupil having been admonished by their teacher.

'Did you burn anything that day that might have been of interest to me, Mary?'

'No Inspector, we'd only just lit the fire when you arrived. We'd burnt a few old Christmas cards, that's all.'

'Nothing relating to Friedmann then?'

'No, nothing.'

'I'll just have to take your word for that, Mary.'

'You will I'm afraid, Inspector.'

Neil fixed her with a long stare, searching her wrinkled face for evidence of her truthfulness. The old lady could only absorb so much humiliation. She glared across at Neil. 'I can assure you Inspector, I *am* speaking the truth.'

'Well it's not worth dwelling on now is it?' Neil raised a conciliatory palm, acknowledging Mary's display of irritation. 'Tell me, what were you doing during the evening of Hogmanay in 1941, the night before Dugald was killed… do you remember?'

'I can tell you exactly where I was, Inspector. The same place I went every Hogmanay night during the war, Glendaig House. The Laird, Sir Brodric Macleod, always laid on a lavish party for the local community. Just about everyone went along.'

'So the Mathesons and the Grants would have been there too?'

'Och aye, of course. The Grants worked on the estate and

Callum being the local Minister, well, he and Anna were always invited.'

'Did anything notable happen that night?'

'What do you mean... *notable*?'

'Anything out of the ordinary, anything at all.'

Mary considered the question for a second or two. 'No, nothing that I can recall. Other than Ursel twisting her ankle when she was stripping the willow with Ramsay, the Laird's son. He was in the RAF, home on leave. His squadron had moved up to Wick, only a train ride away, so he'd come down for the party.' She searched her memory again. 'No, the party was a great success, just as they were later in the war.'

'Okay, and whilst we're being honest with one another, can you tell me anything more about Dugald's death. Murdo implied that there had been some sort of argument before he was killed and events weren't as he initially described them. So, were you ever told anything about this argument?'

'Och, Mr Strachan, I don't know anything about an argument. I just heard they'd been out stalking and there'd been a shooting accident. My understanding was that Murdo *wasn't* present.'

'Sounds silly, but you're sure Dugald's demise had nothing to do with this fellow Max Friedmann.'

'For the last time Inspector, no, why should it have been? You seem obsessed with the notion that young Max had come here during the war. It was an accident Inspector, just an accident, nothing more, nothing less.'

'Okay, one last thing Mary. Are you sure you don't know where I might find Isobel Grant?'

Mary shook her head in disbelief. 'The answer is the same as the one I gave you when you first came here... *no*. Like I said, she's probably long dead by now.'

Neil massaged his lower lip. 'Do you recall her married name? Ursula Stuart thought it had remained as Grant. I considered it unusual, you know, them both having the same surname?'

'Aye, it was Grant, but I don't know why you find that strange. You're either a MacDonald, a Macrae or a Grant around these parts, you must know that to be the case?'

'Aye of course, that's what Ursula said. Stupid of me to think otherwise.'

'Will that be all, Inspector? I'm feeling a little weary, what with all these questions and the like. I'd like to go and lie down for a while if you don't mind.'

'Of course, Mary. I need to get back to Inverness. I think we've covered everything.' He returned his cup and saucer to the draining board. 'Thanks for the tea, I'll see myself out.'

Sitting in the MG, stroking an excited Tam, Neil peered through the windscreen towards the sombre-looking farm house beyond the gateway to the Mains. On the face of it, Mary's account of her life in wartime Glendaig had been entirely credible. Yet there were nagging doubts still lingering within him. Doubts as to the true candidness of both Mary and her long-time friend and neighbour Murdo Stuart.

The drive back along the shore of Loch Coinneach was always pleasant, but today, with the weather near perfect, the prospect was particularly alluring. Neil had retracted the roof of the MG and was heading out of the village, savouring the throaty growl of the little car's re-conditioned engine. As he approached the church he came across the minister, Duncan Mackay, struggling to progress with his old mower along the uneven verge that skirted the graveyard wall. Neil pulled up next to him and swept away the strands of hair that had settled across his brow. The minister released the throttle of the mower and the engine died instantly.

'Out in the wee toy again, Inspector. It does look impressive, you've done a marvellous job. Must have taken some considerable time to get it looking like that.'

'Thanks, I like to think of it as a boyhood dream that came good... thanks to the generosity of you taxpayers!'

Mackay leant heavily on the handle of the mower, panting

gently. 'You don't fancy having a go?' he asked, grinning and gesturing towards the grass-encrusted mower. 'I'm just about all in.'

'Doesn't the church have willing gardeners within their congregations these days?'

'Aye, but my willing gardener's laid up with a bad back, I'm afraid. So how are you progressing with the investigation into the skeleton found on the beach?'

'Very slowly I'm afraid. We've had a few false leads. Seems like just when you think you're getting somewhere, you get knocked back.'

'Sounds like how I feel, mowing this verge.'

'I'm afraid some of the more senior members of your flock have wanted to keep things frustratingly close their chests. That doesn't help.'

'By senior members, I take it you mean Mary Galbraith and Murdo Stuart?'

Neil switched off the car engine and squinted at the minister, intrigued by his response. 'How perceptive, nothing much gets past you Reverend. Where did you pluck those names from?'

'I just use my eyes and ears, that's all. Your visits are always registered by those who lurk behind darkened windows. News travels, Inspector. Surely such an observation is no surprise to you?'

'No, of course not, and what do your *eyes* tell you.'

Mackay grinned back at the detective. His expression could barely disguise the fact that he was considering his answer carefully. After a pause he said, 'I suppose there no harm in mentioning...'

'Mention what?'

'Your two *seniors*, Mary and Murdo. They've been visiting the church on a number of occasions recently. More to talk than pray, I'd wager.'

'That's interesting. So definitely out of the ordinary, these visits?'

'Aye, without a doubt. Murdo never comes to church on a Sunday, let alone the middle of the week. I've come across them two or three times, huddled in one of the back pews, deep in hushed conversation. When I've appeared, they've taken their leave almost immediately.'

'Thanks for that Reverend, it tells me a lot.'

'Nothing sinister I hope?'

'Not necessarily, but I'm convinced they know things that they are keeping from me. As to what, I don't have the slightest idea just now.'

'Well, I wish you luck Inspector. If there's something to be told, then I'm sure you will be able to persuade them to unburden themselves of whatever it is.'

'As things stand Reverend, I have about as much chance of achieving that as you would.'

Neil started the MG's engine again. 'I hope the gardener's back on his feet next time I'm passing.'

'Fear not Inspector, I'm praying for him… every time I get this mower out of the shed.' With a flamboyant wave, he tugged again on the starter cord.

The run to Camuscraig was not disappointing. The Cuillins on Skye were fully visible for once, only the smallest puffs of white cloud hung about their dark pinnacles as they shimmered ghostlike through the distant haze. Seals basked on the rock-strewn shoreline that bordered the loch, their long glistening backs arched in the sun. Neil glanced across at Tam; the spaniel was sitting like a statue, his brown eyes fixed on the road ahead, ears flapping wildly in the warm slipstream that rushed past the speeding car. All seemed as it should be at that moment in time. Unfortunately, contentment is rarely an emotion that lingers and two days later, news would be received which tended to validate that assertion.

Chapter Thirty-One

Thursday 18th June

Brodie relaxed his bulky torso into the sumptuous cushioning of his leather chair. It squeaked as he swivelled it gently to and fro. An extended arm reached out across the desk, the fingers attached to it tapped out a rhythm on the light-coloured wood. The DCI, head tilted slightly, seemed more focussed on his drumming fingers than his DI's review of the Glendaig enquiry. The constant noise began to annoy Neil, and he raised his voice slightly to drown out his boss' gesture of impatience. He could be such an infuriating bastard at times.

When Neil stopped speaking, there was a short delay before Brodie's gaze shifted upwards to meet his own. 'So you're on the trail of this Isobel Grant then, and you think she can provide you with the answers you need to put this job to bed?'

'If she's alive, then maybe she could be very helpful.'

'That's what concerns me Neil… *if she's alive!*' He took a slug from his favourite coffee mug, emblazoned with the Ross County FC crest and liberally dappled with the splash marks of previous drinks. Brodie grimaced at the taste of the cold coffee and returned the mug to its mat. 'What exactly have you done to locate her?'

'The usual; checked the electoral roll, locally and roundabouts. I've spoken to the local authorities, the pension people at the DWP, but it's like finding a needle in a haystack; there are thousands of Grants… and quite a few Isobel Grants, not to mention Robert Grants. I'd be ringing people for ever more.'

'What about their last address, it was on the Glendaig Estate wasn't it? Have you tried the estate office?'

'Aye, of course, but they left in 1979. There's no record of any forwarding address kept after all these years.'

'Do you think this woman Mary Galbraith knows where she is, even though she's denying it?'

'It's difficult to tell, she's not the easiest person to read. For all I know she's being honest with me and hasn't a clue.'

'Well everything seems to be up in the air still,' concluded Brodie, shaking his head slowly. He was reading a copy of the crime report, printed by Neil especially for his perusal. 'You still have an unidentified body, a second empty grave and no answers. This name Max Friedmann keeps popping up, but how he fits into all this remains a mystery... and that'll probably remain the case if the old folk of Glendaig have their way.'

'Aye, it doesn't look too hopeful,' Neil conceded, an air of fatalism creeping through him for the first time.

'We need to bring this enquiry to a close very soon Neil. I accept that pernickety bugger at the fiscal's office wants to cover all angles, so do what you can to placate him. A name to go with the bones would be nice, but we can't keep chasing shadows. We'll pull the plug on this at the end of the month, agreed?'

'Aye, I suppose so,' Neil agreed, emitting a longish sigh.

'Don't worry laddie, I've got plenty of stuff to keep you busy from then on, fear not!' Brodie reinserted all the papers into the box file and closed the lid with an exaggerated pat of the hand. He leant across to return the box to Neil, swivelling in his chair as he did so.

Neil tucked the box under his arm and got up. 'Sir?'

'Yes, Neil.'

'How exactly did you manage to wheedle that chair out of Admin? Surely you need crowns on your shoulders before you're entitled to a furniture like that?'

Brodie looked up slowly, his brow deeply furrowed. Then a wry smile crept across his face as he tapped the side of his bulbous red nose with an equally bulbous forefinger. He said nothing and looked back towards his computer screen. Then, as Neil disappeared through the door, he called out; 'Just tread carefully when you speak to those senior citizens over at Glendaig. Remember, you'll be their age before you know it.'

Neil, amused by his boss' advice, began to tidy his desk in readiness for an early finish to the day. It was nearly five o'clock, but he had one thing left to do. He hit the *compose email* tab on his computer screen and tapped out Matthias Fuchs' email address in the template that appeared. His German colleague needed to know about the now confirmed link between Max Friedmann and the Matheson family in Glendaig. Fifteen minutes later he'd logged out of the system. He'd done all he could that day and savoured the prospect of an evening at his favourite bar in the city with Cat and some close friends.

He emerged into the car park of police headquarters fumbling in his jacket pocket for his car keys. Swinging them from a finger, he set off around the edge of the red brick parking bays, many of which were still populated with the private vehicles of the headquarter's workforce. Then, as he reached the rear of the car parked adjacent to his own, his mobile phone began to vibrate and then ring. He contemplated ignoring the call, fearful of the possibility that he may have to take the long walk back to his office. The number displayed on the screen was not immediately familiar so, with a deep intake of breath, he pushed the green button. 'Hello, DI Strachan.'

The female voice at the other end was muted, trance-like, yet vaguely familiar. 'Hello Mr Strachan, is that you?'

'Aye, Neil Strachan speaking, who's this please?'

'It's Ursula, Ursula Stuart.'

'Oh hello Ursula, what can I do for you?'

'I think it's more a matter of what I can do for you, Inspector.'

He sensed a shakiness in her voice, a component he'd not

recognised before. 'Is everything okay Ursula? It's just... you seem upset about something.'

There was a silence, then a muted sob. 'My husband passed away this afternoon Inspector, it's been a bit of a shock I'm afraid.'

Neil was stunned. *Murdo dead?* 'I'm so sorry Ursula, what on earth happened?'

'It was that damned heart of his, must have just given up on him in the end. I suppose I was half-expecting it. But that's just it, whether you expect it or not it still comes as huge shock. He collapsed at home, in the garden to be precise. They sent an air ambulance to take him to Fort William, but he couldn't hold on. DOA I think they call it... so matter of fact.'

'Is there anything I can do for you Ursula, anything at all?'

'No, thank you, my family are with me now. I just wanted to pass on something Murdo said when we were waiting on the paramedics arriving. He told me to tell you to have another look in that box of photos. There are some envelopes in there. He seemed to think there was something on those envelopes that would give you a clue as to where you might find Isobel Grant.'

'Is that all he said? Nothing more specific?'

'No, he was struggling to remain conscious. That's all he could manage. I just thought you'd want to know.'

'Thank you Ursula, and thanks for the call. I'm sure this is the last thing you want to be discussing.'

'It was his last wish, and I needed to honour it. I'm not doing it for you, Inspector. I'm doing it for him.'

'I understand, but thank you all the same.'

'Look, I must go now, there's someone at the door.'

'Okay, I'll be in touch... Ursula?'

'Yes, Inspector.'

'Why do you think he spoke up, I mean now after all this time?'

'Because I told him to. I'm sick of all these secrets. Satisfied, Inspector?'

The line went dead. Neil stared at the blank screen on his phone, still trying to come to terms with the news about Murdo Stuart. Did *he* push Murdo too hard, was this in some way his fault too? The heart condition must have been a major factor of course, but did he drive the old man over the edge? He slipped the phone back into his pocket and turned back towards the glass doors of reception and ultimately the exhibits store.

He was just in time to catch the property clerk, a dour looking ex-constable, whose placement in the role had been interpreted by him as a delegation of supreme power over all other mortals. The stout little man was just about to lock up and head for home. His initial reaction to Neil's request for Mary's box of photos and envelopes had been less than accommodating. However, a few strong words from Neil had re-established the two men's relative positions within the organisation's pecking order, and the door to the store was duly opened.

Having signed out Mary's box of documents he headed for his office, his heart still pounding from the run up the stairs. Prising off the lid, he emptied the contents onto the desk and sifted through the various documents until he found one of the envelopes. He examined it closely, turning it over and over, before concentrating on its interior. There was nothing, just a handwritten address... *Mrs Mary Galbraith, Rowan Cottage, Glendaig, Ross-shire* and an IV40 postcode. The stamp was first class and the post mark illegible. He selected another and studied it with equal thoroughness. Again nothing, certainly no more than what he'd picked up on the first time he'd gone through the box.

There were a dozen envelopes in all, the handwriting on the front was the same, the addresses were all written in the same way, and spelt the same. Neil grunted, disappointed by the lack of any revelation. Was this Murdo's way of having one last joke at his expense? Surely not, he wasn't that type.

With the contents back in the box, Neil headed for the stairwell once again. He glanced at his watch. It was now twenty past five and the clerk would have certainly gone home. He tucked the box firmly under his arm and ran down the stairs to reception.

The house was empty when he got home. Cat had no doubt arrived earlier and taken Tam for a walk. There was a stillness about the place when the dog was absent but he knew the peace wouldn't last for long.

Having removed his jacket and tie, and armed with an excessively large glass of Chilean Merlot, he delved into the box once again. This time he separated the envelopes from the other documents and placed them on his lap in a neat pile. He sipped slowly from his glass and examined the envelopes one by one. It didn't take long, there was nothing at all to see. What on earth was Murdo referring to?

He returned the glass to the coffee table next to him and picked up the first of the envelopes. For no reason in particular he raised it close to his nose and sniffed. What he'd hoped to achieve was anyone's guess. Perhaps it was the possibility that there may have been a faint trace of perfume or some other aroma embedded in the paper. Not that an olfactory clue of this nature would move things forward. It was a pointless exercise anyway. All he could detect was the faint mustiness of an object that had been stored away, containerised for years.

Unperturbed, he turned the envelope over and lifted the flap, aiming to conduct a similar nasal examination of the interior. As he raised the open envelope to his nose, his eye detected something on the inside of the crumpled triangular flap. Nothing distinctive, just a disturbance in the surface of the paper. He looked again, closer this time, blinking and trying to focus on the small indentations present on the paper. He could see more clearly now. They were words and figures written on the inside of the flap, probably in pencil, but erased with some considerable pressure. Try as he might, he couldn't read the words, but there was no doubting some of the letters, a *T*, a *W* and an *S*. The *W* was in upper case, and beneath he could make out the figures *8* and *2*.

Examination of another envelope revealed no evidence of any word erasures, just a row of figures, or that's what he thought, but the next one did… a similar combination of letters and numbers. There was the *W* again, and an *R* this time. In fact, the majority of the envelopes' flaps bore some evidence of something having been written on them and then erased. The frustrating thing was that he couldn't discern what had been written. He was tempted to highlight the letters in pencil, just as Agatha Christie's detectives may have done, but he knew he had to wait. Impatient as he was, it was the forensic scientist who would stand the best chance of unravelling the mystery of what had been written on these envelopes.

Cat arrived home whilst he was still examining the envelopes. Tam ran into the room panting heavily, his tail a blur of furious movement. Neil stroked the fine blonde hair above the wide excited eyes and called out; 'Come and have a look at this will you?'

Cat appeared from the hallway and patted her partner on the head. 'Not another attempt to get me to do your job for you!' she joked, and took a sip from Neil's now half-empty wine glass. He looked up at her disapprovingly.

'See if you can read what's been written on the inside of these envelopes. The words have been rubbed out, but you can still make out the impressions in the paper.'

Cat selected the envelopes one by one, straining to read the wording on the insides of the flaps. Having contemplated the last one for nearly a minute, she put it down. 'Nope, I haven't a clue, I can just about read the odd letter and number, sorry.'

'No worries,' said Neil rising off the sofa and pouring Cat a glass of wine. 'I know a man who will be able to.'

Fraser Gunn sealed the last of the evidence bags which each contained one of the envelopes from Mary's box. 'I'll get these off today, but I warn you it'll take a few days to get anything back from them.'

By *them*, he meant the Forensic Documents and Handwriting Section, whose laboratory was down in Glasgow. 'Can't you give them a call, and call in a favour or something?' Neil pleaded. 'I've got Brodie on my back…'

'Don't tell me,' said Gunn. 'He's set his alarm clock for the end of the month and when it goes off, the plug gets pulled on this job.'

'Oh, so you know?'

'Aye, he told me… after he'd finished ranting about the forensic support bill for, I quote, *"a load of old bones".'*

'Sorry Fraser, I'm afraid his keen sense of prioritisation has really kicked in as far as this enquiry's concerned.'

'Don't worry Neil, I told him it was all your fault and then suggested that he'd spent so much already, he might as well see it through to the end, value for money and all that!'

'Christ! What did he say?'

'I left him sucking on the end of his pen, and staring out of the window.' Fraser grinned and walked through the door, raising his free hand as a gesture of farewell. 'I'll be in touch,' he called out as he disappeared from view.

Neil returned to his computer screen. He hadn't checked his emails for a while, and the inbox contained over fifty messages. He scanned them quickly. Most of them were of little interest. Force policy updates, leave requests and the like. But half way down the list he did find something worth reading. It was a message from Dr Paul Miller at the Imperial War Museum. His eyes ran along the lines of text, urgently seeking something of interest.

Hello Neil,

It was good meeting you last month. I was wondering how the enquiries were going your end. Matthias tells me the remains don't appear to be those of Max Friedmann. Shame in a way, I was never one for unsolved mysteries!

Get to the point man, I can hear you say! Well, Matthias mentioned that you *were interested in U-boat sinkings in early '42. We agree with him, having studied our sources, that there were no <u>confirmed</u> sinkings in UK coastal waters at all during the month of January '42. However, you may be interested to know that we managed to dig out the operational logs for the seaplane base at Oban.*

Information from within those records indicates that an RAF catalina (flying boat used for anti-submarine operations), operating from Oban, attacked what they believed to be a U-boat running submerged to periscope depth in the Cuillin Sound between Isle of Rum and Point of Sleat, 0500hrs 1/1/42. Depth charges were dropped in the vicinity of the periscope wake. It seems the aircraft couldn't hang around due to lack of fuel, so the outcome of the engagement is unknown.

I've also had sight of a document relating to a survey done of the area by marine archaeologists during the late nineties, but nothing was ever found. Not inconceivable that the sub sank elsewhere, having been damaged. Have forwarded this to Matthias to conduct further research into the unconfirmed sinking in the Atlantic on 8/1/42. He'll get in touch if he comes up with anything.

    Best regards
    Paul Miller

Neil read the email again. Perhaps the escape had been successful after all… Friedmann gets picked up by a U-boat, only to get sent to the bottom of the Cuillin Sound, or elsewhere, by the RAF. Unlucky or what? He snatched the copy of the email from the printer, acknowledging the fact that this meant nothing… nothing at all. It was just another unsubstantiated theory.

He tucked the sheet of paper into his file and tapped out an acknowledgement to Paul Miller. In it, he summarised his progress with the enquiry and as he sat reading it over before hitting the "send" button, he realised just how little he had, in fact, *progressed*.

Chapter Thirty-Two

The little cluster of mourners that huddled around the graveside seemed reminiscent of a scene from an old movie. Neil had been spared the sombrous experience of attending a burial until now and this, the grimmest of ceremonies, had been an unwelcome reminder of the darker side of life. He looked away, up towards the summit of Stac Coinneach Dubh, preferring to focus on its cloud-shrouded summit than intrude on the suffering of the Stuart family.

He'd chosen to maintain a discrete distance from the black-clad principle mourners. They stood in rigid silence, heads bowed, solemn expressions of grief etched on each of their faces as they listened to the Reverend Mackay. The minister spoke in low tones, declaring that Murdo would now be delivered into God's care. It seemed no more than a hollow promise to Neil, but then he did consider himself to be an irreligionist. No doubt Mackay's words would be of comfort to some.

Other local residents clustered nearby, also retaining a respectful distance as the interment ceremony reached its final stage. The hollow thud of soil tumbling onto wood, accompanied by the intermittent sounds of a woman's sobs drifted across the cemetery on the light breeze. Neil shivered as he stood in quiet contemplation and watched Murdo's family bid him one final farewell.

Once the interment had been completed, Ursula, flanked by Siobhan and son Gordon, was escorted away from the grave, followed by other members of the family and friends. Her face grey with grief, she exchanged glances with Neil as she passed. She continued for a few yards before stopping and steering her escorts around towards him.

He stepped forward from the sanctuary of a lichen-encrusted headstone. It bore the weatherworn epitaph of some long-forgotten habitant of this far flung community; *Robert Drummond, aged 72 years, died 1810*. Ironically this memorial stone, a symbol of his death, was now the sole reminder of his life.

'Thank you so much for coming, Inspector,' Ursula whispered from beneath her wide-brimmed hat.

'I'm so sorry that I'm here in these circumstances Ursula, please accept my sincere condolences.'

'I blamed you initially for this,' she said in a subdued tone.

'Mother!' Gordon looked shocked.

Ursula reached out for Neil's hand. 'Don't worry Inspector, the sentiment faded as quickly as it came. I was just lashing out at anyone and everyone. Murdo's time was limited, we all knew that. *He* chose to become embroiled in whatever it was he got himself involved in.' She opened her handbag and pulled out a small crumpled beige envelope. 'You may find these interesting and, before you ask, I have absolutely no idea how he got hold of them.'

She handed Neil the envelope and managed a weak smile. 'I suppose these are the proof you were looking for... that dear old Murdo had some involvement with the Germans, somewhere along the line. One thing's for sure, he didn't get these serving in the armed forces because he never served in them, he was in a reserved occupation.'

Neil's fingers probed the inside of the envelope. Inside was a length of ribbon, coloured red, white and black. It had faded with age, and at one end a frayed hole was present in the material. He recognised it immediately from the description provided by Paul Miller and the photographs in Matthias Fuchs' book. Whilst the Stuarts looked on in silence, Neil delved into the envelope again.

This time he produced a small oval-shaped metal badge. Inset within a gold wreath was the representation of a warship ploughing through the waves. The wreath was surmounted by an eagle clutching a swastika.

'Where did you find these, Ursula?' Neil asked, running an inquisitive finger over the still-shiny decoration.

Gordon provided the answer. 'We were going through Dad's desk, looking for some insurance papers. These were sitting at the back of a small drawer behind a pile of old bills.'

'Have you any idea what they are, or where they may have come from?' Ursula was studying his reaction with some interest. 'I believe this material is German, possibly the tunic ribbon of the Iron Cross Second Class. It was worn on the buttonhole of the tunic, see this hole here?'

Ursula leant towards him. 'What about the badge?'

'It's obviously a German wartime decoration of sorts. I'll have to take further advice. The interesting thing is, the man whose remains we believed we'd found – Max Friedmann – well, he would have worn this ribbon. He also had other decorations which we didn't find at the site where we found the remains. Perhaps these are his!'

'Please let me know, Inspector. I do hope you get to the bottom of all this, I really do.'

'Thank you Ursula, and thank you for these.'

'Won't you join us for a wee drink… to Murdo's memory, back at the house?'

'Aye, I think I'd like that Ursula.'

'Good, we'll see you shortly then.'

She drifted off with her immediate family in tow, stopping further along the path to accept the condolences of another assemblage of local people. Neil carefully folded the order of service, hesitating to view the photograph on the front cover. The smiling face of a younger, fitter Murdo Stuart smiled back up at him, dressed in a tweed suit and matching deerstalker hat. It was a photo taken high on the hill, no doubt during a stalking expedition decades previously. Underneath was the caption…

In loving memory of Murchadh Kenzie Stuart
1921–2009

He tucked the folded document into his jacket pocket and then followed the remaining mourners to the car park. It had been a good turnout for a man clearly respected within his community, but as he walked amongst the diminishing crowd, he couldn't help wondering whether any of the black-clad mourners were just a tiny bit relieved that some long-kept secret had been buried alongside Murdo that day.

Lochview had been thronged with well-wishers when Neil arrived. He'd enjoyed a small dram, and had engaged in conversation with Siobhan and Gordon. They'd been joined by the Reverend Mackay who clearly had a taste for the malt whisky. Neil couldn't fail to notice that the quantity of golden spirit still remaining in the minister's glass had diminished to almost nothing, and in a fraction of the time it had taken to sup his.

As his companions reminisced about the deceased, his idiosyncrasies and unique qualities, Neil's eyes met those of Mary Galbraith's across the crowded room. She scowled back at him, as if to warn him to keep his distance. Neil decided to heed the warning on this occasion, and drained his glass. He said his goodbyes and headed for the door, imagining the glares of two dozen pairs of eyes burning into his back. Once outside he shook his head in disbelief, dismissing the notion, and a little fearful of the paranoia that seemed to have taken hold of him.

The drive back to Inverness had been uneventful and quicker than anticipated. Neil strolled into his office, nodded to the two colleagues who were passing in the opposite direction, and slumped heavily into his chair. He tipped the contents of the brown envelope out onto his desk and examined them again as he loosened, and then removed the black tie he'd been wearing for the funeral.

Were these Max Friedmann's? His sense of excitement was nonetheless tempered by doubt. He fired up his computer and searched the web for *German military decorations*. An image of the metal badge lying in front of him soon filled the screen. He read the associated text beneath the photograph. It was the *Kriegsmarine* Destroyer War Badge, the *Zerstörer-Kriegsabzeichen*. The decoration had apparently been designed by the well-known German artist; Paul Casberg of Berlin. The destroyer on the badge had been modelled on the *Wilhelm Heidkamp*, a ship that had gone down fighting with her 313 man crew during the First Battle of Narvik in April 1940. He read on:

Instituted on June 4, 1940, the badge was initially issued to all those destroyer personnel who had taken part in the Battles for Narvik. It was also presented to personnel attached to E-Boats and Torpedo-Boats. Eleven months later, when they received their own distinctive badge, the Destroyer War Badge would only, solely, be issued to Destroyer personnel.

Neil ferreted through the file on Friedmann that Fuchs had provided during his visit. There was no mention of the destroyer war badge amongst his decorations. In fact, Friedmann had never served on a destroyer. Put simply, the medal was most certainly not the Spanish Cross or the U-boat War Badge as he'd hoped.

He reached for the phone, and dialled Matthias Fuchs' number. A young woman answered in her native tongue, but when she discovered the identity of her caller, she continued the conversation in perfect English. '*Kapitänleutnant* Fuchs is not here at present Herr Strachan. He has been lecturing at the Naval Academy today, and is due back this afternoon. I will get him to call as soon as he returns if you would like?'

'Thank you, I'll await his call.' Neil replaced the handset and picked up the coloured ribbon.

'If these don't belong to Friedmann, who the hell do they belong to?' he muttered to himself, 'and how the hell did Murdo Stuart get hold of them?'

'Talking to yourself again, Neil?' Fraser Gunn stood beaming down at him, papers in hand. 'How was the funeral this morning?'

'Depressing, like most funerals, but I did get these given to me by Ursula Stuart.'

Gunn leant over Neil's shoulder. 'Umm, looks like more German medals to me,' he deduced correctly.

'Aye, you're right, there're no flies on you Fraser! This one's the Destroyer War Badge, and the ribbon, well I'm almost sure it's from the Iron Cross Second Class. It was worn through the buttonhole of the tunic. I assume that's what the hole's for.'

'Interesting,' came the slightly sarcastic reply. 'What do you call someone who's become a medal nerd? They must have a name… something ending in *ologist* I assume?'

'Don't take the piss, Fraser. So what brings you up here to where the humans hang out?'

'I have something *equally* interesting to show you my friend.'

He placed a batch of papers in front of Neil and stood back. 'Your envelopes. The guys down in Glasgow have come up with something on the insides of some of the flaps.'

He leant forward again and turned the first page over to reveal a blown-up photograph of one of the envelopes. 'The words had been written in pencil and erased using a rubber, as you correctly assumed. The thing is, such erasures leave minute particles of rubber in the paper, so we sprinkle a powder of dyed Lycopodium spores onto the document and hey presto! Words appear. The magnified image here shows the words *between the waters* and underneath are some figures which I assume are a date.'

Neil examined the photograph. Sure enough the figures were clear to see: *21/5/82.*

Gunn pulled out a chair and sat down before carrying on. 'The words are always the same on every marked envelope, but the so-called dates, if that's what they are, all differ. If our assumption is correct they range from 1980 to 1983. There are eight examples in all. The remaining four envelopes only have dates written on the flaps.'

'*Between the waters*, what on earth does that mean?' Neil was resting on his elbows, his chin perched on clenched hands.

'Like I said before Neil, you're the detective, but if you want my opinion; I think it's some sort of code, possibly advising the recipient of important dates, if that's what they are.'

'Umm, it seems furtiveness is worryingly commonplace in that village.'

'You know, I think you may be right. Oh, and another bit of trivia for you. The dates erased from the envelopes always relate to a *Friday*, and are always about two weeks after the dates on the post marks. May be that's a coincidence, of course.'

'Best I get my code-breaking hat on then and try and get to the bottom of this so-called code.'

'Best you do.' Gunn turned to leave.

'By the way Fraser, what exactly are *Lycopodium spores*?'

'They're from a type of fern Neil, very useful little plant. It has all sorts of uses, from fireworks to condoms! Good luck,' he called out as he drifted through the door.

Neil, his curiosity partially satisfied, returned to the papers that Gunn had presented to him. Each envelope which bore the phrase and dates had been photographed and enlarged. The words were clear now, having been treated with the magic spores and magnified considerably.

He turned to his keyboard and brought up a diary page for the year 1982. The 21st May was indeed a Friday. His next search was 1980, then '81 and '83. All the dates, and that's what they all appeared to be, were definitely Fridays! He felt compelled to just ask Mary Galbraith; she had to know, surely? But no, she was best left alone for a while. He recalled the strange look she'd given him earlier that day, as if to join Ursula in saying; *this was your fault*. His bet was that she'd deny any knowledge of the erasures. After all, they didn't come from *her*, these envelopes, but he had a good idea who they did come from.

He picked up his mug, intending to get himself a coffee. As he rose from his desk, the phone rang. The voice at the other end was familiar, perfect English with a trace of an accent. 'Good afternoon Neil, Matthias here. Sorry I missed your call earlier, and thanks for the email, I only read it this morning I'm afraid. Interesting developments, eh?'

'Yes I think so, but there's something else I wanted your advice on.'

'Go ahead, I only hope I can help.'

'I attended a funeral today, in Glendaig. A man called Murdo Stuart died suddenly last week. He was living in Glendaig during the war.'

'Ah, I recall his name from the email. That's very unfortunate.'

'Yes, it is, very. I think you must have gathered from my message that I've no doubt that he knew more about the graves on the beach than he was letting on.'

'I did get that impression, yes.'

'Well, his widow handed me an envelope at the funeral containing some interesting items. There was a short length of ribbon; red, white and black, with a small hole cut at one end. I have a feeling it's the buttonhole ribbon of the Iron Cross Second Class.'

'From your description, I would say you are correct. Friedmann himself was awarded such a decoration.'

'The thing is Matthias, I don't think it belonged to him.'

'Oh I see,' came the surprised reply. 'Why do you think that?'

'Because the other item in the envelope was the Destroyer War Badge and Friedmann never received that, did he?'

'No, he did not. He never served on destroyers. I assume you are confident that your identification of the medal is correct?'

'Oh yes, no doubt at all.'

Neil could hear a sigh of disappointment at the other end of the line. 'Tell me, what is on the back of the badge?'

Neil retrieved the medal from his drawer. 'It's a shiny silver colour with a horizontal fixing pin, and the words *Schwerin Berlin 63.*'

'Ah, and the ship portrayed on the badge is silver-coloured, surrounded by a wreath in gold, yes?'

Neil flipped it over. 'That's right.'

'What you have there is an early example of the badge. It's made of tombak, a type of brass alloy. The later versions were made of fine zinc and were a flat grey colour.'

'So you're suggesting that the recipient of this badge was awarded it early in the war?'

'Yes, my guess is the recipient may well have been a veteran of the Norwegian campaign in 1940. The award was created initially for the destroyer crews who served at the battles for Narvik.'

'Yes, I know, I read the notes about the badge online.'

'I'm afraid many badges like this were awarded, but it does provide us with a vague clue as to the possible recipient, should a name come into the frame.'

'Aye, I agree, I'm just hoping a name does come into the frame soon. My time working on this case is fast running out I'm afraid.' Not wishing to dwell on the subject of time limits, he quickly moved on. 'Paul Miller informs me that a U-boat was attacked off the southern end of Skye on 1st January '42.'

'Yes, the details are very vague though. I can tell you nothing more than he has. There's no record of the incident in *our* archives.'

'What about the U-boat that went down on 8th January, have you found out any more about the circumstances surrounding its loss?'

There was an awkward pause at the German's end of the line. 'I must confess I've been unable to do any further research during the past week. Lecture commitments I'm afraid. I do have a free couple of days from tomorrow, so will do what I can.'

'Please do Matthias, as I said, time's running out on this one.'

'Point taken my friend, I'll get back to you on Monday, have a good weekend, *ja*?'

Neil replaced the receiver. His head slumped forward, dejection beginning to flow through him. He felt empty, lifeless like a shrivelled balloon at the end of a party. Sitting quietly, his torpid eyes followed the grain patterns on the surface of his desk.

'Cheer up Neil, it may never happen.'

A uniformed Inspector breezed through the office and dropped a batch of files on a desk close by. 'That's just it, mate, I think it has.' Neil managed a weak smile.

His colleague shot him a bewildered glance. '*What* just has?'

'My failure to get a result on this job over at Glendaig. I've just about run out of time and ideas, and I've come up with more questions than bloody answers.'

The Inspector grinned. 'Och, don't worry about it Neil, it's not your average crime enquiry is it? Brodie going to pull the plug on it then, eh?

'Aye, I reckon so.'

'Well you know what they say about the first forty-eight hours being critical in any criminal investigation. I'd say a seventy-year delay would be an uphill struggle for any detective to get to grips with… including you, boy wonder.' He gave Neil a reassuring pat on the shoulder as he passed by. 'There's always plenty of crime in the *present* to solve, should those of the *past* be too great a challenge for you!' He stopped at the door. 'You know what the answer is, Neil?'

'What's that Malcolm?'

'You should submit a report to the Chief. Get him to set you up with a bloody time machine!'

Neil, cheered by the light-hearted exchange, launched a plastic cup in the Inspector's direction. 'Piss off and direct some traffic or something,' he growled.

However, when the joker had gone and silence once again gripped the empty office, the reality of the situation emerged once more. For all the banter in the world, nothing had changed. He *had* just about run out of time.

Chapter Thirty-Three

The hum of the shower pump in the en suite woke Neil with a jolt. He'd been dreaming about something strange… not unusual for him, but couldn't quite remember the gist of the imagery. His eyelids, still heavy with sleep, reluctantly rolled upwards but then clamped shut again as a shaft of sunlight settled upon his face. He turned his head away as it danced across the pillow to the tune of the gently swaying curtains. When he opened them again, he could just make out the blurred image of Cat's naked form standing in the shower cubicle. Her pose reminded him of the statues he'd seen on holiday in Rhodes, aesthetically pleasing to the eye, as she slowly revolved under the cascade of steaming water. He watched, mesmerized, as she squeezed the moisture from the long blonde locks that lay plastered against her pale skin. Then, reluctantly, he diverted his gaze towards the alarm clock on the bedside cabinet. *Ten forty-five. Christ!* They were supposed to be at his mother's at twelve!

He leapt out of bed evoking an irritable glare from Tam who lay curled up, foetus-like at the end of the bed. Cat had vacated the shower cubicle and was towelling her hair vigorously as Neil hurried past her and slid back the screen door.

'My God, your eyes remind me of cigarette ends,' she jested, stepping aside to allow him past.

The couple had been out with friends the previous evening. It

361

had been a welcome opportunity for Neil to briefly focus on something other than the realisation that he'd wasted a month chasing shadows in Glendaig. He knew the truth was slipping away from him, and was at least thankful that a hot curry and a skin full of lager had temporarily numbed the growing sense of nonaccomplishment that lingered within him.

Having wolfed down a light breakfast, Tam was walked, and they set out for Cromarty at eleven thirty. It was another glorious day, the sky was clear blue to the east, and only a scattering of puffy white clouds hovered over the distant mountains to the west. Neil had removed the MG's canvas roof, allowing its slipstream to rush noisily over the exposed windscreen. Tam, who was happy to sit on Cat's lap, sheltered from the relentless rush of air. He sat proudly, monopolising the view ahead as he stared through the glass, his snout raised in arrogant disregard for his fellow passenger.

They made the Kessock Bridge in good time and, having crossed the Moray Firth to the Black Isle, the drive became more scenic. The quieter road east from the A9 passed through gently undulating fields and pine woods, before finally giving way to wider tracts of farmland. As they sped along towards Fortrose, the road hugged the northern shore of the Firth before snaking its way through the ancient cathedral town. The little car slowed and Cat peered out from behind Tam's flapping ears. She was confident now that she could be heard above the howl of the wind.

'You're quiet,' she observed, her voice raised slightly.

'Oh I was just thinking about this case I'm working on.'

'Surprise, surprise. What about it?'

'Just mulling things over, considering whether I'd followed up on everything I could have done.'

Cat smiled, and squeezed his arm. 'You've still got some time yet. I'm sure something will crop up.'

Neil gave her a fleeting glance as he changed gear. 'I'm not so sure. I have a sixty-eight-year-old body I can't identify, possibly a German naval officer, but if I'm honest I don't really know for sure.

Then there's a second empty grave, two elderly women communicating to each other in code, and now another set of German medals that appear out of the blue. So many unanswered questions. And what about this term *between the waters*, what do you reckon to that?'

'Well I assume it refers to a place, perhaps where two rivers meet... or an island or something.'

'Like Skye, you mean?'

'Possibly, or what about here, The Black Isle, lying between the two firths?' Cat stroked the dog's ears. 'I think those dates on the envelopes are dates of meetings, and *between the waters*, well that's probably where they met, out in the middle of nowhere where no one would see them.'

'I don't know why they didn't just speak on the phone, it would have been a damn sight easier.'

'Perhaps they didn't have phones then?'

'Well Mary Galbraith certainly does now. The thing is, we're talking about the eighties aren't we. That's well over twenty years ago. It may all be irrelevant anyway, because Isobel Grant may have died by now.'

'But it is intriguing isn't it? Secret codes and such like.'

'You read too many thrillers, let's change the subject, eh?'

They'd left Fortrose and were on the last leg of the journey down to the picturesque little town of Cromarty, which nestled at the end of the Black Isle peninsula. The road now descended gently, down through fertile fields towards the small cluster of Georgian merchant's houses and Victorian fishermen's cottages that made up the historic Burgh. In the distance were the hills of Sutherland, rising ghostlike in the haze beyond the sparkling waters of the Cromarty Firth. Several grubby-looking oil platforms stood in the waters of the Firth, eyesores that in Neil's view were a blot upon an otherwise perfect vista.

There's the *Cromarty Rose* out there,' said Cat pointing. 'She's still going strong despite the rumours.'

The little car ferry could be seen slowly chugging across the Firth to Nigg on the far shore. Sunlight flashed off the windows of the two cars that stood upon her deck. It was a summertime scene that had been repeated day in, day out, for as long as Neil could remember. 'Aye, there's talk of replacing her at some stage. Still, she looks as if she's got a bit of life left in her yet.'

There was a lull in the conversation for a minute or two, then Neil turned to his girlfriend. 'When are you going to put that flat of yours on the market then?'

Her blue eyes focussed on him as he checked the rear view mirror. 'So you haven't changed your mind then, you're still happy to have a woman around the house?'

'Aye, of course, it could be a distinct advantage!'

'I'd have to have an equal say as to how things are done, in the house I mean.'

He shot her an anxious glance. 'What do you mean exactly?'

'Well, decor, things like that. Oh, and how long the laundry basket remains full!'

'No problem, that's what I meant by it being a distinct advantage!'

'Of course, there needs to be a trade-off here. I'll wash your boxers if you wash my car!'

Neil smiled. 'It's a deal... I think you've drawn the short straw though.'

'Aye, no doubt about it! Okay, I'll pop into the estate agents next week and get the ball rolling.'

'Good, that mortgage you're paying could be coming to me as rent.'

Cat wasn't going to take the bait. 'In your dreams,' came the reply; it was the one he was expecting.

They exchanged smiles as Neil manoeuvred the MG down a narrow alley between the ends of two substantially-large stone houses. At the end was Shore Street, with its quaint Victorian lampposts and far reaching views. Their destination was away to their left; one of several large houses that faced the sea. *Crumbathyn* was a rambling old merchant's house, constructed of coral-coloured stone that extended to three storeys. The Georgian sash windows could have done with a coat of paint, but generally the property retained its period splendour. Its elegant frontage looked out across Shore Street towards the blue-green expanse of the North Sea.

As Neil opened the wrought iron gate, Rona Strachan appeared at the front door wiping her hands on a garish coloured apron. She was an authoritative looking woman in her late fifties, edging towards plump, with neatly styled mousy coloured hair. She looked every bit the no-nonsense district nurse, a position she'd held locally for over a quarter of a century.

'Goodness you two, on time for once,' she joked as she embraced Cat and then her son. Tam shot past her and into the house, uninterested in any form of greeting ritual and eager to explore every room. Why he did this repeatedly was anyone's guess, because he'd thoroughly examined every nook and cranny of the old house on numerous occasions.

Welcoming formalities completed, the couple headed for the sitting room, one of a number of underused rooms that led off the long dark hallway. Rona and her husband had bought the property for a knock-down price in the mid-eighties, just after she'd been successful in getting the community nursing job. Neil's father had spent much of his working life away from home on oil rigs in the North Sea. He came home at weekends, but the long periods of separation had eventually wrecked the marriage. He now lived in Aberdeen with his new partner, allowing Rona to stay on in the house she loved.

Neil had tried to persuade his mother to find something smaller, but she would always dismiss his representations. She never missed an opportunity to remind him that there would always be plenty of room for his children, *if* he got his act together and made an honest woman of Catriona, as she always called her. He'd given up arguing, preferring instead to leave the inevitable to a time that fate dictated.

However, the unceasing levels of energy that his mother seemingly continued to possess, meant that this wasn't going to be any time soon.

As Neil entered the sitting room, he first detected the faint but unmistakeable aroma of cheap men's cologne. A glance around the door confirmed the identity of the *culprit*, such was Neil's detestation of the stuff. 'Ah, Great Uncle Euan, how are you doing?'

The old man's beaming face appeared from behind the Sunday paper. 'Hello son, good to see you, and where's the lovely Cat?'

'Here, Uncle Euan.' Cat appeared at Neil's shoulder and gave him a little wave. Euan found her use of his family title particularly endearing, and she in turn found his playful yet harmless flirtations a source of mild amusement.

Euan eased himself out of the chair, waving away Cat's protestations that he should remain seated. He was tall, lean, and always immaculately groomed for a man of his advancing years. Beneath his thinning white hair there was still a sense of mischief present in his dark eyes. It was a physical trait that had never really diminished since his youth, when he was serving as a constable in the then Ross and Cromarty Constabulary. The evidence of this was clear to see in the various photographs he'd repeatedly shown his nephew over the years.

As a boy, Neil had often studied the glossy monochrome images belonging to his uncle. They were an insight into a simpler way of life, depicting the proud-looking individuals who once plied the northern Highlands, keeping the peace and investigating the relatively few crimes that were committed within the region's remote and scattered communities. They were men who, more often than not, patrolled alone, and astride two wheeled transport rather than being incarcerated in the fast, high-tech patrol cars of the modern age.

Euan had seen much change in his time. His force amalgamated twice, initially with those in the County of Sutherland and then again in the seventies to form the force in which Neil currently served. He retired three years later in the rank of sergeant, having been posted to both east and west coasts, but always at the sharp end, and always in uniform.

'Where's that mad bloody dog of yours?' he bellowed. 'Making a nuisance of himself upstairs no doubt.'

As if on cue, Tam trotted into the room carrying a shoe and collapsed, exhausted, on the hearth rug. 'Ah there you are you young scoundrel, come here laddie and see your old Uncle Euan.' Tam duly obliged, and positioned himself at Euan's feet, ready to receive any affection that the old man wished to dispense.

Family news was next on the agenda whilst Rona clattered around in kitchen, making final preparations for lunch. 'So what's going on in your lives?' Euan looked across at Neil and Cat who were relaxing on the large leather sofa by the window. Whilst awaiting an answer, he refocused his attention on the task of packing a generous pinch of tobacco into the bowl of his pipe.

Neil squeezed Cat's hand. 'I suppose the latest news is that Cat's moving in with me permanently. She's putting her flat on the market next week.'

Euan looked up again, this time with a gleam in his eye. 'About bloody time too,' he retorted, thrusting the stem of the pipe between his teeth. He pointed at Neil, his expression fixed. 'Now don't let me hear you've been taking advantage of the lassie. Remember she's no' yer housekeeper.'

Neil laughed and patted Cat's thigh. 'I hardly think that's going to happen.'

Cat punched him playfully on the arm, causing him to wince. 'You're bloody right it's not.'

'That's my girl,' Euan chortled as he applied a match to his pipe.

At that moment Rona appeared in the doorway. 'Did I hear Catriona's moving in with you, Neil?'

'Aye Ma she is, I can't resist the inevitable any longer.' Another punch landed on his arm, this time with significantly more force.

'Well I'm very pleased for you both. I don't suppose there'd be the sound of wedding bells in the air any time soon then?'

'Och, for God's sake Ma. Look, now you've made Cat blush. Give it a rest will you.'

Rona turned away, suitably admonished. 'Sorry, me and my mouth. Now come along you lot, to the table… and you Euan, put that damned pipe out. Your brother would turn in his grave if he knew you were smoking in here.'

'Your father always liked the smell of pipe tobacco,' Euan protested, but nevertheless did as he was told.

'My father might've liked the smell, but he never would've smoked in the house against my mother's wishes.' Rona glared at him over her shoulder as she disappeared down the hallway.

'Come on Uncle Euan,' said Neil, placing an arm around the old man's shoulder. 'We'll have a dram after lunch. She can't complain about that. After all, Gramps never had any objections when it came to cracking open a bottle of malt!'

The little family group mustered in the dining room and settled around the antique cherry wood table. Lunch was duly served and consumed, during which Rona fired a relentless barrage of questions at her son and his partner regarding their plans to cohabit. Euan listened in silence as he repeatedly topped up the diners' wine glasses. Meanwhile, Tam lay under the table, ever watchful, should the humans be careless enough to drop a morsel of food from their overcrowded plates.

As the grandfather clock in the hall struck half past two, Rona rose from the table to clear the plates. Cat offered to assist and ushered Neil and Euan into the sitting room. Neil poured out two generous tumblers of single malt, and began to update his uncle on his latest mountaineering exploits. 'I haven't had the time to go off hill walking of late, what with the new job and everything.'

He plopped an ice cube in each glass and offered one of them to Euan. 'I managed to do the Beinn Alligin ridge back in April. Then got up to the summit of Sgurr Mhor. It was something of a scramble, but worth it for the view across the Torridon range.'

'So how many of the Munros have you bagged now then?' Euan asked.

'Seventy at the last count, a couple of hundred still to go… if I get that far.' Neil reclined onto the sofa, and took a sip from his glass. 'I can see this new job with the Major Enquiry Team is going to keep me busy all hours for the foreseeable future.'

'Well don't you let it take over your life son and remember, whatever you do, make time for that lassie of yours, you've got a good one there.'

Rona's head appeared round the door. 'Catriona and I are going to take Tam for a walk, we'll be back shortly.' She disappeared into the hallway and there followed a series of frenzied whimperings as the spaniel's excitement reached fever pitch. Then the front door slammed shut and a sense of quiet gripped the house once more.

Euan raised his glass, 'Slàinte! Here's tae ye. Your mother tells me you've been working on this case over on the west coast. The skeleton found on the beach?'

'Aye, it's certainly been a challenge. So much so that I'm getting nowhere with it and the boss is breathing down my neck, threatening to pull the plug on the whole thing. He reckons it's a job for archaeologists, not detectives.'

'Well, he may be right, but if the fiscal thinks otherwise, then there's little he can do other than let you get on with it, surely?' Euan rested his glass on the table next to him and reached for his pipe.

'My DCI doesn't see it that way… hey, you're asking for trouble if you light that thing up in here, y'know.'

'Aye, aye of course.' Euan reached for his tobacco pouch and lifted the flap. 'Come on then, give me the run down. You never know, a fresh perspective on things sometimes pays dividends.'

'I doubt it, but no harm in giving it a try.'

Neil then embarked upon a detailed commentary, outlining his progress to date. Whilst he did so, Euan sat quietly listening, sucking on his unlit pipe between sips of whisky. When his nephew finally fell silent and reached for his own glass, he sat for a few moments, nodding gently as he reflected on what he'd been told.

'Well well, that's some case for you to cut your teeth on!'

'It's different, I'll grant you that.'

'Seems to me, you need to get another angle on the sequence of events that unfolded over in Glendaig… from someone new, this lady Isobel Grant for example.'

'That's if she's still alive. I might well be heading up a blind alley with that line of enquiry.'

'Now, now laddie, that's not the attitude to adopt here. The first rule of detecting is to follow all leads until they're utterly exhausted. *Never assume anything* my old sergeant used to say. No, we've got to find this woman, or at least establish that she *is* deceased.'

'And just how do you propose *we* to do that? I'm fairly certain I've done all that I can to find her.'

Euan gestured with his pipe. 'The envelopes, they're the key to this. You say a number of them had the words *between the waters* written on them, and with different dates.'

'Aye, the dates on the flaps appear to be about two weeks beyond those on the post marks, and they all refer to Fridays.'

'Interesting, and you're sure they're from this woman Isobel Grant, no one else?'

'That's what I believe. Some of the envelopes matched the size of a number of greetings cards signed Isobel and Robbie. Robbie was the husband's name. Murdo Stuart also referred to them as being a clue to finding Isobel, so I'm satisfied they're from her.'

'What do you make of this phrase, *between the waters*?'

Neil shrugged, 'I personally think it's somewhere where they went to meet, somewhere remote perhaps; an Island on a river, or even somewhere *between* two rivers?'

'It galls me to say this, but have you tried that infernal thing, the Internet?'

'Of course I have. All that comes up are biblical references and music related stuff.'

'Umm,' Euan rubbed his chin with the end of his pipe. 'What about a translation, English from the Gaelic perhaps? You know how keen we are up here to cherish the native language. It may be that if you can find out what the phrase means in the Gaelic, then you have another possible line of enquiry. It may be nothing but it's worth a try.'

'You may have a point there,' said Neil. 'Tell me, do you know whether there are any other ancient names for the Black Isle, other than the direct translation from the Gaelic?'

'You mean *An t-Eilean Dubh*?'

'Well we all know that one. No, I'm thinking of some ancient Pictish phrase, something like that.'

'Why do you ask?'

'Well, Cat suggested on the way here that *between the waters* could refer to the two firths bordering the Black Isle. It's not inconceivable perhaps that the term may refer to this area, around Cromarty.'

'Good point,' said Euan wagging his finger by way of acknowledgement. 'I can't really help on that score… but I think I know someone who can.'

'Who would that be?'

Euan prised himself out of his chair and stuffed his beloved pipe into the pocket of his cardigan 'Just follow me son, and I'll introduce you to him.'

Chapter Thirty-Four

Rona and Cat were crossing Shore Street when Neil and Euan emerged through the open gate at a lively pace. 'And where are you two off to in such a hurry?' Rona stood open-mouthed, keen to discover their intended destination, whilst Cat smiled knowingly.

'If I'm not mistaken, they're sneaking off down to the pub.'

'No, no, lassie, you're wrong as usual. I'm shocked that you should inflict such a slur upon a man whose reverence for the Sabbath has never been in question.'

'Ahh, don't give me that,' said Rona, with a dismissive shake of the head. 'I'm not so sure you can even spell the word Sabbath!'

'If you must know, we're going to find Duncan Buchanan.'

'Duncan! Well that confirms it then, you're away to the pub, because that's the only place you'll find him at this time of day.'

Euan turned away. 'Come on son, there's no convincing some people.'

Neil waved to the two women and walked quickly to catch up with his uncle. 'Do you mean Duncan Buchanan of Buchanans the Undertakers?' he asked.

'Aye, one and the same.'

They were now walking along the grassy tract of land that bordered the rocky foreshore. Behind them, the wooded slopes of the headland known locally as the "Sutors" rose up above the town. To their right, the North Sea glinted in the late June sunshine.

'So how is Duncan the undertaker qualified to advise on the history of the Black Isle then?'

'Believe me Neil, there's nothing old Duncan doesn't know about these parts. He's even written a book on the subject.'

'Never!'

'Aye, a dark horse, eh? And he's chair of the Cromarty and Black Isle Local History Group.'

'Okay,' said Neil, 'I'm suitably impressed. So where do we find him, in the pub as my mother suggested?'

'Och no, he'll be out at the end of the old north pier at the harbour, fishing no doubt. You won't find him in the pub before six.'

As they passed by the whitewashed Victorian lighthouse and turned the corner by the clubhouse of the local boat club, the harbour came into view. It was a simple affair; two stone piers extending out into the Firth. The southernmost provided access to an offshore breakwater via a short bridge. The northern arm curved away from the shore for seventy metres, its head stopping short of the breakwater to form the entrance to the little harbour. Between these old eighteenth-century piers, a variety of small boats bobbed up and down against a narrow pontoon. Their fenders creaked and groaned in harmony as the tiny vessels rode the gentle swell.

Euan turned right onto the north pier and led his nephew over the uneven, weed-strewn cobbles that extended towards the seaward end of the structure. 'Watch yourself out here, these old stones take no prisoners,' Euan warned as he picked his way over a variety of different coloured mooring ropes and coils of rusty chain.

With their destination in sight, Euan called out to a solitary figure propped up against the round pillar that marked the end of the pier wall. The figure, a man at least ten years younger than Euan, turned in response to the call and removed a small cigar from between his lips. He expelled a thin column of blue smoke skyward and tapped ash onto his yellow boots. In his other hand was a fishing rod, the line running out at an oblique angle, carried away upon the ebbing tide.

The fisherman greeted Euan with a vigorous handshake. 'Decided to take up fishing at last, eh Euan?'

Duncan Buchanan was in his late sixties. He was a portly man, but his apparent bulk may have been exaggerated by the thick woollen fleece he was wearing. There were remnants of stubbly black hair skirting his ears, and a sparse beard that had faded to grey at the chin. Perched astride his drinker's nose was a pair of sunglasses, the lenses heavily smudged around the edges. It soon became clear why this was the case. He repeatedly pushed the glasses back up the bridge of his nose with a stubby thumb and forefinger.

Euan extended an arm towards Neil. 'Duncan, you remember my great nephew, Neil?'

Duncan Buchanan wiped a hand on the front of his grubby blue jeans and shook Neil's. 'I've nae set eyes on you since you were a wee laddie,' he announced with a softly lilting highland accent. 'You're a *polisman* now I hear, and a bigwig too, apparently.'

'Nothing too bigwiggish, Duncan, just Inspector, that's all.'

'Detective Inspector, at thirty. Nothing wrong with that son,' Euan interjected. 'In my day you'd have had a foot in one of Duncan's boxes before you ever got to that rank.'

Euan placed an arm around Neil's shoulders and gave him a friendly hug. 'We've come to pick your brains Duncan. That's if you can tear yourself away from the fish for a while.'

'Och, the fish've all buggered off over to Nigg it seems. So you have my undivided attention gentlemen, fire away.'

Duncan wound in his line and propped the rod up against the wall behind him. Meanwhile, Neil suspected that his uncle was about to unleash a barrage of questions on his behalf. He cleared his throat, hoping to prevent any imminent verbal emanation from Euan's direction. It worked perfectly. Not only did his new assistant remain silent, but he now had Duncan's full attention as well.

'I'm not sure whether you've read in the papers recently, about the discovery of some skeletal remains over on the west coast?'

Duncan nodded. 'I didn't read it in the paper, but I did see the report on the TV news. Are you involved with the case then?'

'Aye, I am. I've been given the job of identifying the remains and finding out what happened to the poor fellow.'

'Didn't they say the bones had been there years, something to do with a wartime sailor or suchlike?'

'The bones are old, but we're not sure whose they are just yet.'

'It all seems very interesting. So where do I feature in all this?'

Neil looked across at Euan, who was clearly eager to get in on the conversation. But the old man took the hint and decided to remain silent. Neil turned back to Duncan. 'It's a long story, but I'm trying to trace a woman who lived over at Glendaig around the time the remains were buried. I think she may be able to enlighten me as to what happened back then. It is possible she may be dead by now, but I need to find out one way or the other.'

'And you think I may know her?' Duncan looked puzzled.

'No, but I think that you may be able to help me unravel a clue that may, just may, put me on the right track.'

Euan couldn't help himself any longer. 'I told Neil about your involvement with the local history group, and your unrivalled knowledge of the Black Isle.'

Neil took up the conversation again. 'This woman, her name is, or *was*, Isobel Grant. She sent a series of letters and cards to a relative in Glendaig during the nineteen-eighties. We've found some sort of cryptic wording on the envelopes and thought on the off chance the phrase may have some connection with the Black Isle.'

'A cryptic phrase you say?'

'Aye, *between the waters*. The Black Isle came to mind for obvious reasons, due to its position between the two firths. Have you ever heard of it referred to in that way before?'

Duncan grinned. 'No, I've never heard of the Black Isle referred to as *between the waters*...'

Neil let out a disappointed sigh. 'Well that's knocked that theory on the head then.'

Duncan, still grinning, wasn't finished though. '...I was going to say that I do know someone who lived on the Black Isle who *did* describe his own lands in that way.'

'Who?' Neil and Euan both craned forward, impatiently awaiting Duncan's response.

'William the Lion, King of the Scots between 1165 and 1214. You know, the king who gave us our royal standard bearing the lion rampant.'

Neil seemed taken aback. 'I'm familiar with the story of William the Lion, but was hoping for a more up-to-date connection perhaps.'

'Sorry, that's the best I can do I'm afraid.' Duncan now had a wounded look about him.

'Just hear him out, please,' said Euan.

'Okay, so how was William the Lion connected to the phrase *between the waters* then?'

'Well, according to the Chronicle of Melrose, do you know what that is?'

'Isn't it some form of historical narrative, written by the Cistercian monks at Melrose Abbey?' Neil was struggling with his memory, but his history degree did clearly count for something!

'I'm impressed,' said Duncan. 'Yes, it's reputed to be one, if not *the* foremost narrative source for the history of Scotland and Northern England in the twelfth and thirteenth centuries. Well, according to the chronicle, in 1179 as I recall, William the Lion and his brother David led a large and powerful army into Ross and there fortified two castles, one named *Dunscath*, and the other *Etherdouer*.'

'And how does the phrase, *between the waters* fit into all this?' Neil asked, confounded.

Duncan raised a hand, urging patience. 'Etherdouer, or "Edirdovar" as it's since been called, has been interpreted as meaning *between the waters*!'

'I see, and does this castle still stand today?'

'Well it's a ruin now. It was one of the oldest inhabited houses in Scotland you know. Then it was used by the military during the last war. Since then, it's just been left to crumble.'

'So where is this castle? On the Black Isle?'

'Aye, it is as it happens. The castle was built in a distinctive red brick and so became known as *Caisteal Ruadh* – or red castle – in the parish of Killearnan on the south shore of the Black Isle.'

Neil's eyes widened, and then a knowing smile crept across his face. 'You mean Redcastle, the small village by the side of the Beauly Firth?'

'That's right laddie, did you not know the story? It's without doubt one of Scotland's most significant historical sites.'

'I have to admit I didn't, Duncan.'

'Och, I don't know what they're teaching kids in school these days... and you've been out of school a wee while, young feller.'

'You're lucky I've even heard of William the Lion,' Neil joked.

'Aye, I suppose.' Duncan retrieved his rod and reached up to remove a tangle of seaweed from its hook. 'Do you think Redcastle is where your lady and her friend went to meet?'

'Perhaps, what better place, a ruined castle in the middle of nowhere. I'm not so sure where this will take me though, I've a feeling I may run into a dead end, literally!'

'Then again you might not. Remember what I said to you earlier?' Euan's features crumpled into a frown, frustrated by his great nephew's continued pessimism.

'I know, I know,' Neil replied, 'and I'm grateful for the suggestion. It's such a tentative connection, that's all, but I'll look into it all the same.' He extended a hand to Duncan, who repeated the process of wiping his own on his jeans before grasping Neil's and shaking it once again.

'Good hunting, Neil. You'll have to let me know what comes of it, if indeed something does, that is!'

'I will, and thank you Duncan, you've been really helpful.'

Duncan, fishing rod in hand, turned away mindful of the falling tide and, with a flick of the wrist, cast his line back into the sandy-brown water that swirled about the narrow harbour mouth. Neil and Euan negotiated their way back around the variety of marine debris that lay around the pier.

'So what do you think, worth following up the Redcastle theory?' Euan was ever hopeful that his nephew would be open-minded to the suggestion his friend had just made.

'Aye, of course. I said I would.' Neil stopped dead and turned to face Euan. 'But let's be honest, this is all a bit far-fetched isn't it? Ancient kings, monks' chronicles, whatever next?'

'Have you come up with any other ideas?' Euan argued.

'No, point taken,' said Neil, defeated.

They turned the corner towards the lighthouse and the grassy area beyond. Glimpses of the shoreline were now all that were visible between the numerous caravanettes and holidaymakers' cars that continued to throng the open space. Their occupants lolled about on tartan rugs, picnicking and enjoying the view, uninterested in the two men who strolled past deep in conversation.

Euan pressed home his advantage. 'I accept Duncan's theory is somewhat speculative, but you should never dismiss it. I've successfully solved a number of crimes in my time where the information that led me to the culprit came from the most bizarre sources.'

Neil seemed unimpressed. He focussed on the path ahead, quickening his pace. 'For example?' he asked without turning his head.

'Well, let me see. One such case was back in the early fifties. I recall being sent to investigate the theft of lead, off a chapel roof, up at Brora. I had not the slightest clue who was responsible. It had to be someone local, well that was my theory anyway. I'd stopped at a garage on the A9 to fuel up the motorbike. It was several miles from the scene of the crime as I recall. This old dear was coming out of the shop next to the garage. She came up to me and asked whether I was up that way looking into the lead theft. "Aye," says I. So she says, "You'd be wise to pay young Rory Campbell a visit. He's most likely stashed the stuff in the old burial chamber up beyond their croft." When I asked her why she thought he was responsible, she said, "Because his grandfather did the same back in '23!"

Euan tittered to himself as Neil waited for the story's climax to be revealed. 'And was it young Rory Campbell who was responsible?'

'Well, I didn't believe her at first, dismissed the idea just as you would, but something inside me told me to go and look, so I did. I crept up to the old chamber in the dark and there it was, all the bloody lead from the chapel, and two others!'

'You'd need a warrant to do that today! So did Rory confess to his crimes?'

'Och, sure he did, spent six months in Porterfield Jail.'

'Okay, but at least you got a result on that occasion. This connection with Redcastle is pure supposition, and even if Isobel did meet Mary there in the eighties, where does that leave me in terms of finding Isobel?'

Euan grabbed his arm. 'The moral of the story is; all things are possible, never dismiss anything. Now that's all I've got to say on the matter.'

They walked on in silence, joining Shore Street once again and a minute later turning into the gateway at Crumbathyn. Tam met them at the door, tail wagging furiously. 'Ah you're back. I've just made tea,' Rona called out from the kitchen. 'I'll bring it into the front room.'

When she arrived with the tray, Euan was impatient to recount the conversation they'd had with Duncan Buchanan. 'Didn't you visit Redcastle on your nursing rounds, Rona?' His eyes followed her as she approached Cat and handed her a cup and saucer.

'Aye, but not for a few years now,' said Rona. 'It's a nice wee place though, Redcastle, very neat as I recall.'

'Did you have many patients over there?' Neil peered at her through the steam from his cup.

'A few, mainly elderly, and generally infirm. They'd have falls, or bash themselves and need bandaging up from time to time.'

'Don't suppose you remember any names do you?'

'Of course I do. I never forget a patient's name. There was old

George Farquharson, he was a nice chap, lived just along from the castle. Let me see, another old fellow called Tasker, I don't recall his first name. He was diabetic, moved into residential care in Inverness eventually.'

Neil smiled. 'No one called Grant then? I thought you might just have made my job a little easier.'

'Sorry dear, don't recall any Grants. More tea Catriona?'

Rona replenished Cat's cup and sat back into her favourite wing-backed armchair. She pushed the spoon around in her cup and placed it on her saucer. Then she surprised everyone, suddenly looking up and vociferating loudly. 'I'd almost forgotten, I used to go and see old Annie Bain at Castle Croft twice a week. After her hip replacement it was. How could I forget her? What a lovely old lady she was. Ex-headmistress, lifelong spinster, proud as punch. It was always a pleasure spending an hour with her, having a chat over a cup of tea. She had no one you see, sometimes I was the only person she'd see all week, very sad.'

'Didn't she have any family at all?' Cat asked, intrigued by Rona's nursing recollections.

'Not that I knew of,' Rona replied. 'The couple next door were very good to her, did her shopping every week and looked in on her every day. Aye, they were very nice. Umm, I forget their names now.' Then a second or two later; 'No, I do remember, Robbie and Morag were their names. He'd been a stalker on an estate somewhere over in the west. They had a daughter, Jeanne, as I recall.'

Neil had been taking little interest in the conversation up until then. The name Bain had certainly not excited him, but now he was interested. He'd dropped the magazine he was reading and was now staring at his mother intently. She smiled back at him. 'Are you alright dear? Only you look as if you've just seen a ghost!'

'Not seen one Ma, but you may have just given me a wee clue as to where I might find one!'

Rona looked mystified, but the significance of what she'd just said had not passed Euan by. He winked triumphantly at his nephew.

'There you go son, whenever you've got an enquiry on the go that's going nowhere, the oldies are always here to give you a hand.' He stuffed his pipe in his mouth, only to find himself at the receiving end of one of his niece's penetrating glares. He smiled weakly and withdrew the device, returning it reluctantly to his pocket.

Chapter Thirty-Five

Monday 29th June

Neil was well-acquainted with the road to Redcastle. Back in 2005, he'd spent several evenings conducting observations at the various parking areas along the route. The local police had received a series of disturbing reports from motorists, complaining that they'd been shot at as they'd driven along the narrow road skirting the Beauly Firth. It had transpired that the culprits were two local youths from a farm nearby. They'd been caught red-handed by members of Neil's proactive team, who'd been driving the route repeatedly for over a month in an attempt to flush out the so-called gunmen. As it happened, the weapons being used were ageing air guns; not exactly high powered rifles, but nevertheless potentially lethal.

Instances of crime in this area were, however, few and far between, and Neil hadn't driven along this lonely stretch of road since. It had been wintertime when the airgun incidents were being investigated. The landscape had been bleak, a windswept vista of leafless trees and ploughed fields. Just the odd splash of yellow had survived from the last resilient blooms which clung to the clumps of broom that grew by the roadside. Today was different; a collage of different shades of green welcomed Neil as he turned onto the narrow lochside road. A patchwork of fields lay to the north, backed by small clusters of dense woodland. To the south, the Beauly Firth shimmered in the morning sun as it lapped against the muddy foreshore. In the distant haze, traffic on the A862 could just be made out, like ants scurrying through the summer landscape.

Neil was in no hurry. If asked, his excuse would have probably been that he was enjoying the drive, but the reality was that he was anxious. This was probably his last chance to get to the truth. The clues he'd uncovered during his visit to Cromarty the day before had provided a tiny chink of light in what was proving to be a very dark tunnel, but his mother's connection with Redcastle had lapsed nearly five years previously. She'd given him directions to the small stone cottage that had been the home of Robbie and Morag, the couple who'd been such a support to the elderly Annie Bain, but would they still be there? Could Morag be Isobel Grant? He'd tried to look them up on the electoral roll when he'd arrived at the office, but the website had been down. *We are experiencing technical difficulties, please try again later* it had said. Fate seemed to have become his enemy, but fate couldn't obstruct him now. He was just ten minutes from discovering whether he'd managed to track down the last remaining link to Max Friedmann, and possibly the mysterious events that had occurred in wartime Glendaig. If not, it was all over. The man who'd been gunned down on that lonely beach would probably be laid to rest in a grave marked simply... what was it Tomas Zeigler had said...? *Ein Deutscher Soldat.*

The minutes ebbed slowly away. Neil could sense his stomach tightening as he swept into the tiny village of Redcastle. The road curved sharply to the right, past a black and white sign which informed travellers that they were entering Milton of Redcastle. As he negotiated the bend, a small blue hatchback passed him at speed, heading in the opposite direction towards North Kessock. It was travelling a little too fast in his opinion but, having said that, it wasn't unusual for the locals to treat speed limits on these narrow roads with a sense of disdain.

The village now came into view; first a telephone kiosk, then a cluster of neatly presented cottages, some whitewashed and some of local stone. Lush green verges, neatly tended and edged with white stones, indicated to the passer by that this was a community that cared. *Good for them,* Neil thought to himself as he eased his foot off the accelerator, trying to recall the directions his mother had given him. He was now passing a brightly-painted wooden fishing boat, a decorative centrepiece for the village, its blue hull planted with a variety of colourful heathers. Behind the dry stone wall against which it rested, and obscured by trees, stood the castle that gave the village its name, now in a state of ruinous disrepair.

A junction lay ahead, guarded by a gate lodge built in the Victorian style with distinct bright red gables. He would take the left turn here, opposite rickety wooden gates from which a gravel driveway led up to the castle.

Having turned into another, even narrower lane, Neil slowed again to a snail's pace. He was seeking a track off to the left and found it without difficulty fifty yards further on. In fact it was more than just a track; its surface had not long been metalled and led downhill towards a cluster of farm buildings and scattered dwellings. Beyond their roofs, away in the middle distance, the Beauly Firth now dominated his field of vision.

Standing together by the side of the narrowest of country lanes were two tiny cottages. They were similar structures to those he'd seen elsewhere in the village, built of random stone with a distinctive pinkish hue. Small dormer windows peeked out from their slate roofs, looking down upon colourful cottage gardens that were laid to lawn and bordered by mature shrubs. Parked on a hard standing outside the southernmost cottage was a silver Volvo estate bearing a local registration plate. This was good news as, according to his mother, the first cottage he passed would have been Annie Bain's place. He stopped by its weather-cracked gate for a better look. A fading name sign confirmed that this first property was indeed Castle Croft. He moved on, stopping again beside the Volvo. The second cottage had an identical gate; freshly painted in green, and in a significantly better state of repair, but it was the name of the property in the form of a slate sign plate affixed to the porch that evoked a sudden sense of excitement within Neil. The name, etched in the Celtic style, read *Edirdovar.*

So this could be it, *between the waters,* the cryptic location scrawled on the envelopes. He parked a little way along the lane and walked back. The gate squeaked as he opened it, but that was the only sound beyond that of the gulls which circled noisily overhead. Then, tentatively, he opened the door to the porch. Inside was a second, identical door, obscured in part by the copious number of coats that hung from hooks spaced along the wooden panelled walls. He looked for a bell push but there was none, so he knocked firmly on the door. There was no immediate sound of movement within, so he rapped again, several times; still nothing.

Outside the porch, a paved path snaked its way around the corner of the property. Neil decided to follow this route past the small cottage-style window that provided a view into the tiny sitting room. He glanced in as he passed by; the room was dark and empty. It was comfortably furnished in a style that tended to suggest the occupants were of an older generation. A cluster of framed photographs adorned the top of the dark wood sideboard. The other surfaces within the room, including the mantelpiece, provided a resting place for a disorderly array of small ornaments.

He turned the corner, passed through another low gate, and found himself in a rear garden that extended some way beyond the cottage. The beds provided a blaze of summer colour against the neatly trimmed hedges that marked the property's boundary. A small patio had been laid up to the back wall, upon which stood a large teak table and four chairs, all of which were shaded by a green parasol.

Neil stopped and looked around him. Initially he could see no one, but then his eye detected movement some way down the garden. A woman was kneeling on a cushion by one of the flower beds, vigorously turning the soil with a small trowel. Neil estimated that she was in her sixties, but she was too far away for him to be sure. He emitted a small cough and said loudly; 'Hello, sorry to disturb you.' The woman immediately turned her head, clearly startled by the intrusion. She heaved herself up with some effort and walked slowly towards him, pulling off her gardening gloves as she did so.

'Hello there,' she called out, 'can I help you?'

'Possibly,' Neil replied, 'I'm looking for a lady called Isobel Grant. I thought she might live here?'

The woman stopped a few feet away, as if to maintain a safe distance from this young stranger who'd just breezed into her garden. He could see her more clearly now, and reckoned he'd estimated correctly. She was probably in her early sixties, yet her straight grey hair, styled neatly to her jaw line, and skilfully applied make-up provided the casual observer with a possibly distorted image of her age. It was the lines that criss-crossed her face and neck that gave the game away. Having said this, she was stylishly dressed in blue jeans and cream corduroy shirt, giving the overall impression that she was relatively well-off.

'And you are…?' She stood, head tilted to one side, her pale blue eyes opened wide, awaiting a response.

'Sorry, my name's Neil Strachan, I'm a police officer from Inverness.' He took his warrant card from his trouser pocket and flipped it open. She fumbled for the expensive-looking glasses that were hanging on a cord around her neck and raised them to her eyes without putting them on, then she leant forward to inspect Neil's ID.

'Umm, Detective Inspector, should my mother be concerned?'

'I hope not. Do I take it from your last comment that Morag and Isobel Grant are one and the same?'

The woman hesitated before confirming the assertion. 'Yes Inspector, you can. So you also know the name my mother uses these days, then?'

'Why the change of name? Jeanne isn't it?'

'Goodness Inspector, you are well informed. Yes, I'm Jeanne Guthrie, Isobel's one and only daughter. How do you do Inspector?'

Her expression softened as she extended a hand. Neil took it, sensing a hint of apprehension in her eyes.

'To answer your question in part Inspector, she decided to use my grandmother's name, which incidentally is also *her* second name, back in the late seventies. My parents moved here in 1979. They lived over on the west coast at Glendaig before that, but I expect you know that too?'

Then came the million dollar question. 'Yes, I did, and are both your parents still living here?'

'If you're asking are they both still alive; yes, they are, both hale and hearty. Mum is eighty-nine, and Pops turned ninety-five in March.'

'That's a very good age, he must be doing something right!'

'Aye, he does have a few health issues, but all things considered he's as strong as an ox. That's why they're out; my husband has taken them across to Raigmore Hospital to see an eye specialist. Pops has got cataracts you see.'

'And when are you expecting them back?'

'I can't say exactly. They only left a few minutes before you arrived. You probably passed them!'

'Were they in a blue hatchback?'

'Aye, that's it.'

'Then yes, I believe I did pass them.'

His face must have said it all. Jeanne grinned. 'Speeding were they Inspector? I keep telling Richard, that's my husband, to take it easy!'

'They weren't hanging around, that's for sure.'

Jeanne's grin subsided. 'Can I ask why you're here, exactly?'

'Aye, of course. We've discovered the remains of a man on a beach near Glendaig. We believe he died during the war, and we're trying to identify him. We thought your mother might be able to help, bearing in mind she lived in the village during the war.'

'I thought it might be about that, we read about it in the paper. Tell me, how did you know my parents lived here?'

'Oh, just put two and two together…'

'Was it Murdo Stuart?'

'No, it wasn't. Did you know Mr Stuart?'

'Aye quite well, but I haven't seen him for a good while, neither have my parents.'

'Did you know that he'd died recently?'

'Oh no, I didn't. What happened?' She seemed genuinely shocked. 'I'm surprised my mother didn't tell me, she can't have known either.'

'It was heart problems. I understand he'd not been well for some time.'

'That's a terrible shame, poor Ursula. I'm sorry Inspector, you must think me very rude, please come in. Can I make you some coffee?' She extended an arm towards the back door, and ushered him towards it.

'No thanks, I won't keep you long.'

They stepped into a small kitchen populated with oak-panelled units and mottled grey work surfaces, now hardly visible under an overabundance of kitchen clutter.

'Tell me Mrs Guthrie, why did you think that I'd be here in connection with the find at Glendaig?'

'Please call me Jeanne, I hate formality.' She shrugged. 'I suppose I just did, but I think you'd better speak with my mother about all this.'

Neil smiled. 'Oh, I will. I just wondered that's all.'

'Look my parents are very elderly. I hope you're not going to distress them by asking lots of questions.'

'I'll certainly try not to Jeanne, but I must speak to them.'

'Well, if you don't mind Inspector, I'd like to be here when you *do* speak to them. That's if *they* want to speak to you!'

'Aye, of course, that's fine. I certainly hope they *will* want to speak to me. I'm certain I won't need to take up too much of their time.'

'Okay, shall we say ten o'clock tomorrow morning?'

'Fine by me. I'll be on my way for now then.'

Jeanne led Neil into the hallway and towards the front door. The door to the sitting room stood open to his right. Another doorway across the passage was also open. He glanced in as he passed; the space inside was equal in size to the sitting room, but furnished as a dining room. A large polished table monopolised the room, surrounded by six high-backed chairs in the same style. A gleaming silver candelabrum stood in the centre of the table. 'That's a very impressive piece,' Neil commented, as he paused to admire the silverware.

'It was a retirement gift when my father finished work,' Jeanne replied.

'Oh,' Neil nodded in acknowledgement, but his interest was now focussed on something else. A group of silver framed photographs formed a display on the small drinks cabinet that stood in the alcove beside the chimney breast. One of them, in black and white, was of two naval officers in uniform. He could just make out the rings on the sleeves and the double row of buttons on the tunics. The images were too far away to properly identify the pair, though. Neil considered asking who they were, but thought better of it. The questions could wait until the following day.

As he descended the stone steps at the front door, Neil said. 'You were going to tell me *why* your mother uses the name Morag these days?'

Jeanne smiled, a prickly smile that saw the corners of her mouth twitch in silent irritation. 'As I said earlier, I think it best you speak to my mother.'

Neil didn't want to push his luck. He waved goodbye as he opened the gate and heard the front door clunk shut behind him.

His drive back to Inverness was interrupted twice by phone calls. First it was Cat, eager to learn whether the couple living in Redcastle were indeed the Grants who'd lived in Glendaig. 'So when are you going to speak to them?' she'd asked impatiently.

'Tomorrow, hopefully.'

'Well that's great isn't it? This could be the breakthrough you wanted.'

'Let's wait and see, shall we?'

'Aye, aye, of course. It's good news though, eh? Anyway, must go, lots to do.' She blew two kisses down the phone and the line went dead.

Neil sat for a second or two, reflecting on the amusing conversation he'd just had with his partner. He shook his head in mild disbelief and tossed the phone onto the seat next to him.

Luckily, the next call came just before he reached the Kessock Bridge. Having pulled off the A9 into a parking area he just managed to press the *call accept* button before it went dead. 'Hello, is that you Neil?'

'Aye, it is.'

'Good morning Neil, Matthias Fuchs here. I'm afraid I didn't recognise your voice.'

'Morning Matthias, sorry, it must be the traffic noise. Have you got any good news for me?'

'Actually, I do have some good news…'

'I'm all ears, don't keep me in suspense.'

'Well, I've gone back into the *BdU* records over the weekend. Checked out those two U-boats that were sunk in January '42. One, the U-93, was sunk out in the North Atlantic by the British destroyer *Hesperus*. Thankfully, the site of the sinking was accurately recorded and some of the crew were rescued and taken into captivity.'

'Okay, what about the other one?'

'Ah, this is more interesting. The U-114, a type-seven C-boat, under the command of *Kapitänleutnant* Felix Von Bramsdorf, left Bergen in Norway in the early hours of Christmas Day, 1941. Von Bramsdorf's orders are not clarified in the records. The only surviving paperwork refers to the departure as a "special duties deployment". The fate of U-114 is recorded officially as "failed to return, presumed lost" on 8th January 1942.'

'So are you saying, the 8th is merely the date of the *record*, not necessarily the sinking?'

'Exactly.'

'It's possible then, that she was sunk some considerable time before the 8th.'

'Yes, that's entirely possible.'

'So… if her crew hadn't been able to get off a signal to *BdU*… and the British were unaware they'd sunk her, or at least damaged her so badly that she sank sometime later, then…'

'…Then the location and time of her sinking would be unknown to all… exactly.'

'Neil was thinking fast. 'Is there any other good news?'

'Yes,' came the reply. 'The lack of information available as to the fate of U-114 prompted me to have a look at archived *Kriegsmarine* documents from the U-boat base at Bergen. My search led me to the diary of one of the naval staff officers who served at the base, a man called Günter Lange. He speaks of the excitement and speculation that was rife at the time of U-114's *unexpected and secretive* departure. Then, sometime later he mentions the sadness he felt when the boat was *finally* posted as missing.'

'Interesting use of words,' suggested Neil.

'Yes, they are indeed,' said Fuchs, 'and it gets better.'

'You're going to say that the commander of the U-114 held all the decorations we've found over here on our beach?'

'He certainly was a holder of several of them, including the Knight's Cross, but sadly not with oak leaves. And of course his rank does not correspond with that indicated by the sleeve rings on your piece of uniform.'

'So how does it get better then?'

'Ah, well, there were two crew members on the U-114 who received the decorations you have recently acquired from Mrs Stuart. One was *Obersteuermann* Jacob Witt and the other, more interestingly, was the boat's first watch officer; a colourful character called *Oberleutnant Zur See* Jürgen Reiniger. He certainly would have worn the tunic ribbon of the Iron Cross Second Class, *and* the Destroyer War Badge. He was awarded it after the second battle of Narvik in April 1940.'

'What about the other medals we found on the beach?'

'No, he was never decorated with the Knight's Cross, or the Iron Cross First Class. And I'm afraid the *ärmelstreifen* for an officer of his rank were two gold rings only.'

'Not so helpful then.'

'There is something else. Reiniger was at one time a good friend of Max Friedmann's. They trained as officer cadets together in 1932. Reiniger is even reputed to have saved Friedmann's life following the sinking of the sail training ship *Niobe* in July of that year.'

'Really! Thank you Matthias, the circumstantial evidence is certainly building up, but I'm afraid that's all it is so far. Still, this is all really interesting.'

Neil went on to inform Fuchs of his planned meeting with Isobel Grant the following day. Having promised to update him as to the outcome, they exchanged pleasantries, mainly in respect of the weather conditions in both their countries, and their conversation then came to an end. Neil drove on, passing between the giant spans of the Kessock Bridge and gazing across to the column of white smoke that climbed skyward from the timber mill near Dalcross Airport. He was still trying to make sense of what he'd just been told. Was the U-114 the submarine sent to collect Max Friedmann? Was it the boat attacked by the aircraft from Oban, and where did it lie now? Were the medals found in Murdo Stuart's drawer those belonging to Jürgen Reiniger, U-114's first lieutenant? His fingers gripped the steering wheel more tightly, causing his knuckles to whiten. He sighed, and murmured, 'Perhaps Isobel Grant, you can provide me with the answers to some of these questions at last.' But he wasn't going to hold his breath!

Chapter Thirty-Six

The day had dawned grey on that last Tuesday of June. The brightness of the previous day hadn't lasted and now rain threatened the Northern Highlands. Neil was running late, and it was nine forty-five by the time he'd turned off the A9 and threaded his way down the hill to the side of the Firth. He turned on his windscreen wipers, sweeping away the small splashes that had begun to spatter the glass. Ahead and to the west, the sky had turned darker and a silvery veil of rain now obscured the distant mountains. Neil increased his speed. He didn't want to be late on this of all days.

The number of vehicles he encountered along the way could be counted on one hand, and so he made good time along the dampened road to Redcastle. He pulled up outside Edirdovar at five minutes past ten. The little blue hatchback was parked on the driveway to the side of the house and Jeanne's Volvo occupied the same position in which he'd seen it the day before.

Having sat quietly for a moment or two gathering his thoughts, he grabbed his briefcase and climbed out of the car. Initially he'd been reluctant to take the items that had been recovered from the beach. Call it tempting fate! But then she... they, *may* have seen them before, so he'd taken them just in case.

His approach had been anticipated, and the front door opened just as he closed the gate. Jeanne stood in the doorway, dressed more formally this time in dark slacks and pale blue twin set. Behind her stood an elderly woman, petite and slightly stooped. Her features were indiscernible, darkened by the shadow that fell heavily across the hallway.

'Come in Mr Strachan, before you get wet.' Jeanne stood aside to let Neil pass by her. The elderly woman stepped forward into the shaft of light that had flooded through the open door. She extended a spidery hand.

'Good morning Inspector Strachan, I'm Morag Grant. I believe you've heard of me by my birth name, Isobel?'

Neil took her hand and shook it gently. 'Pleased to meet you at last Mrs Grant.'

He could see her clearly now. Her face was heavily masked by make-up, disguising the deep wrinkles that furrowed her leathery skin. Her white hair was cut short in a bob, revealing the lobes of small, button-like ears, but it was her eyes that gave her away. They were still as piercing and intense as they were in those old photos, their colour resembling pale blue marble, having lost none of their youthful vigour.

'Thank you Inspector. Please go through, my husband's in there.'

Neil followed her instructions, leading the two women into the cramped sitting room. As he emerged from behind the open door, a sumptuous green Draylon sofa came into view. Sitting at one end, almost consumed by a scattering of cushions, was a frail old man, almost bald but for a down-like mantle of wispy white hair. His once large frame was now diminished by significant age, but Neil estimated that he still exceeded six feet in height. A white pencil line of a moustache adorned his upper lip, and the thick lenses of dark horn-rimmed spectacles masked his dark watery eyes. He smiled, and raised a shaky, albeit welcoming hand as Neil walked into the room, but initially said nothing.

Neil crossed to where he was sitting. 'You must be Robert?'

He took the frail hand and introduced himself. The dark eyes examined him for several seconds before swivelling towards his wife, as if seeking her approval before speaking. In those few silent moments, a jolt of recognition surged through Neil. His heart must have sensed it too, because he could feel it suddenly thud against his chest. Perhaps it was the long straight nose, or even the dark eyes. Whatever it was, he was in no doubt.

'Perhaps we should start again Robert, or may I call you *Max!?*'

Neil's eyes flashed across towards Isobel, as if seeking independent confirmation of his assertion.

The old man then gave a little cough, as if wishing to regain the policeman's attention. In a slow, husky voice, his first words seemed to take an age to fully absorb. 'Max will be fine. So Inspector, it would seem that my advanced years have not rendered me totally unrecognisable.'

The old man grinned, briefly revealing an even row of pearly white dentures. Neil stood in startled silence, his eyes fixed upon the one-time U-boat ace. 'It *is* true Inspector, I can assure you of that. I'm sorry that I can't get up to greet you. My leg's not so good these days.' He tapped the walking stick that stood propped up against the arm of the sofa.

'The old wound you sustained in the Irish sea in 1940?' The words flowed out of Neil, as if he were a ventriloquist's dummy being controlled by some unseen force.

'That is indeed correct, Inspector. I see you have been doing your research.'

For the first time, Neil detected just a hint of a foreign accent, now almost indistinguishable from his own. 'Sit down, please.' Max indicated an armchair next to the fireplace. 'Jeanne, go and fetch that photograph from next door.'

Neil watched Jeanne leave the room, as he still came to terms with what he'd just learned. She returned seconds later with the silver-framed image that he'd noticed the day before.

'This is Pops with his brother,' she announced in a low tone, handing the frame to Neil. 'Handsome, weren't they?'

'Very,' Neil agreed as he looked at the picture. He instantly recognised Max, dressed smartly in his number one uniform and standing proudly next to his brother Otto. Both carried the two sleeve rings of an *oberleutnant zur see*. Max then broke the silence.

'It was taken in February 1940, two months before Otto was killed. He was a gunnery officer aboard the heavy cruiser *Blücher*. She was sunk by shore batteries in *Oslofjord* in Norway.'

'How old were you in this photo?' Neil asked.

'Just twenty-six. Otto was two years older.'

'No Knight's Cross here then?'

'Oh no, only the two Iron Crosses, and some other bits from the Spanish war.'

Neil could see the resemblance between Max and his brother, it was the smile and the squint of the eyes, as both men posed in what must have been strong sunlight.

Isobel had taken a seat next to her husband on the sofa. She placed a reassuring hand on his knee, prompting him to respond by placing his atop hers. 'Would you mind making some coffee, dear?' Isobel enquired of her daughter.

'Sure,' said Jeanne dutifully, and left her seat on the arm of the sofa to head for the kitchen.

There was an uneasy silence, time needed for Neil to compose himself. Then he spoke. 'Well, this is a surprise. We thought we'd recovered your remains from a beach over at Glendaig.' He immediately regretted his choice of words. They seemed incredibly banal. It was an opening salvo that in no way reflected his usual aplomb.

Max patted the top of his wife's hand whilst giving her a brief sideways glance. 'No, Inspector, fortunately it was not me.'

Isobel's pale lips relaxed to form a smile. 'We always feared our past would catch up with us one day. I'm just surprised that it's taken quite so long. We're grateful that the loyalty of our friends and family has enabled us to live here in peace for all these years, aren't we dear?' Her husband merely nodded in agreement as she squeezed his hand.

'I assume then, the local people here in Redcastle have no idea who Max really is?' Neil looked first at Isobel, and then across to Max.

'No, absolutely no one Inspector. To them we are Morag and Robbie Grant, retired stalker and wife from over in the west.'

'So has your adoption of the name Grant been formalised?'

'You mean, when we were married? Yes, it was, eventually.'

'What do you mean... *eventually*?'

'Tell him what happened,' Max prompted. 'He'll find out anyway.'

Isobel shifted awkwardly on the sofa. 'My Uncle Callum married us at the church at Glendaig in 1946, more to placate those within the community than anything else.'

'I don't get it, you got married *just* to please the community?'

'...And the family, Inspector, except the ceremony wasn't legally binding. No paper record was ever made in respect of the event.'

'Why?'

'Simply because we didn't have any identity documents for Max at that stage and even if we had, we didn't want his name appearing on any official registry record. It was too soon after the war had ended. You see, we wanted to be together, but this was the only way... you know how religious people were in those days... life would have become very difficult indeed.'

'So Callum officiated at a sham marriage, so that you could live together under the noses of the locals... very compassionate of him! Did your family know that it wasn't legal?'

Only my parents and Aunt Anna... and Callum of course. They weren't entirely happy with the arrangement, but I think they understood the predicament we were in.' She grinned. 'Surprisingly, it was Uncle Callum who came up with the idea. I suppose his involvement in the whole affair knocked him off course from the unflinching moral values he once possessed. I remember him saying, "at least you will be married in the eyes of God, I suspect the need for paperwork won't concern him too greatly." So we went ahead with it, on the understanding that we agreed to formalise the arrangement as soon as we could do so. I don't think anyone else outside of our immediate family group had even considered the paperwork side of things! Sometimes I think it would've been best if we'd left things as they were then, and just got on with our lives.'

'What happened to make you change your mind?'

'We wanted to make things official, partly for Jeanne's sake, and partly to honour our promise to the family. We did it for us too of course.'

She tipped her head onto Max's shoulder. 'So we decided upon a civil ceremony in Switzerland, in 1979. We thought it was a safe bet by then, especially as there wouldn't be any record of the marriage retained over here. The disappearance of Max Friedmann would have been long forgotten, or so we thought.'

'It seems from what you've just said that it hadn't been forgotten.'

'No, a Swiss journalist managed to get hold of our marriage record, and put two and two together. Then he got a colleague at his paper's London office to investigate further.'

Max now took up the story. 'So we left Glendaig in a hurry, went and lived with Jeanne, before getting this place a year later.'

'Did the journalist give up the hunt then?'

'Yes, he was met with a wall of silence in Glendaig, realised he was getting nowhere I suppose, so he went back down south with his tail between his legs.'

'So you are now officially married and using the name of Grant?'

'That's right Inspector,' Isobel confirmed with a nod.

'What about passports, things like that? Surely not having the usual identity documents would have eventually caused you problems?'

'Oh, that side of things has never been a problem,' Max explained. 'The house and all the bills are in Jeanne's name. We've never needed them for identification, and we've never needed to go abroad. Our bank account is in Morag's... sorry, Isobel's name so no, the need for passports never arose until the late seventies. I was able to get a Swiss passport before we were married. I'd managed to get a copy of my birth certificate by then, and of course my mother was Swiss so I was eligible.'

'I see, so you've been living under the radar for all these years, and no one has ever revealed your true identity, amazing!'

Isobel was smiling again, more widely this time, revealing her obvious sense of pride at the achievement. 'You know Inspector, not a day goes by when I don't say a prayer for all those people from Glendaig who've gone to their graves having kept our little secret safe for more than half a century. We thought we may at last join them in the knowledge that it had been buried forever, but it seems that is not to be.'

'I assume Murdo Stuart was one of those people who kept your secret safe?' Neil looked from one to the other. Isobel was first to respond.

'Aye, he certainly was, and now even he's gone I hear. He always struggled with it I'm afraid. Not one for secrets was Murdo. I feel so sorry for Ursula and the family. He never told them you know. It was eating him up.'

Jeanne interrupted the flow, returning with coffee and biscuits. 'You didn't tell me Murdo had died Mother.'

Isobel looked a little embarrassed. 'Sorry lassie, Mary called me a few days ago. I'm afraid it had slipped my mind.'

Jeanne handed Neil a mug, apparently satisfied with her mother's explanation. She fixed him with a protracted stare. 'Before we go on,' she said, as if wishing to set out her conditions for the interview to continue. 'You need to know that I've discussed your visit with my parents, and they feel that the time has come to unburden themselves of all the secrecy that has plagued their married life. They've decided to answer your questions and explain what happened back in 1941. But please bear with them Inspector. This was a distressing time for them, and dragging up the past as we must surely now do will be as painful an experience as it was then.'

Neil listened respectfully as she delivered her little speech, his solemn expression resembling that of a schoolboy being dressed-down by his teacher. 'I understand fully Jeanne, but I do need to hear the full story, whatever it is.'

Isobel reached out to her daughter as she resumed her position on the arm of the sofa. 'Don't fuss now lassie, we're tough old birds, your father and I. Actually it's quite a relief to be able to talk about the past after all this time.'

Neil placed his mug on the occasional table that stood beside his chair. 'Personally, I have to say I'm relieved to hear that you want to tell me what happened back then. If anything, my interest lies in the historical significance of your story. Officially of course, I'm here to enquire into the identity of the remains that were buried on that beach, and to try and establish what happened to him.'

The old couple once again exchanged reassuring glances, then Isobel looked across towards Neil. 'I think we can help you with both of those aspects of your investigation, Inspector.'

'I see, that's good to hear. I'm afraid I may have a considerable number of questions to ask. Perhaps the best way to begin is for me to listen to what *you* have to say, then perhaps we can clarify anything afterwards.'

Isobel nodded in agreement. 'Of course Inspector... is this the point when you caution us not to say anything that will incriminate us?'

Neil looked surprised. 'Not unless I considered you to be suspects in a crime. No, I'm here to speak to you as prospective witnesses, that's all.'

'You may change your mind when you hear what we have to say,' said Max with a glint in his eye.

'Well, I'll keep an open mind for now,' Neil replied. 'I think it's more important that I just listen to what you have to say, don't you?'

'As you wish, Inspector. I hope you have plenty of time.'

'All the time in the world, Isobel.' He looked across at her enquiringly. 'Sorry, do you mind if I call you *Isobel*?'

'Of course not.' She prodded her husband. 'He uses the name

Robert these days, but he still likes to be called Max sometimes!'

Max interjected. 'I was born Max *Ruprecht* Friedmann you see. Ruprecht is Robert in German. I thought Robert would be more acceptable if I was to remain in Scotland for the duration of the war.'

Isobel took up the story. 'I believe you know how Max and I first became acquainted, Inspector?'

'You believe *I know*?'

'Aye, Mary told me you'd taken her box of letters and photographs, and that you'd discovered that Max was known to us before the war.'

Neil grinned, and shook his head. 'Your cousin Mary certainly knows how to keep a secret.'

'She's been such a support to us,' Isobel agreed. 'So you know that Max's mother Katharina and Anna Matheson were sisters?'

'I do, they were from Kreuzlingen in Switzerland I believe?'

'Well, they were born there,' said Max as he sipped his coffee. 'Kreuzlingen is a small town on the border with Germany. These days it's become swallowed up by the city of Konstanz. That's where *I* was born, in the hospital there. My mother was having difficulties with the birth and was admitted as an emergency case. So, although I always considered myself Swiss, officially I was born German.'

Isobel took up the story again, explaining how Anna and Katharina had left their native Switzerland to embark upon very different lives. Neil listened with interest as she told a tale of youthful romance, separation, and eventual tragedy.

The sisters had been born to a German banker, Gustav Eichel, and his Swiss wife Else. They had spent much of their later childhood in Zürich, living in the fashionable northern outskirts of the city. The girls had attended the same schools and had accepted employment at the bank at which their father was Vice President.

Then, as young women in their early twenties, they had both been tempted by the prospect of life abroad. In 1911 Anna had moved to the Scottish capital, Edinburgh, where she'd been offered a position as nanny to the children of one of her father's banking associates.

Katharina had moved north, to the German city of Kiel, two years earlier. She had received an invitation to stay with a favourite aunt, who'd lived in an imposing nineteenth-century villa in the pleasant tree-lined district of *Blücherplatz*. It had been an offer too good to turn down and her parents had supported the proposal. So from then on, the sisters had lived very different lives but had always managed to remain close, more often than not through their letter writing.

Whilst living in Edinburgh, Anna had met and fallen in love with Callum Matheson, a young priest, who'd taken a living as curate at her local parish church. They'd later married in the village of Glendaig, where Callum's father had also been a Church Of Scotland Minister.

In Germany, Katharina had entered into a relationship with a young naval cadet, Karl-Heinz Friedmann. The couple married in 1912 and were soon blessed with two sons, Otto and Max.

When hostilities broke out between Britain and Germany in 1914, the sisters' husbands both responded to their countries' call to arms. Karl-Heinz was already serving as an officer in the *Kaiserliche Marine*, Germany's Imperial Navy. Callum left his position in the Edinburgh parish to become a chaplain with the Royal Scots Fusiliers.

Then, in May 1916, tragedy struck the Friedmann family. Karl-Heinz's ship was severely damaged during a ferocious engagement with British warships at the Battle of Jutland. The elderly cruiser sank quickly with few survivors. Karl-Heinz was amongst those lost, and his remains were never found.

Katharina, grief-stricken by the news, made plans to return to Zürich with her sons. She was eventually persuaded by her father-in-law to remain in Kiel, where he would continue to support the family. So she remained in their little house in the district of Ravensberg where Gerhardt Friedmann, a retired Vice Admiral, and his wife Viktoria helped bring up the two boys. During this time, Katharina also became close to another naval officer; Bruno Steigler, one of her husband's oldest friends. Steigler was serving on a U-boat and was often away for weeks at a time. He was a kind man, acting as a father figure to Otto and Max, and the boys loved to hear his tales of daring from the waters around Britain when he returned from patrols.

In 1919, upon his safe return from France, Callum became Parish Minister at Glendaig when his father, Walter, retired. Soon afterwards Ursel, a daughter, was born; a sister to young Dugald who'd arrived during his father's absence in 1915.

Anna and Callum had lived at the parish Manse until Callum's retirement in 1955. Isobel recalled how Anna had come to love Glendaig, with its random cluster of grey stone and whitewashed cottages strung out along the shoreline of Loch Coinneach. She painted a picture of a woman who was at her happiest wandering with her children across the boulder-strewn slopes of Stac Coinneach Dubh, or "Black Kenneth's Hill" as the locals called it, under which the village nestled.

Max also contributed from time to time, reminiscing about the family holidays spent in Glendaig in the twenties and thirties. He told how they would often pause on their frequent family walks to listen to the wind rustling through the low clumps of heather, and take in the breath-taking scenery before them across the Sound Of Sleat, westward towards Skye and its snow-capped Cuillins. It had all seemed so perfect.

Katharina's personality had been moulded by the tragedy at Jutland, and Isobel commented that there was not the same sense of mischief in her smile that was present in her sister. She was happy enough though, according to her son. Happy to be with her beloved Anna and happy to be free, albeit temporarily, from the dominance of her in-laws and their draconian ways.

In the years following the Great War, Katharina and her sons often returned to Switzerland and spent weeks at a time with her parents. During the summer months they would also visit Scotland, where they would enjoy long holidays with Anna and her family.

'We visited regularly up until 1932,' said Max, before draining his mug. 'My mother seemed to be spending more time in Zürich from then on. My grandfather died in April of that year, and my grandmother did not enjoy good health up until her death in '38. So I came on my own, once in 1932 before I started my naval training, and then again in 1935.'

'Aye,' said Neil, confirming his recollection of the visit. 'I've seen a photograph taken of you during that last visit, up on the hill with Isobel and Mary.'

'Oh yes, I remember that snap. Ursel took it with her father's camera. I recall the weather was particularly fine that year. The four of us were out every day, walking, picnicking, you name it. Yes, I was very close to my family in Scotland, especially my cousin Ursel. Isobel was *also* her cousin you see, through her mother Morag's side. Morag and Callum Matheson were sister and brother.'

'What about Dugald, how did you get on with him, Max?'

'Dugald?' Max scowled. 'No, he never liked me at all.'

Isobel seemed happy to elaborate. 'My cousin Dugald despised all things German, Inspector. He was the product of the public school system between the wars. Taught by bigots; crusty old men who'd returned from the trenches to infect the next generation with the same xenophobic beliefs that they themselves had adopted. He was a sullen, reclusive child and clearly jealous of the attention his German cousins enjoyed during their visits. In hindsight, I suppose there was a sense of predestinate inevitability about it...'

'About what exactly, Isobel?' Neil asked.

'That Dugald, from a young age, was set on a path that would see him plunge into the depths of infamy, had it not been for those around him who risked all to protect his reputation.'

Neil didn't entirely understand what she was getting at, but decided not to labour the point at that stage, preferring to allow the couple to tell their story in their own time. '...And Mary Galbraith, how did she fit in?'

Isobel answered again. 'Mary's also my cousin... on my father's side. He and Mary's mother, Elizabeth were also brother and sister.

I suppose it was typical of a small community. Everyone related to everyone else in some way or another. Mary and I were of a similar age, so we became quite close… but not as close as I was to Ursel.'

'It must have been a very happy time for you all,' said Neil. 'Halcyon days as they say?'

Isobel handed her empty mug to Jeanne. 'Yes, they certainly were, up until 1935 that is. I was fifteen, and Max twenty-one. I was hopelessly in love with him by then, besotted if I'm honest. You know how it is, teenage girls fall in love very easily at that age, especially when in the presence of a dashing young naval officer. The Queen and Prince Philip spring to mind, and the same happened to Max's mother when she met his father in Kiel, all those years ago.'

She smiled affectionately at her husband, her blue eyes almost sparkling. 'I knew he was fond of me, even then, but of course not in a romantic sense. I was six years younger than him after all, still a child in his eyes. He told me he'd been seeing a girl back in Germany. I remember her name even now… Else Gotz, wasn't it?'

Max grinned, acknowledging that her memory had not failed her. She wiped away a stray tear with a tissue supplied by her daughter. 'I thought he would eventually marry her you see, and was distraught when he left that last time.'

She laughed. It was the sort of laugh that develops from a sob, when emotions clash. Max took up the story so that Isobel could wipe her eye again

'It became more difficult to keep in touch after that last visit. I was rarely given the opportunity to take leave. The *Ubootwaffe* was being built up rapidly and my boat was dispatched to patrol the waters around Spain in late '36. Operation *Ursula* they called it. Germany had pledged to support Franco during the Spanish Civil War.' He chuckled to himself. 'The reality was quite different… we were practising for what was to come. When I returned to Germany, I attended an endless succession of training courses and then, not surprisingly, it was all too late and our countries were at war!'

Neil took a few seconds to absorb what he'd been told. 'I see.

So the next time you saw each other was when?'

'It was Hogmanay, 1941,' said Isobel, reaching across and grasping Jeanne's hand. She took a deep breath. 'It was probably the worst, and I'm almost ashamed to say it, the best night of my life.' Her eyes had glazed over as more tears welled up and began to track down her cheeks.

Max nervously caressed the carved ivory head of the walking stick that leant against the arm of the sofa. 'Perhaps I should explain what happened, prior to my meeting up with Isobel that evening, Inspector?'

'That would probably be a good place to start, Max.'

Neil sat enthralled as the old man told of his capture and eventual escape from the train. He went on to describe his journey across to Glendaig to meet up with Von Bramsdorf's U-boat. Then he fell silent, as if exhausted by the painful reminiscence, suddenly lost for words. He pulled out a handkerchief and dabbed his eyes, first one, and then the other.

'Do you want to carry on, dear?' Isobel once more placed a hand over his.

Max shook his head. 'No, you tell him, tell him everything.'

'Are you sure?'

'Just tell him what happened, Isobel,' he said, his voice faltering.

1 9 4 1

Chapter Thirty-Seven

The jaunty tones of fiddle and accordion drifted through the tall creaking pines. The tune was a stately *Strathspey*, accompanied by the muffled sounds of joyous laughter. Chinks of light flickered from behind the heavy drapes that were drawn across the tall windows of Glendaig House. Anywhere else, the ARP wardens would have been quick to administer a warning, but tonight was Hogmanay. The second full year of war had but an hour left to run and the restrictions that went with it were now being relaxed to allow a time-honoured tradition.

The annual Hogmanay ball at Glendaig House had been a feature of local life since Victoria's reign. The Laird at the time had introduced the event to celebrate the end of the campaign on the Crimean peninsula, and to welcome home the local men who'd survived the conflict with the Russian Empire.

Not once had it been cancelled, not for the Kaiser nor the Führer, and tonight was no exception. Sir Brodric and Lady Lilian Macleod had cunningly overcome the ARP issue by inviting the local wardens to the event and plying them with generous measures of single malt. One of the ageing officials, Sandy Macrae, leant precariously against one of many suits of armour that lined the walls of the splendid gothic entrance hall. He regarded the comings and goings from the nearby ballroom between sips from a large crystal glass and tapped his foot to the music. Another guest hurried by in search of the lavatory. His urge to relieve himself was not so pressing that he didn't have time to offer the warden a humorous rebuke for not enforcing the blackout efficiently.

Macrae was quick to defend his reputation. 'Why on erth would thae Germans want tae bomb Glendaig Hoose anyway. T'was that bloody *German Geordie* who built it in the first place.'

His reference was to the Hanoverian King George the Second, who'd commissioned the building of the turreted mansion as a hunting lodge soon after Jacobite rebellion.

The amused guest patted the elderly historian on the shoulder and whispered in his ear. '...And *Italian Charlie* would've been on the other side too no doubt, now that Mussolini's joined the fray.'

Macrae swayed forward, before recovering his balance from a near critical angle. He was grim-faced, startled by the enormity of the revelation that the Young Pretender could have been allied to the Italian dictator. He stared blankly at his new friend. 'Aye man, you're bloody right. Christ what a mess it could've been.'

His attention was then diverted as the massive carved doors to the ballroom flew open. The ceilidh band was now blasting out an accompaniment to *stripping the willow*. Macrae could just about make out the party guests through the dense airless fug, spinning each other around and whooping with delight. Then, through the haze beyond the doorway, Ursel Matheson emerged, grimacing from the pain of a twisted ankle. She was supported on one side by her cousin Isobel and on the other by a kilted Ramsay Macleod, the Laird's son, who was home on leave from the RAF. Ursel's pained expression did little to mask the realisation that her long-awaited opportunity to dance with the dashing Ramsay had been scuppered from the start, but he had acted most gallantly when she howled in his ear, having turned her ankle on the polished wooden floor.

As the threesome struggled past Macrae, Callum and Anna Matheson appeared from behind them. 'What on earth has happened?' Anna exclaimed, placing a reassuring hand on Ursel's arm.

'Och, it's nothing at all Mother. I've just twisted my ankle, being flung around by this brute here.'

She grinned as she tilted her head accusingly towards Ramsay. In response, the young man's cheeks became flushed as he tried to defend his honour. 'I can assure you it was just an accident Mrs Matheson. I wasn't overdoing it.'

Anna smiled. 'I'm sure you weren't Ramsay dear. It's just one of those things.'

'We'd better get you home lassie,' said Callum, clearly concerned about his daughter's welfare. 'I'll go and get the car right now.'

'Oh please don't fuss Father. You and Mother must stay here to see the New Year in. Isobel will drive me back to the Manse, and she'll stay with me until you get home.'

'Are you sure, darling?' queried Anna. 'We're more than happy to come with you, so that Isobel can stay here.'

'Yes of course Mother. I'm not allowing Isobel the opportunity to get her claws into Ramsay here when I'm sat at home nursing a sprained ankle. Oh no, indeed not, I need to keep my eye on her.' She nudged Isobel, as if to invoke a response.

'It's not a problem, *really* Aunt Anna, I'm more than happy to go with Ursel.'

'Well, if you're sure,' said Anna.

'Would you like me to drive you?' Ramsay asked, in an attempt to make up for any previous wrongdoing on his part. His request was met with a mischievous grin from Ursel. It was not wasted on her father though, who quickly interjected; 'That won't be necessary, thank you Ramsay. I'm sure your parents would prefer you to remain here.'

Ramsay shrugged. 'Well, if you're sure.'

'We're sure,' confirmed Callum, who'd failed to notice his daughter's display of face-pulling just beyond his field of vision.

The little group continued on their way, Ramsay opening the heavy oak door to allow the cortège to pass through.

Once Ursel was safely inserted onto the front passenger seat of her father's black Austin Ten, Anna and Callum retreated towards the house and disappeared through the doorway where Ramsay was waiting.

Isobel slid into the driver's seat and fumbled around for the ignition. Ursel leant across towards her and winked. 'We'll find a wee something to see the New Year in with, don't fret!'

Isobel grinned and released the handbrake. She was not used to driving Callum's car, and the vehicle lurched forward as she released the clutch. She steered to the right, following the curve of the gravel driveway as it dipped away between towering rhododendron bushes. Almost immediately, Ursel shrieked as a dark figure appeared in the dim light from the hooded headlamps. Isobel braked heavily, bringing the car to a halt, almost skidding on the loose gravel. The figure slowly approached the car, swinging a bottle limply from the left hand. It was Dugald, Ursel's brother, wearing officer's khaki battledress over a kilt of Seaforth Mackenzie tartan.

The dim light from the car's headlamps caught the brass buckle of his webbing belt as he manoeuvred himself around the car to the driver's-side rear door. It flew open and he slumped in, slamming it behind him. The young women quickly detected the sweet aroma of digested liquor as Dugald slouched across the back seat, fumbling with the buttons on his battledress blouse.

'Good evening ladies, off home so soon? The party's hardly started.'

His grinning face loomed out of the darkness as he leant forward between the seats. Isobel felt a finger caressing her cheek and jerked her head away instinctively. 'My God you stink Dugald. Get out will you.'

'My, my Isobel, and this being *my* father's car too. That's a little harsh isn't it?'

Ursel swung her head around. 'Isobel's taking me home Dugald. I've twisted my ankle. So unless you want to go back to the Manse with us, get out now please.' She winced as the fumes from Dugald's breath entered her nostrils.

'I think that's a splendid idea, seeing the New Year in with two bonnie lassies such as yourselves. Drive on Isobel, please do.' His face retreated into the darkness as he reclined across the cracked leather seat.

The two women exchanged glances, then Ursel turned to confront her brother again. 'I mean it Dugald. Get out now or...'

Dugald's head appeared again, teeth clenched, eyes charged with anger. '...Or what sis? What exactly will you do? Run to Daddy as usual?' He turned again to Isobel. 'I believe I asked you to drive on, cousin Isobel. So perhaps you'll kindly oblige, if that's not too much to ask?'

His head withdrew again, and the sound of a cork being removed from a bottle could be heard from the back seat. Isobel threw the car into gear and accelerated away down the drive. Dugald meanwhile, drank contentedly from his bottle of malt. The time was now eleven fifteen.

They sat in silence as Isobel drove along the coast road towards Glendaig. The moon appeared intermittently from behind fast-moving clouds, providing the illusion that it too was racing across the night sky. Snowflakes splashed onto the windscreen at random intervals, but it was the frost that sparkled on the asphalt like a carpet of tiny diamonds which concerned Isobel most. She gripped the steering wheel tightly, praying that she'd avoid any lethal patches of ice as the car cruised on through the night. Her relief was palpable by the time they reached the sanctuary of the Manse, and the slush-spattered Austin came to an eventual halt outside the front door.

'I'm most grateful to you, driver,' Dugald slurred as he climbed out of the car and sauntered off towards the house, the whisky bottle still trailing from his left hand. Isobel opened the door for Ursel and assisted her up from her seat. Ursel let out a shriek as she hopped onto her good foot.

'My God, that brother of mine can be truly beastly at times,' she declared through clenched teeth.

It was a slow hobble into the house, but the two women

managed adequately without the assistance of their male relative. Having reached the sitting room, Isobel lowered Ursel into a sumptuously-upholstered armchair, raising her injured ankle onto a footstool. Ursel let out a sigh of relief. 'Home at last, eh Isobel,' and then in a raised voice, solely for the benefit of her brother; 'and no thanks to you, Dugald dear.' She scowled, a gesture of her displeasure towards her now absent sibling, then her face brightened as she pointed to the drinks cabinet.

'I fancy a wee gin. What about you, Issie?'

'Not until I've bandaged that ankle,' warned Isobel.

'They're in the bathroom cupboard, the bandages,' Ursel called after her as she disappeared through the door in search of a suitable binding.

Ursel attempted to manoeuvre her leg into a more comfortable position, failing to notice Dugald appear from the hallway. He ambled across to the heavy mahogany dresser that stood at one end of the room and pulled open one of the small doors in the base. Ursel looked up when she heard the chink of glass on glass. Dugald had selected three crystal tumblers from the cupboard and placed them neatly in a line on the nearby table. He then uncorked a bottle of his father's best pre-war Glenlivet and poured himself a generous glassful. He took a sip and savoured the aroma that hung in the glass. 'Umm, excellent as always. Care to join me in a wee dram, sis?'

'No thank you Dugald, I'll wait for Isobel.'

'Suit yourself.' He took another mouthful, flinching as the powerful spirit flowed down his throat.

Isobel reappeared with a roll of bandage. 'Here we go,' she announced as she knelt down beside Ursel, unravelling the bandage. Dugald looked on, still sipping his whisky as she carefully began binding Ursel's ankle.

'My, you would have made a wonderful nurse,' he slurred, his voice laden with sarcasm. He drifted around the chair, positioning himself behind the kneeling Isobel. Then without warning, he stooped over her so that their cheeks almost touched. Isobel's features contorted in response to the miasma of whisky fumes that hung on Dugald's breath. When he spoke, the effect became more intense, and Isobel turned her head away.

'Oh, that's not very friendly, not even a little peck on the cheek for your favourite cousin?' Dugald whispered as he straightened up.

Isobel spun back towards him, her blue eyes burning into his with such ferocity that he reeled away from her, half-expecting a slap. 'We've been here before Dugald. Let's not go there again, or you may live to regret it.'

Ursel, sensing Isobel's fury, sat forward and pushed Dugald away. 'Leave her alone for heaven's sake. Don't you understand she has no interest in you, Dugald?'

Dugald stood up and adjusted the waist strap of his battledress blouse. He licked his lips. 'Oh, on the contrary sis, I think she loves it. The quiet ones should never be underestimated.'

Ursel pointed an accusing finger at her brother. 'I'm warning you Dugald. Don't think I don't know what went on five years ago.'

'Ah, so we've been telling tales have we lassie?' He looked down at Isobel and sneered. 'What *have* you been telling her, Isobel? That I dared to kiss you, is that it?'

Ursel pointed an accusing finger towards him. 'It was more than that Dugald, and you know it. You're drunk. Don't repeat it tonight… or you'll have me to contend with.' The intensity of Ursel's glare now matched that of Isobel's. Dugald held her stare for a few seconds but his eyelids became heavy, prompting him to look away, defeated. He knew he was onto a loser, so he slowly withdrew like a wounded stag, and returned to the bottle he'd left on the table. Isobel watched him nervously as she resumed the task of bandaging Ursel's ankle.

Whilst Dugald tugged impatiently at the cork he'd plunged back into the whisky bottle, the telephone rang in the hallway. Ursel turned to him. 'Can you get that? It's probably Mother checking to see if we got home safely.'

Dugald didn't reply, but did as he was told and picked up the black Bakelite handset, placing it to his ear. 'Hello, Glendaig Manse.'

There was a pause. 'Aye, this is him. Who's this?'

The two women looked up, an expression of bemusement on both their faces. It clearly wasn't Anna or Callum Matheson, so who else would be calling at this of all times?

'Oh, hello Lachlan, what is it?' Dugald listened, swirling the remaining whisky around his glass. 'Are you sure Lachlan?' Then; 'Did you see who was in it?' He nodded. 'No bother Lachlan. When was this?' Another pause. Then; 'Good lad, well done Lachlan. I'll make this worth your while if I find them.'

Dugald replaced the receiver onto its cradle. He looked at his watch. 'Eleven forty. I haven't much time,' he muttered, and made for the hallway in a half run. Isobel followed him.

'What's going on, Dugald? Was that Lachlan MacDonald on the telephone?'

She found him in the hallway, struggling into his heavy army greatcoat. He looked back at her, his face flushed with excitement. It was as if the dulling effect of the whisky had suddenly vacated him, like a spirit exorcised by a priest.

'Aye, that simpleton Lachlan MacDonald over at Camuscraig. He thinks he's seen those bloody Germans drive back through the village and head out this way.'

Isobel stared at him wide-eyed. 'So what are you going to do now, Dugald?'

Ursel had managed to hobble to the hall doorway. She'd heard what Dugald had just said and turned back with some difficulty, making for the telephone. 'I'll call Father up at the big house. He'll know what to do.'

Dugald yelled after her. 'You can do what you want, sis. I'm going to find the bastards and put a stop to their little game… whatever it is they're up to.'

Isobel tugged on his sleeve. 'For heaven's sake Dugald, you may be wrong about this, but if they *are* who you say they are then they may be dangerous. You're going to get yourself hurt. Heavens, they may have guns.'

He brushed her hand away from his sleeve. 'As if you care, Isobel. Anyway, I'm going to pick up your father's rifle first, then I'll have no problem stopping them in their tracks.'

Isobel glared at him. 'The rifle's in the scullery at Seal Cottage. You can't just walk in and take it. You have no right.'

'Just watch me Isobel. Let's just say I'm commandeering it on behalf of the war effort. I'm sure your father will understand.'

He opened the door, allowing the icy wind to surge into the hallway. 'As I recall the door's always open at the back... and the ammunition's kept in that old chest in the kitchen, yes?'

She didn't reply, which to him amounted to an affirmative response. He smiled, then turned and marched out into the swirling snow.

Isobel called out to Ursel. 'Tell your father that Dugald's going to get my father's gun. Tell them to get here quickly.'

She followed Dugald out into the darkness, wrapping a shawl around her shoulders that she'd found lying on the chair in the hallway. The temperature was hovering close to freezing, inducing a shiver deep within her. She buried her chin into the folds of the material as her eyes struggled to adjust to the darkness. A view of Dugald climbing into the driver's seat of the Austin slowly emerged, prompting her to hurry across to the car and throw open the passenger's door. Dugald had started the engine and was in the process of selecting first gear when Isobel flopped into the seat beside him.

'You can't do this Dugald. I won't let you take that rifle. You're drunk, and you're going to kill someone. Listen to me, you may be making a terrible mistake.'

The car lurched forward, wheels spinning as Dugald heaved the vehicle around and headed for the open gateway. 'You didn't have to come with me. I never asked you to. In fact you can get out when we reach your place. But please don't get in my way Isobel. I wouldn't want to hurt you.' He ran his finger across her cheek. 'Just do as you're told, or get out now,' he snarled, and turned to concentrate on the road ahead. Nothing more was said whilst they drove the short distance to Seal Cottage. Isobel was thankful for the silence. It gave her time to think as she frantically sought a solution to what was surely going to end in tragedy. Dugald, on the other hand, seemed steely calm. She glanced across at him and wondered what he was thinking. Was it tactics, or was he relishing the thought of being the local hero, halting the enemy in their tracks? One thing was for certain, he didn't look like a man who cared whether or not he may be wrong, and who was about to embark upon a course of action which would attract universal condemnation.

The car practically skidded to a halt outside Seal Cottage. Dugald leapt out and sprinted toward the building, leaving Isobel to fumble with the door release. By the time she reached the door at the rear of the cottage, he was emerging with Donald Grant's prized BSA sporting rifle slung over his shoulder. In his right hand he carried a tattered cardboard box containing more than a dozen .303 high velocity cartridges.

Isobel stepped into his path and screamed; 'You can't do this Dugald! Please listen to me.'

He looked straight through her, oblivious to her pleadings, aggressively brushing her aside, causing her to stumble and fall. By the time she'd picked herself up and returned to the car, Dugald had started the engine again and was about to pull away. She leapt into the vehicle, just as it moved off.

'You had your chance Isobel. I'm not stopping again. So keep your mouth shut and stay out of the way, do you hear me?'

Isobel shook her head in despair, but remained silent. Her heart thundered against her chest as she played out the various outcomes in her mind. Perhaps the car and its mysterious occupants had turned off somewhere, and would not be found. Unlikely though in these parts; there weren't many options as far as alternative routes were concerned! No, all she could hope for was that Callum and her father had been alerted to what was happening and were heading their way.

Dugald, meanwhile, was focussed on the road ahead, accelerating up the slight incline that led past by the church and out of the village towards Camuscraig. The windscreen was clear now, the earlier snow shower having all but petered out. To the west, the moon appeared briefly between billowing columns of slow-moving cloud, bathing the wintry landscape in a ghostly pale light.

On the ground, the thick frost that had aroused caution within Isobel earlier still presented a real hazard, its luring sparkle still visible in the light of the headlamps. But it was a hazard that Dugald seemed impervious to as he sped along the shore of Loch Coinneach, his foot firmly applied to the accelerator pedal.

The war-ravaged year of 1941 had finally reached its death throes and, according to Isobel's watch, had just over five minutes to run.

Chapter Thirty-Eight

As the narrow road wormed its way around the great expanse of water that lapped at the cliffs beneath it, the uphill gradient became steeper, pegging the little car's progress back to just twenty miles per hour. Dugald cursed as the engine note dropped off, and pumped the accelerator pedal aggressively. Their speed was little more than a crawl when they reached the blind summit that marked the end of the climb. Once over the crest, the car's speed began to pick up rapidly. Dugald now applied more pressure to the accelerator, and switched off the lights. He knew that beyond this point any light from their masked headlamps would herald their approach from some way off.

He leaned forward, his eyes straining into the darkness as he steered the car by the light of the now glowing moon. Isobel grasped the sides of her seat, praying that her cousin would slow down. Sensing the road was levelling out he did exactly that, slowing to a crawl as the car now negotiated a winding stretch of road. The glistening surface of Loch Coinneach was closer now, stretching away to the west like polished metal. Half-hidden by a low cliff, Eilean Ceann-Cinnidh loomed up from the silvery water, the wiry firs growing from its upper slopes easy to see, silhouetted in the moonlight. Small wavelets broke gently against the piles of scree that rested beneath its grassy bulk, foaming white as they teased their way around and between the ancient stones.

But it wasn't the scenery that prompted Dugald to bring his fist down heavily onto the steering wheel, though. It was the sleek pencil-shaped object lying one hundred yards off shore that invoked a real sense of excitement within him.

U-114 had stopped her engines and now lay still, her wake slowly fading from view. There was no sign of life on the submarine's long hull as it rose and fell with the tide, but after several seconds, Dugald's eyes had become sufficiently accustomed to the gloom to clearly make out movement on the bridge.

'There you go lassie, I knew I was right… Huns!'

Isobel wanted to speak, but the words just wouldn't come. She was, in a way, relieved that the scene before her *did* tend to support Dugald's assertion that the occupants of the car were indeed enemy agents or suchlike. Yet her sense of relief was quickly snuffed out by the realisation that the level of threat had just soared. Was her cousin really going to take on the entire crew of an enemy submarine? Not to mention the occupants of the mysterious car that were likely to appear at any second. Was he that courageous or was it more a case of suicidal arrogance? Isobel feared that the latter was driving her headstrong cousin to risk both of their young lives.

'We must get help Dugald, we must. You can't take this on alone, we'll both be killed without a doubt.'

Dugald ignored her plea. He'd turned off the engine and they were now cruising silently down another slight incline. He knew that the road became wider further along. It was a well-known passing place used by the locals, but also served as a lay-by. This, he believed, would be the place where the occupants of the other car would choose to alight. So he brought the little Austin to a standstill some distance short of the lay-by. He chose to park half on the verge, effectively hidden from the lookouts posted on the submarine behind the thorny mass of broom that clung to the cliffside. It was, he believed, a good tactical position looking down unseen upon the U-boat from above, but also a safe distance from the lay-by so that his car remained hidden in the darkness, at least until it was too late for the men in the other vehicle to take any serious evasive action.

He turned to face Isobel, staring at her fixedly, as if he were absorbing every detail of her face one last time. Then he half-whispered; 'Leave this to me, Isobel. If I wait for anyone else to arrive, I could miss the opportunity to stop these bastards. Now I'm telling you, stay here in the car. Don't interfere, and if things get a bit hairy, take yourself off back to Glendaig on foot, do you understand?'

Isobel glared at him, her face almost obscured by shadow. 'I think you're mad,' she hissed through clenched teeth and turned her head, staring blankly through the windscreen. Dugald mumbled something unintelligible and placed the palm of his hand gently against her cheek. He smiled, one of his sickly, dismissive smiles, then eased himself out of the car and closed the door quietly behind him. Isobel then sensed the back door open and cold air rush into the car behind her. Dugald retrieved the rifle and scooped up a handful of ammunition from the box, dropping the shiny cartridges into the pocket of his greatcoat. He then removed the magazine from the weapon and delved once more into the box, calmly loading five rounds and then slotting the magazine back into its housing next to the trigger guard. The door closed, and Isobel watched as his profile faded into the darkness beyond the car's long bonnet. Her attention then switched to a pair of dimmed headlamps, pinpricks of light heading towards her from the west. She closed her eyes, dreading the moments to come, and wiped away the tears that now stained her cheeks.

Outside, Dugald had seen the approaching headlamps accompanied by the distant sound of a car engine. Beneath him, he could also hear the faint sound of footsteps on metal, interspersed with the sound of men's voices carried on the breeze. He edged into the broom and dropped to a squat before working the bolt on the rifle and easing a round into the breach.

Phoebus' Morris Eight came to a halt in the lay-by, just as Dugald had predicted. Having checked that the safety catch was off, he raised the rifle's shiny walnut stock slowly to his shoulder. He estimated that he was about fifty or so yards from the lay-by, and well within range for a safe shot.

A short, slightly built man emerged from the driver's side of the Morris. He looked around him searchingly before ducking back into the car. Seconds later he was out again, this time with a torch. Low voices could be heard, and then a series of flashes pierced the night, illuminating the signaller sufficiently for Dugald to see the vapour from his breath. He had no idea what was being communicated to the U-boat, but its commander *Kapitänleutnant* Von Bramsdorf certainly did. It was the signal he'd been waiting, and hoping for. *Drumbeater is ready for collection.*

A series of flashes were then returned from the conning tower of the submarine, no doubt in acknowledgement, sending momentary fingers of light darting across the surface of the loch.

Two other men then stepped out of the Morris. Dugald could just make out that one was wearing naval uniform, the other a heavy greatcoat. The voices were clearer now, foreign voices... German voices! All three men stood together by the driver's door, deep in discussion.

The figure wearing the long coat removed it and placed it onto the back seat of the car. Underneath, he wore a thick dark pullover and baggy trousers. He then moved quickly to the boot of the car and opened it.

Dugald crept out from the sanctuary of the broom, steadied himself and lined up his sights on the little group. His mouth was dry; a combination of fear and excitement. It was time to finish this. He stood up, sight bead still lined up on his target. 'You there, stand still and raise your hands... slowly.'

The three men turned towards him, startled, trying to locate the source of the voice through the darkness. Frustratingly there was no compliance with his instruction. Then, to his utter astonishment, a Scottish voice drifted across to him above the strengthening wind.

'Show yourself. Who are you?'

Dugald, ruffled by the unflinching response apparently from one of his own, edged out into the roadway, rifle still raised, eye still squinting through the sights. 'I'm a British Army officer, now raise your hands above your heads or I'll have no hesitation in opening fire.'

On seeing Dugald emerge from the shadows with rifle raised, three pairs of hands slowly extended skyward. 'What now?' *Phoebus* called out. 'We have no weapons.'

'Turn to face the car and place your hands on the roof... do it... now,' came the no-nonsense reply.

As the men turned, Dugald allowed himself a sideways glance towards the U-boat. A small dinghy containing two figures was weaving its way slowly towards the beach below. He was painfully aware that he was carrying a single shot rifle, and had to make a decision fast. He dropped to one knee and swung the barrel of the rifle around to line up the dinghy in his sights, then pulled the trigger. A loud crack echoed off the mountainside behind him as the round tore into the side of the dinghy. He'd done enough. The two occupants paddled furiously to execute a hasty U-turn and headed back to the submarine, crouched low between the vessel's rubber sides.

On the bridge of U-114, Von Bramsdorf watched the action through night glasses. He punched the rusting rim of the tower with a gloved hand and called into the voice tube: 'Obermeyer!'

'Yes, sir,' came the immediate riposte from his navigating officer down in the control room.

'Prepare the boat for sea. Start engines. Await my orders.'

'Aye aye sir.'

'And tell *Obersteuermann* Keissel to prepare another dinghy for the shore party.'

'*Jawohl Herr Kaleun!*'

Dugald, still on one knee, heard the twin M.A.N diesels burst into life. He ejected the spent cartridge case, sending it pinging across the road surface to his right. Then, having slammed the bolt home, he readied himself for another shot.

In the silence that followed the first rifle crack, *Phoebus* cautiously turned his head, hoping the so-called soldier was preoccupied with a reload. He saw the dinghy's paddles thrashing about wildly as the two submariners headed for safety, and rightly assumed that the shot had been fired in their direction. More importantly he was right, the rifleman was indeed busy reloading, and not looking in their direction. He instinctively opened the car door and reached inside, fumbling around for the Walther PPK that he'd secreted under his seat. His hand quickly located the cold metal barrel and he pulled it out of the car, working the slide as he did so. Arms extended, he swung the barrel towards Dugald, his finger already squeezing the trigger. But it was too late. Dugald had managed to complete the reload and had resumed his firing position. He saw *Phoebus* spin around, and was ready. He pulled the trigger again, and as the rifle's stock kicked into his shoulder, another round set off towards the German agent at over 2,000 feet per second. The projectile passed clean through *Phoebus'* heart and exploded from between his shoulder blades, peppering the interior of the Morris with a fine spray of blood, and the expelled remnants of his scrawny back. The force of the shot, capable of taking down a fully-grown stag, propelled the agent back into the car where he lay motionless across the front seats, staring vacantly at the roof lining. The Walther now lay out of reach in the road, some ten feet from the two Germans.

Dugald was busily reloading again. He yelled at them. 'Stay exactly where you are. Move, and you'll both end up like him.'

Reiniger felt helpless. His own pistol was still in the boot of the car and he knew what the likely outcome would be if he made any attempt to retrieve it. The smaller PPK was out of reach. The only option was to make a run for it. They had little or no time to make decisions. He grabbed his friend's arm. 'Quick Max, let's go.'

They set off at a pace across the road and crashed through the dense bracken that grew along the verge, then it was down the steep slope to the beach. Another crack rang out from Dugald's rifle. Reiniger held his breath, waiting for the searing pain that would surely overwhelm him, but it didn't come and Max also seemed to have escaped unscathed. They half-ran, half-fell down the slope, loosening the stones that lay bedded into the sandy soil. Rock debris now cascaded past them as they slid the last few feet to the beach.

On the bridge of the U-boat, Von Bramsdorf had seen his two countrymen make their bid for freedom. He called down to his chief quartermaster; 'Keissel, launch that dinghy now. Make sure the shore party are armed!' Keissel raised a thumb in acknowledgement, struggling to make his voice heard over the sound of the wind and the throbbing diesels.

Reiniger could see the dinghy being prepared on the submarine's casing. He helped his friend up and the two men set off across the beach, zigzagging across the sand in an effort to frustrate Dugald's aim. They were so close they could hear the dinghy hit the water with a distinctive *splat*. Two crewmen climbed gingerly into the little raft, Schmeisser machine pistols slung across their chests.

It seemed like an eternity, but they eventually reached the water's edge. There hadn't been any more shooting. Perhaps the rifleman had run out of ammunition, or possibly his weapon had jammed. Reiniger crouched close to his companion as the cold water from the loch washed over his boots. He caught Max's eye, and smiled between gasps for breath.

'I think we may have...' His words were lost as another loud crack echoed round their heads. Max dropped onto his side and cried out as he grasped his right thigh. He could already feel hot sticky blood soaking through the dark material of his trousers and collecting between his fingers. He yelped, his face contorted by pain. 'Twice in one year, unlucky or what!'

Reiniger had no time to respond. His eyes were searching the beach for the shooter. He could see nothing, just darkness. He turned towards the U-boat. The dinghy was heading in their direction, having just left the sanctuary of the submarine. Reiniger grasped Max under the armpits and heaved him up onto his feet. The wounded man gasped as he positioned himself on his good leg, and with one arm around Reiniger's neck they waded out into the water.

'…What a shame, almost there.'

Reiniger looked back, seeking the source of the voice. It was Dugald, standing at the water's edge, *Phoebus*' Walther in his right hand. 'I think it's best you both come back here. I'm certainly not going to miss from this distance.'

The Germans exchanged glances. Their decision was made without speaking. It was their only option if they were to avoid being shot where they stood. Shivering uncontrollably, they reluctantly paddled back to the edge of the beach.

'Down,' Dugald ordered, reinforcing his instruction with a brief gesture of the hand. The two men complied, and dropped to their knees. Reiniger looked up defiantly.

'So what are you going to do about the men in the dinghy? Soon you will be outnumbered.' His English was fluent but heavily accented.

'I'd better even things up then,' said Dugald with a half-smile. He stepped forward, raised his gun hand until the muzzle pointed at Reiniger's forehead, and pulled the trigger. The young man from Bremerhaven slumped backwards onto the sand and lay still. Seawater lapped around his lifeless head, fogged now by an infusion of blood. From the small hole above his eyes, that same blood slowly snaked its way down the side of his nose.

The crewmen in the dinghy stopped paddling. One of them unslung his Schmeisser and aimed it at the two men on the beach.

Almost immediately, an instruction was bellowed from somewhere atop the conning tower of the U-boat, and the seaman immediately lowered his weapon.

'Sounds like they don't want to play ball, Max.' Dugald grinned. 'Aye, I heard your friend call you Max and thought, surely that can't be my good old German cousin, not here of all places? But yes, it was, I'd recognise you anywhere, even though you look a good deal older now. My, how the war has taken its toll on you it seems, Mother would be shocked.'

Max was equally shocked, especially now that the identity of his assailant was known. 'That was murder Dugald, cold blooded murder. You bastard.' Max's shivering was now a combination of cold and shock. Loss of blood was also taking its toll on him. He began to feel weary, as the will to survive drained steadily from him. 'So what are you going to do now Dugald, shoot me, take me prisoner? Whatever you're planning, let's just get it over with shall we?'

'Well I could take you prisoner, or should I say *recapture* you? What a popular chap I'd be.' He pointed the Walther towards the U-boat. 'Not a lot I can do about that thing, but I can rid the world of you. Another U-boat celebrity meets his end, eh? Not only that, but I can rid myself finally of the Nazi cousin who everyone in the family seemed to adore. You know, they still talk fondly of you now, even though you're the bloody enemy, happily slaughtering our countrymen in their hundreds just because they dare to bring us food from America.' He scowled and raised the pistol in both hands, aiming at his cousin's head.

'You must do what you must Dugald, but just do it… now.'

Dugald stood expressionless, contemplating his next move. Then he swung the pistol away to the right and fired three times in the direction of the U-boat.

Von Bramsdorf ducked behind the rim of the conning tower as the rounds pinged off the metal plating. When he dared to raise his head again, he could see Keissel and another crewmen crouching behind the deck gun. The captain cupped his hands to his mouth and called out to the quartermaster; 'Get that dinghy back and stowed. We must leave now, before the entire British Navy come steaming up this loch.' He dropped again behind the parapet, where his second *wachoffizier* was sheltering. 'This isn't going to work, Wendt. We can't stay here any longer. I can't risk the boat and its crew.'

'But surely we can overpower one man with a pistol, sir?'

'That swine out there knows what he's doing. He's keeping so close to Friedmann, any shot taken by us in these conditions could hit the wrong man. I can't send those two crewmen onto the beach and not permit them to use their weapons. No, Friedmann will have to take his chances, I have a whole crew to consider. If that murdering bastard on the beach has summoned assistance before coming here, then we'll be pushed to get out of this loch in one piece.'

He allowed himself a brief glimpse over the conning tower rim. The dinghy was heading back to the submarine. Dugald stood at the waterline, still pointing the pistol at Max.

'Looks like they're abandoning you, Max,' said Dugald as he ejected the magazine from the Walther. 'Umm, five rounds left. That's more than enough for you.' He replaced the magazine into the pistol's stock and worked the slide, then casually fired another round in the direction of the U-boat. 'Don't want any jams, do we?' He swung the pistol back towards Max and levelled it again. 'Och, I'm sure three dead Germans are as good as two and a prisoner in the eyes of the authorities. Having said that, the little feller had an excellent Scottish accent.'

'He *was* a Scot, one of your own,' said Max, grimacing.

'Och, he was no Scot, he was just a traitorous bastard who richly deserved the bullet that finished him off.'

He cocked the pistol's hammer back just as the throb of the submarine's diesels increased in volume. The calm water around the U-boat's stern began to boil as the twin screws began to turn.

'Just get on with it, Dugald.' Max closed his eyes. His body felt heavy now and his teeth were chattering with the cold. He just wanted to end it. He could hear the sound of the submarine's engines fading as the vessel slipped away towards the mouth of the loch. Now it occurred to him that these would be the last sounds he would ever hear… other than the shot that was about to kill him. *How apt,* he thought, as he waited for that fateful *bang*. Then he heard a woman's voice, a voice he believed he recognised, and his eyes snapped open again.

'Put that gun down Dugald, please. I can't let you kill anyone else.'

Isobel stood silhouetted against the wet pallid sand. She'd picked up her father's rifle from where Dugald had left it propped up against *Phoebus*'s car and was now aiming it directly at her cousin. She struggled to keep the rifle steady at shoulder height, its long heavy barrel wavering against her petite frame. The seconds seemed to pass so very slowly, and her arms began to weaken under the weight of the weapon. She stood impassively, gritting her teeth, about ten yards behind Dugald, waiting for him to comply with her instruction. He looked back at her and produced one of his customary sneers.

'You won't shoot me, Isobel. Besides, the recoil of that thing will knock you over lassie. You'll never hit me, not even at that range.' He turned back to face Max, the sneer still in place. It wasn't a confident expression though, it was more of a hopeful countenance, hopeful that his assessment of the situation was correct. *Surely Isobel would never pull the trigger, and if she did, she would probably miss.* Reassured by his own belief, he raised the pistol again.

'Dugald, no!' Isobel cried out. Then there was a loud crack.

Max saw the eruption of blood and serge as the bullet exited from his cousin's chest, and felt its fine spray pepper his face.

Dugald staggered forward into the shallows, legs slowly buckling as if he were labouring under a heavy load. Then he dropped to his knees, an expression of disbelief etched upon his face. He swayed for a second or two then toppled face first into the shallow water. His two bare legs initially flicked upward, before dropping back. Then he lay motionless, his sodden kilt buffeted gently by the tide.

When she came closer, Max instantly recognised Isobel. She was noticeably older now, not the child he remembered but a beautiful young woman. 'Is that you Isobel, Isobel Grant?'

She was sobbing quietly. 'Max? Max Friedmann?' She ran forward, the realisation gripping her like an iron fist. 'Oh my God, Max!' She dropped to her knees, inches from Max's face, and leant back to get a good look at his blood-flecked features. His hair was plastered across his forehead, wet from the spray, and his dark eyes looked terribly tired, but there was no mistaking it. She embraced him; a gesture that produced a cry of pain.

'Cousin Dugald managed to hit me in the thigh again,' he groaned as he slumped sideways, forcing Isobel to support his body weight. She looked across to where Dugald's body was lying and the tears flowed once more. 'What on earth have I done?' she sobbed. Her body trembled as the enormity of the situation took hold of her.

'You need to pull yourself together Isobel, take this, now.' Max handed her a damp crumpled handkerchief.

'Have you told anyone that you were coming here?'

She nodded between sobs. 'Ursel was calling her father. Everyone's up at the big house tonight.' She wiped away the salty tears that were blurring her vision.

'Well that's good, we need help quickly. Go and have a look at Dugald will you, for what it's worth.'

'Aye, alright,' she stuttered, and crept away gingerly towards her cousin's limp body. Max watched as she checked for any signs of life. She looked across and shook her head. 'He's dead,' she sobbed. 'I shot him in the back. I've killed my own cousin.'

Max beckoned to her to come back to him. 'Look Isobel, you did what you did to protect me. I will stand by you. People will understand. He executed Jürgen there and he was about to do the same to me. He was out of control, war or no war.'

She nodded again, acknowledging the reassurance, and wiped more tears away before regaining her composure to some degree. 'Well, if you're wrong Max, they'll hang me,' she sniffed.

'Nonsense, you mustn't think like that. Now come here and help me off with my jacket.'

She placed her hand on his thigh, just below the ragged blood-soaked hole that oozed beneath his palm. 'Why do you want to do that? You'll freeze out here.'

'I'll be fine, I have a jumper on under the jacket. I just can't bear to see Jürgen's face like that, I have to cover him. Please understand.'

Removing the jacket was not a straightforward task for either party, but they finally achieved it, and Isobel draped the garment gently over Reiniger's head and torso. The couple then sat huddled on the damp sand, her arm supporting his upper body, as they waited for help to arrive.

'Don't worry, Callum and my father will be here any time now... does it hurt much?' Isobel tilted her head towards his and edged closer to him.

'Not much. There seems to be an exit wound the other side of my thigh, so hopefully the bullet went right though. As long as I don't lose too much blood I'm sure they'll be able to patch me up when I get to a POW camp, wherever that might be.'

'Let's worry about getting you to see a doctor first. We'll call Alpin Macrae when we get back to the Manse. He's the village doctor, and a good one too.'

'Well I hope it's quick. I'm feeling really cold now, and a little drowsy, that's not a good sign.'

'You must be in shock.' She untied the shawl that she'd taken from the Manse and wrapped it around his shoulders. 'There, that should help.'

'Thank you.' He buried his chin into the thick material. 'Tell me, how did you learn to shoot like that, and in the dark?'

'It's my father's gun. Dugald took it from the cottage. Father taught David to use it when he was old enough and, me being me, well I pestered him to teach me too. And don't forget, I've been out stalking with my father since I was a child.'

'Well just as well he *did* teach you, or it might've been me lying there now. Not that *anyone* should be lying there at all.'

'Look,' said Isobel, her voice now raised in excitement. 'I think I can see a light up there on the road.'

Sure enough, a group of figures had appeared at the top of the slope. They were carrying lanterns and were calling out. It was her father and Callum Matheson, together with two others.

Max turned to Isobel and wiped away a tear that glistened wet on her cheek. 'It'll be alright, you'll see.'

She smiled weakly as she watched the line of lanterns descend the path towards the beach. 'We're down here,' she called out. 'Come quickly!'

2 0 0 9

Chapter Thirty-Nine

Tuesday 30th June

The drone of a distant lawnmower was the only discernible sound that filled the room. Neil sat in silence, mesmerised by the tale he'd just heard, apparently unaware that his hosts had stopped talking.

'Inspector?'

He blinked, as if startled back into the present. 'Yes, yes. Sorry, I was just taking all this in. So Dugald Matheson was never killed in a hunting accident, as I'd been led to believe. He died the night before, having been shot by *you* Isobel, whilst trying to protect your husband here?' He felt compelled to reaffirm the facts, even though they'd already been fully-absorbed.

Isobel nodded and looked down towards her feet whilst she dabbed the corner of her eye with a tissue. 'I assume this is when the caution becomes relevant, and you produce your handcuffs?'

Neil considered the question, she had a point. Then he smiled. 'I think in these circumstances we can avoid such formalities for now. You did, after all, act in defence of your husband, albeit sixty-eight years ago!' He sat forward, an awkward expression now present on his face. 'I suppose it's only fair to advise you that we will have to take advice from the Procurator Fiscal, and no doubt Crown Counsel in respect of this matter. With that in mind, do you feel you want to carry on?'

Isobel nodded in the affirmative. 'Well we've started now, so we may as well finish. It's just a relief to finally lift the lid on all this awful secrecy.'

Neil sat back, somewhat relieved. 'So we have three deceased persons as a result of this incident on the 31st December 1941. Dugald Matheson, your colleague Lieutenant Reiniger…' his gaze settled upon Max, '…and an unknown male using the code name *Phoebus* who was operating as a German agent in Scotland. Is that correct?'

'Aye, that's correct,' said Isobel. 'It still seems like a terrible nightmare.'

'Can I assume that Dugald Matheson's body was laid to rest where I would expect it to be?'

Isobel seemed shocked. 'Oh yes, of course Inspector.'

She paused to dab her eyes again, allowing Max to make a contribution. 'I think I know what you're implying, but no, Dugald wasn't buried on that beach in some grave that you haven't found yet.'

Neil was relieved. 'It's just, what with two grave sites on the beach, and a hitherto unknown body in one of them well, nothing would surprise me.'

'No, you can be assured that Dugald's remains are where you'd expect them to be Inspector, buried properly in the churchyard at Glendaig.'

'Good, and from what you've just told me about Max's tunic being laid over *Leutnant* Reiniger's body, can I assume the remains we have discovered on the beach are indeed his?'

'You are correct Inspector, poor old Jürgen never made it off that beach. It's something that has haunted us both all our married lives.' Max looked away, choking back tears.

'Okay, let's leave it at that for now, but I do have some other questions about the items we found in and around the grave. Now, what about this agent, *Phoebus*? We found what appeared to be a second grave site next to Reiniger's, but that was empty. Was that intended for him?'

Isobel nodded. 'Yes, he *was* buried there… but only temporarily.'

'So where is he now, Isobel?'

There was a period of silence again, during which the old couple exchanged worried glances. Neil sensed another revelation was on its way. 'Well, Mum?' asked Jeanne, frustrated by her mother's delay in answering.

Isobel let out a little sob. 'He's in with Dugald.'

'There was another silence, more protracted this time. Then a shocked Jeanne placed a hand to her mouth and exclaimed '*Mother*! I don't believe this.'

Jeanne's unexpected reaction prompted Neil to ask; 'How much *did* you know about all this, Jeanne?'

She took a deep breath. 'I knew that my father was a German prisoner of war who'd escaped and ended up in Glendaig, where he was looked after during the war by the Mathesons.'

'What about the shooting of Dugald Matheson and the two other men?'

'I knew some men had been shot, including my father, as he attempted to board a submarine… but not that my mother had shot Dugald.' She looked down at her mother, tears now running down her cheeks.

'Did you ever wonder who these *men* were, Jeanne? The men who were shot I mean.'

'Soldiers, I suppose? The men from the submarine? I don't really know to be honest. No one ever discussed it in detail, not like today.'

Isobel took her hand. 'I'm sorry dear, it wasn't something we felt we could burden you with, not even as an adult. I hope you understand.'

Jeanne looked back across at Neil. 'I was always told that the whole affair should remain a secret because folk might not approve of the fact that a German prisoner of war was being harboured by our family, especially one who'd been a U-boat captain.'

Isobel handed her Daughter a tissue. 'You see, many of the local men, particularly the fishermen working along this coast, joined the Merchant Navy, and a considerable number were lost because of the U-boats.'

'I see,' said Neil. 'You must've been in a very difficult position.'

'Oh, *difficult*'s an understatement,' said Max, his voice faltering.

'Let's return to the events of that night in 1941. Perhaps you'd better tell me what happened after the shootings on the beach.'

'Yes, of course Inspector.' There was a sereneness about Isobel now. 'Well, my father arrived with Uncle Callum, my brother David and Murdo Stuart. David and Murdo were best friends back then, they were inseparable, both ghillies working on the estate for my father. They were shocked to the core, as you can imagine, when they were told what had happened. Uncle Callum was terribly upset, understandably, especially when he learnt that *I'd* fired the shot that had killed his son.'

'He must have been. I suppose there was a fair amount of animosity on his part… towards you I mean?'

Isobel shook her head, and smiled. 'No, not at all as it happens. He hugged me, and told me he understood why I'd done it, almost as if he knew what Dugald was capable of. Deep down, the whole family knew. Like I explained earlier, he was the black sheep of the family… no, his parents had no illusions as to what he was capable of.'

'You seemed to think he was influenced by his teachers at boarding school?'

'Yes he was, but it went far deeper than that. He was not a nice person even at an early age. He was especially jealous of Max and Otto because they were popular members of the family I suppose. You see, he was never king pin when they were around.'

Max interjected sharply with a wave of the arm. 'Tell him about the time he molested you Isobel, he should know about that.' Then he sat back, content that he'd at last exposed Dugald for what he was.

Isobel's cheeks coloured visibly. She turned away towards the window. 'That was years before all this happened, it's not important now.'

'It will help me to understand your relationship with Dugald if I know everything, Isobel,' said Neil softly, his voice loaded with compassion.

Max burst forth again. 'Go on tell him dear, like I said, he should know.'

Isobel avoided eye contact with Neil, preferring to gaze out of the window. 'I was just a teenager at the time, sixteen, something like that. It must have been during the summer of '36. Dugald was home from law school and came to our cottage to see me one afternoon. My parents were out at the time.'

Her voice faded away, prompting Jeanne to place her arm around her mother's shoulder. Reassured, she went on; 'He wanted me to go out for a walk with him, down to the beach by the castle. I said I was too busy. I knew what it would lead to. Well, he wouldn't be told, and I ended up threatening to tell my mother and father that he was pestering me.'

'So how did he respond to that?'

'He became very angry, dragged me into my parents' room and attacked me.'

'*Attacked* you?'

'He tried to rape her,' Max reached out for Isobel's hand.

Jeanne gasped as her mother's trembling fingers clamped around her husband's.

Neil felt he had to ask. 'How did you get away from him Isobel? You must have been terrified.'

'He was a well-built laddie, but I managed to kick him hard in the groin. He went down like a stone and I just ran out of the house. I don't remember where I ended up.'

'She never mentioned it to anyone,' said Max, now patting his wife's knee and keenly aware that she was struggling to regain her composure.

'I always detested Dugald after that,' said Isobel. 'But I tried to remain civil, mainly for his family's sake. The more I dismissed his advances, the more he tried. It was as if I was a challenge for him, something to be conquered.'

Neil sensed that now was the time to change the subject. 'I'm so sorry, Isobel. Are you sure you don't want a break, because we can continue this...'

She cut him short. 'No Inspector I'm fine, really. Where was I? Yes, the beach.' She seemed eager to change the subject too.

'We had to get Max off the beach very quickly because he was still losing blood, and very weak, so Uncle Callum and my father carried him to the car. Then Uncle Callum drove us back to the Manse. When we got there, he told Aunt Anna and Ursel what had happened. You can imagine how they reacted but again, there was no anger towards me, just kindness. Ursel called Alpin Macrae, the village doctor. He arrived soon after... still tipsy from the party as I recall.'

Max chuckled. 'He was more than tipsy, I'm convinced he was operating on autopilot that night.'

Isobel dismissed Max's attempt to inject humour into the conversation and carried on; 'Alpin examined Max and dressed his wounds. He gave him something for the pain and we put him to bed. I was told to sit with him whilst the rest of the family discussed what to do next. I suppose they felt it was best if I wasn't present.'

'And what did they decide?' Neil prompted.

'My father came up to the Manse and I could hear raised voices outside in the hallway. Uncle Callum felt that the authorities should be called immediately, but Aunt Anna and my father persuaded him to wait until all the options had been considered.'

'You say your father arrived at the Manse. What were David and Murdo doing whilst all this was going on?'

'Well, Father had helped them bury the other two bodies on the edge of the beach in the graves you found, whilst they decided what to do. I have a feeling that even then, my father was not going to report the incident. Luckily Aunt Anna agreed with him.'

'What about the guns and the agent's car. What happened to them?'

Max spoke again. 'Donald, that's Isobel's father, told the boys to remove everything and dispose of it.'

'So where did it all end up?'

'In the loch, along towards Invertulloch. There are some steep cliffs close to the road, about a mile this side of the Inn. The loch is very deep there, over a hundred feet. They told me they'd put everything in the car and pushed it over the edge.'

'Not everything, it would seem,' suggested Neil. 'But I'll come onto that later. So what happened to Dugald's body?'

Isobel took up the story. 'He was taken back to the Manse and laid out in the scullery. It must have been nearly three in the morning by then. Everyone was in shock and emotionally exhausted. It was agreed that we would not do any more that night as everyone needed some time to digest what had happened, so my father proposed that we reconvene at the Manse later that morning to discuss our options.'

Neil turned his attention to Max. 'I take it the wound to your thigh wasn't too serious if the doctor did no more than clean and dress it?'

'No, mercifully the bullet had passed clean through the fleshy part, missing the bone completely. He cleaned the wounds and packed them out, then said he'd return early the next morning to have another look. I think he was more concerned about shock and hypothermia than anything else. Anyway, Isobel and Ursel took turns sitting with me that night and, as you can see, I managed to survive!'

'I can't begin to think what must have been going through your minds that night,' said Jeanne, massaging her mother's shoulder.

Isobel looked up at her. 'I was terrified that I'd be arrested at any time, and then hanged for killing Dugald. My parents and brother tried to tell me that it would be alright, but I could tell they were worried sick. After all, I'd just killed a British soldier who, on the face of it, was trying to prevent the escape of an enemy agent and two enemy submariners. I couldn't see myself getting too much support outside Glendaig.'

'Umm, I suppose not,' said Neil. 'Clearly the U-boat men were getting some very bad press at the time.'

'Aye, they were, and then of course we were harbouring an escaped prisoner; not any old prisoner, but a distinguished U-boat ace!' She turned to her husband and smiled. 'We were all very fond of Max... me especially. If he was discovered, then there was every chance that the whole terrible affair would be exposed. It was a horrible predicament, Inspector. We were a respected, law-abiding family up until that night. Then in just a few minutes we'd committed the worst crimes in the book, or so many would have believed.'

The pain of reliving the events of that fateful night had clearly shattered Isobel. She looked vulnerable now, her face wizened, her cheeks stained by tear tracks like crows' feet on clay.

'I think it would be best if we had a break,' Neil suggested again, concerned for her well-being. 'I know this must be very difficult for you all. Perhaps we could continue this discussion some other time, when you're feeling stronger?'

His gesture of compassion was met with a glare from the Isobel. 'Indeed not Inspector. It will never become any easier, whenever it is we discuss it, so I want to do this *now* and get it over and done with.' She got up and straightened her skirt. 'Perhaps you'd excuse me for a couple of minutes, I need to do something with my face.'

'Of course, I need to make a phone call outside, so please take your time.'

When Isobel had left the room, Neil got up too. 'I'll only be a couple of minutes,' he said, heading for the front door.

'I'll make some tea then,' said Jeanne.

'I'd rather have a whisky,' said Max. 'What about you, Inspector? You'd make an old man very happy.'

Neil stopped in his tracks. 'It's a bit early for me, but hey, you've twisted my arm. As long as you don't tell my boss!'

Max laughed out loud. 'I think you can count on me of all people to keep a secret, no?'

Neil was relieved to be outside once again. He took in a deep lungful of air as he walked to his car. The breeze had strengthened since his arrival at the house, and tantalising glimpses of blue had now been revealed by the fast-moving cloud. Once inside the car, he looked at his watch. Just after midday, Alex Brodie would probably be languishing in his office enjoying a leisurely lunch of soup and oatcakes. He dialled Brodie's number and raised the handset to his ear.

'Alex Brodie,' came the muffled reply. Yes, as expected, he had a mouthful of food on the go!

'It's Neil Strachan, sir. Thought I'd update you on the Glendaig case.'

'And *is* there any update Neil?' his boss asked, swallowing hard.

'Actually there is. I've identified the remains from the beach, *and* the individual who shot him. In fact three men were shot dead there, that same night.'

There was no reply from the other end of the line, just a distant choking sound. 'Sir…?'

'Aye, I'm here Neil. I wasn't expecting such news that's all.'

'It's a bit complicated, perhaps we can discuss it when I get back to the office?'

'Aye, I'd like that,' said Brodie with a hint of sarcasm. 'Just a couple of things I need to know though. Firstly, where are the other two corpses now, do you have any idea? Please tell me they're not buried on our patch somewhere.'

'Sorry to disappoint you, sir. They're sharing the same grave in the cemetery next to Glendaig Church. One is Dugald Matheson… you've heard me speak of him.'

'Aye, of course I remember him. You'd been told he'd been killed during a stalking expedition.'

'That's the one. The other chap was a German agent, code named *Phoebus*. I don't know much about him at present.'

There was another lengthy pause. 'Of course Neil, *Phoebus* you say?'

'That's right. Look, I'd better go just now. I'll brief you in more detail when I get back. What was the other thing you wanted to know?'

'I don't suppose you've discovered what happened to that chap Friedmann?'

'Aye sir, I have. In fact we've just been having a cup of tea together!'

'Umm, I see. Look, perhaps we'd better leave it there for now. I'll be waiting when you get back.'

'Okay, bye for now.'

'By the way Neil.'

'Yes sir…?'

'Good work, well done son!'

'Thank you, sir.'

Neil dropped the phone back in his pocket. A broad grin spread across his face as he looked out towards the firth. He'd been looking forward to having that conversation for nearly a month.

Isobel, Jeanne and Max were all present in the little sitting room waiting for him when Neil appeared in the doorway. The women were sipping tea and Max held up a crystal tumbler so that the ice cubes floating in his whisky clanked against the glass. 'Yours is on the table next to the chair. It's a fine wee tipple, if I say it myself.'

'Thanks,' said Neil as he sat down and eyed the generously-large glassful he'd been given. 'Sorry about that, I was just speaking to my boss.'

'Telling him that you'd solved the mystery of the bones, no doubt?' Isobel enquired. She seemed brighter now, her blue eyes were clear once again, and her make-up had been freshened.

Neil lifted his glass. '*Slàinte mhath.*'

Max followed suit, and the ice tinkled again as he sipped from his glass.

'I needed to let him know that I'd be a while. So you both want to continue with this?

'Of course Inspector, what else do you want to know?' Isobel took a long deep breath, her dignified exterior belying the true level of apprehension that still weighed heavy upon her.

'So how did things develop the next day Isobel, when you all reconvened to discuss what to do about Max?

'I woke up early. The dawn was just breaking. I hadn't slept much because Max was restless. Ursel and Aunt Anna came in to take a turn sitting with him. They told me to go home and get some sleep, so that's what I did. I must have slept for an hour or so, that was all. When I got up, everyone else was out, along at the Manse I presumed. So I went for a short walk, just to clear my head, then made my way down there to see how Max was feeling. Ursel met me at the door and told me he was doing fine. My parents weren't there as I'd expected them to be. My mother had gone to tell the McSweens what had happened. They knew Max, so we couldn't really not tell them I suppose. David and my father had gone to pick up Murdo and check that nothing had been left on the beach.'

'And had there been?'

'Apparently not. It was as if nothing had happened. I think they found a few empty cartridge cases, that's all. The car had well and truly been disposed of too, no trace of it at all.'

'How were the Mathesons when you arrived at the Manse that morning?'

'Glum, to say the least. It was as if there was a huge black cloud hanging over the house, but what would you expect…?'

1 9 4 2

Chapter Forty

Callum Matheson sat at the large washed-oak table cradling a mug of tea in both hands. Steam curled up from the hot drink and clouded his spectacles. They were old, wire-framed, with thick little lenses that perched on the end of his button nose in a scholarly fashion. Indeed, Callum looked every inch the scholar. He was a portly man, round-faced with a ruddy complexion. His thick head of hair, akin to ripe wheat, was normally parted neatly to the side, but today it had been neglected and lay compressed against his scalp. His slouched form reflected his melancholic mood as he stared blankly at the teapot that sat in the centre of the table.

Anna pushed a bowl of porridge towards him, but he raised a hand to decline it. 'You have to eat,' said Anna with an unusually impassive countenance.

'I can't face anything,' he replied, having removed his glasses to wipe the moisture from the lenses.

The door to the kitchen opened and Ursel appeared arm in arm with Isobel. An awkward silence then ensued whilst Anna and Callum composed themselves, mindful that their son's killer had just entered the room, but the awkwardness was momentary, and soon overcome.

'I thought my parents would be here,' said Isobel, close to tears. 'Perhaps I'd better go.'

'Nonsense,' said Anna. 'Sit down, I've just made some tea and porridge, do you want some?'

'Tea would be nice, thank you.'

Callum beckoned her over to him. 'Sit here with me, lassie,' he instructed, and welcomed her with a comforting arm. His kindness, and the sense of relief that came from it, was too much for Isobel. Tears began to flow from her already-swollen eyelids down her cheeks and onto her lips, from where she attempted to sweep the salty secretions away with her tongue.

'You have to understand,' said Callum, 'we don't blame you for what happened last night. Heaven help me for saying it, but I may have done the same thing myself in those circumstances. I just don't understand why Dugald became what he was. We certainly never led him down that path.'

Anna joined them and placed a mug of tea in front of her niece. 'It's true Isobel, we *do* understand. Of course we're devastated, but also thankful that Max has survived.' She raised her eyes wistfully and sighed; 'It's all such a mess, such an awful mess.'

'I'm sure God will guide us through this,' said Callum, drawing Isobel closer to him.

'Thank you all so much for your kindness, I really can't begin to tell you how sorry I am,' Isobel whispered between uncontrollable sobs.

Anna smiled. 'Now enough of this, lassie. You go in and see Max. That'll cheer him up.'

'How is he feeling today, Aunt Anna?'

'He's coming on fine. I've been sitting with him for the last hour. He's feeling guilty too, heaven knows why. Dugald had already shot him once, then went back for more. He may be classed as an enemy of this country but he never deserved to be executed on that beach.' She got up from the table. 'Doctor Macrae is coming back at nine, we'll have to see what he says.'

Ursel sat down beside her father. 'What are we going to do Father, about Max I mean, and Dugald and…?'

Callum raised his hand, a plea for her to desist from plying him with such questions. 'I don't know right now,' he replied. 'We have some difficult decisions to make, and we have to make them very soon. Otherwise we're going to end up in more trouble than we already are.' He got up quickly and went to get his coat. 'I'll get everyone together here at nine, when the doctor's arrived.'

The front door slammed shut. Ursel took Isobel by the arm. 'Come on, let's go and see Max.'

At nine fifteen that morning the kitchen was busy again. Those individuals who'd been directly involved in the previous night's events were seated around the old table. Morning sunlight streamed through the small window, bathing the room in a warm glow, as if to burn away the glumness that had so heavily infused its occupants.

Callum sat in his normal place flanked by Anna. To his left sat Ursel and Isobel. Facing them were Donald and Morag Grant, with their son David and Murdo Stuart. Each member of the assembled throng had a mug of tea in front of them. The mood was sombre, each one of them lost in their own thoughts, each one eager to hear the doctor's prognosis.

Then Alpin Macrae emerged from the hallway, drying his hands on a small white towel. He was a small man, slightly stooped, with greying hair distinctively parted to the centre, and with a fringe that flopped across his brow. His face reflected the years of strain as a battlefield medic in the previous war; a war in which his performance in the field hospitals of the Somme had earned him the Distinguished Service Order. 'I've redressed the wound,' he explained in a quiet, official sounding tone. 'I'm of the opinion that the bullet passed straight through the thigh, with no apparent damage to the femur.'

'That's good news, isn't it?' said Anna.

'Well he's not out of the woods yet. There's still infection to consider. I've managed to get hold of some new stuff from a colleague of mine. They call it penicillin. It's still being trialled, but

453

the clinical tests so far have proved extremely encouraging when it comes to killing infections.' He sat down next to Donald. 'I have a colleague at the Northern Infirmary over in Inverness. We can smuggle Max in for an x-ray when it's safe to do so. I just want to confirm there's no femoral damage. Sometimes the path of the bullet can be deflected onto the bone you see but, as I said, I believe it's unlikely in this case.'

'Wait Alpin, are you assuming that we'll be keeping Max here, under wraps so to speak?' Callum looked worried.

'Well yes, I though that's what you'd want to do. He *is* a member of your family is he not?'

'Yes but...'

'Think of it Callum. If you hand him over to the authorities, he'll spend the rest of the war, however long that may be, in a POW camp somewhere. Years possibly. If you keep him here he's hardly going to be assisting the German war effort is he? Not that he wants to, from the conversation I've just had with him. He's exhausted, and he's had a gutful of this war. He's lost his brother, and his friends by the bucket load, and now he's wounded... again! Of course, the other thing to remember is if this incident is reported to the authorities, there will be many questions asked. We mustn't forget, three men have been killed. The facts surrounding Dugald's shooting will surely come out and where would that leave young Isobel here?'

Callum shook his head. 'I'm deeply uncomfortable with the proposal that we should cover all this up. Surely Isobel cannot be held criminally responsible for what she did?'

Alpin frowned, his wide-eyed expression said it all.

'Do you think we can get away with this, Alpin?' said Donald, his deep voice uncharacteristically hushed. Alpin turned his attention to the big man.

'How many people know about this?' He waved his hand around the table at those present. 'Only us in this room.'

'...And the McSweens. They knew something was afoot when we left the party in a hurry. Morag told them this morning.'

'Well they're family aren't they? Surely we can rely upon them to keep their mouths shut.'

'Aye of course they will,' Morag interjected. 'I told them not to breathe a word to anyone about this.'

'What about young Lachlan Macdonald, along the way at Camuscraig?' said Ursel, leaning forward across the table. 'He called Dugald last night and told him about the Germans driving through the village. What's he going to think when it gets out that Dugald is dead?'

'Alright, so we have to deal with him. What about the other partygoers; are they likely to come asking questions?' Alpin directed his enquiry towards the Mathesons.

'No, I don't think so,' Anna replied. 'We said we were leaving to see in the New Year with Ursel at home.'

'So can we all keep this to ourselves? Because one slip of the tongue, and we'll all be for it,' Alpin warned, scanning the faces around the table.

Callum, rubbed his brow vigorously. 'Just a minute, I can't believe what I'm hearing, and from the so called pillars of our community. We have two dead men buried down there on the beach, my son lying dead in the back room, shot in the back, and you're suggesting we can actually cover this up? Don't get me wrong, I understand why and I have no wish to see Max incarcerated, or Isobel at risk of an unspeakable fate at the hands of the judiciary, but I just can't see this affair remaining under wraps.'

'Look,' said Donald, 'we can't change anything now, but we *can* protect Isobel from an unjust fate, and your nephew from years of imprisonment.'

'Possibly worse than that,' said Alpin. 'Max has just told me that the fellow who took him off the train shot two military policemen in the process, which could make Max culpable for their deaths.'

Gasps of surprise rippled around the table. 'God help us, it just gets better and better,' said Callum.

'Well let's not forget, Max has harmed no one,' Alpin reminded him. 'He had little choice in the matter but to go with his colleague.

This is war, and bad things happen in war. For all we know, British servicemen are doing exactly the same in Germany in a bid to escape. It is, after all, their duty to try to escape.'

'You make a compelling case, Alpin. It's a case that I'd expect a military man such as yourself to make.'

'And you Callum, you were a military man once. The thing is, we're not military men now. That all ended in 1918. You're a priest, I'm a doctor, and that's all there is to it.'

'Aye, fair enough Alpin, but I couldn't live with myself if all the people around this table were to suffer imprisonment or worse in the weeks and months to come, because of a poor decision we make now.'

Anna leant across and took Callum's hand. 'Callum, our son was killed because he was about to shoot our nephew, who was defenceless and wounded. He'd already executed another. We know what he was like, and I'm not proud of what he did. I wouldn't want the world knowing that he executed an enemy serviceman in cold blood, effectively committed a war crime. It distresses me to even think about it, and I'm his mother. That's the reality of it. Whatever the rights and wrongs of Alpin's suggestion, we have to make a decision. There's nothing we can do to bring Dugald back, but we can do our bit to ensure Isobel and Max have a future. They're our own blood for heaven's sake so, if we can achieve that, and Max can live here safe and out of harm's way, then I owe that to my sister who, in case you'd forgotten, has already lost one son in this awful conflict.' She sat back and folded her arms, frustrated by her husband's intransigence.

He shook his head, unconvinced. 'I just don't know whether my faith will allow me to go through with this, Anna.'

She glared at him. 'Sometimes your faith has to come second to your family and friends, Callum.'

She turned her attention to the doctor who was sipping his tea. 'How do we get around the shooting of my son, Alpin?'

The doctor placed his mug on the table, and wiped his lips with the back of his hand. 'We say it was an accident. He was out stalking this morning with Donald and the two laddies here. Donald has leant Dugald his rifle, and one of the boys has been carrying it for him. Unbeknown to him, it's been left with a round in the breech. The laddie slips and falls causing the gun to discharge, hitting Dugald, who's walking ahead of him, in the back.'

'Wouldn't it be better if I took responsibility?' said Donald. 'Why involve David and Murdo in this?'

'Because their relative inexperience with firearms would make the story far more plausible, which would *not* be the case if an old hand like you, with all your experience, was carrying the weapon.'

'I'll say that it was me,' said David without hesitation.

'Are you sure?' his father asked.

'Aye, Father, I want to. It's my sister's neck on the line after all.'

Donald ruffled his son's mop of red hair. 'Good for you son.'

Murdo leant forward so that Donald could see him. 'I'd be happy to say it was me too,' he smiled.

'We appreciate that Murdo, we really do, but there's no need to drag you into this any more than we have to. Just go along with our story, that's all we ask.' Murdo sat back, relieved in a way, but also disappointed that he couldn't do more to help.

Alpin continued to outline his plan. 'Donald and Murdo are the only other members of the party, way up on Beinn Caisteal, so there'll be no other witnesses. We can say that the accident occurred later this morning, and it took some time to get his body down from the hill. Late afternoon would be best, which would explain the level of rigor mortis present in the body.'

Anna began to sob, and was immediately comforted by her husband who'd been listening to the doctor with a sombre expression fixed upon his normally jovial features. He said nothing on this occasion, finally hushed by his wife's apparent commitment to the plan.

'I'm sorry Anna,' said Alpin, mindful of the distress he was causing. 'It's just that the plan needs to be credible.'

Anna sniffed as she accepted Callum's handkerchief. 'Go on Alpin, we're alright.'

'You and Callum are here when Donald and the boys arrive. You call me, and I come to confirm the death. There will be some formalities, but believe me, Davie MacAllister will be only too happy to put the whole affair to bed. The witnesses are, after all, highly respected members of the community. Then there's my opinion, and I've been working with Davie for years. He certainly won't want to make too much fuss to add to your grief. I'm confident you'll be able to bury your son with his reputation intact.'

Callum couldn't contain himself. 'Alright, so if your plan works, we can rescue Dugald's reputation. But what about the two men on the beach? You seem to have forgotten them.'

'You can leave them to us, Callum,' Donald asserted, nodding towards Murdo and his son. 'Are you up for it Murdo?'

'Aye Mr Grant, you can depend on me.'

'Good, but you mustn't tell anyone what we've done mind. Not ever.'

'I know, I know,' came the hasty reply.

'What about you David?'

'Of course Father, looks like I'm up to my neck in it anyway.'

'Good lad.'

Callum fixed Donald with a sullen stare. 'Can I ask what exactly you intend doing with the bodies of these poor souls?'

'We'll find them appropriate resting places Callum. I'll even say a few words for them. Best you leave this to me, eh?'

Callum closed his eyes tightly and inhaled deeply. He opened them again, removed his glasses and massaged his nose. His silence confirmed his grudging acquiescence. He knew there was no other way.

'I'll speak to my sister's family up at the farm, *and* Lachlan Macdonald,' said Donald. 'They'll keep this to themselves, believe me.'

Alpin needed reassurance. 'The bodies of these Germans must

never be found Donald. You must be thorough. If not, this whole affair will come back to haunt us.'

'Aye, I know that Doctor Macrae, I'll sort it, believe me.'

'What about their car, what have you done with it?'

'I took it down the track into the woods by the castle. Everything we found lying about is in the boot.'

'Good,' said Alpin. 'Later tonight, the later the better, get the car away down the road towards Invertulloch. You know where the cliffs drop away into the loch, close by the road?'

'Aye, I know the place,' said David.

'Put all the items you've found; guns, clothing whatever, into the boot, and push it into the loch. It's very deep there, so it should sink quickly.'

Donald turned to his son. 'We'll go after midnight, just to be sure nobody's about. I'll drive the car and you can follow me in the truck, David.'

'Where's your rifle Donald?'

'Back in the house, Alpin.'

'That's good. Just in case it's needed as evidence. Give it a good wipe down and then make sure David's had his hands all over it. Yours too I would suggest. They can check for fingerprints these days.'

'Is that likely, Alpin?' said Anna, looking concerned.

'Don't worry Anna, it'll be alright. Better to think of everything though, don't you think?'

Donald placed an arm around Isobel. 'We can get through this,' he declared, eyeing each of the parties around the table in turn. 'Now, is everyone in full agreement with this?' They all nodded. Some murmured "aye" as they nervously exchanged glances with their co-conspirators.

'Callum?' Donald singled out the priest for special attention.

'Aye, of course Donald. I just hope you know what you're doing.'

'Anna, you'd better tell Max what's going on,' said Alpin. 'I'll wait until three o'clock, then I'll call Davie.'

Callum wanted the last word. 'One last thing, Alpin. What if that submarine makes it home? The crew must have witnessed everything. Surely there'll be repercussions from the Germans as to the treatment of their men?'

'Well they're hardly going to call the police here are they Callum? To put it simply, their attempt to rescue their prized U-boat commander has failed catastrophically. The circumstances of it are irrelevant. Making a big deal of it wouldn't exactly be a propaganda coup for them would it? No, my guess is that they will bury the whole affair.'

'Umm, you seem very confident Alpin, but I suppose you have a point.'

Chairs scraped across the flagstones as the little group prepared to leave. Callum fumbled in his pocket for his briar pipe and headed for the door.

Anna, Ursel and Isobel crowded into the little room that once had been Dugald's. Max had not moved; he lay with his head resting upon clasped hands, staring dreamily at the ceiling. When the women knocked and entered, he raised his head and smiled. 'A deputation, should I be concerned?'

Anna shook her head. 'No of course not, Max. We just wanted to tell you what we've decided to do.'

The two younger women sat down on the side of the bed whilst Anna preferred to stand. Max listened as Alpin's plan was explained to him. When they had finished, he looked from one to the other, his clammy brow deeply furrowed, apprehension present in his eyes. 'Are you sure this will work? It will put you all at risk.'

'Nonsense,' Anna replied dismissively. 'We live in the middle of nowhere. If anyone can get away with it, we can. The thing is, we can't afford for it not to work.'

Isobel took his hand. 'If we don't do this, you will end up in a prison camp somewhere, and possibly tried for what happened to the soldiers on the train and, well, let's just say I could be in a lot of trouble for shooting Dugald.'

'Rubbish,' protested Max. 'You were just defending me.'

'Yes, but can we take the chance that a court would see things from our perspective, Max? It's too much of a risk.'

'She's right,' Anna concurred. 'For Isobel to have any defence at all, we'd obviously have to disclose the fact that Dugald intended to shoot you in cold blood, *and* that he'd already shot your friend. If we had to, then so be it. But ideally we'd rather that didn't happen. The ignominy we feel as a result of our son's wicked deeds is distressing enough without having to share the experience with the entire country.'

'Well if you think it's for the best,' Max replied.

'We do think it's best,' said Ursel as she swept her long auburn hair back across her shoulder.

'What about you?' Anna enquired. 'If we were to try to keep you here with us, would you be happy with such an arrangement?'

'But of course, I could not think of anything better.'

'Would you not consider it your duty as an officer to try to return to Germany and take up the fight again?'

He laughed. 'Aunt Anna, I have done my duty already. There is nothing good about this war. Germany is bound to be defeated in time, now that the Americans have entered the conflict. I too feel ashamed of some of the things I have done, sending good men to their deaths for the sake of the Reich. I have lost my father to the futility of war, and now my brother too. Perhaps if I survived, that wouldn't be such a bad thing, especially in my mother's eyes.' He laid back, and grinned. 'Besides, it's unlikely I would get back to Germany in one piece. So far, no one else has, and I believe there was only one successful escape during the last war!'

'It may be difficult to begin with. You may have to spend a lot of your time in the house,' suggested Anna.

'I'm sure I'll survive,' Max replied. 'Anyway, I like it here with all of you.' He squeezed Isobel's hand. 'So why would I worry about being confined in this marvellous old house?'

'Good, that's decided then,' said Anna. 'You realise that even your mother will not be informed of your whereabouts for some time, perhaps for the duration of the war?'

'Yes, I understand that, but I suppose there's little choice.'

'We'll try to get word to her as soon as it's safe to do so.'

'What about my companions, Aunt Anna, what happens to them?'

'Donald will arrange burial somewhere, at least temporarily. It's not ideal. Perhaps we can make some more suitable arrangements later.'

Isobel was quick to add, 'You know they'll be treated with respect Max, and who knows, one day we can arrange for them to go home, wherever that may be.' She and Anna exchanged glances. They both sought vindication for their untruthfulness, and found it in each other's eyes.

'Perhaps I should be trying to get home just for them,' said Max, 'but you know, I have no urge to do so, now that I'm here. I've had enough.'

'Well you just rest, and recover quickly,' said Anna. She turned towards the door.

'What then? After I've recovered I mean?' Max called after her.

She looked back at him. 'We'll just have to wait and see. People around here know I'm Swiss; perhaps you could pose as a relative of mine, stranded in Britain. That wouldn't exactly be a lie… and people aren't going to disbelieve the minister's wife are they? We just need to have faith that we can pull it off.'

Max sunk back into the crisp linen pillow. 'Have you heard of the German poet Friedrich Schlegel, Aunt Anna?'

'No, I don't believe I have Max.'

'He once wrote, *"In life, every great enterprise begins with, and takes its first forward step in faith."* I've always remembered those words; they've inspired me on many occasions.'

'I'll bear Herr Schlegel's sentiments in mind,' she replied with a smile, and closed the door behind her.

Chapter Forty-One

The clock in the hallway had just chimed on the half hour. It was four thirty and snow was falling again. Large white flakes tumbled around the Manse, whispering faintly as they added to the lacy blanket that enshrouded the gravel driveway.

The muffled growl of an approaching motorcycle drifted towards Callum as he stood smoking his pipe by the front door. He watched from behind a haze of blue smoke as the source of the din emerged from the snow-flecked darkness. PC MacAllister, sitting astride his trusty Velocette motorcycle, turned gingerly onto the driveway. He was dressed in a bulky waxed jacket, its collar turned up against the cold. His uniform cap was secured around his well-insulated jowls by a shiny chin strap and his eyes obscured by bulky leather-trimmed goggles.

The motorcycle slowed to a halt close to where Callum was standing. The constable eased himself stiffly from the saddle and propped the machine up against the wall. He turned towards the minister and brushed away the snow that clung cape-like to his substantial shoulders. Gauntleted hands lifted the goggles above the peak of his cap, and he strode across to Callum, removing the gloves as he went.

'Hello Callum, what a terrible start to the New Year, I'm so sorry to hear of your loss.'

'Thank you Davie, come on in.' Callum ushered his visitor into the small porch and helped him off with his coat.

'And how is poor Anna coping?' MacAllister removed his cap and hung it on the hat stand.

'Och, she'll no doubt survive. We have no choice do we?'

'Aye, I suppose you're right there.'

The two men made their way slowly along the darkened corridor and into the kitchen where Anna was waiting with Alpin Macrae and Donald Grant. Greetings were exchanged, and the constable squeezed Anna's arm reassuringly before sitting down at the table.

'Tea, Davie?' Anna asked as she filled the kettle.

'Aye, that would be fine Anna, thank you.'

McAllister's numb fingers fumbled with the small silver button on the breast pocket of his tunic. 'Perhaps you could explain exactly what happened earlier today, Donald. I understand you were present when the tragic accident occurred?' He emphasised the word *accident*, as if to make the point that the jury was still out as far as that aspect of the incident was concerned.

Donald sat down nervously and waited. MacAllister, who'd now managed to release the button, pulled a battered notebook from his pocket and set it down on the table before him. Once the constable was prepared, pencil at the ready, he began to speak. 'Dugald spoke to me last night, along at the big house. He asked whether I'd be willing to accompany him up on the hill this morning...'

'On a stalking expedition?' MacAllister interjected.

'Aye, up on Beinn Caisteal. He always liked to bag a hind or two when he was home during the season. He'd not had the chance at Christmas, because the weather had been so poor, and his leave was coming to an end, so I agreed.'

'And Callum tells me you took your son David with you?'

'Aye, and Murchadh Stuart, one of the young ghillies on the estate.'

'So how did this terrible tragedy unfold then?'

Donald could sense the scepticism in the officer's voice. He wrung his massive hands together, unable to disguise his agitation. He knew how this would be seen in the constable's eyes, but hoped that MacAllister would regard it more as a sign of his distress at having to relive the event.

'We were climbing up to the summit crag, keeping close and in line. I was leading with Murchadh and Dugald was following behind. Young David was bringing up the rear, and carrying my rifle. We spotted a young beast up on the summit ridge and Dugald went for the shot. He missed, so he handed the rifle back to David. We continued the climb, and then I heard a bang. It was so loud, I almost fell over.'

'So you didn't actually see the shot being fired?'

'Well no, but I turned, and saw that Dugald was lying on his front and not moving. David was also lying on his front with the rifle next to him. He was sobbing.'

'What did you do then?'

I went over to Dugald and saw he'd been shot in the back. He was clearly dead. David said the gun just went off when it hit the rock beneath him.'

MacAllister looked across at Anna, who was wiping away a tear from the corner of her eye. 'I'm so sorry about this, but I have to ask these questions I'm afraid.'

'Don't worry,' said Anna, sniffing back the tears. 'You have to do your job, I know that.'

MacAllister turned back to Donald. 'So you're saying that the gun went off accidentally when David fell, is that correct?'

'Aye, that's correct Davie.'

'Umm I see, and this gun, it appears to have been loaded, yes?'

'Aye, David wasn't aware at the time, but Dugald must have fed another round into the breech before handing it back to him, I assume in readiness for his next shot.'

'And did the rifle have a safety catch?' The constable tapped his pencil on the cover of the notebook that, so far, had remained unopened.

'It did, on the cocking piece, but it must have been off. David assumed Dugald would have put it on, before handing it to him.'

'I'll have to ask David about that, but it all seems a wee bit careless if you don't mind me saying so.'

465

Donald nodded. 'Aye, I can't argue with that. David should have checked, but to be fair Dugald was normally very careful.'

Then Callum spoke. It wasn't something his co-conspirators would ever have expected, but his words certainly had an impact. 'Dugald had been drinking heavily the night before, Davie. He shouldn't have been up on that hill this morning, and I would have told him if I'd known he was going, but he was a stubborn young devil, and would have probably ignored me anyway. Personally, I'm not surprised he'd cut corners on that shoot. That was the way he'd do things. It's just a shame that David and Donald now have this on their conscience.'

MacAllister took a second to digest the minister's words. 'I see… perhaps his judgement had been somewhat impaired, especially if he'd been celebrating the night before. Dugald certainly liked his whisky. I discovered that myself only a few days ago!'

'Aye he did that,' said Callum. 'I always feared it would be his downfall one day, and so it has been.'

The constable turned back to Donald. 'And did the laddie seem, *in control* shall we say, when you left this morning?'

'Aye, I believe so.' Donald desperately wanted to build upon Callum's good work. 'He wasn't looking his best, that's for sure, but who does after Hogmanay?'

'Well, I suppose it's advisable to make the most of it whilst you're young enough. Mrs MacAllister and I were tucked up in bed well before the clock struck twelve.' His attention returned to the matter in hand. 'Do you have the rifle handy, Donald?'

'Aye, it's down at Seal Cottage. I can take you along to see it if you like?'

'That would be grand, and is David at home the now?'

'I told him to wait there, aye.'

'Then we'll go along shortly so that I can hear his account. And young master Stuart, where will I find him?'

'He'll be along at his father's croft, Taigh na Beinne, by the Invertulloch road just beyond the big house.'

466

'Right, I'll just make note of our conversation here and then perhaps I could view the body, Doctor Macrae?'

'Certainly Davie, he's been laid out in the scullery.' Alpin, eager to get on with the viewing, headed towards the closed door.

MacAllister was in no hurry though. '…And Donald, for my notes, when exactly did this accident occur?'

'Midday, or thereabouts,' Donald lied.

'When did you arrive back here with the body?'

Donald looked around at Anna, seeking her input. 'Just before Callum telephoned you,' said Anna. 'It must have been just a few minutes before.'

MacAllister referred to his notebook. 'Just before *four* then?'

'Aye,' said Callum. 'That'll be about right.'

'I have to say, you seemed remarkably in control when you telephoned, all things considered.'

'I tend not to display my grief openly, Davie. I've had a lot of practice when it comes to hiding my feelings about things.'

The constable eyed him warily. 'Is that so Callum?' He snapped his notebook shut, and got up. 'Lead the way Doctor,' and he followed Alpin into the scullery.

The room was cold. Ice had formed on the inside of the little window over the sink and the wind groaned around the ill-fitting external door. Dugald's body was covered by a crisp white sheet that draped over the sides of the bleached wooden table upon which he lay. The edges of the sheet wavered gently in the draught. For some reason, the scene reminded MacAllister of the photographs he'd seen of King George the Fifth lying in state, but a good deal less grandiose of course.

Alpin whipped back the sheet to reveal Dugald's pale, expressionless face. He'd been stripped to his underwear and the ragged bloody exit hole to the centre of the chest was immediately evident. 'He was clearly shot from some range, certainly greater than a couple of feet.' Alpin heaved the corpse onto its side and pointed to the smaller entrance wound. 'There's evidence of abrasion around

467

the rim here, where the skin is temporarily overstretched, together with some minor tearing of the wound edges. I've seen this before, when soldiers have been shot from considerable range by a sniper, for example. There's no evidence of powder deposition or searing, which is usually present on close range wounds of less than two feet.'

'What about the exit wound?' MacAllister asked.

Alpin returned the body to its previous position. 'Aye, it's not pretty. What I'd expect though.'

The constable leaned forward to examine the wound. It certainly wasn't pretty. Remnants of skin tissue clung to the clotted blood that had congealed within the gaping crevice. 'Looks more like a large knife wound than a bullet hole,' MacAllister remarked.

'That's because the bullet has been deflected from its course by bone and internal organs. Hence the exit wound occurring in this area of the chest. I'd say there's been massive internal damage done in there.' Alpin pulled up the sheet. 'He's quite stiff now, probably more so than he would've been, had he not been climbing a mountain in freezing conditions at the time of death.'

'I see, so that accelerates rigor mortis does it?'

'It can do, as does the deceased's age, sex and physical stature.'

MacAllister scrawled in his notebook before glancing up again. 'Is it possible that part of the bullet could still be present in the body, doctor?'

'It's not *impossible*, but improbable I'd say. The exit wound may have been partly caused by bone fragments but, in my experience, the type of .303 round used in rifles such as Donald's tend not to shed fragments.'

'And would you say this wound is consistent with such a bullet?'

'Aye, I would, I've seen many wounds like these; the work of a Lee-Enfield .303.'

'What about time of death, would that be consistent with Donald's account?'

'It's difficult to be exact, just from examining the body like this, but I would consider the time of death to have been less than eight hours.' He swallowed hard as the lie slipped from between his lips.

MacAllister looked across at the neat stack of military uniform that lay on a nearby chair. 'I assume they are Dugald's?'

'They are. I take it you'll be wanting to take them with you?'

'No, not on the motorcycle, but leave them here please and they'll be collected. I'll just note down what's here for the time being. Strange, he was wearing this up on the hill?'

'Not really, probably the warmest clothes he's got, especially the greatcoat, and he never wore anything other than the kilt.'

'Aye I suppose so, these soldier laddies are never out of uniform these days.'

Whilst MacAllister sorted through the clothing, checking for any additional signs of violence, Alpin asked; 'So what happens now then?'

MacAllister didn't look up. 'I'll go along and have a look at the rifle and speak to the other witnesses of course. Then I'll head off and make some telephone calls. The body will need to be removed to the mortuary for a post mortem. Then I'll be making my report to the fiscal, and we'll see what happens from there.'

'I see.' Alpin needed to know what conclusions the constable had drawn from his enquiries so far, and thereby gain some indication of what the report might infer. 'Do you think it will be a protracted investigation? I'd hate for Anna and Callum to be unduly prevented from burying their son.'

MacAllister returned his notebook to his tunic pocket. 'Between you and me Doctor, I don't consider there to be any aspects of this terrible incident that would prevent the prompt release of the body. I will need to speak to the other laddies without delay, but the circumstances as they've been reported, and the people involved, hardly give me cause for suspicion.' He leant forward and grinned. 'Unless you believe otherwise, of course?'

'Och no, Davie. I fully concur with your assessment. It's just such a terrible situation to be in, that's all.'

MacAllister made for the door. 'Leave it to me Doctor. I'll get the formalities completed just as soon as I can.'

Having explained to the Mathesons what action he'd be taking when he returned to the police office at Camuscraig, he shook everyone's hand once again. Then he donned his leather coat and cap, before following Donald out into the snow.

When the front door had closed, Ursel and Isobel emerged from Max's room, where they'd been listening at the door. They found Anna and Callum sitting at the table with Alpin. 'How did it go?' Ursel asked.

'He seemed satisfied with our explanation,' said Alpin.

'That's a relief, so what happens next?'

'We wait, and hope that the pathologist and the procurator fiscal see the incident in the same context as Davie MacAllister appears to have done.'

The constable's interrogation of David Grant had not been the solicitous event that Donald had anticipated. His son had been asked to give his own account of the shooting; an account that David had clearly rehearsed, as the fluidity of his story telling had left Donald wondering whether the event had in fact actually taken place. Fortunately, Murchadh had been visiting Seal Cottage when the constable arrived. He sat and listened whilst MacAllister recorded David's version of events. The constable clearly had no inclination to speak to the two ghillies separately.

Once satisfied with David's explanation, he turned to Murchadh, merely asking whether he had anything to add. Having scribbled more notes in his little book, he rose to leave. Morag offered him more tea, but he declined. Then Donald followed this up with the temptation of something a little stronger. This too was declined, but only after some thought. 'I can think of nothing better Donald,' he said, nodding towards the raging peat fire. 'No, Mrs MacAllister will have my tea on the table, so I'd better get on my way. Do you have the rifle for me, Donald?'

Donald duly collected the rifle from the cupboard in the kitchen. He handed it to the constable, still contained within its carrying case. 'When do I get it back, Davie? It's just that I need it for work.'

The constable slung the weapon over his shoulder. 'I'll return it just as soon as I can Donald. Don't you worry.'

The two men went to the door where MacAllister, content that he was out of earshot of anyone else, turned to Donald. 'I have to say to you Donald, I'm not happy that this here rifle was used in such an ill-considered, if not reckless manner up on that hill. I fully expect the fiscal to take dim view too. You know that?'

'I know, I know Davie, I'll speak to David and you have my assurance we'll keep to the rules in future.'

'You do that, Donald.' He moved closer, and half-whispered in the stalker's ear. '...Or you'll be stalking with just your wee telescope in future.' He descended the steps to the path before looking back. 'By the way, you have nae seen any strangers around the village recently by any chance?'

Donald shook his head. 'No, why do you ask?'

'I've been asked to look out for a *POW* who's on the run from a train over Inverness way. It happened sometime last night. I can tell you, I certainly won't forget this Hogmanay in a hurry!'

'Surely it's unlikely he'll head this way?'

'Aye, you're probably right, but no harm in mentioning it though.'

'I'll let you know if I see anyone, Davie. Goodnight to you.'

The policeman raised an arm in acknowledgement as he headed for his motorcycle.

Donald closed the door and returned to the little sitting room. 'That went better than I thought,' he smiled.

'I can't believe he didn't want to question Murchadh,' said David.

'I can,' said Donald. 'The fat wee feller wanted away for his tea!'

471

2 0 0 9

Chapter Forty-Two

'...And did the procurator fiscal accept the explanation given to PC MacAllister?' Neil asked.

'Well yes, he did,' said Isobel. 'Davie knew the community well. He may not have been considered the brightest star in the sky, but the powers that be certainly respected the opinion of the village policeman in those days. There was no reason to doubt what the witnesses had said, and I'm sure his report reflected that.'

'What about the pathologist. Did his findings tie in with Alpin Macrae's?'

'It would seem so. We were a wee bit worried about the discrepancy in the timings, but no one ever questioned them.'

'So Alpin's plan worked without a hitch then?'

'Absolutely. The formalities were completed quite quickly, and we were told to go ahead with the funeral the following week. It was the Wednesday as I recall.'

The sun had at last burnt off the remaining stubborn cloud, and was now streaming through the sitting room window. A shaft of light, laden with tiny dust particles, fell directly upon Isobel's face, highlighting the lines that creased her cheeks and exposing the finger marks on the lenses of her glasses. 'Pull that curtain dear,' she asked Jeanne, raising a hand to shield her eyes. Whilst her daughter complied with the request, Neil continued with the questions.

'Perhaps this is a good time to return to the agent, *Phoebus*. Tell me how he came to be buried in Dugald's grave?'

Isobel lowered her hand. 'My father was adamant that the man known as *Phoebus*, and Jürgen Reiniger, should be buried somewhere secure once and for all... somewhere where they'd never be found. He didn't want to discuss the subject in much depth, and preferred to keep things very much to himself, probably to keep Callum off his back. My uncle certainly wouldn't have gone along with the plan! I know that Father was deeply concerned that if he didn't remove all trace of them properly, and the corpses were eventually found, both shot, then all sorts of attention would be focussed on Glendaig.'

'It seems he was right,' said Jeanne, with a hint of sarcasm.

Isobel ignored her daughter's comment and went on. 'You see, he was never convinced that everyone would maintain their silence if the bodies were found, so he had this idea; that to dig deeper into Dugald's grave and place the other two corpses in, just before the funeral, would be the best option.'

'Did your father tell you this himself?' said Neil.

'No, David told me. Like I said, my father wanted to keep the locations of the bodies to himself. In his view, the fewer people who knew, the better. He warned David and Murdo never to disclose their intentions, but I eventually made David tell me. It was sometime later though.'

'Clearly, not everything went to plan then?'

'No, the night before Dugald's funeral, Father went down to the church with David and Murdo. It was very late, so as not to be disturbed. Together, they dug the grave to a much deeper depth than Willie Craig, the local gravedigger had initially done. The plan was to lower the two bodies in, then cover them with planks of wood and then soil. Anyway, once the grave had been prepared, he sent David and Murdo back to the beach in the little truck that they used on the estate. They were to collect the two bodies and take them back to the graveyard. They would then be buried, and that would be it, hidden for all time.'

476

'What went wrong?'

'Davie MacAllister, that's what went wrong!'

'You mean PC MacAllister turned up unannounced when Murdo and your brother were down by the beach...?'

'You know?'

'Aye, I've seen his pocket notebook entry for that night. Obviously, when I read it I didn't realise the significance of it, but please carry on.'

'Well, Davie got a call down to Glendaig House, to look for some poachers apparently. He must've been on his way home and came across David and Murdo by the roadside with the truck.'

'That's right, it was just before half past eleven.'

'Aye, well, the boys had just loaded the agent, *Phoebus*' body onto the truck, and covered it with a tarpaulin. They were just about to go back for the second body when Davie turned up and spoke to them. They were lucky, because he was in his car that night, rather than the motorcycle. They didn't initially realise it was him you see. I think they told him they'd been over to Camuscraig for a night out and had stopped to relieve themselves, something like that. Anyway, he must've believed them and let them go on their way. He didn't go though and stood by his car smoking his pipe. He said he was going to stay in the area for a while... in case the poachers returned I imagine.'

'So what did David and Murdo do?'

'They took the agent's body back to the graveyard and buried it as planned. Then they drove back to collect the other body just after midnight, expecting Davie to have gone.'

'But he hadn't had he?'

'No, thankfully David had the foresight to stop the lorry some way off and check on foot. The constable's car was still there with Davie inside, sound asleep, so they abandoned the idea, and returned to tell Father what had happened.'

'Did they make any further attempts to collect Reiniger's body?'

'Certainly not that night. I got the impression they were

concerned that Davie was a little suspicious of what they were up to. The risk was too great.'

'Go on.'

'David told me he returned to the beach early the next day to make sure the body was properly buried in the sand, but it was too late to move it to Dugald's grave.'

'He obviously didn't do that good a job, because one of the hands had become exposed somehow. It could have been like that for years, and was only spotted by chance by some hill walkers who'd ventured onto the beach looking for a cairn on the island.'

'It's just a shame Davie wasn't on his motorcycle,' said Isobel. 'Otherwise, all would have gone as it should have done... and perhaps we wouldn't be having this conversation.'

'Most unfortunate,' Neil replied, with a hint of sarcasm. 'Was there not a *Plan B* or something, to bury Reiniger I mean?'

'This sounds awful, but I believe the plan was to wait for the next burial in the graveyard and attempt the same thing. Unfortunately, no one obliged by dying... not until 1948, when Willie Craig himself was buried there! It's a very small community, Glendaig, as you know.'

'So Reiniger remained where he was then?'

'Aye, and as time went by, the will, and I suppose the courage to move him, slowly waned. Father felt it best to leave things as they were and just check the site from time to time.'

'Didn't any of your so called co-conspirators ask any questions as to where the bodies were buried? What about you Max? After all Reiniger was your friend wasn't he?'

Max raised his hands in a gesture of helplessness. 'Of course I was interested, and yes, I did know where they were buried. I too visited the site on the beach until we moved here, so I can say with some confidence; the hand was not exposed initially. Then I became too old to get down that steep slope from the road. I just had to accept things as they were... for Isobel's sake.' He clasped his hands together on his knees and gazed down upon his shiny leather slippers. When he eventually looked up, he was visibly moved, his eyes moist with tears. 'I can only hope these two men can now be given a more appropriate resting place, it's been too long.'

'I'm sure that *will* happen in due course,' said Neil.

'No one else who had knowledge of the incident ever asked about the grave sites as far as I'm aware,' said Isobel. 'I think they just preferred to put the whole affair out of their minds.'

'We'll obviously need to confirm the whereabouts of this man *Phoebus*, and try to identify him. That'll no doubt mean that we'll have to apply for an exhumation order for Dugald Matheson's grave. The two of them can then be buried properly, and any living relatives can be informed.' As an afterthought, he decided to ask the question again. 'Have either of you *any* idea who this man *Phoebus* was?'

His question was greeted with the shaking of heads. 'I was only in his company for a very short time,' said Max. 'All I can tell you is that he was a small man in his mid-thirties, five feet six tall, something like that. He had a Scottish accent, not pronounced, more subtle. He spoke German fluently. Other than that, all I can tell you is what Jürgen told me.'

'Okay, and what did Jürgen say?'

Max trawled his memory for a second. 'I recall Jürgen saying that he came from somewhere near Dumfries, and his father was a schoolteacher. The father couldn't have been a very pleasant character because *Phoebus*, as I recall, told Jürgen that the old man almost threw him down the school well! Oh, and he used the name James something, *Chisholm* I think it was, but I assume that must have been false.'

'Okay, that's really useful, your memory certainly hasn't deserted you,' said Neil, busily making notes. 'Now let's go back to *you* Max. How did you keep you real identity under wraps, when you recovered from your injury I mean?'

Max was yearning to discuss this chapter in his life and sat forward, the faint origins of a proud grin beginning to form around the corners of his mouth. 'I was off my feet for a few weeks, and limited to the house. Then word was slowly circulated around the village that my Aunt Anna's cousin from Switzerland had come to stay. She came up with this very feasible cover story that I was a journalist working for a liberal-minded paper based in Zürich...' He shook his head, in mock disbelief of his own story. '...I'd apparently been relentless in my attempts to expose the Nazi regime for what they truly were, and had criticised the Swiss leadership for their collaboration with the Axis powers. So, having received numerous death threats, I decided to flee and stay with relatives in Scotland. It took me some time, but I managed to find my way across to Portugal, and eventually to Britain.' Now he laughed. It was a laugh that quickly mutated into a chesty cough, and he reached for a handkerchief to muffle the spasm. When he'd recovered, he smiled again. 'Ingenious don't you think? And everyone fell for it too. They even considered me something of a hero!'

'So only the immediate family knew the truth?'

'Yes, and Murdo of course. When I recovered from my injury I went out with Donald, helping him around the estate. He persuaded Sir Brodric to give me a paid position as a ghillie, and I took to the work like a duck to water, as you say over here.'

'You and Isobel must've seen a lot of each other then?'

'We became close friends, and not surprisingly a relationship blossomed,' said Isobel. 'We were, as you now know, *informally* married in August 1946. '

Max interposed. 'We took Isobel's name, *Grant*, even then, and moved into the old bothy on the McSweens' farm. Then Jeanne came along in 1948.'

'Surely eyebrows were raised when you used the name *Grant*, having apparently been married?'

'Not really, we used the excuse that it was probably better to do that than adopt a German-sounding name at the time, being so soon after the war.'

'And what name did you use when you first emerged from your convalescence?'

480

'Robert Eichel, Eichel being my aunt's maiden name.'

'Umm, I see. Understandable I suppose, and during all this time, no one suspected anything?'

'Not a thing,' said Isobel. 'We were amazed. No police came along asking questions, there was nothing in the papers; in fact we couldn't believe our luck. We can only surmise that the authorities thought Max had escaped and were too embarrassed to publicise the fact.'

Max returned his handkerchief to his pocket. 'As you may know the submarine sent to rescue me was attacked off the Cuillin Sound. It must have maintained radio silence as it was operating in British coastal waters, or perhaps the radio aerials were damaged. Whatever the case, it seems the story of what happened on that beach never reached German ears! They must have assumed that the operation had failed, and buried it for fear of it being used as a propaganda tool against them.'

Isobel wanted to continue the story of their life in Scotland. She fidgeted, waiting for Max to finish what he was saying, and ran her hands impatiently across the creases in her skirt. 'When Donald Grant retired in 1957, Murdo became Head Stalker on the estate, and Max became his deputy. They worked together for over twenty years until they both retired in early 1979. It was during that year, just after we'd returned from Switzerland, that the journalist fellow came around asking questions about an escaped prisoner of war living amongst the community. You can appreciate how nervous we became. Murdo was on edge all the time and kept asking if we'd heard anything. I'm afraid I upset him, told him to get a grip. He stormed off from me and things were never the same after that. Perhaps in hindsight my response was a wee bit heavy-handed, but the whole affair prompted us to move on and to live closer to Jeanne and the grandchildren.'

Neil placed his notebook on his lap. 'I suppose it was a good test of everyone's loyalty, this journalist appearing on the scene, asking difficult questions?'

'Aye, it was, but a worrying time all the same.'

Neil then changed tack. 'How did you maintain contact with everyone here in Glendaig after you moved away?'

'We came back on occasions to see people, but it was mostly by letter. Certainly Mary didn't have a phone at the time. My brother had moved to Camuscraig. Ursel moved to Inverness just after the war. Everyone else who'd had any involvement had died, either before or just after our move. My father had gone to live with my brother, until he died in 1980. We used to get the odd visit from David but then he was tragically killed in a car accident near Fortrose in 2000.'

'What about David's family; did they know about Max?'

Isobel shook her head vigorously. 'Oh no, his wife died in 2005 and his two sons moved away, one to Canada, and the other down to England. They never knew about what happened in Glendaig.'

'So really, it was just Mary and Murdo then?'

'Aye, that's right. We sent Murdo and Ursula a Christmas card each year, but never really socialised after we'd moved. Initially Ursel had Skye View Cottage as a holiday home, and we'd go back and spend the odd weekend with her and her husband. We were very close up until her death in 2004.'

Neil opened his briefcase, and took out a plastic evidence bag containing one of the coded envelopes he'd seized from Mary Galbraith's box. He got up and handed it to Isobel. 'So what about the code on the envelopes? Why go to all that trouble?'

Isobel studied the envelope then looked up, a wide grin spread across her face. 'How very perceptive of you Inspector! It was something of a private joke between Mary and I. When we left, around the time the journalist was hanging around the village, we discussed meeting up. Iain was always too busy and wouldn't bring her to us… not that we particularly wanted him to, because I could never trust him not to divulge our whereabouts. So Jeanne would either take me back to Glendaig, *or* collect Mary every so often for a visit. I was paranoid initially that no one should know in advance that we were going to meet, especially Iain. I even had a recurring dream that I'd arrived at Rowan Cottage to find a flock of journalists waiting for me. Silly really, but that's the way it was. Anyway, Mary joked that we should have a code to let her know when I was going to visit, or when she was invited over here. We'd just bought this place, and had researched the name. Max suggested it. I would enter the date of our proposed get together on the inside flap of the envelope, and the words *between the waters*, only if Jeanne was going to pick her up and bring her here. We'd always get to her, or collect her at around eleven in the morning, so no need to mention times. It worked very well until the mid-eighties when Mary got the phone installed.' She sat back and sighed. 'It all seems so juvenile now.'

'You see, your forbears may have cracked our enigma ciphers, but you couldn't crack my wife's,' said Max with a gleeful chuckle.

Neil retrieved the envelope and returned it to the case. 'Ah, but it did lead me to your front door, Max,' he retaliated as he sank back into his chair. 'So is there anyone else alive today, other than Mary Galbraith, who has knowledge of this story?' Neil asked.

The couple looked at each other, considering on the question carefully. Then Isobel shook her head. 'No there isn't anyone at all,' she said. 'I think it's fair to say that the secret was very close to being buried forever.'

'I'm afraid some of us just refuse to die,' said Max, 'and that's been our undoing I'm afraid.'

Jeanne had been silent, listening with interest to her parents' story. 'But wouldn't it have been a terrible shame Dad, if this story *had* been buried, from a historical perspective I mean?'

'That's debatable dear. I suppose some will find it of interest. Which is fine if we're left alone to get on with our lives, however long they may be!'

Neil lifted his case back onto his lap and flipped the catches. 'I've brought some items to show you Max, perhaps you can identify them?'

He threw back the flap, and delved into the case. His hand re-emerged clutching a bunch of plastic bags. He moved across to the sofa and squatted down beside the old man. 'These items were found amongst Jürgen Reiniger's remains, and these were given to me by Ursula Stuart.'

Neil gently placed the bags on the Max's lap. The old man picked up the bag containing the black cross with the oak leaf clasp. Having caressed the medal through the plastic he muttered to himself, 'My God, after all this time, *das Ritterkreuz mit Eichenlaub.* He looked up, visibly moved. 'Sorry,' he said, 'I never thought I'd see this again. It's the Knight's Cross with Oak Leaves. Perhaps I should be saying, *my* Knight's Cross with Oak Leaves! We used to call it the *blechkrawatte* or "tin necktie".'

'So you can identify this as yours, can you?'

Max turned the medal over. 'I believe I can, yes. It is in fact a copy. I purchased it from *Quenzer Und Klein*, the makers, for display on my service suit. The actual award was left with my mother.' He studied the rear of the medal. 'There is an *L* number somewhere, distinguishing the maker. Here it is, exactly as I remember it.' He examined the next bag containing the other cross. 'Ah, yes, this will be my Iron Cross First Class. This is a copy too.' Again, he turned it over. 'As you can see, it has a screw back fixing; this threaded tube was fixed onto the tunic with a round plate. We preferred these fixings on working uniforms, as they held the decoration more securely. Certainly, if you found these items with Jürgen then they are definitely mine, Inspector.'

Neil retrieved the bags and then replaced them with the bag containing the gold sleeve rings and the watch. 'What about these?' Neil asked.

'These are *ärmelstreifen,* the sleeve rings of a *korvettenkapitän*, and from my service suit jacket I would assume.'

'And what about the watch? Would this have belonged to Jürgen Reiniger?'

'It must have, because it isn't mine. These Hanhart watches were very popular with *Kriegsmarine* officers.'

'I understand they were particularly useful on U-boats, is that right?' Neil asked.

'You are absolutely correct, Inspector. You have indeed been doing your homework. Yes, their functions assisted officers with navigational calculations and those connected to the running times of torpedoes.' Max went on to confirm that the tattered fragment of wallet must have been Reiniger's, and that the buttons were, as previously suggested, German naval design from the wartime period.

Neil then showed him the medals that Ursula Stuart had given him. 'Do you recognise these items at all?'

'Well, the ribbon is that of the Iron Cross Second Class. It could have been mine I suppose, or it could have belonged to Jürgen. This one here is the Destroyer War Badge, definitely not mine, but Jürgen served on destroyers so I would guess this may have been his. Murdo must have taken these from Jürgen's tunic. He'd left it in the boot of the car. Then, when he was shot, I couldn't bear to see him just lying there, so I asked Isobel to cover him with my own jacket.'

Neil collected up the bags and returned to his chair. 'I have to say, I'm a little confused. How is it that we found your two crosses at the grave site? My understanding is that decorations, especially ones such as these, would've been removed when you were taken prisoner?'

'You are right Inspector, and they did remove my Spanish Cross and U-boat War Badge, because I'd left them on my tunic. They left the buttonhole ribbon of my Iron Cross Second Class, I suppose a ribbon isn't much use as a weapon eh?'

'So what about these crosses then how did you manage to retain these?' Neil raised the two bags, as if to jog Max's memory.

'I was lucky I suppose. Before I left the U-boat, I cut a small hole in the lining of my jacket and dropped them in. They were precious, and I didn't want them taken from me. I didn't really have time to secrete the others and besides, I didn't want them all clattering about, did I? Anyway, a boy rating searched me when I was taken aboard the British warship, and he missed them. He took all my other possessions from me; wallet, photographs, you name it. Amazingly after that time, when I was searched again on occasions, the crosses remained undiscovered. Of course, when I used the tunic to cover poor old Jürgen, they were still in the lining.'

'Ah, now it all makes sense,' said Neil.

'I feel sure we must have told you everything there is to tell,' said Isobel. She looked across at her husband, seeking his acquiescence.

He nodded. 'I can't think of anything else,' he confirmed. 'Do you have any other questions, Inspector?'

'Yes, I do as it happens,' said Neil. 'It's more of a history-based question if I'm honest.' He produced an ageing manila folder from his case and removed a batch of yellowing papers from within. 'This is the action report, submitted by the captain of the British destroyer *HMS Wareham*, the ship that engaged the U-boat U-500 on 21st December 1941. I believe you were aboard that submarine Max. Am I correct?

'You are correct, Inspector,' said Max as he accepted the folder from Neil.

'There is mention in these papers of a strange-looking contraption fitted to the U-boat, aft of the conning tower. It seems to have remained a mystery as to what exactly that contraption was. I'm hoping you can enlighten me?'

The old submariner scanned the pages of the report before answering. 'I'm sure I can,' he smiled. 'I find it hard to believe that the story has remained such a mystery as you put it, all these years.' He looked across at Neil, as if to anticipate the detective's reaction to the question that he himself was about to ask. 'Does the name *Paukenschlag* mean anything to you, Inspector? Loosely translated it means "Drumbeat".'

'Aye, it does. One of your countrymen, a naval historian, told me about it recently. It relates to an operation where a number of

U-boats headed across to the eastern seaboard of the USA, just after the Americans had entered the war at the end of 1941. I'm told they decimated US shipping because the Americans were utterly unprepared for such an attack.'

'Yes, your summary is essentially correct. It would have had even more of an impact than you describe, but Admiral Dönitz was not permitted to send the twelve boats he'd initially planned for. So it was going to be just six, but unfortunately one dropped out due to technical problems. Evidently, the historians have never discovered that there *was* indeed a sixth boat, prepared at Kiel for departure on 17th December. I was lucky enough to be invited to join the commander, my old friend Werner Hahn, and sail with this boat, the U-500, to take part in the *Paukenschlag* operation. I was on board merely as an observer, acting on behalf of my commanding officer, Admiral Ernst Von Thalberg. He wanted his own eyes and ears present on the operation not only to observe its progress, but also to evaluate the trial of some top-secret equipment that was being carried. Von Thalberg was not happy when I put myself forward to go. He knew that politically it was not a good move and that his superiors in Berlin would have been vehemently against the idea, but I was getting more and more fed up sitting behind a desk, and he knew it. So eventually he caved in, and let me go. I travelled to Kiel via Berlin on 14th December, and we sailed on 17th. Unfortunately things went a little wrong, as you will have read here, and I ended up a prisoner of your Royal Navy.'

'So what exactly was this top secret equipment then?'

'Patience Inspector, I'm just coming to that bit. Our scientists at the rocket research establishment at Peenemunde had for some time been developing the idea of mounting a rocket-based weapon on U-boats. That is no secret, and historians will tell you that Germany was engaged in such trials from the summer of 1942. What is not so well-known is that this project had, in fact, progressed to a stage where the *Oberkommando Der Marine*, the Naval High Command, wanted to commence combat trials. So U-500 was selected to carry a *Wurfgerät* rocket launcher mounted on her upper casing. The contraption could carry six thirty centimetre rockets, capable of being launched against sea and land targets from a depth of fifteen metres. Our brief was to sail into the harbour at New York together with U-123, Reinhard Hardegan's boat, and to engage targets on Manhattan Island. Hardegan, meanwhile, was to attack shipping in the harbour area.'

Jeanne gasped. 'That's shocking, the area would have been devastated.'

'I wouldn't use the word *devastated* Jeanne, not with six rockets. But the damage would have been significant within a small area around Manhattan's financial district.'

'…And the political damage immense,' Neil added, with a shake of the head.

'Exactly,' said Max. 'We knew the American people were not initially keen to get involved in a war with Germany. The view was that Roosevelt would have become nothing less than a pariah in the eyes of his voters following such an attack by U-boats.'

'I suppose this was Germany saying to the Americans; "you're not out of our reach",' suggested Neil.

'Exactly, and it almost worked. Hardegan *did* get into New York Harbour and sank a British tanker on his way out. Of course the damage to American coastal shipping was also severe.'

'So the loss of the U-500 prevented that additional punch, and consequently US opinion was never swayed,' said Neil.

'Exactly right, I was one of three survivors when she went down. One of the other men died shortly after being rescued and the third ended up in Canada, I believe. They wouldn't have been able to say much about the rocket trial because they just didn't know about it. The few members of the crew who did know, all went down with the boat.'

'It's a fascinating story. I suppose then, your commanders were very keen to get you back again, hence the rescue bid.'

'That's right,' Max agreed. 'I don't wish to sound at all conceited, but the reality was that at that time I was considered valuable as a propaganda tool, and a booster of public morale. I also had an in-depth knowledge of both *Paukenschlag* and the rocket programme, codenamed *Seeadler*.'

'And so when the rescue went wrong, your masters must have been more than willing to keep their mouths shut, in order to save face I suppose?'

'Of course, and it would have got the likes of Von Thalberg off the hook too. He would have been praying that the British didn't start boasting about their prize.'

Neil placed the manila folder back into his briefcase. 'Luckily for everyone's sake they didn't, but then again, who'd want to admit to capturing, and then losing, one of Germany's top U-boat aces?'

Isobel patted her husband's leg. 'Well it certainly turned out well for us, didn't it?'

'Am I right in saying that I'm the first person to hear all this; about the rocket trial and the attack on New York, I mean?'

'I suppose you are,' said Max without hesitation.

'And you've never contacted anyone in Germany since the end of the war, to let them know you're alive and well?'

'No, the risk would've been too great. If I became an item of interest, then the incident at Glendaig may have raised its head. We were still unsure as to the possible consequences, and of course Isobel may still have been at risk. My family were all gone by the end of the war. Mother in an air raid, brother killed in action. I only had a couple of distant cousins back in Switzerland.'

'Sorry to change the subject, but can you tell us what happens now Inspector?' asked Jeanne, almost interrupting her father.

Neil pursed his lips and exhaled deeply, considering his answer carefully. 'Firstly, I must submit a report once we've recorded all this officially. My senior officers and the Crown Office will consider the facts and make their decision. We're investigating a series of suspicious deaths here, however old they may be. Having said this, age does play a part, both yours and that of the event itself. There are also a host of other considerations relating to the public interest. My guess is, and it's only a guess at this stage, that we're unlikely to see any proceedings in this case.'

'That's reassuring,' said Jeanne with a sigh, 'and what about the press?'

'That's a more difficult question. This story is incredibly newsworthy and there's significant interest in it already. We'll have to disclose certain facts, of course. You can never underestimate the media I'm afraid and, to add to that, there'll be no shortage of interest from academics.'

'Well it's something we'll just have to live with, as long as Isobel here is protected from the press hounds,' said Max. 'Jeanne is right, it is time this story was at last told, if only for the sake of history.'

Neil glanced at his watch. 'I seem to have been here for hours. If you'd excuse me, I'd better be on my way.' He raised himself out of the chair, sensing the stiffness in his legs. 'Thank you both for confiding in me,' he said as he shook hands, firstly with Max, and then with an emotional Isobel.

'Thank you too Inspector,' Isobel replied. 'Max and I feel a great weight has been lifted from us today. We look forward to seeing you again.'

Having exchanged more pleasantries at the front door, Neil took his leave. He looked back from the gate and waved to the little group huddled by the door. 'Don't worry, I'll be in touch shortly.' The frail old couple, now unburdened of their secrets, waved back. It was a strangely synchronised gesture that made him smile. Then again, he thought, it was nothing more than he would've expected from two people such as these.

Chapter Forty-Three

Kirkallan, Dumfries And Galloway
Friday 3rd July

A gleaming new village name board heralded the end of a long drive and an early start. Neil had slipped out of the house in Culloden around five thirty and had commenced the long slog down the A9 to Perth. He'd forgotten how extensive a country his homeland was, but the journey was now almost over and his one remaining challenge was to locate the village school.

Kirkallan was a classic example of what geographers would call a linear settlement, with its brightly-painted cottages hugging the busy main road that ran through the village. The map here had remained unchanged for centuries, there being little new development beyond the Dumfries to Lockerbie road. Certainly there was nothing greater in stature than the school and the parish church, the stone tower of which peeped above the slate roofs, thereby maintaining a watchful eye on its "flock".

The school was situated in the very heart of the village. It was built in the classic Victorian style, and with similar materials to the church, all under a grey slate roof. The large casement windows, now replaced with PVC, were the only obvious sign of modernisation. Even these retained their original painted lintels, matching the large red front door. Behind the dry stone wall that enclosed the school grounds stood a purple sign informing visitors that this was Kirkallan Primary School, and the headmaster was Mr Malcolm Haugh BA.

Neil pulled into the small car park. He took in a deep lungful of fresh air as he at last emerged from the stuffiness of the car, before heading off along the path, following the sign to *Reception*.

Inside, the building had been stripped of its Victorian dreariness and now smelt of new paint. The atmosphere was further lightened by the distant sound of laughing children that drifted along the corridor.

'Can I help you?' A middle aged woman dressed in a smart two piece tweed suit had appeared from a nearby office. Above the door hung a wooden sign saying *Reception*. Neil produced his warrant card and introduced himself. 'I believe Mr Haugh is expecting me?'

'Oh yes of course Detective Inspector, follow me please.'

The receptionist marched off along the corridor, her arms swinging smartly by her sides. Neil followed at a distance reflecting on his own schooldays, when he recalled the receptionists had wielded far more power than even the headmaster!

The woman stopped at an open doorway and indicated to Neil that this was his destination. As he entered, a small man in his late forties with curly black hair and matching moustache was rising to greet him. 'Malcolm Haugh,' he boomed, as only a headmaster could. 'Welcome to Kirkallan. Goodness, you've had a long journey today.'

As they shook hands, Haugh turned to the woman who'd remained standing by the door. 'Can you bring us some coffee, Margaret? That okay with you, Inspector?'

'Aye, that would be fine, thank you,' said Neil, who'd been hanging out for a cup for the last fifty miles.

Haugh dropped back into his chair and observed Neil from behind the pile of exercise books that teetered on the edge of his beech wood desk. 'Sit down Inspector, please. Tell me how we can assist with your enquiries. I believe you're trying to trace someone locally. Am I correct?

'Aye, that's right,' said Neil. 'I'd better explain, I'm afraid it's a wee bit complex.'

The headmaster sat silently, hanging on Neil's every word as he summarised the investigation at Glendaig and why his enquiries had led him to Kirkallan. When he'd finished, Haugh let out a little whistle. 'Whoa, that's some story Inspector, so you're trying to identify this mystery man known as *Phoebus*?'

'Well, we've applied for an exhumation order so that we can recover his remains. Naturally, I'd like to identify him, if I can.'

'Of course, and I assume you must have some information to suggest that he came from around here?'

'We believe his father was a village schoolteacher from somewhere near Dumfries.'

'Well there are over a hundred schools in this region Inspector, and that's not taking into account the considerable number which have closed since the war.'

Oh, I understand that Mr Haugh, it's just that your old school house appears to be the only one that has a well in the grounds!'

Haugh nodded in agreement. 'Aye we do, but are you sure *ours* is the only school around her that can boast such a feature?'

'So it seems, according to the lady at the Education Department in Dumfries. She was saying what a headache it was getting the thing capped to comply with health and safety regulations.'

'That's certainly true,' Haugh agreed, 'and if it's the lassie I'm thinking of, she's been working in that office since the beginning of time, so I think she'd know if this was the only such well.'

'That's just what *she* said,' confirmed Neil with a grin.

Haugh leant across to his right, disappearing briefly beneath the desk. He reappeared holding a large leather-bound ledger, liberally caked in dust. 'I got these out in case they'd be helpful. They're the old school registers dating back to the 1890s.' He prised opened the volume, releasing a small cloud of dust from between the pages. 'Let's see, this one covers 1899 to 1901. What year were you thinking of?'

'I believe the man was in his mid-thirties, so how about 1910 as a starting point? I doubt he would have been at school before then. In fact, even that date may be a little early!'

'Okay.' Haugh placed the register back on the floor. The curly black hair bobbed about behind the desk for a couple of seconds before his flushed face appeared again. 'Here we are, 1911 to 1913. Let's have a look see.'

He opened the register and scanned the pages cursorily before turning them. 'Interesting,' he muttered as he sampled a page towards the end of the volume. 'The teacher during this period was a chap called Richard Wallace Balfour. I actually recall his name because he supposedly ran the school here for a considerable period of time, up to the end of the war as I recall. But look here, in the summer of 1912 there's a boy registered at the school by the name of *Harold Balfour*. Richard's son perhaps?' He spun the register around and lifted it over the clutter for Neil to see.

The page had been completed in immaculate copperplate. The entry was dated Monday 15th July 1912, and followed by twenty names. At the bottom of the list was *Harold Balfour*, followed by the teacher's signature, *Richard Wallace Balfour*. 'I suppose it's entirely feasible that Richard would have been teaching his own children?' enquired Neil.

'In those days, without a doubt. There was little choice in a village this size and with only one teacher available.'

Margaret's footsteps could now be heard echoing along the tiled floor of the corridor. She appeared through the doorway and distributed mugs of coffee to the two men. As she placed a plate of biscuits on the desk Haugh said, 'Now, Margaret will know about this Mr Balfour. She knows everything there is to know about the history of this school!'

Margaret stood back, the tray held protectively against her substantial chest. Her features had now softened, pleased to be valued by the head and included in the discussion. 'You mean the teacher, Mr Balfour?'

'Aye, Richard Wallace Balfour, what do you know about him Margaret?' Haugh looked up at her, wide-eyed, as he selected a biscuit.

Margaret inhaled deeply, as if in preparation for a prolonged speech. 'Richard Wallace Balfour was teacher at this school from 1905 until the end of 1944, when he retired to a cottage down in the village. He was the longest-serving teacher to have taught here. In fact, he spent his entire teaching career at this school.'

'Poor bugger,' Haugh remarked, between mouthfuls of biscuit. 'I don't know how he did it.'

Margaret frowned, displeased by either his use of words or, more probably, his interruption. She smiled condescendingly and went on. 'When he retired, the school sports day team cup was named after him. It still resides in the cabinet in my office.'

'Well, I didn't know that,' said Haugh genuinely surprised.

'Then you should look more closely Headmaster, but I do concede that it hasn't been used at such events since the sixties.'

'What about his family?' Neil asked. 'Do you know anything about his personal life?'

Margaret resumed her lecture. 'He was married to a woman from Castle Douglas and they had two children, a boy and a girl.' Then, at last, came the information he'd been hoping for. 'His granddaughter Emily Irving still lives in the village. She's in her mid-seventies now.'

'Is she from the son's side, or the daughter's?'

'The daughter's I believe.'

'Do you know where Emily lives, Margaret?'

'Aye, of course I do Inspector, you turn right from the school, back through the village and past the inn, *The Bonnie Moorhen*. You'll see a wee house on the same side as the inn with grey harled walls; that's her place.'

Twenty minutes later, Neil was parking his car directly outside the newly harled house. The name *Ballochmyle* was displayed on slate beside the wrought-iron gate, from which a crazy-paved path led to the front door. Either side of the path were two neatly mown lawns.

Both were sharply edged, with borders containing impeccably sieved soil and a variety of flowering heathers.

Neil heard the doorbell ring within the house but heard no movement. He rang again and there was still no answer. Frustrated, he turned away, seeking the car keys he'd dropped into his jacket pocket. Then, to his relief, he heard the door open behind him. He turned to see a tall slim woman, seventy something but well-preserved for her age, wearing an apron coated in flour. She wiped her hands on a tea towel and produced a disarming smile. 'Sorry about that. I was busy baking, and had the radio blaring.'

Neil retraced his steps, and introduced himself. 'Could I spare a minute of your time? I wanted to ask you about your Uncle Harold Balfour? I believe he *was* your uncle?'

The woman seemed surprised. She brushed away the strand of mousy blonde hair that lay draped across her left eye and squinted at him. 'You mean my mum's brother Harold?'

'Aye, I believe so Mrs Irving.'

She ushered him inside. 'You'd better come in then, I'm intrigued.'

He was taken through to a large newly-fitted kitchen, strewn with the paraphernalia of baking. The oven hummed in the corner as Emily Irving removed her apron and sat down at the large pine table, directly opposite Neil.

'Margaret along at the school tells me your grandfather was the local school teacher for many years?'

'Aye that's true enough.'

'And he had two children; your mother, and a son called Harold?'

'That's right, but I never met Uncle Harry as he was called. I was only two when he went missing at the beginning of the war.'

'*Missing* you say? Have any of your family heard of him since then?'

'Certainly none of the family. It was always thought he'd settled in Ireland, but we can't be sure. Funnily enough one of my mother's friends seemed to think she'd seen him several years ago walking around the village, as if he was looking up his old haunts, but I'm not so sure.'

'You didn't believe this friend then?'

'Och no, she was away with the fairies that one! So what's your interest in my colourful uncle, Inspector?'

'I'll try and keep this brief,' said Neil, and commenced yet another retelling of the Glendaig story. By the time he'd finished, an expression of enlightenment had crept across Emily's face. It wasn't exactly the reaction he'd expected, but hoped against hope that this was indeed a positive sign.

'So you think Uncle Harry was a German spy, do you?' Emily questioned.

'What do *you* think?' Neil replied.

'I think you're probably right. I don't know much about him, but my mother certainly told me enough. Would you like a cup of tea?'

'No, thanks I've just had one up at the school. So what do you know about your uncle?'

'Wait a second,' she said, raising a finger and disappeared into the hallway, returning a minute or so later with a large photo album. She laid it on the table in front of Neil and stood by his shoulder, flipping through the leaves. Eventually she stopped at a page covered in black and white holiday snaps. She tapped one of them with her finger. 'That's him there, on holiday at Brighouse Bay in the early twenties. He must have been in his mid-teens by then.'

'He's not, how shall I put it...'

'You mean he's *puny*, Inspector?'

'Well, perhaps that's a bit strong...'

'You'd be right though. My mother always used to say he was undernourished. She must have been blessed with *his* height as well as her own. Anyway, that's the only photo I have of him, apart from a couple of posed baby shots with his parents.' She sat down again and pulled out a folded sheet of paper from the back of the album.

497

'So why am I inclined to think Uncle Harry was a German spy? Have a read of this.'

Neil took the document from her and unfolded it. He quickly realised that it contained a handwritten biography of her uncle. It was more than he could have hoped for... and the little fellow was certainly a colourful character it seemed!'

'Where on earth did you get this, Mrs Irving?'

'From my mother, bless her. I asked her to write down all she knew about her relatives whilst she still remembered everything. I'm a bit of a genealogist you see, and was researching our family tree with my son at the time this was written.'

Neil read the notes again, during which time Emily sat patiently thumbing through the photo album.

Harry James Balfour did indeed attend the local school, and was taught by his father, who appeared to be every bit the tyrant that he'd been portrayed as to Reiniger. Young Harry never saw eye to eye with him, but there could be no doubt that Richard had prepared his son well for an academic life beyond Kirkallan.

At eighteen, Harry initially went off to university in Edinburgh to study languages, and then in the mid-twenties travelled to Heidelberg in Germany to study politics and German at the city's ancient university. Having graduated, he remained an employee of the university until around 1933 when, through contacts in the academic world, he was offered a post as translator at the German embassy in London. For a time he was personal translator to the then ambassador, Leopold Von Hoesch. Then after Von Hoesch's untimely death, his employment there continued during the run up to war under the notorious Joachim Von Ribbentrop.

During his time in Heidelberg, Harry met and fell in love with a fellow student; an Austrian called Teresa Haas whom he married in London in 1934. The couple lived in west London, choosing to remain there when war broke out in 1939. Initially they retained their liberty, Teresa having been categorised as a category B alien requiring supervision only, but in 1940 after the failure of the

Norwegian campaign, things changed. Spy fever had spread throughout Britain, and enemy aliens were then considered in a different light. Harry and Teresa were both arrested and interned. Initially they were both sent to the Isle of Man. From there, Teresa was deported to Australia on the liner *Eidothea*. Tragically, she appeared to have died from pneumonia during the voyage. Meanwhile, Harry remained on the Isle of Man, moving from camp to camp. Then in September 1940, having been told that he was due to depart for Canada, he somehow managed to escape, never to be seen or heard of again, by anyone!

'So you see Inspector, good old Uncle Harry was definitely a prime candidate for recruitment as a spy!'

'There's a lot of detail here, did your mother remember all this herself?'

'I'm afraid not, it would've been a damn sight cheaper if she had. No, it's amazing what you can find out, certainly if you're prepared to flash your credit card about to the right people.'

'I'm sure. So I wonder why they didn't return to Germany when diplomatic relations were suspended in 1939. Surely they would have been better off there?'

'Because Inspector, Teresa Haas was a Jew. Germany was not a good place to be at that time if you were a Jew. Things weren't much better for her here because the British authorities had no interest in the religious or spiritual backgrounds of these people. To them they were enemy aliens; nothing more, nothing less.'

'I see, and why was Harry interned? He was British after all.'

'We can only assume it was because of his connections with the German embassy, perhaps his political views were of concern, who knows?'

'How did he escape, do you know?'

'The staff at the Manx Museum told us he was being taken to hospital for something or another. He climbed through a toilet window on the first floor and scaled down a drainpipe. The theory was that he managed to get off the island, probably to southern

Ireland. There were always fishing boats coming and going from the other side of the Irish sea apparently.'

'Do you think I could borrow that photograph for a while Mrs Irving? I'd really like to show it to someone.'

'Be my guest.' She eased the photo from its sticky mounts and handed it to Neil. 'Good luck with your enquiries, Inspector. In a way I hope it is him; no one likes a mystery do they? Certainly not within their own family.'

'There is something else you can do for me that may help confirm things one way or the other,' said Neil tentatively.

'Anything to help, you only have to ask.'

'Can you provide me with a DNA sample, just a mouth swab? It may assist us.'

'Of course, help yourself.'

Having completed the formalities with the sample, and been furnished with a copy of Harold Balfour's biography, Neil stepped out of the front door into the bright summer afternoon. The comforting sound of bees filled the warm air as they hummed around the hanging baskets suspended from the porch. Neil swatted one of the insects away as he skipped down the steps by the front door. 'This is probably a long shot, Mrs Irving, but the German agent I was talking about; he used the name *James Chisholm* on at least one occasion. Does that name mean anything to you?'

Emily leant against the door frame and pursed her lips, searching her memory for any trace of the name. 'No Inspector, nothing comes to mind. Sorry.'

'Okay, and what about *Phoebus*? We think that was his German code name.'

On hearing this, her eyes widened and she let out a little laugh. Then, pointing along towards the pub sign further along the road, she said. 'You see the pub along the way, *The Bonnie Moorhen*?'

'Aye.'

'It's named after a poem by Robbie Burns. One of my grandfather's favourites it was. The fourth verse goes something like this…' She rattled off the words to an accompaniment of frenzied bees:

'*Auld Phoebus himself, as he peep'd o'er the hill,*
In spite at her plumage he tried his skill;
He levell'd his rays where she bask'd on the brae.
His rays were outshone, and but mark'd where she lay…'

She too waved away one of the annoying little insects. 'He's an old fellow out hunting the moorhen you see. You can read the poem in the pub; it's painted on the wall in the bar.'

'Thank you very much Mrs Irving, I might just pop in for a sandwich and do just that!' He gave her a wave, and turned left out of the gate.

There were signs that the pub had been extensively renovated, but mercifully the old architectural features had been lovingly preserved; a glimpse of the past still existing within a scene from the present.

Emily had been right; the old Burns poem had been reproduced in full across one of the pale yellow walls. The distinctive eighteenth-century Caslon font told of the elusive qualities of the moorhen when hunted by *Auld Pheobus* and his chums. Above the flowing text a painting of the bird, with its dark plumage and distinctive red and yellow beak, graced the upper part of the wall.

Neil swallowed the last of his coffee and brushed away the crumbs from the baguette he'd just dispatched. The landlord was deep in conversation with an elderly man sat at the bar and huddled over a pint of "heavy". They looked over as Neil got up, self-consciously scraping the legs of his chair across the flagstones. Having made payment, waves of appreciation were exchanged and he ducked through the low door and back onto the street.

The unique fragrance embedded into the fabric of the CID car reached his nostrils as he climbed into the driver's seat. It was strangely comforting; a medley of faint aromas ranging from cigarette smoke to takeaway curry, the remnants of several years of unrelenting police service.

Neil gazed out towards the line of trees behind the school, pondering his next move. He flipped open his mobile phone and dialled the number he had for Matthias Fuchs. This time, the German replied promptly and in his native tongue, but switched effortlessly to English on discovering the identity of his caller. The two men exchanged the usual greetings, and then it was down to business.

'Matthias, I need you to do a little research for me. I need to find out whether a man called Harold Balfour ever became involved with the *Abwher* during the war. He was an employee at your embassy in London just before the conflict.'

'Do you think he was the agent you were telling me about, this man *Phoebus*?'

'I do as it happens, and I may be able to prove it through DNA.'

Fuchs sounded impressed 'That's very good news Neil. Has the exhumation gone ahead yet?'

'The paperwork's been done, we're just waiting for the go-ahead to start digging.'

'I'm pleased that you have another means of identifying this man, Neil, because I don't know how complete the *Abwher* records are. I suspect most of them were destroyed before the fall of Berlin.' There was a pause, so that he could consider his options, then he added; 'I do have a contact at the *Bundesarchiv* in Freiburg. They house many of our wartime military records. I'll give him a call.'

'Thanks, I'll email you with more information when I get back to the office.'

'Excellent. I'll forward it to my contact as soon as I receive it.'

Neil tossed the phone onto the passenger's seat and started the engine. With his lips tightened into a satisfied smile, he pulled out onto the road and headed east for Lockerbie and the motorway to Glasgow.

Epilogue

Never in its history had the little church at Glendaig accommodated so many worshippers at one time. Certainly not since it's construction in the 1730s. There hadn't been sufficient room to accommodate everyone inside the lofty, oak beamed nave, so a small group of latecomers had clustered around the open doorway. They listened in silence, straining to catch the muted voices of the various speakers who, one by one, took their turn to step up to the pulpit. Occasionally, the breeze would reward them with snatches of speech, together with the usual coughs and echoes that always provided an accompaniment to such proceedings.

Maintaining a discreet distance by the crumbling boundary wall were members of the press, together with a solitary TV camera crew from Germany's *Das Erste* network.

Amongst those standing in the late summer sunshine, were Tamsin and Mike Kirkwood. They'd made the journey up from Lincoln, keen to witness the final chapter in this dramatic story that had been born out of their macabre discovery back in May.

The sound of organ music interrupted their thoughts, as movement could be discerned from within the church's shadowy interior. Then, slowly, a sombre looking Duncan Mackay emerged from the porch followed by two coffins draped in the red yellow and black of the German naval ensign, and carried shoulder high by naval ratings of the *Deutsche Marine*. The cortège slowly and silently snaked its way along the path and around the side of the church. They were followed by a steady stream of mourners that continued to spew out of the church, many wearing military uniform. The soft clatter of camera shutters, snapping to capture the scene, drifted across the graveyard from the assembled press corps.

Having left the path behind, the minister glided spectrally across the newly mown grass, his feet hidden beneath his flowing cassock. He passed slowly between randomly-leaning headstones, finally halting before a line of rowan trees that stood just inside the boundary wall. In the shade of their foliage were two freshly-dug graves, both marked by simple headstones. They bore the Germanic cross pattée and the inscriptions; *Jürgen Reiniger 2.2.12 to 31.12.41* and *Harold James Balfour, "Phoebus", 15.7.06 to 31.12.41.*

The mourners clustered several deep around the two graves whilst the Reverend MacKay completed the formalities of the committal. All present stood in silence as the two coffins were simultaneously lowered into the ground. Six riflemen drawn from Germany's modern day submarine service raised their weapons skyward and unleashed a volley of shots. As their echoes died away, Max Friedmann shuffled forward, supported by an emotional Isobel. He plunged his hand into the pocket of his jacket and pulled out his Knight's Cross. With a flick of his bony wrist, he dispatched the medal into Reiniger's grave. It came to rest on the coffin lid with a hollow thud, prompting Max to raise his arm in shaky salute. He then repeated the process with the Iron Cross that Neil had returned to him earlier, this time into Balfour's grave. Max smiled weakly as he glanced across towards Emily Irving who was standing next to him. She acknowledged his gesture with a gentle embrace, an expression of her gratitude that her uncle's sacrifice had been acknowledged.

Once the formalities had been concluded, the crowd then began to thin as the mourners started to drift away towards the car park. Neil turned away too, but something drew him back. Stepping up to the graves for one last time, he gazed cogitatingly into the peaty voids. He looked up, distracted, as a butterfly rested briefly on Reiniger's headstone, basking in the last rays of summer. Sunlight flashed from the silver edging of the Knight's Cross that lay upon the coffin lid. There was an air of peace about the place, somehow enriched now that the sound of human chatter had subsided. Now there was quiet, interrupted only by the soft tireless breeze and the faint distant mewing of a buzzard.

'Not a bad place to end up,' Neil muttered to himself. 'Not a bad place at all.'

'Yes, I agree,' came a hushed voice from behind him. 'I'm not disturbing you, am I?'

'Not at all Mary, how are you keeping?'

'Och, so so. Age is no friend I'm afraid.'

Neil turned towards the old lady. He was surprised to see that she wasn't alone. Mary Galbraith was standing arm in arm with Jeanne Guthrie. 'You kept your secret well Mary.'

'Oh I don't know about that, Inspector. You always knew I was hiding something didn't you? I just wanted to say I'm sorry I wasn't more helpful. I hope you now understand why.'

'Of course I do Mary, I admire your loyalty to Isobel, and I can assure you I will be leaving you all in peace from now on.'

'Just as long as Isobel is free from worry at last, I hear they're not taking any action against her, is that right?'

'Yes, that's right, the Crown Office have decided that it wouldn't be in the public interest to pursue the matter, just as we expected.'

'That's good to hear, thank you Inspector. By the way, Jeanne has something for you.'

The younger woman held out a small torn photograph. 'I believe you've been wondering what happened to this?'

Neil took the old monochrome print and saw that it was a picture of Max as a young man, dressed smartly in tweeds and leaning on a stick. He was looking down to his right, smiling at someone standing beyond the frayed edge of the image. 'Dad was working as a ghillie when this was taken. It was torn from the photograph that you were looking at in Rowan Cottage. Mary gave it to my mother just after it was taken. Mum was understandably touchy about having Dad's photo displayed anywhere at the time. She eventually gave it to me and I've always kept it.'

'I knew it was Max she was looking at,' Neil confided 'There was an intensity to her smile, identical to that photo taken up on the hill in 1935. It seemed to me to be a smile for someone special.' He grinned and handed it back.

'Thanks for showing me.' He patted the old lady's arm. 'You take care of yourself Mary.'

'I'll certainly try young man.'

He left the two women by the graveside and headed for the car park. Cat was waiting by the MG, comforting a fretful Tam whose head and shoulders filled the open window on the passenger's side of the car. Matthias Fuchs stood next to her, stroking the dog's head. The two men shook hands. 'An impressive turn out I think,' said the German with a broad smile.

'Yes, I think so.' Neil agreed. 'The honour guard was certainly a nice touch.'

'Yes, it was most fortunate that one of our submarines was paying a goodwill visit to your naval base at Faslane.' He stooped to open his briefcase. 'No Mr Brodie today then?'

'No, he's away at a conference somewhere down south.'

'I see, well here's the information on Harry Balfour I promised you.' He handed Neil a folder, stacked with papers. 'Interesting character, Mr Balfour. He appears to have been connected to the *Link* Organisation of fascists during the late nineteen-thirties, whilst he was living in London.'

'The *Link* organisation?'

'Yes, it was an organisation established in 1937 to promote Anglo-German friendship. It functioned mainly as a cultural organisation, although its journal was indeed pro-Nazi. In London particularly, the group attracted anti-Semites and pro-Nazi sympathisers. It closed down shortly after the outbreak of war in 1939.'

'I see, so he had affiliations with British-based fascists.'

'Yes, he most certainly did, no doubt encouraged by his masters within the embassy.'

'But what about his role as an agent, did your contact at the *Bundesarchiv* find out anything?'

'Indeed he did, more through luck than anything. The name *Phoebus* appears in an internal memo written by a *Kapitän* Wichmann. He was the *Leiter*, or head of the *Abwher's* regional office in the Knochenhauerstraße in Hamburg. Wichmann's team concentrated mainly on naval intelligence, almost exclusively concerning Britain and the USA. It was responsible for intelligence work connected to the planned invasion of Britain and, in the second half of 1940, they dispatched a significant number of agents to Britain.'

'So around the time that Balfour went missing from the Isle of Man?' Neil interjected.

'Exactly. The memo was addressed to one of Wichmann's staff officers. In it, the *Leiter* requests him to make contact with *Phoebus* through an intermediary in the Irish Republic, directing him to attend a meeting with Wichmann's representative in Dublin. We believe this was to be a briefing prior to Balfour's departure for Scotland.'

Is there no official record of Balfour being signed up by the *Abwher*?' Neil asked, as he caressed his dog's ear.

'In a word, no. Up until now, there has been no known connection between Harry Balfour the embassy translator and *Phoebus* the *Abwher* agent.'

'That seems strange.'

'Not at all Neil. We must not forget that many of the *Abwher's* documentary records were destroyed prior to the fall of the Reich in 1945. It is entirely possible that Balfour *slipped under the radar*, as you like to say. Anyway it's all in there for you to read.'

'Thank you Matthias, fortunately we got a positive DNA match with Balfour's niece, so I believe we've just about tied up all the loose ends.'

'That's gratifying to hear Neil. So now we can go to bed with it, eh?'

'I think you mean *put it to bed*,' said Cat, trying to suppress a giggle.

Fuchs blushed. 'Yes, yes, how foolish of me, I really shouldn't experiment with your strange little sayings!' He offered his hand again. 'It was good working with you Neil, and if you ever find yourself in Flensburg please look me up.'

'I'll certainly do that Matthias. Do you have transport?'

'Oh yes, the Flag officer at Faslane kindly provided us with a minibus, so I'm fine. Thank you for asking.'

Neil and Cat climbed into the MG, much to Tam's delight. 'I do like a man in uniform,' said Cat as she fastened her seatbelt. 'Especially him!'

'You're incorrigible,' Neil replied as he selected first gear.

'But I like detectives best.' She grinned as she placed her hand on his thigh.

Neil eased the MG out onto the road and turned right towards Camuscraig. The Reverend MacKay waved from the church door as they accelerated away, prompting Neil to respond with a short blast on the car horn.

The sun was now high in the sky, shrouding the distant mountains of Knoydart in a shimmering haze. Neil squinted across towards the rocky knoll of Eilean Ceann-Cinnidh as it came into view. The boughs of the pines that topped the little islet danced in the breeze, their lacy foliage vivid green against the blue of Loch Coinneach.

He pulled up on the lay-by, directly opposite the beach where the whole drama had begun. He killed the engine and gazed out in quiet contemplation of what had gone on there years before.

'This is where it all happened, isn't it?' Cat asked as she opened her door.

Neil snapped back into the present. 'Aye, that's right. Do you mind if we have a wee stroll down to the water?'

'No of course not, lead the way.' They crossed the road and

descended the path to the beach. Tam headed straight for the shoreline, barking wildly at a flock of resting seagulls. Neil stood silently, surveying the scene.

'It's lovely here,' said Cat, almost in a whisper. She took hold of his hand and rested her head on his shoulder.

'It's almost impossible to imagine what went on here,' said Neil, shaking his head in disbelief. He looked up as the gulls that Tam had discourteously chased off wheeled and dived above them.

'Do you think they'll ever discover any additional evidence of Friedmann's capture, or the cover up on the British side?' Cat asked.

'You mean in support of Max and Isobel's account of what happened?'

'Aye, an official record, or a letter, something like that.'

Neil picked up a length of driftwood and hurled it along the beach for Tam to chase. 'It's always possible, although someone somewhere did a pretty good job at the time removing all trace of any such record. One thing's for sure, the historians will give it their best effort, now that the story's out.' He wrestled the piece of wood from Tam's mouth. 'At least I've done my bit.'

'You certainly have,' Cat agreed. 'I'd go as far as saying that any changes made to the history books as a result of this case, will in no small way be down to your persistence in getting to the truth.'

'…And that's some achievement, when you've got big Alex breathing down your neck!'

They both laughed as a sudden gust of wind whipped up the sand, stinging their faces like thousands of tiny needles. Neil instinctively closed his eyes, and somewhere in his subconscious he swore he could hear the distant throb of engines and the sharp crack of a gun. Then, as the breeze intensified again, he felt more grains of sand sting his cheeks. For all the world they could have been snowflakes, tossed about on an icy December night. He shivered briefly, and opened his eyes again. Then, with a smile he placed an arm around Cat's shoulders.

'Come on love, let's go home. Places like this belong to the past.'

Author's Note

Operation *Paukenschlag*, often referred to as "The Second Happy Time", lasted from January 1942 until August of that year. German U-boat commanders called it the "American shooting season", taking full advantage of the United States' unpreparedness for war to attack the country's merchant shipping. In all, 609 merchantmen were sunk along America's eastern seaboard, totalling 3.1 million tons; roughly one quarter of all shipping sunk by U-boats during World War Two. Only twenty-two U-boats were lost during this period.

During the course of the operation the commanding officer of U-123, *Kapitänleutnant* Reinhard Hardegan, was ordered to penetrate New York's harbour. He did this on 15th January 1942 using only a tourist guidebook as a navigational aid. His visit was short-lived due to the lack of targetable merchant shipping, but U-123 did manage to sink the British tanker *Coimbra* on his way out of the harbour.

References to the use of rocket-powered weapons during the operation are purely fictional. However, the concept of mounting rockets on U-boats was a reality. The idea was raised in 1941, during a conversation between Dr Ernst Steinhoff, an engineer at the Peenemunde rocket development facility, and his brother *Korvettenkapitän* Fritz Steinhoff, commander of U-511. This resulted in the commencement of trials in the summer of 1942. The tests were deemed successful, but the lack of a suitable guidance system for such a weapon and the priority being afforded to the V-1 rocket programme meant that staff at the facility could not devote sufficient time to the initiative.

The project was resurrected in 1944 when three U-boats, secretly equipped with rocket launchers, deployed against Soviet harbour facilities and ships moored in the Black Sea. This historic event proved to be the first combat use of a submarine-launched missile.

No German prisoner of war ever successfully managed to complete a "home run" from the United Kingdom during World War Two. Numerous escape attempts were made, but all were subsequently foiled.

Other than the fictional character Max Friedmann, at least twenty-nine members of the *Ubootwaffe* received the prestigious Knight's Cross with Oak Leaves. Of these, seven were killed during the war.

Glendaig and the area of the West Highlands featured in the book are of course fictional, as are any references to Scottish nobility connected to the area of Knoydart.

Historical comments relating to other locations within the Highlands, such as Redcastle and Cromarty, are in the main factually correct.

The characters in the story are all fictional, other than those historical figures mentioned in passing such as Admirals Karl Dönitz and Alfred Saalwächter.

I have, as far as possible, attempted to accurately reflect the policing and judicial processes that would be followed in a case such as that featured in this book. Any technical inaccuracies are my responsibility alone, and will only have been included so as to suit the plot.

Acknowledgements

Whilst a considerable amount of the research for this book was conducted using online resources and in Scotland itself, I am thankful for the reference material provided in David Fairbank White's excellent account of the Battle of The Atlantic, *Bitter Ocean*, and also James Miller's book, *Scapa*.

I am particularly grateful for the assistance provided by the excellent web resources at *uboat.net* and *uboatarchive.net*, whose comprehensive records of the U-boat war and the men who served in them was without doubt invaluable.

My sincere thanks also go to my family, whose unceasing encouragement and support has inspired me to realise my dream and to publish this, my first novel.

Clive Allan 2013

Born in 1959, CLIVE ALLAN is a native of West Sussex, living near Chichester with his Scottish born wife. In 2008, he retired after thirty years police service, ending his career as an Inspector at Gatwick Airport. He now divides his time between the Sussex coast and his cottage in the Scottish Highlands.